TREACHERY AT
LANCASTER
GATE

By Anne Perry and available from Headline

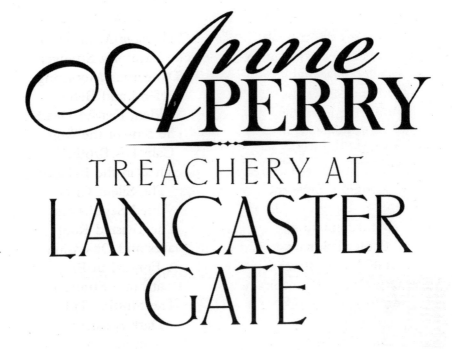

Anne Perry

TREACHERY AT LANCASTER GATE

headline

First published in 2015 by
HEADLINE PUBLISHING GROUP

1

Cataloguing in Publication Data is available from the British Library

ISBN 978 1 4722 1955 8

Typeset in Plantin by Palimpsest Book Production Limited,
Falkirk, Stirlingshire

Printed and bound by
CPI Group (UK) Ltd, Croydon, CR0 4YY

Headline's policy is to use papers that are natural, renewable and recyclable
products and made from wood grown in well-managed forests and other
controlled sources. The logging and manufacturing processes are expected
to conform to the environmental regulations of the country of origin.

HEADLINE PUBLISHING GROUP
An Hachette UK Company
Carmelite House
50 Victoria Embankment
London EC4Y 0DZ

www.headline.co.uk
www.hachette.co.uk

To Flora Rees

Chapter One

PITT STOOD in the middle of the street looking at the smouldering ruins of the house. The fire brigade had thoroughly hosed the small bursts of flame here and there, and the water puddled on the floor and settled in the craters left by the bomb that had detonated forty-five minutes ago. Now it was midday but the sky was still clouded with smoke and the stench of it was everywhere.

Pitt moved out of the way as two ambulance men lifted a wounded man on to a makeshift litter and carried him out to the waiting ambulance. The horses were shifting their weight impatiently, obedient as they were trained to be, but they knew the smell of burning in the autumn air, and each crash of collapsing timber startled them.

'That's it, sir,' the white-faced constable said to Pitt. Perhaps it was the smoke that stung his eyes, but more probably it was emotion. All the dead and the injured were police as well: five of them altogether. 'That's the last of them out.'

'Thank you,' Pitt acknowledged the words. 'How many dead?'

'Hobbs and Newman, sir. We didn't move the bodies.' The constable coughed and tried to clear his throat. 'Ednam, Bossiney and Yarcombe are pretty badly injured . . . sir.'

'Thank you,' Pitt repeated. His mind was teeming with thoughts, and yet he could not come up with anything to say that would give any real comfort to the constable. Pitt was head of Special Branch, that discreet part of Security that dealt with anything that was considered a threat to the nation, such as sabotage, assassinations, bombings, any form of terrorism. He had seen destruction and violent death too many times. In fact, before Special Branch he had been in the regular police, like the dead men, but dealing primarily with cases of murder.

But this was a deliberate attack directed specifically at the police: colleagues he had known and worked with over the years. He could remember Newman getting married, Hobbs's first promotion. Now he had to search this wreckage for what was left of their bodies. The fact that he had known them should not make any difference. Everybody had one life to keep or lose. Probably everyone had somebody for whom their death was devastating. And if they did not, was that not even worse?

He turned and started to move slowly, picking his way so as not to disturb what was left of the situation – the evidence, if it could be called such. They already knew it was a bomb blast. Passers-by had heard the explosion and seen the rubble flying, and then the flames as wood caught fire. There were glass shards everywhere from exploded windows. Two people were close enough to be witnesses. Now they were sitting in the back of an ambulance, its doors open as one of the drivers finished binding up a gash in an arm and spoke to them quietly. Both looked battered and shocked, but Pitt would have to speak to them. They might have seen something that would come to matter, however slightly. Sometimes it was what someone did not see, an absence that had meaning, realised only afterwards.

Pitt spoke to the man first. He looked to be in his sixties, white-haired, dressed in a formal coat, as if he had been on his way back home from church. There were cuts on the right side of his face, and a burn across his cheek, as if a piece of flaming wood had caught him. All his right side was smeared with dust and there were small burns to the fabric of his clothes.

Pitt apologised for disturbing him, asked his name and where he lived.

'On my way home from church, God help us,' the man said shakily. 'Who are they? What kind of people would do this?' He was frightened, and trying desperately not to show it in front of his wife. He must have been walking on the outside, as a man would, and she had been closer to the blast and was more seriously hurt. It was her arm the ambulance man was binding, and already the blood was beginning to seep through the bandage as he added another layer. His glance to Pitt told him to hurry up.

'Did you see anyone else in the street?' Pitt asked. 'Anyone at all? Any witnesses might help.'

'No . . . no, I didn't. We were talking to each other,' the man replied. 'Who would do this? Is it more anarchists? What do they want?'

'I don't know, sir. But we'll find out,' Pitt promised. 'If you remember anything, let us know.' He handed the man his card, wished the woman well, and then with a nod to the ambulance man he walked back towards the house. It was time to go in and look at the bodies, gather whatever evidence there was.

He skirted around a block of fallen masonry, picking his way carefully. He could taste burning in the air and yet it was cold.

'Sir!' a fireman called out. 'You can't come in here! It's . . .'

Pitt kept on walking, his feet crunching on broken glass. 'Commander Pitt,' he introduced himself.

'Oh . . . well, watch where you put your feet, sir. And your head.' He glanced upwards at a broken beam that was hanging at a crazy angle, swaying a little, as if it could become detached and fall off any moment. 'You still shouldn't ought to be here,' he added.

'The dead men?' Pitt requested.

'It's dangerous in here,' the man pointed out. 'They'll not be going nowhere, sir. Best you let us get them out. The blast killed them, sir. No doubt about that.'

Pitt would have liked the excuse not to look at the bodies, but there was none. He might learn nothing useful, but it would be a beginning of facing the reality and coming to terms with it.

He was standing in front of the fireman. The man was pale-faced, apart from the black ash smudges. His uniform was filthy, and wet. When he had time to think about it, he would realise he was cold as well.

'That way, sir,' the man said reluctantly. 'But be careful. You'd be best not to touch anything. Bring the whole lot down on top o' yourself.'

'I won't,' Pitt responded, beginning the awkward journey and trying to avoid tripping. If he fell he would almost certainly bang into a jutting wall strut, a piece of smashed furniture or something dangling from where the ceiling used to be.

The floorboards were half up, torn by the blast. It must have been a large bomb and, to judge by the burning and the angles of the broken wood, he was near the centre of it. What on earth had happened here in the quiet house on a pleasant London street near Kensington Gardens? Anarchists? London was full of them. Half the revolutionaries in Europe had either lived here or passed through. In this year of 1898 there had been less terrorist activity than in the recent past, but now, almost at the close of the year, it seemed Special Branch's sense of ease was misplaced. Was this the dying blow, or the first outrider of another storm? Nihilists in Europe had assassinated President Carnot of France, Tsar Alexander II of Russia, the Spanish Prime Minister, Cánovas del Castillo, and, earlier this year, the Empress Elisabeth of Austria-Hungary. Perhaps the violence was coming here to England as well?

In front of Pitt there was a body, or what there was left of it. Suddenly he could not swallow and he thought for a moment that he was going to be sick. One leg was entirely gone, one side of the chest caved in under part of a beam from the rafters. But, forcing himself to look at the half of the head left, the face oddly unmarked, Pitt could recognise Newman.

He would have to go and see his widow; say all the usual words of grief. It would not help, but its omission would hurt.

He stared at the body. Did it tell him anything, other than what the fireman had already said? There was no smoke on Newman's face. His left arm was gone, but when Pitt looked more closely he saw his right hand was clean. Did that mean he was already inside here when the bomb went off? He had not battled his way through smoke and rubble. Why had he come here? Trouble reported? An alarm of some sort? Following someone? A meeting already arranged? An ambush?

He turned and moved away, dizzy for a moment. He took a deep breath, steadied himself and moved on.

The second body was half obscured by fallen plaster and wood, but it was far less obviously damaged. There was little smoke or dust on Hobbs's face and his pattern of freckles was easily recognisable. Pitt studied him as dispassionately as he could, trying to learn something from the way the debris lay around him. The police surgeon would be able to tell him more, but it appeared that Hobbs had been caught by surprise, and much further from the site of the explosion than Newman.

Pitt was still staring at the surroundings when he heard footsteps somewhere behind him. He turned and saw the familiar figure of Samuel Tellman picking his way through the plaster, water and charred wood. Tellman had been Pitt's sergeant when they were both at Bow Street. It had taken them a long time to be comfortable with each other. Tellman had distrusted anyone with a background as humble as Pitt's, but who spoke like a gentleman. To him it seemed that Pitt's accent was affected, as if Pitt thought himself superior. Pitt felt no reason to explain that his speech was the product of having been educated along with the son of the country house where his father had been gamekeeper, until he was transported to Australia for theft. His mother had remained as laundress, and Sir Arthur Desmond had seen the young Pitt as a companion to his son, and a spur to excel him in class. The whole story was a wound that still ached on his father's behalf, and something Tellman did not need to know.

Years working together had taught them a mutual respect, and a loyalty.

'Good afternoon, sir.' Tellman stopped beside him.

'Good afternoon, Inspector,' Pitt replied.

Tellman stared down at the body. 'I'm your liaison with the police, sir.'

Pitt had expected someone to provide liaison, partly because he was Special Branch, not in the regular police himself, but mostly because the victims were the police's own men. Their internal loyalty was not unlike that of soldiers in an army at war. An officer facing danger had to have an absolute trust in those who stood beside him, or at his back. It was his lifeline.

Pitt nodded. It would be good to work with Tellman again – but on anything other than this. Emotions were too raw.

'Looks like they were right here when it went off,' Pitt observed. 'Newman must have been closest to it.'

'Yes. I saw. What kind of a bloody lunatic would do this?' Tellman's voice was tight, as if he were controlling it with difficulty. 'I want freedom for all men, and food, and houses, and the right to come and go. But what the hell good does this do? These men never did anything to them! Which anarchists did this anyway? Spanish? Italian? French? Russian? Why in God's name do all the bloody lunatics in Europe come and live in London?' He turned to face Pitt. 'Why do we let them?' His face was white, two spots of colour in his lean cheeks, anger in his eyes. 'Don't you know who they are? Isn't that what Special Branch is supposed to be for?'

Pitt hunched his shoulders and drove his hands deeper into his pockets. 'I don't make the policy, Tellman. And yes, I know who a lot of them are. Mostly they just talk.'

The disgust and the pain in Tellman's face was more powerful than words. 'I'll find them and hang them – whatever you want to do about it.' It was a challenge.

Pitt did not bother to answer. He understood the emotion behind the words. Right at this moment he felt much the same. He might feel differently when he learned who was responsible. Some of the men branded as anarchists had done no more than protest for decent pay, enough to feed their families. A few of them had been imprisoned, tortured and even executed, simply for protesting against injustice. Driven far enough, he might have done the same.

'Why were these men here?' he asked Tellman. 'Five of them, at this quiet house right on the Park? It can't have been an inquiry. You don't need five men for that. There's no one else dead or hurt, so the house must have been empty. What were they doing?'

Tellman's expression tightened. 'I don't know yet, but I mean to find out. If this was something to do with anarchists, they would have told Special Branch what was going on, so it must be something else.'

Pitt did not take that as totally for granted as Tellman did, but it was not the time to argue. 'Anything known about this address?' he asked instead.

'Not yet.' Tellman looked around him. 'What about the bomb? Bombs are your business. What was it made of? Where was it put? How did they let it off?'

'Dynamite,' Pitt told him. 'It always is. Detonating it is simple enough with a fuse. Just make it long enough not to reach the bomb itself before you can get away.'

'Just like that? That's all?' Tellman asked bitterly.

'Well, there are more complicated ones, but not for this purpose.'

'Like what?' Tellman demanded.

'Upside-down bombs,' Pitt said patiently as they both turned and made their way gingerly back towards the open air. The stench of burned wood and plaster was overpowering, filling the head, stinging the nose and throat. 'You make a container with two halves, carefully perforated. Keep it up the right way and it's safe. Turn it upside down and it explodes.'

'So you carry it in the right way up, and hope someone turns it over?'

'Make it into a parcel. Put the strings tied on the other side, or the name of the sender, or anything else you like,' Pitt answered, stepping over a fallen beam. 'It works very well.'

'Then I suppose it's a miracle we don't all get blown to hell.' Tellman lashed out and kicked a loose piece of wood, which flew in the air and crashed against a wall still standing.

Pitt understood the violence. He had known some of these men also, and hundreds of others just like them, working hard at an often thankless job, underpaid for the danger it too often involved. He had done it himself for long enough.

'Dynamite is controlled,' he said as they stepped out on to the pavement. The street had been closed and there was no traffic. One fire engine still remained. The ambulances were gone. The closed-in wagon for the morgue was waiting at the kerb. Pitt nodded to the attendant and the police surgeon. 'I don't think we can learn anything more,' he said quietly. 'Give me your report when you can.'

'Yes, sir,' the police surgeon responded, taking it as his cue to enter the bombed building.

'Controlled,' Tellman said sarcastically. 'By whom?'

'It's not for sale,' Pitt replied, walking slowly along the pavement away from the still-smouldering wreckage. 'They use it in quarries, and occasionally in demolition. You'd either steal it from there, or buy it from someone else who had stolen it.'

'Like anarchists,' Tellman said sourly. 'Back to where we started.'

'Probably,' Pitt agreed. 'But as you pointed out, it doesn't seem to fit in with their purposes.'

'Maybe they just hate everybody, or else they're so damn crazy they don't care.' Tellman stared across towards the bare trees in Kensington Gardens, a black fretwork against the sky.

'I suppose you know what you're doing, letting them stay in Britain.' He didn't inflect it as a question, but he might as well have. 'Personally I'd rather they went home and blew up their own cities.'

'Speak to the firemen.' Pitt did not bother answering the challenge. 'See if they can tell you anything useful. We can see from poor Newman's body roughly where the bomb went off, but the pattern of burning might place it even more closely.'

'And how will that help?'

'It probably won't, but you know as well as I do that you don't prejudge the evidence. Get it all. You know what to look for! And find out whatever you can about who lives in this house, what they look like, when they come and go, who visits them, what they say they do and, if possible, what they really do.'

'You don't need to tell me how to do police work,' Tellman said angrily. He seemed about to add something more, then bit the words back. He stood still and looked at Pitt for several seconds, then turned away. The grief was there in his face.

'I know,' Pitt said quietly. 'Sorry . . .'

He remembered Newman at his wedding, the way his young bride had looked at him. No one should end up as he was now.

'I'm going to the hospital,' he said gruffly. 'One of the injured men can at least tell me why they went to that house.'

He walked smartly towards the Bayswater Road where he could get a hansom quickly. He needed to feel as if he were doing something with a purpose. St Mary's in Paddington was not far, a few minutes' ride up Westbourne Terrace to Praed Street and he would be there.

There was a stationary cab close to the kerb, as if the driver had known he would be needed. 'St Mary's Hospital, Paddington,' Pitt said as he got in.

'Yes, sir,' the driver replied gravely. 'You'll be wanting me to hurry,' he added.

'Yes, if you please.' Pitt wanted to speak to the injured men, if they were still conscious and not in the operating theatre – or dead. No one had been able to say how badly hurt they were.

It seemed like an endless journey, and yet in other ways far too short.

Pitt got out, paid the driver and thanked him.

'Ye're welcome, sir. You just catch the bastards!' the driver called after him.

Pitt half turned and raised his hand in a swift acknowledgement. There was nothing he could promise.

The doctor in charge told him that he couldn't see the patients. They were still in great pain, and heavily dosed with morphine.

Pitt explained again who he was. It was one occasion when a uniform with plenty of buttons and braid would have helped.

'Special Branch,' he said yet again. 'This was a bombing, Dr Critchlow. Right in the middle of London. We have to catch the perpetrators and stop them before they do it again.'

The doctor's face paled and he bit back his insistence. 'Then be quick, Mr Pitt. These men are in a bad way.'

'I know that,' Pitt said grimly. 'I've just been looking at the dead.'

The doctor winced, but did not say anything more. Instead he led Pitt briskly along the corridor to a very small ward where four beds were filled with men in different states of treatment. Two of them appeared to be unconscious, but could have been merely silent, motionless in suffering.

The most senior of the injured was Ednam, and he was awake, watching Pitt as he approached. His face was bruised and there was a dark red, angry burn across his left cheek. His left arm was bandaged from the shoulder to the wrist and his leg was propped up and heavily bandaged so whatever treatment it had received was concealed. Pitt guessed it was broken, and probably burned as well. When Pitt asked quietly if Ednam could speak to him, he looked back guardedly, taking a moment or two to recognise him. Then he relaxed a fraction, with just an easing of the muscles around his mouth.

'I suppose.' His voice was dry. Clearly his throat hurt, and probably his chest, from inhaling the smoke.

'If you can tell me anything,' Pitt replied.

'If I'd known there was a bloody bomb I wouldn't 'ave gone!' Ednam retorted bitterly.

'Why did you go?' Pitt asked. 'And with four other men? That's a big force. What were you expecting to find?'

'Drugs. Opium, to be exact. Big buy there, we were told.'

'By whom? Did you find any evidence of it?'

'We barely had time to look!'

Pitt kept his voice soft.

'Was anyone else there?'

'Apart from us? Not that I saw,' Ednam answered. 'But the information came from a good source. At least . . . one we've trusted before.' His voice was now little above a whisper. The effort to speak cost him dearly. 'Newman and Hobbs are dead, aren't they?'

'Yes.'

Ednam swore until he couldn't get his breath any more.

'I need to know your source,' Pitt urged, leaning forward a little. 'Either he set you up, or someone else set him up. He may be able to identify them.'

'I don't know his name. He calls himself Anno Domini.'

'What?'

'Anno Domini,' Ednam repeated. 'I don't know if he's religious or what. But we've had a few good tips from him before.'

'How? Do you talk with him? Get letters? What?'

'Letters, just a line or two. Delivered by hand.'

'Addressed to you?'

'Yes.'

'By name?'

'Yes.'

'Telling you what?'

'Where a purchase will be or where drugs are stashed.'

'How many arrests have you made on this information?'

Edman's eyes did not leave Pitt's face.

'Two. And found about two hundred pounds worth of opium.'

More than enough to establish trust; in fact enough to raise the funds to buy a small house. Pitt could not blame Ednam for following the lead. He would have himself.

'Do you think he was setting you up?' he asked. 'Or was someone else using him?'

Ednam thought for a few moments, his face tense with concentration. 'I think someone else was using him,' he said at last. 'But it's a guess. Find who's behind this. I want to see them hang.'

'I'll try,' Pitt promised. It was one of the rare moments when he agreed. Usually he found hanging a repulsive idea, regardless of the crime. It was an act of revenge that reduced the law to the same level of barbarism as those who had broken it.

He walked over to the bed opposite and found Bossiney. It was a nurse who told Pitt his name. Pitt spoke to him only a few moments. He was very badly burned and must have been in savage pain, drifting in and out of consciousness.

Pitt walked over to the nurse, who gave him a bleak smile and would not confirm or deny anything. She had hope that he would survive, but would not commit herself to more. The emotional exhaustion at the witnessing of pain was there in her face.

Then Pitt went to the bed closest to the window where Yarcombe was lying staring at the ceiling, his face almost blank. A glance told Pitt that his right arm was missing from the elbow downwards. Pitt struggled for something to say and could find nothing that was remotely adequate. His own right hand clenched till his nails bit into the flesh of his hand, a sweet reminder that it was there, real and alive.

'I'm sorry,' he said awkwardly. 'We'll get them.'

Yarcombe turned his head very slightly till his eyes focused on Pitt. 'Do that,' he replied in a whisper. 'They set us up!' He added something more, but it was unintelligible.

Pitt left with his head pounding and a vague, sick feeling in his stomach. He did not ask the doctor in charge what chances any of the men had of recovery. He knew that all he could do was guess.

He arrived back at the Special Branch offices at Lisson Grove to find a message waiting for him to report to Commissioner Bradshaw of the Metropolitan Police. It did not surprise him. Bradshaw would be deeply upset about the bombing and remiss in his duty if he did not contact the head of Special Branch. Pitt had wanted to return to Lisson Grove only to see if there was any further information he could give to Bradshaw.

Stoker knocked on his door almost as soon as Pitt had closed it and looked at the papers on his desk.

'Sir?' Stoker said as soon as he was inside. He was a man of few words, but this was brief, even for him.

'Nothing more,' Pitt replied. 'Hurt very badly. Yarcombe lost an arm. Nobody can say if they'll live or not. Ednam doesn't look fatal but you can't tell what's inside. Or how bad the shock will be. He says they went there on a tip-off that there would be a big opium sale. They expected a degree of resistance, and they didn't want anyone escaping with the proof.'

'Was there any?'

'No.'

'Any idea who set them up?'

'Man they know only as Anno Domini.'

'What?' Stoker looked startled.

'Anno Domini,' Pitt repeated. 'No idea why. But Ednam said he's been reliable before.'

'Setting them up for this,' Stoker said straight away.

'Looks like it. Tellman's our police liaison. You'd better check on all the potential bombers we know of.'

'Already started, sir. Nothing useful so far. But I suppose if it was someone we know, we'd have had wind of it before.' He made a grimace of unhappiness. 'At least I damn well hope we would! We've got enough men infiltrated into their groups. I've already spoken to Patchett and Wells. They don't know a thing. But dynamite's easy enough to get, if you have the right connections.'

Pitt did not argue. Unfortunately it was true, hard as they tried to prevent it. 'I'm going to see Bradshaw,' he said.

'Yes, sir.'

Pitt was shown into Bradshaw's office immediately. This time there was no pretence at being busy with more important things, as there had been on occasion. Bradshaw was a good-looking man in his early fifties. His thick hair had little grey in it and he had not yet developed any surplus body weight. He was well-dressed, as always, but creases of tension marred the smoothness of his face.

'How are the men, Pitt?' he began without ceremony the moment Pitt was in and had closed the door. He waved towards one of the elegant chairs but did not bother with an invitation.

'Two dead, sir,' Pitt replied, walking over towards the desk, his feet silent on the heavy Turkish rug. 'Newman and Hobbs. Ednam, Bossiney and Yarcombe injured. Yarcombe lost an arm. Too early to say if they'll recover.'

Bradshaw winced. 'It's police who were killed,' he said sharply. 'It was a police case.'

'Yes, sir.'

'Do you know what it was about?'

'A very large opium sale.'

Bradshaw's face paled, the muscles in his jaw tight. 'Opium,' he said quietly. 'Have you . . . have you any idea who is involved?'

'Not yet . . .'

'Why is Special Branch taking the case?' His voice was hard-edged, challenging. 'What evidence have you that it's terrorists? Do you know who's behind it? Did you know before?'

'No, sir. We were not consulted until after the bomb went off

14

this morning. It was one of their informers who lured them to the meeting, and with information that caused them to bring five men, rather than just a couple.'

'They had an informer? How do you know that?'

'I got it from Ednam when I saw him in hospital.'

'Poor devil,' Bradshaw said softly. 'Who is this informer?'

'Always communicates by letter. Calls himself Anno Domini.'

'Educated man?' Bradshaw looked surprised.

'Possibly. He suggested it was a very large drug sale. Addiction to opium is no respecter of age, class, wealth or anything else.'

Bradshaw's face was tight, and a little pale. 'I know that, Pitt. I presume you're looking for this man?'

'Yes, sir. And working with the police.'

'But what are you doing?' Bradshaw pressed.

'Looking at all our contacts, asking our usual informers . . .'

'Do your anarchists deal in opium?'

'Possibly. But they certainly deal in dynamite.'

Bradshaw sighed. 'Yes, of course they do. Damn them.' He regarded Pitt bleakly, his face filled with pain. 'I suppose you've inherited a network of spies from Victor Narraway? You must have some ideas. Or am I out of date?'

Pitt had a retaliation on the tip of his tongue, but he knew better. 'We'll do our best, Commissioner,' he said gently. 'And I will keep you personally aware of any progress we make. On a day-to-day basis, I will be working with Inspector Tellman.'

Bradshaw nodded. 'Anything you want that we can help with . . .' he said grimly. 'I imagine you have your own men.' It was not a question. He had no liking for Special Branch, and no wish to lend any of his force to do their work.

The first thing Pitt did was to visit the bereaved families. It was the worst duty in all police or Special Branch work, and it could not be passed off to anyone else.

He was exhausted when he finally went back to Lisson Grove

and heard from Stoker the reports coming in, the threats, attacks, rivalries, anything that would give them a place to start. He had found no reference to the address in Lancaster Gate, and no one at all using the soubriquet 'Anno Domini'.

It was late when Pitt arrived home in Keppel Street, just off Russell Square. There was a thin rime of ice where the pavement was wet. The street lamps were haloed by a faint mist, softening the outlines of the houses, blurring boundaries between them.

He climbed the steps to the familiar door with a sense of peace, as if he could leave the violence and the grief of the day behind him. He slipped his key in the lock and went inside, closing it with a slight noise deliberately. He wanted somebody to know he was home, even though it was late, and seventeen-year-old Jemima and fourteen-year-old Daniel would already have eaten, and possibly even gone to bed. Charlotte would have waited up for him. She always did.

The light was warm and bright in the hall.

The parlour door opened and she stood there, the lamplight on her hair bringing out its auburn tones. She came towards him, concern in her face.

He took off his hat and coat and hung them up where they could dry out, then turned and kissed her gently.

'You're cold,' she said, touching his cheek. 'Have you eaten anything? Would you like a roast beef sandwich and a cup of tea?'

He suddenly realised he was hungry and, sensing his response before he spoke it, she turned and led the way to the kitchen. It was always his favourite room anyway. It smelled of clean scrubbed wood, of the freshly ironed linen hanging on the airing rail winched up to the ceiling, sometimes of new bread. There was a large wooden table in the centre, and a Welsh dresser with blue and white ringed plates arranged on it, and a few jugs. Copper pans gleamed on hooks on the wall.

For years it had been the heart of the house. All kinds of people had sat here long into the night, talking of plans, easing defeats, helping each other to believe in victory. Gracie had come here as a maid when she was still a child. She was married to Tellman now, but there were moments when Pitt still missed her, as if he could hear her voice and she were only in the pantry, or the hall. Now it was Minnie Maude who had taken her place, but she had not Gracie's sharp tongue, or bright, stubborn courage – not yet.

He pulled out a chair and sat down as Charlotte moved the kettle over on to the hottest part of the oven hob, and began to slice the beef.

'No horseradish,' he reminded her. It was part of a ritual. He never had horseradish. He liked pickle.

She nodded very slightly. 'It was in the newspapers. They didn't give names. Did you know any of them?'

He hesitated, but only for a moment. 'Yes. Newman was one of them. I . . . I told his wife.'

Charlotte stood motionless for a moment, the tears filling her eyes. 'Oh, Thomas, I'm sorry! I remember her at her wedding – she was so happy! This is terrible.' She swallowed, trying to control her emotion. 'And the others?'

'I've seen them, but Newman was the only one I really knew.'

'Are the injured ones going to be all right?'

'It's too early to say. One of them lost an arm.'

Charlotte didn't try to say anything comforting, and he was glad of it. She cut the bread, spread a little butter, then laid the beef thickly, adding pickle. The kettle boiled. She warmed the teapot, put in three spoons of tea, then added water and carried it all to the table.

'What are they saying in the papers?' he asked as he picked up the sandwich and bit into it. It was rich and sharp.

'Anarchists,' she replied. 'They're frightened. Everything seems so uncertain. It's as if there is violence in the air and you never know quite where the next attack is coming from.' She poured the tea ready for him and a cup for herself. 'I suppose that's what they're aiming for, isn't it? The kind of fear that disables people and makes them do stupid things.' It was not a question. It was what she believed. She said it aloud because she wished him to know she understood.

He swallowed his mouthful and took another.

'In thirteen months we'll be into the 1900s.' She sipped her tea. 'A lot of people seem to think it will be different, really different. Darker and more violent. Why should it change? It's only a date on a calendar. Or is it a self-fulfilling prophecy? We'll make it happen by thinking about it so much?'

He was too tired to discuss it, but he recognised the fear in her voice. She wanted an answer, not a palliative.

'Things are changing,' he agreed quietly. 'But they always are.'

'Small things.' She shook her head. 'Not big, like the changes people want in Europe. America hasn't yet signed a peace treaty with Spain, and there's going to be even more trouble in South Africa. We shouldn't be fighting there, Thomas. We're not right.'

'I know.'

'There are assassinations, bombings,' she went on. 'We haven't had that before, not all over the place. People are restless about poverty and injustice. They want change, but they're going about it in all the wrong ways.'

'I know that, too. We're doing what we can. This looks like an opium sale gone wrong.'

'Two police killed and three badly injured!' Charlotte protested. 'They weren't shot, that whole building was exploded and set on fire!' Then she saw his face. He had done what he could to clean the ash and soot out of his hair, but he had not had a chance to put on a clean shirt. There was not only soot but scorch marks on his cuffs, and he must smell of charred wood.

'I'm sorry,' she whispered. 'I suppose I'm as frightened as everybody else, except that I'm frightened for you too.'

'That I won't catch them?' he asked, then instantly wished that he hadn't. What could he say to undo it?

'That too,' she said candidly. 'But also for you not to be hurt.'

18

'I've been in the police since before we met, and I've not been seriously hurt yet.' He smiled. 'Scared stiff a time or two. And one way or another, we've solved most of the big cases.'

She nodded slightly and smiled, keeping her eyes on his.

Nevertheless he was worried. He had men embedded in all the major anarchist groups he knew of, and there had not been even a murmur of an atrocity like the bombing at Lancaster Gate. Nothing at all. He had been completely blindsided. Would Victor Narraway have known? Pitt had been promoted on Narraway's own recommendation, when Narraway was dismissed. Had Narraway overestimated him?

He reached out across the table and put his hand over Charlotte's, but he did not say anything. He felt her fingers curl up and close around his.

Chapter Two

IN THE morning Pitt dressed in old clothes and deliberately took on an even more casual appearance than usual. He made a point of not shaving. He set out early, while Charlotte was still occupied upstairs, so she would not see him and guess what he was going to do. There was no point in worrying her unnecessarily.

Later he would find out how the injured men were doing, he resolved as he closed the front door behind him and walked along the icy pavement towards Tottenham Court Road. There were newspaper sellers out already and all the headlines were about the bombing in Lancaster Gate. Some cried out for justice, many for revenge. The reports were all laced with fear.

He crossed over into Windmill Street. It was a risk going to the Autonomy Club himself. Usually he had less memorable-looking men frequent the place, build up an identity and pass unnoticed. Now he felt as if he did not have the time for such slow-yielding efforts.

He reached the door and went in. There was a bar, and a restaurant that served good, inexpensive food. He could have breakfast here while he observed and listened.

He entered the restaurant with no more than a glance from the half-dozen or so men sitting staring into coffee, or beer. Some were talking quietly to each other, others ate in silence. Two had pamphlets they were reading. As usual, most of what conversation there was, was in French. It seemed to be the language of international passion and reform. At Narraway's instruction, he had struggled to learn enough to understand most of what was said, and on rare occasions to join in. Oddly enough, he found himself gesticulating with his hands in a way he never did when speaking English. It seemed to fill in some of the gaps when he could not think of the word he wanted.

The owner of the place, who lived here with his family, came over to the corner table where Pitt sat, and bade him good morning in French.

Pitt replied, and asked for coffee and whatever form of bread was available. He did not like coffee, but to have ordered tea would have marked him out as indelibly English, a stranger, and memorable. He did not want to be remembered. He was just one more scruffy, dispossessed and angry man who could find no place in ordinary society.

Two more people came in, a man and a woman, speaking Italian, which he did not understand. The man had a grim expression on his face and crossed himself two or three times in a sign of piety and resignation.

They were joined by another man, who was heavily bearded and had high cheekbones. He spoke in a language Pitt could not identify, then they all reverted to French. Suddenly he understood most of what they said, even though to begin with they did not raise their voices.

They mentioned the explosion and the deaths several times, and shook their heads in bewilderment. They seemed to have no idea who was responsible.

Pitt's coffee came, and he paid for it, fishing for pennies in his pocket.

He remained for another hour as the place filled up. Finally a small, dark-complexioned man came in, glanced around, then saw Pitt. After speaking casually to half a dozen other people, both men and a few women, he sank down in the seat opposite Pitt, asking permission in heavily accented French.

'Bad business,' he said, shaking his head from side to side. He spoke very quickly now, watching for the proprietor to approach him and take his order. 'Surprise, eh? Don't you think so, Monsieur?'

'It surprised me,' Pitt agreed.

'Pity about that,' the man commiserated. 'Think it surprised everyone.'

'That's odd,' Pitt took a sip of his coffee. He disliked the flavour, and it was no longer hot. 'You'd think someone would know.'

The proprietor hovered by, and Pitt's companion looked round, exchanged a few words as if they were long familiar, then gave his order. He did it as smoothly and comfortably as if he ate here every day. When the proprietor was gone, he turned back to Pitt, but he looked down at the scarred tabletop. 'You would, wouldn't you?' he agreed, as if there had been no break in their conversation.

They sat in silence for several minutes, as two strangers might, while they drank their coffee. Both were listening intently to the babble of conversation around them.

'I've nothing to tell you,' the man said finally. 'But if I ever have, I'll do it.'

'Sales,' Pitt mumbled. He was referring to dynamite, and his companion knew that.

'Bits,' he said. 'Here and there. Not enough for that, that I know of. I'll look.'

Pitt stood up. 'Be careful,' he warned.

The man shrugged and did not reply. He pulled his coat collar up higher and shambled out towards the door.

Pitt waited a few minutes, then stood up and walked between the tables without glancing either side. He went out into the street where it was fractionally warmer than before, and beginning to rain. He went round the corner to Charlotte Street, to a small grocery store called Le Bel Epicerie. This was another favourite place for anarchists, run by a passionate and generous sympathiser.

He waited in the queue, listening and passing the time of day. The bombing in Lancaster Gate was mentioned, but greeted with indignation by a large man with a beard and crumbs on the front of his coat.

'Damn fool!' he said angrily.

A much smaller man next to him took exception. 'Not for you to criticise,' he snapped back. 'At least he's doing something, which is more than you are!'

'Something stupid,' the bearded man retorted. 'Nobody even knows who it is! Could have been gas mains blowing up, for all the public knows. Fool!'

'That's only because you don't know who it is,' the small man sneered.

'And I suppose you do?' a third man joined in.

'Not yet! But we will,' the small man said, as if he were certain. 'He'll tell us . . . when he's ready. Maybe after he's blown up a few more bloody police.'

Pitt kept his temper and a calm face, as if the man were speaking of blowing up some derelict building, not human beings, men he had known and worked with.

'Gets the attention,' he murmured.

The bearded man glared at him. 'You want attention, then? That what you want? You in your nice warm coat!'

Pitt glared back at him. 'I want change!' he said equally aggressively. 'You think it's going to come some other way?'

The small man smiled at him, showing broken teeth. A customer was served, and left with a paper bag in his hands. The queue moved forward.

Pitt went on and kept appointments that in more usual circumstances Stoker would have kept. He needed to do this himself. He was haunted by the fact that he had seen no warning of this

23

bombing. Five policemen had been lured to a specific site, and had gone, believing it to lead to a large illicit purchase of opium. Their source was one that had proved reliable in the very recent past and there had been no clue to the sudden appalling violence. What sort of a person would do such a thing? If it had not been an anarchist protest, then what? What conceivable purpose was there in killing these policemen?

Pitt had men infiltrated in several groups of protestors, anarchists, nihilists, following Narraway's advice, as well as his own experience. It was an old dictum: 'keep your friends close, and your enemies closer'.

'Nothing,' Jimmy said as they sat over yet another pint of ale in one of the dockside public houses. It was narrow and crowded, straw on the floor, steam rising from the rain-sodden coats. The smell of beer and wet wool filled the air. Jimmy was a long-time informer, a lean man, almost graceful, were it not for one slightly withered hand, which he carried always at an odd angle.

'Don't believe you, Jimmy,' Pitt said quietly. 'It was yesterday morning. Somebody's said something. I want to know what.' He had known Jimmy for years, and getting information out of him was like pulling teeth, but in the end it was usually worth the trouble.

'Nothing useful,' Jimmy replied, his dark eyes watching Pitt's face.

Pitt knew the game. He also knew that Jimmy wanted to tell him something, and he would stay here until he did. 'Who says?' he asked.

'Oh . . . one feller and another.'

'Who says it's not useful?' Pitt persisted. 'We'll get to who told you in time.'

'No we won't!' Jimmy looked alarmed.

'Why not? Unreliable?'

'Don't try that one!' Jimmy warned, shaking his head. 'You're sunk, Mr Pitt. This Special Branch in't good for yer. Yer used ter be a gentleman!' It was an accusation, made with much sorrow.

Pitt was unmoved.

'Jimmy, what have you heard? Two policemen are dead, and more are likely to be. This information could be important, and I can promise you, if I don't find whoever it is did it, I'm going to go on looking, and that's going to get unpleasant.'

Jimmy looked affronted. 'There's no need for that, Mr Pitt.'

'Get on with it.'

'Yer won't like it,' Jimmy warned. Then he looked again at Pitt's face. 'All right! Yer won't find a whole lot o' help coming because there's talk o' them police being bent, on the take, like.'

'You don't bomb buildings to get at police on the take,' Pitt said carefully, watching Jimmy's eyes. 'You find proof of it, and turn them in. Unless, of course, they've got something on you?'

'Turn them in, right? Who to?' Jimmy asked with disgust. 'Yer lost the wits yer was born with, Mr Pitt? They're bent all the way up, or as high up as I'm likely to get.'

Pitt felt his chest tighten and the smell of beer was suddenly sour.

'Revenge bombing?' he said with disbelief.

Jimmy's voice was heavy with disgust. 'Course not. In't you listenin' at all? I dunno what it's for. But nobody's weepin' a lot o' tears over a few coppers getting blown up. Not like they would if it was butchers or bakers or 'ansom cab drivers. Nobody's going ter take risks ter find out for yer.'

Pitt frowned. 'Doesn't make a lot of sense, Jimmy. You give information about a sale of opium to the police, someone will go, but you can't know in advance who it will be. Revenge is personal. If you kill the wrong ones, then the right ones will come after you. You've tipped your hand.'

Jimmy shrugged. 'Think wot yer like, Mr Pitt. Some o' them coppers is as bent as a dog's 'ind leg. I'm tellin' yer.'

'You'll have to do more than tell me, you'll have to prove it.'

'I'm stayin' out of it!' Jimmy said fervently, and lifted up his beer, avoiding Pitt's eyes.

Pitt paid the bill and went outside into the rain.

When he arrived back at Lisson Grove, a couple of fruitless hours later, he was followed within fifteen minutes by Stoker, looking cold and fed up, his face bleached with tiredness.

'Nothing?' Pitt guessed as Stoker closed the door.

'Nothing I like,' Stoker replied, walking across the short space to the chair opposite Pitt's desk and sitting down in it. 'We have a reasonable chance of tracing the dynamite, if whoever it was got it through an anarchist cell. It might take time, so that if he comes from the Continent he could be well back there by then. But he could be within a day anyhow.'

'Anything to suggest it's a foreign anarchist?'

'No. To be honest, sir, it sort of smells more like a home-grown one with a grudge.' Stoker watched Pitt's expression carefully as he said it, waiting for his reaction.

'Then you'd better start looking more closely at those anarchists we know,' Pitt conceded. 'Something's changed, and we've missed it. Any ideas?'

Stoker drew in a deep breath, and let it out. 'No, sir. Frankly, I haven't. We've got men in all the cells we know about, and they've heard nothing beyond the usual complaining about pay, conditions, the vote, the police, the trains, just the usual. Everybody hates the Government, and thinks they could do it better themselves. Most of them hate people who've got more money than they have, until they get more money. Then they hate the taxes.'

'Something different – anything,' Pitt said quietly. 'Any change or shift in pattern, someone new, someone old leaving . . .'

Stoker looked exhausted. There were deep lines in his bony face.

'I'm looking, sir. I've got every man hunting, but if they ask too many questions they'll be under suspicion, sir. Then we'll get nothing, except maybe some more good men killed.'

'I know. And make damn sure you're not one of them!'

Stoker smiled a little uncomfortably. He knew what Pitt was referring to. Almost two years ago, on an earlier case, he had met a woman named Kitty Ryder. In searching for her he had become fascinated, and when he had at last met her he had fallen in love. Now he had plucked up the courage to ask her to marry him, and the wedding was set. She knew what he did to earn his living, and that the dangers were considerable. She understood and did not complain. Nevertheless, Pitt was determined that Stoker would go to his wedding alive and well, and on time.

'No, sir,' Stoker agreed. 'I know better than to rush it.'

Pitt came home late and had barely finished his evening meal when the doorbell rang, and Charlotte answered it. She returned to the kitchen not alone, as Pitt had expected, but with a woman of striking appearance a couple of steps behind her. She was in her fifties, at least ten years older than Charlotte, but beautiful in a quiet way, which seemed to grow more intense the longer one looked at her.

Pitt rose to his feet.

'I'm sorry,' the visitor said. 'I see this is an extremely inconvenient hour, but I would not have come had I thought I would find you in at any other time.'

From another woman the remark would have seemed strange, but Isadora Cornwallis was the wife of the previous Assistant Commissioner of Police who had been Pitt's superior when he was at Bow Street. Cornwallis and Pitt had been more than just colleagues; there was a trust between them from heavy and hard-fought battles. Side by side they had faced some bitter enemies. One of the worst had been Isadora's brother. She had shared grief with both Cornwallis and Pitt, and found a very deep love with Cornwallis. Although at first it had seemed hopeless, because she was still married, her husband, the tragic Bishop Underwood, had then died.

'I'm afraid that's true,' he agreed. 'Would you like a cup of tea?' He glanced at the clock on the dresser. 'Or a glass of sherry?' Then he wondered if they even had sherry. It was not something they drank unless they had company, which was rare enough. 'If we have it,' he added.

'Tea would be excellent,' she accepted.

Charlotte shook her head at Pitt, as if she was surprised he had not taken as much for granted.

'I'll bring it through to the parlour,' she said quickly.

He knew that Isadora would not have come without good reason. He searched her face for a moment for signs of grief or fear, and found none. Had Cornwallis been ill it would have been written there in her demeanour, however she might seek to disguise it.

In the parlour the curtains were drawn against the winter night. The fire was long settled in hot coals in the grate, filling the room with warmth.

Isadora sat down in the armchair opposite Pitt's, and he took his own.

'I have come to give you some information that I regret deeply having to pass on, but it may have something to do with the bombing at Lancaster Gate. I give it to you in confidence, and the trust that you will treat it as such, and act on it only if it should prove to be as I fear.'

'Of course.' He was uncertain what she could possibly know that might have to do with the bombing. Were it anything of a police nature then it would be Cornwallis who would know. Surely she was not going to tell him something indiscreet, even secret? It was beyond his imagination that she should betray her husband's trust.

She began as if the whole subject distressed her. There was a tension in her voice and her hands were stiff on her lap, her usual grace completely absent.

'I assume that you have learned very little so far?' It was a tentative question. Clearly she did not know how much she could ask without being told, albeit courteously, that it was confidential to Special Branch.

'Nothing at all as to who it might be,' he answered honestly. 'The only avenue of approach we have is to find out how the dynamite was obtained. That is very probably through one of the usual sources for any anarchist.'

'Are you certain it is an anarchist behind this?' she said very seriously.

It was as if the temperature in the room had dropped. A chill gripped him. She was going to say something specific, painful, not speculation intended to be helpful, because perhaps Cornwallis knew something that she had suddenly realised might be relevant. Of course not. He should have known that. If it were Cornwallis's information, he would have come with it himself.

'No,' he answered. 'I don't see any anarchist purpose in killing our police. We tolerate them here because they are where we can see them. We have moderately good relationships with the countries they come from. They would like many of them extradited back, but they would execute them, or imprison them for life. Our own home-grown anarchists are more trouble, but so far major bombings are not their style. Sabotage, insurrection and strikes are more useful to them. Why do you ask?' He sounded impatient. He had not meant to, but he was tired and still heavily weighed down with grief.

Isadora was measuring her words very carefully. 'Of course it is likely that anarchists provided the bomb, or at the very least, the materials for it,' she said. 'But it seems possible that the motive was not political, in the sense of seeking a change in the entire system of government . . .'

'I assume you don't have any specific evidence, or you would not hesitate to say.' He leaned forward a little. 'But tell me what you suspect. I will take it as an observation, a suggestion only.'

She took a deep breath and let it out very slowly, giving herself time.

'There is a young man whose family I know moderately well. They are socially in an important position . . .'

With difficulty Pitt forced himself not to interrupt to urge her to reach the point. He found his hands clenching.

'About four years ago,' she went on, 'I don't know the exact date, he had a bad riding accident. His back was injured and he took some time to recover.'

Was she going to be so circumspect that in the end what information she gave would be meaningless?

'The injury still causes him considerable pain,' she went on. 'But I think the most severe legacy of the event was an addiction to the opium he was given in hospital during the worst of it.' She was obviously finding it difficult to tell him, not for lack of understanding, or of the words to describe it, but because in a sense she was betraying what might have been perceived as a confidence, or at the best, information gained in an unspoken trust.

'He is still taking opium?' Pitt tried to make the narrative easier.

'I think so. He does not mention it, but I have seen him in differing moods, and with the anxiety and constant unease where one knows he is . . . addicted . . .'

'If it is for pain, then I presume his doctor prescribes it for him.'

'Of course. But I am not sure that is still the case, or if it is, if it is in the amounts he wishes.'

Pitt was uncomfortably aware that Isadora's account, like the police being lured to the Lancaster Gate house, seemed to centre around opium.

'And you are afraid that he is buying opium himself?' he concluded. It had not been made public that the raid had been intended to capture dealers in drugs. Did Isadora know somehow? Through Cornwallis? He could have told her, if he knew. He was no longer Commissioner. He might consider the information not to be privileged – not from her, anyway. 'Does your husband know you have come to see me?' he asked.

She winced. 'No. He is not aware of Alexander Duncannon's . . . frailty. I prefer that it remains so. I have no obligation to act regarding opium. I can assume that it is legally prescribed and not enquire. He might feel that he could not.'

Pitt was puzzled. 'But you came to tell me? I don't understand.'

She was quick. 'You seized on the opium,' she said. 'Did the bombing have something to do with opium?'

'Is that not why you mentioned Duncannon, and his addiction?'

She smiled ruefully. 'Don't play with me, Mr Pitt. I am well used enough to it with my brother, and with my first husband. I am really quite good at it, absurd and insulting as that is. I came to you, even though it is difficult for me, because Alexander is addicted to opium. He is a charming but unstable young man, highly intelligent and well educated, who has a passionate hatred for the police. It amounts to an obsession, a crusade against them. He has made no secret of it, but I think many people assume it to be merely part of his rather eccentric style of living, perhaps an attempt to be accepted by the company he chooses to keep, possibly even as a rather desperate form of rebellion against his father, who is a wealthy and formidable man who once had high expectations of his only son.'

'Do you mean it is a pose rather than a real addiction?'

'Some believe so.'

'And you?'

'I believe it is an addiction,' she said very quietly. 'I like him. I have spent time in his company, occasionally, at concerts, lectures, and even at some functions when he and I were equally bored by the niceties being exchanged.'

'He hates the police? Is that because he has sympathy with anarchist connections?' It was not unusual for young men of wealth and privilege to have sympathies with the poor, and aspirations to see the politics changed. They saw it as a just cause on whose behalf to rebel.

'No,' Isadora said simply. 'He believes that a large proportion of the police are deeply corrupt, and they are being shielded by other police, for reasons of their own, perhaps because they are also corrupt, bribed and possibly afraid. Or simply some of the many who prefer not to see that which makes them uncomfortable, or would change them if they acknowledged it. To take action would be expensive to them, even dangerous.'

Perhaps after his own questioning, and the whispers he had heard, Pitt should not have been surprised, and yet he was. It was even more startling that Isadora Cornwallis, of all people, should feel strongly enough about it to come to him, without confiding in the husband she loved so deeply, because he had once been Commissioner of the very police they were speaking of.

'Do you believe him?' he asked.

She had not expected anything quite so direct. It was clear from the sudden widening of her eyes.

'I believe it is what he thinks,' she answered. 'A dear friend of his was convicted and hanged a couple of years ago. Alexander did everything he could to save his friend, certain that he was innocent. He failed, and Dylan Lezant went to the gallows. Alexander never really got over it.'

Pitt remembered the case. He recalled with a chill that that, too, was to do with a drug arrest that had gone wrong. Lezant had been arrested after he shot a totally innocent man who merely happened to be passing.

'I recall the case.' Pitt nodded. 'Tragic. Alexander believed Lezant's story? I suppose that's natural enough, if they were friends. Was Lezant also addicted?'

'Yes, but Alexander was still certain that he was innocent.'

'So who shot the bystander?'

She shook her head very slightly. 'Alexander believed Lezant's story that it was the police themselves.'

Pitt was startled.

'Why would they do that, for heaven's sake?'

'Carelessness . . . panic,' she said. 'But then they had to blame someone else, because they shouldn't have had guns with them anyway. I know what you think: a young man who was devoted to his friend, perhaps the one person who understood his addiction and did not blame him. He believed what he had to, to preserve his own emotional values and possibly even to justify the battle he put up to save Lezant from the rope – and failed. Who knows all the reasons why we do things? Maybe least of all ourselves.'

He could not argue with her. 'So you think Alexander could have placed the bomb that blew up the Lancaster Gate house, killing two policemen and critically injuring three more? Is that not . . . extreme?'

'Yes, it is,' she agreed. 'And I very much hope that I am totally mistaken. Believe me, I debated long and deeply whether I should even mention it to you. It seems disloyal to my friends. Maybe it is worse than that. I am not certain John would approve. I suppose that is obvious, since I have not told him.' Now her face was pinched with a painful memory. 'But I know that people you have loved, that you have known all your life, can be quite different from what you have supposed. Why would you even entertain the idea that they are really strangers to you, full of passions that you did not dream of?'

He knew now that she was speaking of her brother, who would have been willing to see her blamed for a crime she had not committed. She would never know if he would even have seen her hanged for it, without speaking out to save her with the truth.

The shadow of that time was there in the room. What did she recall of it now? It had been years ago. It was Pitt who had saved her. It was also Pitt who had caused the downfall of her brother, and his death, in another case, after that. So much old pain. And yet Isadora had come to him now with this, not choosing to look aside, not even choosing to confide in Cornwallis. Was that not to wound the man she loved, rather than to protect him from having to look for such a vile truth?

Or because she trusted Pitt to face it, whatever the cost?

'I'll speak to Mr Duncannon tomorrow,' he promised. 'Where can I find him?'

She had wanted him to do that; it was the reason she had come. And yet now she also looked stricken. The die was cast. It was too late to change her mind.

With stiff fingers she opened her reticule and passed him a small piece of paper. On it was written the address of the flat in which Alexander Duncannon lived. He was of the social class and income that did not need to have any occupation, except whatever he chose with which to pass his time.

'When might I find him there?' he asked.

'I would try about ten o'clock in the morning,' she answered. 'I don't imagine he will be an early riser. Later, and he might have gone out. He has friends.'

'Thank you. I will find another reason for talking with him,' Pitt promised. 'I certainly will not mention your name.'

She hesitated for a moment, at a loss for words herself. Then she gave a brief smile and allowed him to escort her to the door, and the street where her carriage was waiting.

Pitt found Alexander Duncannon not at his flat but at an art exhibition three blocks away from the Automony Club. The man at the door told him who he was. Apparently he came often. A dark, slender young man. He looked about twenty-five. He was standing alone in front of a large painting of a country scene. Labourers stood with scythes in hand. The August sun shone out of a clear blue sky on to the golden cornfield. A few scarlet poppies burned bright at the margins.

Pitt had grown up in the country. This looked idyllic, and quite unreal to him. It had a kind of beauty, but it was set back from the smell of the earth, the relentless heat of harvest time, the ache of backs too long bent.

'Do you like it?' he asked.

The softness of youth was in his cheeks when he turned, but there were hard shadows around his eyes. He was clearly familiar with pain. He smiled, suddenly and charmingly. It lit his face. 'No,' he said with candour. 'Do you? Or have you not looked at it long enough?'

Pitt smiled back. 'How long do I need to look at it in order to like it?' he asked.

Alexander was amused. 'I don't know, but longer than I have. What do you not like about it? It's pretty enough . . . isn't it?'

Pitt decided in that moment to engage him in an honest conversation. 'Is that what you think it should be, pretty?' he asked.

'You don't like pretty pictures?' He took him up on it instantly, and – from the grace of his posture and the sudden life in his eyes – with pleasure.

Pitt gave it consideration. 'No, I think I don't. At least not if it is at the expense of the real. Artifice has its own kind of ugliness.'

Now Alexander was eager, his eyes alight.

'Do you know the place?'

'Not recognisably.'

Alexander laughed. '*Touché*,' he said cheerfully. 'But are you familiar with what it is meant to be? What it was, before it was sentimentalised?'

'Many like it, yes,' Pitt admitted, for a moment caught back in memory so sharp it was almost physical.

'Funny. I don't,' Alexander shrugged. 'And yet I know it's wrong. Perhaps one develops a distaste for the artificial, don't you think?'

'Yes, I agree.' Long ago, before graduating to murder cases, Pitt had worked with theft, especially of fine art. He had learned a lot more about it than he had expected to, and found it gave him great pleasure. He need not tell this young man who he was, not just yet. Special Branch was not police. No such disclosure was required. 'It is an emotional lie,' he added.

Now he had Alexander's complete attention. 'How perceptive of you, Mr . . .?'

'Pitt.' There was no escaping giving his name without just the kind of dishonesty he had spoken of. 'Thomas Pitt.'

'Alexander Duncannon.' He held out his hand.

Pitt shook it. 'There has to be something better here, surely?' he asked. 'What do you like?'

'Ah! Let me show you something lovely,' Alexander responded. 'It's very small, but quite beautiful.' He turned away and began walking rather unevenly towards the next room.

Pitt followed, interested to see what the young man would like.

Alexander stopped in front of a small pencil drawing of a clump of grass depicted in intense detail. Every blade was perfectly drawn. In the heart of it was a nest of field mice. He stared at Pitt, waiting for his verdict.

Pitt looked at the picture for several moments. He was uncomfortable. Alexander had shown him something that was truly beautiful. His appreciation of it revealed some part of himself. He was not going to break the silence. He would wait until Pitt delivered an equally honest answer.

'That's real,' Pitt said sincerely. 'I almost expect them to move. I can smell the dry earth and hear the wind whisper in the grass.'

Alexander did not hide his pleasure. For a moment in time they stood side by side and looked at the drawing. Then Pitt dragged his attention from the tiny lives caught both by a man's pencil and by his heart, and thought again of bombs, burning wreckage and dead police.

'Wonderful,' he said quietly, 'how a man can catch something so small, and make it eternal. Thank you for showing me.'

'Worth it, isn't it?' Alexander replied, his thin face alight. 'The whole trip, just to have seen that. Life's full of small things that matter passionately. Absurd – a man that doesn't, and mice that do.'

'You say that as if you had someone in mind?' Pitt prompted.

Suddenly the pain was back in Alexander's face, and a startling bitterness. 'Too many,' he replied. 'People dead, who shouldn't be. People alive who do only harm.'

Pitt remembered what Isadora had said about Alexander's friend, hanged for a murder Alexander was certain he had not committed. He felt faintly deceitful in broaching it, but perhaps this young man had nothing to do with the Lancaster Gate bombing either. He would be pleased if that proved to be so.

'Indeed,' he said quietly, looking at the next painting, a rather flat still life with flowers. 'Anarchists, for example. Destroy everything and create nothing.'

Alexander did not reply for several moments.

Pitt was about to speak again.

'Sometimes it's only the destroyers who get noticed,' Alexander answered then. 'Everybody remembers whoever assassinates a president that oppresses his people and puts to death hundreds of the poor who dare to protest. Who's going to remember the man who drew the mice? Are you?'

Pitt felt a moment's embarrassment. He had been too absorbed in the drawing to look for the artist's name.

'No,' he admitted. 'Who was he?'

Alexander smiled, a wide, flashing radiance then instantly gone, and the darkness swept back in again. 'I know. You said, "Who was he?" Natural enough, I suppose, but actually it was a woman. Mary Ann Church.'

'And the anarchists?' Pitt said.

Now Alexander's face was shadowed and his body tense, visibly so, even under his beautifully cut jacket. 'I wouldn't tell you, even if I knew.'

Pitt did not hide his surprise.

Alexander shrugged. 'Well, perhaps if I knew, and they got the wrong people, and were going to hang them, I would,' he amended. 'Justice is a very big thing, kind of ugly and beautiful at the same time. Like that tiger over there!' He pointed vaguely.

Pitt searched the paintings on the far wall.

'I can't see a tiger.'

'That's rather my point,' Alexander replied. 'There are some more nice things in here, if you look. I must go.' He turned and walked away, and as Pitt watched him he was aware of a considerable limp, as if the young man's back gave him constant pain, one he could only rarely forget.

Pitt walked back to look again at the mice, tiny, pulsing with life, and now immortal, at least in the mind.

Tellman came to Pitt's office late, just as Pitt was thinking of going home. Tellman looked tired and his lean face was pinched with unhappiness. He stood stiffly in front of Pitt's desk. He would not sit down until he had been given permission. It was as if he were making a statement that he did not belong here. He had an overcoat on, but no gloves, and Pitt noticed that his hands were red from the cold air outside.

'Tea?' Pitt offered. These days he had someone who would make it for him and bring it.

'I've little to report,' Tellman replied. 'Not be here long enough time to take tea. But thank you . . . sir.'

'Yes, you will,' Pitt told him, pulling the bell cord for someone to come. As soon as they did, he asked for tea, and biscuits as well.

Reluctantly Tellman took off his coat and hung it on the coat stand by the door, then sat down.

'Haven't got anything very helpful yet, sir,' he repeated. 'Been to all our usual informers, and nobody seems to have anything. Sorry, but it looks as if you've got a new and very bad sort of anarchist in the city. Might have got the dynamite from one of the quarries inland a bit. Bessemer and Sons is missing a noticeable amount. A dozen sticks or more. Reported it unwillingly. Didn't want to look as incompetent as it seems they are. Somebody's head will roll for that. Probably the foreman's.'

'Any idea who took it?' Pitt asked. It could be a lead, and so far the only certain direction in which to look.

'Working on it,' Tellman replied.

The tea came, with biscuits, and Pitt thanked the man as he left.

Tellman glanced at it reluctantly, but could not resist the fragrant steam and the suggestion of warmth. He took a biscuit and bit into it, clearly suddenly hungry.

'You find anything?' he asked with his mouth full.

'I'm not sure,' Pitt replied. He looked at Tellman's tired, unhappy face, and knew that he was still deeply shocked by the violence of the bombing. Of course policemen were killed in the line of duty every now and then, and there were traffic accidents, even train wrecks where the casualties were appalling. Buildings burned, bridges collapsed, sometimes floods caused terrible damage. But this was deliberate, created by human imagination and intent, and directed specifically at police, men that Tellman knew.

'Not sure?' Tellman said with surprise. He put his mug down, no longer warming his hands on it. 'What do you mean?'

'Isadora Cornwallis came to see me, privately, so this is confidential,' Pitt told him. 'If she chooses to tell her husband that's up to her. I don't want it getting back to him through police gossip. I'm telling you it was she simply so that you know what I learned was not lightly given, or something I can afford to ignore.' He watched Tellman's expression to be certain he understood.

'What does she know about anarchy?' Tellman pursed his lips, doubt in his face.

'Some anarchists come from privileged backgrounds,' Pitt told him. 'They aren't all peasants or labourers with a pittance to live on.'

Tellman stared at him, waiting.

'She is acquainted with a young man of excellent family who has a profound grudge against police, whom he believes are corrupt,' he continued. 'He also has possible connections with anarchists. So far it is only philosophical, so far as we know, but he would certainly know where to go to purchase dynamite, possibly stolen from a quarry such as Bessemer and Sons, who you say are presently missing about a dozen sticks.'

Tellman put his hands back around the mug. 'What's his complaint about the police? Maybe they were just keeping order, and he thought he was above having to accept it and behave himself?'

'He thinks it's a great deal more serious than that.'

'Like what?' Tellman said sharply.

'Like police accidentally shooting a passer-by, and then blaming an innocent man, Dylan Lezant, and seeing him hang for it.'

'Oh, yes?' Tellman sneered. 'And who says he's innocent? His friend the anarchist sympathiser?'

Pitt put down his own tea. 'Tellman, what actually happened doesn't matter. If this young man thinks it did, then that's what he's going to act on.'

'That's what he says,' Tellman argued. 'Have you any reason whatever to think he isn't just an ordinary bomber who thinks he can terrify us into doing whatever political madness he wants?' There was an edge of challenge in his voice, as if Pitt had deliberately suggested there were some justification, some weakness or error on the part of the murdered police.

Pitt measured his reply carefully, but he felt his own anger rise, even though he understood the depth of Tellman's loyalty, and the reality of his grief. He had seen those broken bodies himself.

'I don't know,' he admitted. 'I don't know if he had anything to do with it. I'm telling you that we can't rule him out as a possibility.'

'What's his name?' Tellman asked.

'I'll deal with it, for the time being.'

Tellman froze, the colour flushing up his cheeks. 'You don't trust me to tread softly with this young gentleman of yours?' His voice was strained, his jaw tight. 'I'm an inspector, Commander Pitt. I'm just as capable and used to speaking to quality as you are, even if I'm not raised in a country house, or married to a lady. And maybe I appreciate the ordinary policemen, like those in the hospital, or the morgue, a bit more than you do.' He put his mug down and rose to his feet. 'I answer ultimately to the Police Commissioner, not to their lordships in Parliament. I'll find the man that set that bomb, whoever's son he is.'

Pitt was momentarily taken aback. He had not been sensitive to just how deeply Tellman had been hurt by this; or, to tell the truth, by how profound his loyalty was to the force that had given him both his purpose and his identity. There was an element of truth that Pitt had changed his sense of identity when he left the police and joined Special Branch. He'd had no choice, if he were to succeed in his new position. The change had not been of his choosing. He had been forced out of the police because he had solved a crime by finding an unpopular answer, one that offended those with the power to ruin him.

He had joined Special Branch as the only other group that could use his skills, and could afford to defy the powers who wanted him ruined.

Pitt remained sitting. 'You can't defend yourself against the charges if you don't know they exist,' he pointed out. 'You may prefer that I don't tell you in future, should there be anything further in it. If that is the case, then I shall have to take it directly

41

to Bradshaw. But I would rather not. He doesn't know the dead men personally; you do.'

Tellman looked confused. He had made something of a fool of himself, and he was now aware of it, but unwilling to step back.

'I suppose you'd better tell me,' he said unhappily. 'Somebody has to fight for the men. God knows, two of them are dead and more could follow them.' He met Pitt's eyes defiantly, with challenge in his glare. 'I'm not going to let them be murdered, blown apart, burned and crippled, then when they can't speak for themselves, blamed for it as well.'

Pitt hesitated only a moment. If he allowed Tellman to get away with that, something would be lost between them.

'Is that what you are suggesting I am going to do, Inspector Tellman?' he asked quietly.

Long tense seconds of silence hung in the room before Tellman answered.

'That possibility won't arise . . . sir,' he answered, rose to his feet with a curt nod, and walked out.

Pitt leaned back in his chair feeling acutely miserable. He had had no choice but to inform Tellman of Alexander Duncannon's charge, because it could be part of the case. In fact, at the moment it was the only lead they had. But he had not handled it well.

His last visitor of the day was completely unexpected, and did not come to Special Branch in Lisson Grove, but was waiting for Pitt when he finally arrived home at Keppel Street. He had barely got through the front door and hung his wet coat on the rack in the hall when Charlotte came out of the parlour. He knew the instant he saw her face that something was disturbing her.

She smiled, but there was a warning in her eyes. She came forward and kissed him gently, just a moment of sweetness he would dearly like to have clung on to, but she pulled away.

'Jack has come to see you,' she said almost under her breath.

'There is something about which he is deeply concerned. I'll leave you to talk to him in the parlour. The fire's burning up well and there is sherry, if you want to pour him a little. I'll be in the kitchen.' And after a moment of meeting his eyes again, she turned and went down the corridor and around the short corner into the kitchen.

Pitt opened the parlour door and felt the warmth of the familiar room close around him. It was quiet, full of pictures of the family, ornaments they had collected over the years. The picture over the mantel was a good reproduction of a Vermeer painting of a quiet harbour with sailing vessels and Dutch quayside buildings against a gentle sky.

The curtains over the French doors to the garden were drawn closed, keeping out the winter.

Jack Radley stood near the mantel shelf, handsome, well-dressed as always. Whether he was at his ease or not, he always managed to look it. He had a natural grace. He straightened up as Pitt came in and closed the door.

'Sorry to call without warning,' Jack said. His smile was slight, and worried.

Pitt went over to the decanter on the side table and without asking poured two glasses of sherry. He did not particularly like it, and he took less for himself, but it gave him time to order his thoughts. Jack Radley was the second husband of Charlotte's younger sister, Emily. He had begun as a remarkably handsome and charming young man about town with good breeding and absolutely no money. The fortune was Emily's, inherited from her first husband, Lord Ashworth.

But Jack had taken his opportunities very seriously. He had worked hard to become a Member of Parliament, fighting a seat on his merit, rather than accepting a safe one where he could afford to be idle. He had earned his present position in the Foreign Office. In fact, he had been extremely unfortunate not to be in an even higher one. A misjudgement, a loyalty betrayed, had robbed him of a position his diligence warranted.

He sipped his sherry. 'Thanks. Rotten night. Feels like January already. I'm sorry to disturb you. You must be frantic with this appalling bombing.' It sounded like a casual remark, but Pitt knew it was not. Jack was becoming politically adept. Beneath the charm, he seldom wasted words.

'Indeed,' Pitt nodded. 'I imagine you would much prefer to be at home with Emily. So what brings you here?'

Jack smiled sincerely this time. 'Can't waste time playing diplomatic games with you, can I, Thomas? Very well. To the point. I believe you have been to interview Alexander Duncannon. Whether it has anything to do with this bombing at Lancaster gate or not, people will assume that it has. That has to be taking all your time and attention right now.'

'Of course. Yes, I went to see Duncannon. Why does that concern you?'

'Are you aware of who his father is?'

'No. Nor do I care.'

'Then you had better begin caring.' Jack's smile had vanished and his face was marked with concern. There were lines Pitt had not noticed before around his eyes and mouth.

'Why?' Pitt said levelly. 'If Alexander Duncannon is involved in the murder and maiming of five policemen, I don't care who his family is, I will charge him with it.'

Jack kept his temper with difficulty. 'Thomas, don't pretend you are naïve. You've been in high office long enough to know that things are seldom that simple. Haven't you lost enough position being thrown out of Bow Street – largely for political ineptitude, for solving a crime with an answer, albeit true, but unacceptable to those in power? I'm not asking you to lie, or to let a guilty man go, or arrest an innocent one – just wait a few days – a week maybe . . .'

'Wait for what?' Pitt asked.

'Until a certain contract of major importance has been negotiated,' Jack replied. 'I can't exaggerate how much it matters. It is with a provincial government in China, concerning making a free port on the China Sea. The boost to trade will be immeasurable. In Britain thousands of people will benefit. The work it will promote will make them richer and safer, once this contract is signed. That's all I can tell you, so please don't push me for more.'

'Why on earth should I hold up investigation of a bombing because of that?' Pitt asked curiously. 'I don't see any connection.'

'Godfrey Duncannon is the only man who has the skills and the connections to negotiate it successfully. If his son in under investigation, or there is even a suggestion of it, it will handicap him enough to jeopardise the whole matter. The Chinese don't trust us easily, which after the Opium Wars is hardly surprising! I wouldn't trust us.'

'Replace him with someone else,' Pitt said. 'Let him advise them from somewhere where he isn't seen. They can report to him, and he can put his knowledge there, without anyone knowing.'

Jack lost patience. 'For God's sake, Thomas! It's his standing, his reputation, his charm that matters! Of course we've got other people who could be schooled to say and do the right things. I could do it myself, with a bit of guidance. But I don't have Godfrey's personal connections. He's spent a lifetime making friends, building up a network of obligations and debts of honour and gratitude within China. That sort of thing takes time, which we haven't got if we go back to the beginning.'

Pitt hesitated.

'We need Duncannon,' Jack insisted. 'I've no idea if his son has anything to do with the case or not. It's possible he could have got himself caught up on the fringes. Solve it without his help. Or leave it a week or two until the treaty is sealed. Please!'

'I'm not sure that I can,' Pitt said slowly, searching for words as he went. 'If the rest of the investigation comes back to him, I can't tell the police not to question him.'

Jack's face was tense, his voice hard-edged. 'What can he tell you? That someone he spoke to bragged that he knows where to get dynamite? You'll get that through another source. Don't tell me you only follow up one man, one overheard piece of conversation? You must have men in every cell of anarchists worth bothering with. Even I know about the Autonomy Club. You must know of a dozen other such places. Alexander Duncannon might be the easiest source for you to question, and the safest. He's a damaged young man in plain sight, and you can go and find him without having to look. He had a bad accident and is still vulnerable. Leave him alone, Thomas. Get the same information somewhere else.'

Pitt saw the anxiety in Jack's face and knew there was far more that he was unable to say. But was it about the contract that he could not go into detail, or was it his own stake in the matter? Jack had made too many serious errors of judgement over the last few years. He had done no more than any other man in his place might have, but the results had been on the brink of catastrophe. Treason and murder had been involved. Jack was a diplomat, not a member of Special Branch. He had trusted people everyone else had also seen as above suspicion, and been wrong, but he had been close to these men; had worked hand in glove with them. It was Pitt who had learned the truth, and put together the pieces that formed a far different picture.

But as it was, Jack would be seen, at least by some, as being easily fooled, with flawed judgement, not safe to promote to higher office. Was that what troubled him this time? He could not afford to be closely allied to another man stained by scandal, let alone mass murder, and anarchy was close to treason!

'He hasn't given me any information,' Pitt said. 'He is possibly a suspect . . .'

'In bombing the house in Lancaster Gate?' Jack asked incredulously. 'Don't be absurd!' But even as he said it, his voice wavered minutely. 'Why on earth would he do such a thing? He has unsuitable friends, that's all. He's young. Twenty-three or four. I had some unsuitable friends at that age. Didn't you? No, I suppose you didn't. You were probably walking the beat in some domestic suburb and helping old ladies across the road.' There was anger in him now. Or was it fear?

'Probably,' Pitt agreed. 'Whereas you were helping the young ones.'

Jack blushed very faintly. He had moved from one country house to another, as a cheerful, handsome and hugely entertaining guest. He had never intended to marry any of the highly eligible young ladies. He would not have been acceptable to their families because he had no money with which to support them. But everybody liked having him as a guest. He made them laugh, he flattered them, he was nice to everyone. He dressed beautifully and rode a horse with skill and grace. He was wise enough never to drink more than he could hold, and had more sense than to sleep with the wife of anyone who mattered. In fact he was discreet enough never to damage anyone's reputation at all. They were not skills everyone possessed.

'Perhaps I deserve that.' He gave Pitt a rueful look. 'Please, Thomas, I'm asking you.'

'I'll try,' Pitt conceded. 'And certainly I will be discreet about questioning Duncannon. That's as far as I can go.'

'Thank you.' Jack nodded, a faint smile touching his lips at last. He picked up his sherry, turning the glass slowly and letting the firelight sparkle from the cut edges of the crystal.

Pitt raised his as well, but it was a gesture, an agreement.

Chapter Three

TELLMAN SAT beside the fire in his own home, the place he most loved to be. It was a small house, one he could afford without anxiety, but in a neat row of other houses along a quiet street. He did not know the neighbours well, but his wife, Gracie, did, and liked them. Several of them were other young women, like herself, with small children. They were all respectable. Gracie had wanted a house like this, with her own husband and her own children, for as long as she could remember dreaming about anything at all.

She had been born in the East End, in poverty, and with no education. She had begun work at thirteen, as a maid for Charlotte and Pitt, almost as soon as they were married. She was still barely five feet tall, but with enough spirit in her for two people twice her size. Charlotte had taught her to read and write as well as how to cook and generally keep house.

Tellman sat in the rocking chair in the corner of the warm kitchen and watched as Gracie fed their daughter. It was a sight that was infinitely pleasing to him. Nothing in the world would ever matter quite as much as this.

Little Christina looked at him once or twice, puzzled, because he had not picked her up and cuddled her, as he usually did. He had a heavy cold, and he did not wish to give it to her. He probably missed the touch of her face more than she missed him. He smiled at her now, even though he did not feel like it.

The bombing had horrified him, especially since the victims were fellow police, and in the course of their duty. But his job had caused him to see a great deal of violence and tragedy over the years. What disturbed him more deeply was the talk of corruption. Of course people made mistakes, everyone did, and sometimes the results were serious. He had no doubt that at times people lied, either to protect themselves, or someone else. Men had been known to keep the odd few coins, perhaps even a guinea, almost a week's wages.

Tellman despised it, but he would have faced the guilty man. He had done, on occasion. You did not go behind a man's back; you gave him the chance to put it right.

But two men were dead and three men crippled, and might yet die. Tellman had been to the hospital and seen them, not to ask any questions, but out of respect. They had looked awful. Bossiney would probably live, but he was in agony from the burns that had devastated half his face. Yarcombe was silent, stunned by the loss of his limb, unable to grasp that it was not there.

Ednam had been more consumed by fury at the attack on his men than at his own pain. At least that was how it had seemed. He had glared at Tellman and demanded from him an oath that he would find who had done this, and see them hanged for it.

Tellman had replied that he would do it regardless of oaths or pressure or threats, and he had meant it. It had taken an effort to forgive Ednam for even asking.

Now Pitt was saying that the strongest lead they had, one they could not ignore, was that the whole atrocity was a revenge against police corruption so vile it had ended in the deliberate hanging of an innocent man!

It was nonsense, of course. The man who made the charge must be mad. In any other circumstances Tellman would have pitied him, for something had clearly unhinged his mind. Apparently the man hanged was a close friend.

If anyone had so terribly damaged those Tellman loved, would he have lost his balance, his wits, maybe even his morality? He could not bear to think of it.

He stood up now and walked over to Gracie. 'Sorry,' he said quietly. 'I'll carry her up.' He smiled at Christina, who put her head to one side and slowly smiled back at him. Suddenly he was choked with emotion. He reached forward and picked her up, holding her close, smelling the sweetness of her, soap, warm wool, smelling faintly milky.

'C'mon, angel,' he said a little harshly. 'It's your bedtime.'

He carried her up the stairs and into her room, next to theirs, and where, with the doors open, they could hear her if she cried. He took off the blanket around her and again marvelled at the embroidery on her nightgown, little flowers worked in pink. He remembered Gracie stitching it, only a few months ago. How quickly babies grow. Every day was precious.

He tucked her into the bed and kissed her. 'Good night,' he whispered.

'Night,' she answered, closing her eyes. She was probably asleep before he reached the door.

Back downstairs again his mind returned to the question of corruption.

For Tellman, growing up poor, the scrawny, undersized son of a factory labourer, to be a policeman was an honourable job. It was a position that earned respectability, and the regard of the community. People who had never noticed him as a child now looked to him for help. And he gave it, with pleasure.

It was Thomas Pitt, years ago, when they had both worked in Bow Street, who had made him see what a good job it was, what courage and honour there was in it. They were men who spent their days, and sometimes their nights as well, seeking the truth, wherever it led them, fighting to see that justice was done and people were kept from injury, loss, fear of the people they could not fight alone.

That was why he found Pitt's attitude now so acutely painful.

He could not tell him that. Of course he understood that Pitt's job had changed and he could not afford a loyalty to the police rather than to Special Branch. But it still seemed like a denial of what he used to care about, the men he had worked beside in the past, not so long ago.

Tellman was tired and his head ached. The hot tea had eased his sore throat a little, but his face ached across the bones of his cheeks. He was in for a really heavy cold.

Gracie looked at him with a rueful smile.

'Yer should take a day in bed,' she told him. 'Just sleep as much as yer can. It won't send it away, but it'll 'elp.'

'I can't,' he answered firmly, mostly to convince himself. Nothing sounded better than bed just now. 'I've got to find out all I can about this bombing.'

'What can you find, if it's anarchists?' she asked reasonably. She sat down sideways on one of the hard-backed chairs at the kitchen table. The room reminded him a little of the Pitts' kitchen. It had the same coloured china; although it was a different pattern. It was still blue and white. And there was a copper-bottomed saucepan hung on the wall by its handle. Gracie seldom used it, but she liked the beautiful, gleaming colour of the metal. He had seen her polish it countless times. The fact that it was hers always made her smile.

On the dresser where most people would have had special plates, there was a little brown china donkey. He had bought it for her in a market one day, and she had loved it. She said it reminded her of a real one she had known, and she called it 'Charlie'. He looked at it now and smiled. This was home, and he longed to be able to stay here until his cold was better. It would almost certainly be wet tomorrow, and the sting of the east wind could slice through even the best woollen coat and scarf.

'If it's anarchists then it isn't crooked police,' he answered. 'I'd give a week's salary – a month's – to be able to find that.'

'Do you think it could be?' she asked. Gracie never ran away from a problem; at worst she would creep around and attack it from another angle. She was the bravest, and the most stubborn person he knew. He admired it in her, even loved it, but it still frightened him. She may be only the size of a ninepenny rabbit, but she had more fight in her than a weasel.

She passed him a soft cloth rag and he blew his nose fiercely.

'That means you think it could be,' she said very quietly.

'That means I don't know how to prove it wasn't,' he argued. 'We make mistakes, but we aren't corrupt. Gracie . . . if you'd seen them, you'd want to put a spit through whoever did it and slow roast them over the fire!'

'You knew them, didn't you, Samuel?' she said, biting her lip.

'It could have been me leading that raid on the house.' He met her eyes and saw the pain in them, as she imagined what the other men's wives must be feeling now.

'But yer weren't,' she said flatly. She sniffed. 'Do yer know what it were about?'

'No. It looks like an opium sale.'

'That's not what you do, opium!'

'What difference does that make?' he demanded. Why was she arguing? 'What if it'd been paintings, or jewellery? Then it could have been me!' he said sharply.

She sat absolutely still, her face tight with pain. 'I know that. Yer scared for next time they send you somewhere?' She reached forward to touch his hand, and then changed her mind. 'I wouldn't blame yer.'

'No, I don't think so,' he answered quite honestly. 'I think I feel sort of guilty, because they're in the morgue, blown to pieces, or in hospital burned and broken – and I'm sitting in my own house in a warm kitchen complaining 'cos I've got a cold. What makes me different, Gracie? How come I'm alive an' they're dead? Or maybe dying! Yarcombe lost his arm.'

'I dunno,' she admitted. 'But it 'appens all the time. Mrs Willetts down at number twenty-three died when her babe was born. An'

I'm as fit as the butcher's dog. Nobody knows the reasons, Samuel. Least not yet. Maybe one day. I got one reason . . .'

'Like what?' he said after a moment. He really did not want to know, but she seemed to be waiting for him to ask.

'We're goin' to 'ave another baby . . .'

Suddenly a wave of emotion swept through him, as if there were a fire inside him, filling him up. All the rest of the kitchen melted into shadows and all he could see was Gracie sitting sideways on the chair, the lamplight on her face, a little flushed, her eyes bright.

This was his home, his family, more precious than anything else in the world. It was all he needed for happiness. He must look after them, keep them safe, see that they were always fed, sheltered, happy. Whatever job he had to do, he must do it well. This was his greatest calling in life. He must always look after them.

'Say something!' she urged him. 'Are yer pleased?'

Tears choked him. 'Of course I'm pleased.' he said, reaching for the cloth again and blowing his nose fiercely. 'I'm . . . I'm happier than any man has a right to be.'

'Then get up to bed and sleep,' she ordered. 'Sleep termorrer too.' She gave him a quick hug, which he returned quickly, tightly, but still argued.

'I can't, I've got to go to work. I need to prove to Pitt that this is anarchists, and nothing to do with the police!'

Tellman felt thick-headed and his throat was sore when he woke up, but he pretended he was better. However his first words to Gracie were punctuated by a hacking cough, so her total disbelief was understandable.

'Go back to bed,' she said gently. 'I'll bring yer up an 'ot drink, and a nice crisp slice o' toast. I got some good, sharp marmalade.'

For an instant he hesitated. He could hear the rain against the kitchen window, even though it was warm inside. She must have been up for some time, because the cooker was hot and the whole kitchen was comfortable, the air soft to the skin.

'Yes,' he said huskily. 'But I'll have it down here. Got to go and see more about the injured men again.' He knew he must look into whatever they had in common. Was it them in particular the bomber was aiming at? Or police in general? Anybody to pay for the one he thought was corrupted? He sat down at the kitchen table. He could see by the clock on the dresser that he was late already, but he could afford ten or fifteen minutes more. Perhaps the rain would ease.

Gracie opened the door to the hot coals and put a slice of bread on the toasting fork. While he waited he poured himself a large mug of tea.

She brought him the toast, crisp and perfect. He thanked her for it, and reached for the butter. Then he spread the marmalade on and bit into it. It was delicious and piquant enough to taste, even thick-headed as he was, and totally robbed of the sense of smell.

'What are you looking for?' she persisted. She never gave up.

'Lots of things, maybe,' he answered, swallowing the first mouthful.

'Like what?'

'Was it those particular men,' he said to begin with. 'Do they usually work together, or was it for a special case?'

'Why?'

'So we know if it was the case they were attacked for, or if it was them the bomber wanted,' he explained.

'Why would an anarchist care who it was?' she asked, taking a second piece of toast off the fork and putting it back on so the other side faced the coals.

'They wouldn't,' he answered with his mouth full.

She stood up and brought over the toast. They were large slices, thick and crisp.

'What are you saying, Samuel? That it weren't anarchists? Who, then? Wot is it?' She looked at him steadily, eyes unwavering.

He did not want to face the alternative. Sometimes he wished she were not quite so quick. At times she knew him better than he knew himself – quite a lot of times, actually.

'Yer mean they was after them police in particular?' she concluded.

'I have to make sure it wasn't,' he evaded the answer.

'So what'll you do? Give it back to Mr Pitt, then?' She was not going to leave it alone.

'If it was anarchists, I suppose so. That's his job.' He realised he was not sure if that was what he wanted to do. There was a discomfort at the back of his mind, a need to defend his own men from the smear of corruption that had been suggested. And more than that, the victims were police. They deserved justice, a settlement of the case with people accused and tried, and if they were guilty, then hanged as well. It was a monstrous crime.

'Except I don't want to,' he said instead. 'I want to follow it all the way, and see the end of it.' He looked up at her and saw the anxiety in her sharp, bright little face. Although she was well into her twenties, and expecting her second child, there was so much in her that was still like the quick, brave, confrontational little girl he had first met years ago, when he was Pitt's sergeant and she was his opinionated little housemaid. She had challenged Tellman, contradicted him, and far too often been right. He had tried very hard not to fall in love with her, and failed utterly. It had taken him years even to catch her attention, let alone her respect. At least that was how it seemed.

Now she looked at him tenderly, the same way she looked at their child.

He felt a wave of emotion wash over him completely, and concentrated on his toast as if it had been a complicated masterwork.

'They're police, and they're dead, or worse,' he said finally.

'I'm alive. They're my own people, Gracie. I've got to find out what happened to them, and who did it. I've got to show people that police are good men doing a job that shouldn't get them killed. I owe them that . . . them that are gone, and all them that are still here, and still out on the streets.'

'Be careful,' she warned. 'Somebody did it. They in't going ter want you finding them. Don't let 'em kill you too, Samuel.'

She was doing everything she could to hide her fear, but he saw it. He did not want her frightened, hurt in any way, but if she had not been afraid for him, that would have settled over him like a darkness, a loneliness he had not felt since the day she had said she would marry him. If anything did happen to him, could she possibly miss him as much as he would miss her?

Perhaps losing an arm, a leg, not being able to look after her, would be worse than being dead?

'I'll take care,' he said firmly, and then before she could argue, or get any more emotional, he ate the fresh toast with one hand, and poured himself more, hotter tea with the other.

The first thing Tellman did was go to see Whicker, Ednam's immediate superior. If he asked the right questions he might be able to kill this rumour before it went any further. As he got off the omnibus and walked along the windy street he framed the questions in his mind. If there were minor errors, a little dishonesty here and there, would he report it? His own sense of justice said that these men were suffering more than enough. They might not ever recover sufficiently to return to the force anyway. You don't kick a man when he's down.

Was it to do with the case Pitt was talking about? Were all these five men involved in it? That was a place to begin.

And if they did work together, how would anyone outside the force know that?

He would have to be extremely tactful about it, avoiding the reason for his inquiry. He hated investigating his own, as if he thought those dead or damaged men were somehow at fault for the disaster that had struck them down. And everyone else would hate him too.

He turned the corner, stepped over a couple of deep puddles, and went in through the police station doorway. He went to the desk and introduced himself to the desk sergeant on duty. The place seemed bare, and even drabber than usual, as if the bereavement could be felt in the wood and linoleum and the iron locks on the doors.

He asked to see whoever was in charge.

The sergeant nodded and sent a constable with a message. Five minutes later Tellman was in Superintendent Whicker's office in the best interview chair and facing Whicker across the desk. Whicker was perhaps fifty-five, solid, greying at the temples and with a ragged moustache.

'Of course they worked together now and then,' he said tartly when Tellman asked. 'Doesn't your station co-operate, er . . . Tellman?'

'Yes, it does, sir. And I know when they do,' he added.

'What is it you're expecting?' Whicker frowned. 'You already know that they went mob-handed because they were expecting a big purchase of opium. There could have been half a dozen dealers or buyers there. People who trade in that kind of stuff expect trouble, you know. They come prepared, and they can be violent.'

'But they don't plant bombs in the rooms and blow them up,' Tellman pointed out. 'Bad for business to kill yourself, not to mention your customers. They were set up!' He said the words between his teeth, the hot anger and guilt, and the fear of death all making his voice almost choked. 'I need to know if the bomber meant to get these men, all of them, or just some of them . . .'

'For God's sake, man!' Whicker retorted violently, his face suffusing with colour. 'They don't care who they get! They're anarchists. They want chaos – terror – panic! You'll never catch them if you chase after reasons!' There was pain in his eyes. He had lost five men.

Tellman sat still, fighting not to lose his own control.

'We don't know that, sir. There are rumours around that they meant to get these men particularly. I want to kill that as soon as I can. If it was revenge, I want to be able to prove to anyone that it was unjust, and none of us did anything out of order.' He leaned forward. 'I want to get these bastards, and knowing why they did it is about the only chance I've got of finding out who they are. I want them on trial, then I want them on the end of a rope. Don't you?'

Now Whicker was pale. His heavy hand on the desk holding a pencil looked as if he were about to snap it in half. 'Of course I do. They were my men, dammit! I know they had the odd failing now and then, but they were good men, policemen. What is it you're imagining? I'll show you all the records you want. You'll see they were all just as good as your own men. I'll show you, and I'll show the bloody newspapers that are looking for blame. And I'll show bloody Special Branch! They should have seen this coming, and stopped it!'

Tellman found himself answering before he considered whether it was wise or not.

'No matter how hard we work, sir, or how clever we are, we can't stop all crime, and Special Branch can't either. What we can do is catch the bastards afterwards. Now if you'll let me see those records, I'll be much obliged.'

The records were brought to him, and he spent a long, miserable day searching them. It took him a little while before he found the Lezant case that Pitt had mentioned. He could see immediately that the five men injured in the bombing had been involved.

A constable brought Tellman a cup of hot, over-strong tea, and he was so absorbed he forgot to drink it until it was cold.

The case centred on another suspected sale of opium, on the

information of an informer considered reliable, but named only as 'Joe', which could have been anyone.

The arrest had gone badly wrong. The two young men, both addicts, who were presumed to be the buyers, had turned up, but the seller had not, nor had they apparently found him later.

The disaster was that one of the young men had been carrying a gun, and was extremely tense and jittery. In Ednam's opinion, he was needing his drugs and almost out of his mind from withdrawal symptoms. A passer-by had chosen this alley as a short-cut home. The young man was so highly strung he had completely lost his nerve and shot the passer-by, killing him immediately. He had realised what he had done, and turned to run away.

The police could then show themselves and chase both young men. They caught the one who had fired the shot, but the other had escaped. Tellman looked for a description of him, but it was so vague as to be useless. He was average height, possibly thin. He looked in the faint lamplight to be dark.

Dylan Lezant was charged with murder.

Tellman read the report again, slowly and even more carefully. All five men said exactly the same thing, agreeing on the details. But then they were so few, and so general, there was nothing much to disagree about. It was not a complicated story where disagreement on details was to be expected.

It was a simple tragedy, correctly handled.

He read on, looking to see if there were any questions later, and found none. The seller of opium was never found. But then when he read about the shooting in the newspapers the next day, he would very naturally have moved his place of doing business.

Tellman stopped for a few minutes, rubbed his eyes, tired of reading handwriting, relatively neat as it was. He was glad of a fresh cup of tea and a couple of biscuits.

Then he began on other reports, including financial ledgers. He had always been good at arithmetic. It had a kind of logic to it that he liked. There was a right and a wrong. It balanced itself.

He was working on accounts of money from robberies, arrests, stolen goods receipts. He checked the addition and found an error. He tried it again, and realised someone had read a five for an eight. Easy to do, especially when you were tired and had probably been working all day. A man could easily be too eager to go home to his family, a warm hearth and a decent meal, to check his additions. Not everyone found numbers easy.

Working on a little further, he found more, a seven mistaken for a one; threes, fives and eights written carelessly, and misread.

He went back to check all of them, and realised that in every case, the error was to make the bottom amount less. It only added up to a few pounds, but a pound was a lot of money. A few years ago, it had been a constable's weekly pay.

He closed the ledger and sat back. Another thing he had noticed, much as he did not wish to: all the errors had happened when Sergeant Tienney was on duty.

What had happened to the money? His pocket? Someone else's that he owed? Bribes? Tellman hated the thought, but he would have to follow it up, sooner or later, whether it had anything to do with the bombing at Lancaster Gate, or not. Who was paying whom? And why?

It left him with a sour taste, as if something clean and long loved had been soiled. Did it take him any closer to finding out who had planted the bomb? Possibly. More probably not.

Two days later there was nothing further gained of value, and Tellman was still choked up with cold. He had spent the day with Pitt, going over and over the physical evidence. The construction of the bomb was simple enough. Even with so little of it left, it was easy to tell that it was a container of dynamite, stolen from Bessemer and Sons, and set off with a fuse, almost all of which had been destroyed in the fire the explosion had caused. No doubt that was exactly what was intended.

Tellman walked the last half-mile or so home from the bus stop through the thickening fog. The only traffic was the occasional hansom cab going over the cobbles. He could hear the clatter of hoofs and the hiss of wheels in the water before he could see the lights. It was a night any sane man was at home beside his own fire, not out turning over and over lies and stupidity in his mind and trying to find excuses he knew were worthless.

He saw the lights of the Dog and Duck tavern, golden yellow and warm. Someone opened the doors and came out, laughing and waving his hand. Tellman succumbed to temptation and went in. He was not ready to go home yet. However much he tried to pretend that everything was all right, Gracie would see right through it. She would know he had found something wrong. They were only small things, but like a piece of grit in the eye, painful, and unforgettable. And, like a sore eye, he kept rubbing at it.

Were the money errors anything to do with the bombings? He had found no connection between them and any of the men who were injured. The Lezant case was sad; the passer-by had been killed by mischance. He had been thoroughly investigated, and found totally innocent.

He was chasing errors, repetitive petty theft. Yes – police corruption, but very small.

He sat on one of the bar stools and ordered a pint. It was warm inside, and damp from wet clothes steaming in the heat from the fire over in the great hearth at the far side of the room; from too many warm bodies; and now and then beer slopped over on to the straw-covered floor. Normally he did not like such places, but tonight it was good, perhaps because it was so very normal.

The barmaid brought Tellman's beer and passed the time of day, but she could see his mood, and she did not pursue conversation. Tellman was glad of a small table out of the way where he could watch others but remain essentially alone.

He was troubled, afraid of what all these small errors might mean. If someone else were to look at Tellman's work, would they find as much unaccounted for? He did not think so.

61

Did that make him a better policeman? Did details matter? Or was he losing himself in them because he was good at it, and sometimes it was an escape from the larger picture of violence, dishonesty and waste?

Could all this be anything to do with the bombing at Lancaster Gate? Hardly. There was no pattern big enough for that. It was all pennies and sixpences. He would never have taken any notice of it at all had he not been looking minutely to find some connection between the bombing victims that could lead him to who had deliberately tricked them into going to the house at Lancaster Gate, and then detonating a bomb that would kill or maim all of them. Hardly over a few pence here or there. It would be laughed out of court – and deservedly so.

Then why did it matter?

He finished his ale and went to the bar and ordered more. The barmaid was a big woman, friendly, her shock of hair falling out of its pins as she strove to serve everyone. Not the kind of woman he found attractive at all. But this evening her warmth was welcome, her cheerful, meaningless chatter a good distraction.

He must find out more about Tienney, and the financial errors, although he strongly suspected that whatever petty carelessness he had committed, it was trivial. Grubby, of course, but of no consequence. It could have nothing to do with the bombing. It was just a small, grubby bit of regular theft that might never have been discovered if he were not looking for corruption.

What if he did not report these accounting anomalies to Pitt? What if he said there was nothing? Or better still, was replaced by someone else, someone who would not expect police to be better than another man, above temptations of any sort? Someone who cared less. Maybe someone with a little less childlike idealism, who did not think of police as the guardians of law, of the vulnerable, whoever they were, gentleman or pauper.

But that might also mean someone who did not care about protecting the police themselves. The police could only survive if they could rely on each other's loyalty. If you were chasing a thief into a dark alley, with nothing but a truncheon to defend yourself, then you relied absolutely not only on the courage of the man beside you, but on his absolute loyalty. And that of the man in the street, who saw your uniform as a badge of honour – like a soldier's battledress. It was a statement of whose side you were on always, whatever it cost.

When had that started? He thought back to being a boy, only briefly. There were too many things about it he preferred to forget. He was not that person any more. He wasn't hungry, scared, runny-nosed, scabby-kneed, always feeling on the outside. He was a grown man with a purpose. He had been that for years, even since he had joined the police, part of an army for good, someone who belonged.

He had felt that purpose more deeply when he had started to work with Pitt. Pitt was a tall man, strong, someone who had come from an ordinary enough background. But Pitt knew what he wanted to be, and he believed in himself. Tellman had modelled himself on Pitt.

It had worked well. Now he was an inspector himself, a rank he would never have imagined reaching, even a few years ago. It was his duty to protect the police from attack inside or out. Without loyalty they lost their greatest shield, and weapon. And you could not expect loyalty from men to whom you would not give it. It was when it was costly that it counted.

And he owed it to Gracie and his little girl. And the new baby coming. That might be a son! Someone who would want to follow in his footsteps, be like him.

He stood up, leaving the last few inches of his ale, paid his bill, and walked out into the thickening mist.

Gracie was more aware of the gravity of the situation than Tellman. The next morning, after Tellman had left for work, she left her child sleeping quietly in the winter sun, in the care of the woman who came and did the heavy cleaning. She would spoil her, and take delight in doing it, but she had had several of her own, and knew exactly what to do, or not do. Her face lit up at the prospect. Playing with a happy baby, just able to talk, was far more agreeable than scrubbing a floor, even a small one that was pretty clean anyway.

Gracie caught the omnibus to Russell Square, and then walked along to Keppel Street. Of course she did not know if Charlotte was in, but there was only one way to find out. She was sufficiently early to make it very likely. She needed advice, and there was no one else anywhere who would be wiser, or more generous, to give it.

She was fortunate. Charlotte was still at home. She had planned to go out, and changed her mind.

'My errand is of no importance at all,' she assured Gracie. 'You are an excellent excuse to avoid it. Come in and have a cup of tea.'

'It's too early for elevenses,' Gracie said a little awkwardly. This was not really a social call. Her reason for coming was important, and urgent. Tea was a pleasantry that did not matter.

Charlotte looked at her more gravely. 'Something is wrong. What can I do?'

Instead of the kitchen where Gracie had worked all her years from thirteen to well over twenty, Charlotte led her into the parlour, and closed the door behind them.

'Sit down, and tell me,' she directed, then took the seat that was usually Pitt's, and offered her own to Gracie.

Gracie had been worrying about how to word it all the way here on the bus, but now suddenly it was easy. The years disappeared and it was as if they were back in the old days when they had faced all kinds of cases together and Gracie had been part of the family, free to give her opinion like anyone else. Even Lord Narraway and Lady Vespasia had listened to her . . . sometimes.

'Samuel's been looking at all these police what was hurt in the bombing,' she said earnestly. 'He doesn't tell me much, but I know 'im. He's found bad things. I know that because 'e says nothing. If it was all right, he'd say so.' She looked down at her hands, which were very small, but very strong. 'He's a dreamer inside, you know. 'E thinks they're all as straight as 'e is. But they in't. I know that.'

'I know it too,' Charlotte agreed. 'But if he accepted that, then he might not have the loyalty he does, and it's that which makes him special, and able to keep going even in the hardest cases.'

Gracie said nothing. Now, suddenly, it was not so easy. She had not come here for comfort; she needed to have a plan of some sort, something practical, if it all went bad.

She looked up at Charlotte. 'Wot if they was bombed because they was crooked? On the take, like?'

Charlotte could remember very clearly what Pitt had said about the bombing, and how specifically those police had been lured to the Lancaster Gate house. It was a bitter thought, but not one she could dismiss. They might have to face it.

'That seems very extreme,' she said slowly. 'If anyone had proof of stealing, or lying, wouldn't they try to report it to police higher up, who would stop it themselves? You could do that without any damage to yourself. If necessary you might be able to write an anonymous letter, if you were afraid of reprisals.'

'I thought o' that,' Gracie answered. 'It must be that there's police 'igher up protecting them.' She shook her head. 'Samuel thinks the police are kind o' heroes. Like knights in armour, to protect the rest of us. Like King Arthur, all sworn to protect the innocent. 'E knows better, o' course.' She sighed. 'But yer gotta believe in something ter keep on going back all the time, an' fighting against fear, an' doubt an' . . . an' just giving up. We all got our fairy stories. But I wish I could protect 'im from finding out the bad ones are bad enough to 'ave been the reason for this.' She looked at Charlotte, studying her face, wanting to see the confidence in it that Charlotte could prove her fears ungrounded.

Yet if Charlotte did not understand, or were willing to deny it too, that would be even worse.

Did that mean that Gracie believed it?

No! . . . Yes? No . . . it meant she knew the possibility was there, and had to be faced.

It was several more moments before Charlotte answered.

'They have to find the corruption, if it's there,' she said, biting her lip. 'And then they will discover where the deepest loyalties are. Choices between right and wrong are easy. It's the ones where you have to decide between two rights, or two wrongs that hurt, and maybe you never know which would have been the better.'

'The police are going to say it should be to yer mates on the force,' Gracie said. 'The ones as 'ave watched for yer when you was tired, a bit slow, made a mistake, or could 'ave been knifed if they 'adn't been there. If yer don't know which side yer mates are on, nobody's going ter fight. Samuel says then, if yer going into a dark alley an' yer don't know what's in front of yer, yer gotter be sure as hell what's behind yer.'

Charlotte did not argue. Gracie could see the conflict in her face, and the helplessness to find a way out of it.

'I know,' Charlotte agreed. 'And yet if the police don't keep honour to the truth but choose to protect those of them that lie, or twist evidence, steal little things here and there, take bribes to look the other way, what happens to the rest of us?' She shivered. 'It's like a building that's got woodworm in the joists and rafters. One wormhole's nothing: ten thousand and the whole thing caves in on your head.'

'So wot are we gonna do?' Gracie at last said the unavoidable.

For an instant there was a spark of dark humour in Charlotte's eyes at her automatic inclusion, and then it vanished. This was too serious for any kind of laughter.

'We are feeling bits wot really hurt.'

'I don't think there's anything you really can do,' Charlotte answered. 'If there is, I've never found it.'

A moment of surprise flickered across Gracie's face, as if she had never considered Pitt vulnerable in the same way. Then quickly she moved on to the practical. 'Wot *are* we going to do?'

Charlotte threw away the last vestige of doubt. 'You are going to look after your family. I am going to visit my sister, who knows all kinds of people, and ask her to find out all she can. Who knows how high up this may go?'

Gracie bit her lip. 'An' if it does?'

'I'm not sure. But an idea of the truth is the only place to begin.'

Gracie smiled a little lopsidedly. 'Thank you.'

Chapter Four

EMILY RADLEY sat by the fire in her boudoir, that lady's sitting room where she received her closest women friends in comfort. There was tea on a tray on the carved cherry wood table, and small sandwiches of thin white bread, with wafer-thin slices of cucumber from the glasshouse. She stared at her sister, Charlotte.

'Oh dear,' she said quietly. 'Yes, I do know Cecily Duncannon, but not very well.'

'Then please get to know her better,' Charlotte said gravely. 'This is a terribly serious matter. I need to know for Tellman, and even more for Thomas.'

Emily's mind was racing. Years ago, when Pitt had been a regular policeman and not in Special Branch, where so much was secret, she and Charlotte had both meddled in his cases. Sometimes they had been at the core of solving them. Of course it had also been dangerous, now and then, and they had made mistakes. But still she missed the passion and the involvement. It gave a sharpness to life. It mattered, in fact, more than the social niceties to which she gave so much time now, the surface rules that hid deep tides of intrigue and emotions she guessed at, but seldom saw.

Was it possible Cecily Duncannon was concealing an agonising secret, albeit one she did not acknowledge to herself, for fear of what it would mean?

'I like her,' she said quietly. 'I don't want to do this . . .'

'Then let Thomas tell you what their bodies were like!' Charlotte replied. 'Or how the injured men are—'

'I didn't say I wouldn't!' Emily responded quickly. 'I just . . . I just don't like it! How does Thomas do it every day?'

'Choosing not to look at it doesn't make it go away,' Charlotte told her. 'Please . . . just find out what you can. Maybe Alexander's innocent? Wouldn't it be worth something to prove that?'

Part of Emily did not want to touch it: but there was another part that ached to be involved again, to search and disentangle the truth, to live in a reality that was both beautiful and painful, but shorn of the shallow pretence that gave such a superficial comfort.

'Of course I'll help,' she said firmly. 'How could you think I wouldn't? Do you think I've lost all heart?'

Charlotte smiled, quick to apologise. 'Of course not, or I would hardly have come.' She took another sandwich. 'Thank you.'

Emily took a sandwich herself. 'How is Gracie?'

'Expecting another child, and desperate to protect Samuel.'

'From disillusion?' Emily smiled back and felt a sudden stab of fear herself. Her own husband, for all his ease and confidence of manner, was desperately vulnerable too. If Alexander Duncannon were guilty, then his father would be jeopardised also, and with him the contract, and Jack's career. Jack could not afford another diplomatic failure, however much it was in no way his fault. Misjudgement could ruin a reputation, no matter how innocent, and it would not be his first.

'Yes. Pretty complete,' Charlotte replied to the question about Tellman, but it was about Jack too, and they both knew it.

'I'll begin tonight,' Emily promised. 'I have a perfect opportunity.'

A few hours later Emily sat in front of her dressing table looking-glass and regarded herself critically. She was Charlotte's younger sister, delicately fair, with hair that curled naturally about her face.

Her skin was porcelain fair, it always had been, but she noticed now the tiny lines around her eyes and mouth as she rapidly approached forty. Character and wit lasted far longer than beauty. In the last year or two she had been obliged to accept that. To do it with grace was the only attitude that made sense and Emily had always been the pragmatic one. She had never been the idealist, the passionate dreamer that Charlotte was. Tonight she thought of the past and the adventures they had shared, and determined that she would do all she could to help, use the courage, wit and judgement she used to have.

She was wearing a gown in one of her favourite shades of soft green, a colour that always suited her. She had emeralds and pearls in her ears, and around her slender throat.

Jack stood behind her, meeting her eyes in the glass. For a moment there was a flash of admiration in them, just long enough for her to see it, and be satisfied. At the beginning of the year she had had a bleak few months when she feared it was gone. He had seemed distant, even a little bored. She had realised with a blow hard enough to bruise that she had taken his devotion for granted.

She must learn from how much that had hurt, and make sure she was never so cavalier with him again. To be comfortable, take the sweetness as if it were hers by right, was not only arrogant – even in time boring – it was also dangerous.

Now she smiled back at him in the glass.

'Are you ready?' she asked. She was not referring to his appearance. As always, he was immaculately dressed. She was referring to his preparation for a gathering in which his position as Member of Parliament and junior minister at the Foreign Office was going to be tested in relation to this contract, on which many fortunes rested. And she knew of danger to it that he did not – if Charlotte were right.

He swallowed before replying. She knew him well enough to see small signs of tension in him others would not have noticed.

'Yes.' He always spoke positively. It was a habit gained in his earlier days when everything rested on chance and uncertainty, and a brave face was part of his armour. Charm was a mixture of many things, but always included a subtle blending of modesty with confidence, an air of belief in the good. 'There's everything to play for,' he added. 'Godfrey Duncannon is the perfect man to guide this through.'

'Who's against it?' She turned round on the padded seat and looked at him earnestly.

'Sir Donald Parsons,' he replied. 'I would like to know why.'

She was surprised. 'Doesn't he say?'

'Oh, yes.' He smiled and gave a slight shrug. 'He will quote so many reasons that it makes me wonder which of them is the real one, or if any of them are. It might be something we haven't even thought of.'

She understood immediately why that was an obstacle. She had been in Society quite long enough to know that in order to do battle with anyone and have a chance of winning, you had to know what they really wanted, not simply what they said.

'I see. What can I do to help?'

In some situations she was the best ally he had, and lately he had had the grace to acknowledge it.

'I would like to know what Parsons really wants, but I would also like to understand Godfrey Duncannon a lot better,' he answered. 'Not that I hesitate on the contract, which is more like a trade treaty for a vast amount of money, just a lot easier to negotiate. I have looked into that for myself.' He smiled ruefully. 'I'm less trusting than I used to be.' He was referring to past errors that had cost him dearly.

She did not say anything. It was a delicate subject. He was referring to the occasions when he had served with more loyalty than judgement. Pitt had had to resolve violent and bitter issues too close to treason for anyone to escape easily, even if they were as innocent as Jack had been. No one had put it into words, least of all Emily, but his ambition to succeed, without any help from Emily's connections or her money, had been a considerate part of it.

'The contract is good,' he said again. 'But I am relying heavily on Duncannon to negotiate it. He has known the other parties for a long time and they will deal only with him. They trust him completely. I will be interested to know why. I've looked, and I can't find anything powerful enough to explain it.'

She frowned. 'Isn't his past record enough? He's been a brilliant success in business himself, and without the slightest shadow on his name.'

'I've thought that before,' Jack said quietly.

She rose and came round the stool to stand in front of him. She ran her fingers over his lapel, although it was already perfectly smooth. 'He's not a politician, you know. You don't have to be quite so wary.'

'Yes I do,' he replied. 'This could be worth millions of pounds altogether, the livelihood of thousands of people. And I can't afford another error, however little I'm really to blame.' In spite of his attempt to be optimistic there was an urgency in his voice. 'My name will be connected with it. People will know that. They won't bother to ask in what way. I can hear them perfectly. *Oh, really? Wasn't he connected with that contract with China? Better not have him. Not sound, you know? Choose someone else.*'

Emily could see the dark shadow in his eyes. He was speaking lightly, even smiling, but he was passionately serious underneath. She knew him well enough to be certain he was also afraid.

She took it seriously. 'I will do all I can to help, I promise.' She thought of Charlotte, and Thomas, and Samuel Tellman, but she did not mention them. Jack had enough to worry about already.

He kissed her lightly on the cheek. 'Thank you.'

The party was held in a magnificent home just off Park Lane. They were helped by the footman to alight at the portico of the front door. Liveried footmen seemed to be everywhere. The night was cold but dry, and lamps gleamed like so many fairy moons, reflecting off the horse brasses of the carriage that drew up behind them. Then as the woman alighted, the diamonds in her tiara blazed briefly, and the pale satin of her skirts gleamed.

Jack and Emily went up the steps and through the wide, carved front door. Once inside the rustle of taffeta was louder than the murmur of polite voices, and now and then the raised tones of the butler announcing this or that important person's arrival.

Emily had once been 'Lady Ashworth'. She was quite happy now to be 'Mrs Jack Radley', especially when his name was followed by 'Member of Parliament'.

They stopped for a moment at the top of the stairs, and then went down the two or three steps into the already considerable throng. They had timed it perfectly: early enough to be polite, late enough to be interesting.

Two of the first people Emily was introduced to were Sir Donald Parsons and his wife. Emily was glad Jack had warned her in the carriage on the way here. Parsons was an impressive man, not above average height but with a sweep of black hair and enormous eyebrows that lent a fierceness to his aspect that his features did not quite support.

Lady Parsons looked somewhat in awe of him, but Emily thought she saw a hint of amusement in the pale blue eyes that interested her far more.

'How do you do, Lady Parsons?' she said with a sweet smile, when they were introduced. She could be just as docile as anyone, if she judged it politic. 'How nice to meet you,' she added. 'I have heard so many delightful things about you.'

Lady Parsons looked momentarily confused, as did her husband. She was the first to recover. The two women looked at each other, and knew exactly where the power lay.

'People are very kind,' Lady Parsons murmured, and the

amusement was back in her eyes – just a momentary light, then gone again.

There was no answer to such an observation, and Emily knew it. It was something to be noted for later. Never underestimate such a woman, or imagine for a moment that she did not notice everything.

Parsons made some harmless remark, and Jack responded. Emily kept her smile, appearing to listen intently, until they were joined by their host and the conversation became general.

The men moved away, deep in discussion of international trade and finance.

Lady Parsons looked at Emily, her face still impartially polite.

'Do you know anyone here?' she enquired. 'May I introduce you to people you may care to meet?' It was a delicate way of suggesting that Emily was a stranger in Society, perhaps in need of assistance.

Emily could feel the prickle of anger already. How dare this woman suggest Emily was a nobody? She increased the sweetness of her smile. 'How kind of you,' she said innocently. 'I am sure there are many . . .' she hesitated delicately, '. . . ladies more familiar with the diplomatic scene than I and with whom you have been friends for years. I should be most grateful for your generosity.'

Lady Parson's smile widened, then suddenly froze as she recognised the implication of her considerable seniority. She was perhaps ten or twelve years older than Emily, not the twenty Emily suggested.

Emily continued to smile expectantly.

Lady Parsons did not flinch. 'We are on opposite sides in the affair of this contract,' she said quite calmly. 'But I think I shall like you. You are a great deal deeper than you look, and quicker, I think?' The amusement was back in her eyes, now quite openly. It was an offer of friendship with a barb inside.

'It doesn't do to appear too clever,' Emily replied. 'People keep up their guard.'

'I am tempted to say that you are in no danger,' Lady Parsons said sharply, 'but I think that is unnecessary. It rather betrays a need to win, don't you think? Those who must always have the last word become rather tedious.'

'I agree,' Emily said. 'To be tedious is the ultimate flaw in a woman's character.'

Lady Parsons laughed quite openly. 'Oh, my dear! Did Oscar Wilde say that?'

'Not that I am aware of,' Emily replied, raising her eyebrows in surprise. 'I have discerned it for myself in endless political parties.'

'A pity you are too well-born for the stage,' Lady Parsons observed. 'You might do well.'

'I could never remember other people's lines,' Emily replied.

'Come. I shall introduce you to some of the people I know.' Lady Parsons had a very gentle but insistent hand on Emily's arm. 'I shall enjoy the experience of seeing what they make of you.'

It was pointless to argue, and Emily thought it might be profitable for her to see the wives of the 'opposition' to the contract. She would tell Jack about it later.

She was walking beside Lady Parsons, acknowledging various acquaintances, when she caught a glimpse of Godfrey Duncannon about twenty feet away. He was standing talking to a woman who was at once beautiful and delicate. She looked over forty, but with an innocence of someone younger. She was paying intense attention to him as if she dare not miss a word he said. He in turn was bending very slightly to listen to her, his attention also total. And yet his posture was not in the least romantic; it appeared more to be a recognition of her fragility, and her dependence upon his care.

The light shone for a moment on the diamonds at her slender throat, and gleamed on the warm apricot silk of her gown. Then she lowered her gaze, and he smiled and moved away.

Emily realised that she had made a mistake, seeing only the profile view of the man. It was not Godfrey Duncannon at all, just someone who had a certain resemblance to him in build, and the bone structure of his head. He did not even have the same colour of hair. Indeed, this man was at least a couple of decades younger.

She gave herself a mental shake. She should be careful she did not address somebody by the wrong name! Or even worse than that, assume she knew someone she really did not!

She accompanied Lady Parsons for a further twenty minutes or so, meeting a few more people of interest, then parted from her with a promise to meet again in a few days. Apart from its usefulness, it was a friendship she would enjoy. Difference of view has always been more interesting than incessant agreement, sincere or not.

She set about moving towards Cecily Duncannon much more determinedly. They had met several times already and the liking between them was quite natural. Cecily was about ten years older than Emily, and still a handsome woman. In fact, middle age became her more than youth had done. Her dark hair was streaked with dramatic silver and where she had been a trifle bony in youth, now her broad shoulders were less obvious, and she had learned to carry herself with unusual grace.

She saw Emily and smiled with unaffected pleasure. She excused herself from the two ladies of uncertain age with whom she had been making conversation and walked towards Emily.

'I saw you were engaged with Mrs Forbush and her sister,' she said with a smile. 'Some parties seem to last for days!'

Emily knew exactly what she meant. So many conversations felt as if they ended up almost exactly where they had begun.

'I suppose time doesn't really stand still?' Emily replied, not intending it a question to be answered.

'I used to be so nervous at events like this,' Cecily confided with a rueful little gesture. 'Godfrey was always at ease.' She glanced to her left where Godfrey Duncannon stood talking to several men of middle years, wide of girth, and decorated with orders of one sort or another. They were talking, frequently two at a time, and all nodding agreement. Godfrey, iron-grey haired and immaculately dressed, was either completely at ease, or else a superb actor. The resemblance to the other man, earlier, was an illusion. Someone was telling a story, smiling as he did so and waving his hands around.

Godfrey laughed as if delighted by it. Everyone looked satisfied.

'Women are allowed to gossip, indeed expected to,' Emily said a little ruefully. 'But we are not supposed to tell any jokes! Or even listen to them!'

'A pity,' Cecily answered. 'The invented jokes allow you to laugh, which is wonderful. It's the real absurdities and the ridiculousness of life that hurt. And you cannot help seeing them.'

Emily caught a note of sadness in her voice, perhaps even fear. She glanced at the other woman's face momentarily. If it were really sadness or fear Emily had detected, she did not want Cecily to know that she had seen it. There were things one did not speak of so that they could never be denied, even when it was kinder to do so.

Deliberately Emily started on a new subject. It was chatter, a means of expressing that they were friends, without saying anything so overt and clumsy.

'I just met Lady Parsons,' she said lightly. 'In other circumstances I think I could like her. She is not at all as bland as she appears.'

'I expect not many of us are as we appear,' Cecily said, staring across the room. 'I would hate to think I was readable at a glance. It would be like one's nightmare of having accidentally gone out into the street in one's underwear!'

Emily laughed deliberately, as if she thought Cecily had been at least half joking. But was it possibly not a silly dream so much as an underlying fear of having something specifically read so easily?

'Especially in this weather,' she added. 'I wonder if we shall have snow for Christmas.'

'Do you go to the country for Christmas?' Cecily asked. 'It's such a family thing, it's rather nice. The city gets so grubby when all the snow turns to slush.'

Emily looked at Cecily's face, the strong bones, the ivory skin, the black sweep of eyebrow. There were faint shadows around the dark eyes that powder could not hide. Was it concern over the contract her husband was negotiating, and which seemed to matter so much? Or something far more personal?

'I'm afraid with so many feet, and so many wheels, that always happens in the city,' she replied. 'I love Ashworth Hall in the middle of winter, with all the fires burning and the country outside mantled in snow. But I'm afraid that this year we will almost certainly have to stay home. The contract . . . international trade doesn't wait for holidays.'

Cecily was still looking across the room at her husband. 'No,' she agreed. 'We cannot afford to assume we will win. It matters intensely to Godfrey . . . as I imagine it does to all of us.' She included everyone, but Emily knew she meant Jack. Did Godfrey's career really rest on it in anything like as much as Jack's did? Godfrey Duncannon had made a fortune. Everything he touched had prospered. She had heard that it was Cecily's money origin-ally, inherited from her father, that had been the foundation of their wealth, but Godfrey had multiplied it many times over, and risen to a pinnacle of respect he might not have dreamed of as a young man. Could this possibly matter to him as much as it mattered to Jack, who was still so very much making his way?

She refused to think of what could happen to his career if in the next election he did not hold his seat! The thought was always just beyond the edge of her mind, but it cost some effort to keep it in check. It was not a matter of money, but of self-belief.

She had seen the doubt in him, the loathing of being dependent on her.

'Yes,' she murmured in agreement. She wanted to know more, but there were questions one did not ask.

She remained a little longer in pleasant, light conversation. After they were joined by several others, she excused herself and gradually worked her way over towards the most beautiful woman in the room, her great-aunt Vespasia. She had been Lady Vespasia Cumming-Gould, a courtesy title inherited because her father had been an earl. Now she was Lady Narraway, because recently she had married Victor Narraway, who had been head of Special Branch immediately preceding Pitt. A scandal had robbed him of that position. Pitt had redeemed Narraway's reputation, but too late to reinstate him in office. He had been sidelined to the House of Lords. However, he had realised his deep love for Vespasia and at last found the courage to ask her to marry him. It was not that he had doubted his feelings; he had been afraid to lose a friendship he valued above all others by telling her its nature, and making the old ease between them impossible.

Now Emily and Vespasia stood close to each other, momentarily out of conversation with passers-by, and Emily seized her chance. Vespasia was not her aunt by blood, but by her first marriage to Lord George Ashworth. However, their ever-deepening friendship over the years, their sharing of triumph and disaster, had created a bond deeper than that of mere kinship. Emily knew that Vespasia felt an even closer bond with Charlotte and Thomas, but she had long ago ceased to mind about that.

Vespasia's face lit with pleasure when she saw Emily. In her youth, Vespasia had been celebrated throughout Europe for her exquisite features and the strength and delicacy of her bones, her flawless skin. Now it was the wit and the passion in her face that arrested the attention, the courage and grace of her carriage.

'I was hoping you would find a few moments from your duties,' she said warmly. 'How are you, my dear?' She held out her slender hand, blazing with a single emerald ring.

'Enjoying myself,' Emily replied, accepting it momentarily with an answering smile. 'At least some of the time.'

'I should hate to suspect you of dishonesty,' Vespasia said drily. 'The conversation is deadly, but perhaps some of what is not said is interesting, don't you think? I noticed you in conversation with Lady Parsons.'

Emily laughed. 'I hear what you are not saying,' she observed. 'She is far more perceptive than I had thought. Her husband is the chief opponent of this contract, you know?'

Narraway moved closer to them and it was he who answered. He was a slender man, not so very much taller than Vespasia, lean and wiry, his eyes so dark as to look almost black. His thick hair was shot through with silver, and time had improved and refined his features rather than dulling them.

'We do know,' he agreed. 'But, I think, not all of his reasons. That would be very interesting to find out, and possibly useful.'

'Jack wants me to learn what I can about Godfrey Duncannon,' Emily responded. She wanted to ask Narraway if he could tell her if he knew anything, but even though she had known him for some years, she did not dare to presume on the acquaintance to ask. He was a man who had known many of the secrets of the great and powerful. It had been his job, just as it now was Pitt's. But Pitt appeared so much more open, approachable. Would he become like Narraway, eventually? Would he see the private darkness within all kinds of people, and smile and hide it . . . until it became useful to him?

Involuntarily she shivered.

It was Vespasia who answered. 'Then you had better continue to enjoy your friendship with Cecily Duncannon,' she advised. 'But I think it will not be easy for you.'

Narraway looked at her with surprise, his dark eyebrows raised.

Emily understood. Vespasia did not mean that Cecily would

not continue to like Emily. On the contrary, the warmth would remain, and increase. What she meant was that learning the source of someone's pain, understanding their secrets because they trusted you, silently if not openly, faced you with dilemmas to which there was no happy solution.

'I know,' Emily said gently. It was an admission she had avoided making to herself. It was so much less challenging not to know, to sail through life, through relationships of any sort, seeing only what you wished to, never the layers below the surface, where the light was.

'Has Cecily Duncannon such painful secrets?' he asked quietly, although the fact that he phrased it so exactly made it clear that he knew the answer.

'Of course,' Vespasia replied.

'To do with Godfrey?' he persisted.

'That I don't know. It's possible.'

'His future is secure,' Emily put in. 'And, as far as I know, his reputation is above criticism. Jack has looked into it most carefully. He can't afford to have his own reputation tied to another disaster.' She regretted the harshness of the words the moment she had said them. Of course both Vespasia and Narraway knew about the past disasters. Narraway probably knew more than Emily did herself. It still sounded like something of a betrayal to remind them.

Vespasia understood. 'I was thinking of her personal life,' she said. 'I do not think Godfrey is always an easy man.'

'A mistress?' Narraway said with a smile that seemed like genuine amusement. 'I think not. He is far too careful for that. Unexpected passion can catch most people, but I would stake a lot that he is not one of them.'

'A lot?' Emily asked immediately. 'A contract that apparently matters intensely to the fortunes of some, and the survival of many?'

'Yes,' he replied almost without hesitation. 'He has never allowed any kind of emotion to cloud his honour, or his ambition.'

Vespasia gave a wince so slight only Emily caught it and read it correctly. She had watched Cecily's face and seen the shadows in it. Maybe they had less in common than Emily had thought. She had loved Jack from the beginning, at least in part because he had always been a friend. They had talked about all kinds of things in the earliest days of their acquaintance, because then he had had no aspirations to marry her, not even any thought that it was possible. There had been none of the awkwardness of a courtship, the forced propriety, the tensions. They had laughed together, given confidences and been open about thoughts, ideas and even feelings. That had never changed.

Of course, there had been misunderstandings, even rifts between them occasionally, but they had occurred when the friendship was strained, the laughter and ease temporarily vanished.

Had Godfrey Duncannon ever offered Cecily such warmth? Perhaps he had not that ease to give to a woman? Sometimes the perceived differences were too great to bridge.

If that were so, was it any of Emily's right or privilege to discuss it? Not if it had no bearing on the contract. Some griefs could be endured only because no one else knew of them.

The next moment, they were joined by Jack, who greeted Vespasia and Narraway formally, introducing them all to Godfrey Duncannon, who accompanied him. Immediately the conversation became general: where people were going to spend Christmas, in the city or at some country estate; what theatre or opera was playing, and whether the performances were as good as others they were familiar with; and of course what the weather would do.

Emily listened and watched, keeping a demure look of interest on her face.

'We'll have to make the best of it in the city this year,' Duncannon said to Emily on the subject of Christmas. 'You could attend the midnight service at Westminster Abbey or, of course, St Paul's if you prefer. They both have such a sense of history it makes one feel very much part of a great unity, past, present and into the future.' He smiled at her, and she had a sudden awareness of his charm. Its source was not warmth in the usual sense, but rather more an intense intelligence, an appreciation of a multitude of things, each of which was beautiful to him.

She smiled back at him. 'I imagine the Abbey will be a little crowded.'

'Filled to the very doors,' he agreed. 'The music will be sublime, and everyone will be singing their hearts out. It isn't just the great organ, or the choir, or even the numbers, it's the joy of the people, the wave of belief. If you wish, I'm sure I can arrange a decent seat for you.' There was complete assurance in what he said; generosity certainly, but also pride. He knew he could do it, and it pleased him, as when a man strikes a perfect shot at golf, and the ball sinks into the hole, as he knew it would.

She would like to have had the rank and the confidence to decline, but she did not, and they both knew that.

'Thank you,' she said graciously. 'It is an experience I am sure I would never forget.' She felt she should say a little more than that, so she added. 'It is very kind of you.'

He was pleased. He inclined his head in acceptance of her gratitude. He did not once glance at Cecily.

The conversation continued along other lines and Emily listened dutifully. They spoke of international affairs, other people's lives, political news and speculation.

Twice Emily accidentally caught Vespasia's eye, and knew exactly what Vespasia was thinking. She restricted her smile with some difficulty. It would seem light-minded – or worse, mockery. She made sure not to catch Vespasia's glance again.

Finally Vespasia herself inclined her head politely and excused herself on the grounds of seeing an acquaintance she should not seem to ignore. She took Emily's arm. 'Come, my dear, I'm sure Lady Cartwright will be pleased to meet you.'

'Thank you.' Emily murmured, the moment they were out of earshot, 'Who is Lady Cartwright?'

'No idea,' Vespasia replied. 'For heaven's sake, what a cold man! Is he always like that?'

'Duncannon? I think so. Perhaps not in his own home . . .' She let the suggestion trail.

'You mean in the bedroom,' Vespasia replied. 'If so, one might be better off sleeping through the whole thing.'

Emily kept her face straight with difficulty. 'I think he is nervous about the contract. Many people over-talk when they are anxious. It does mean a great deal to him. Or perhaps he is afraid of you?'

Vespasia smiled. 'I hope so.' Then suddenly she was serious. 'You may be right about this contract. Victor will not discuss it with me, and I am perfectly sure he knows a great deal.'

'And he is in favour of it?' Then Emily wondered if she perhaps should not have asked. Would apologising make it worse?

'Very much,' Vespasia replied unhesitatingly. 'But there will be those who lose. Or, of course, who have political objections.'

'But not ethical ones?'

'I don't think so. And those are the ones that matter.'

Emily looked at her with surprise, not that she should think so, but that she should say it. It seemed naïve for Vespasia.

Vespasia laughed. 'I am not being sanctimonious, my dear! It is that good men will fight for an ethical cause, and they are the hardest to beat, partly because one is not ever certain that one wishes to.'

'Is Godfrey Duncannon a good man?'

'I don't know,' Vespasia admitted honestly. 'There are times when he is certainly tedious enough that one would believe he wishes to give that impression. But whether his exhaustive knowledge comes from intelligence as well as the overwhelming desire to impress, I don't know.'

'Or the wish to dominate the conversation and keep it off all personal matters,' Emily suggested.

'Ah,' Vespasia said gently. 'How perceptive of you. That could indeed be it. We are about to meet another man who is exhaustingly righteous.' She smiled with a grace that disguised all dislike. 'How nice to see you, Mr Abercorn. Emily, may I present Josiah Abercorn. My niece, Mrs Jack Radley.'

Abercorn was the man Emily had earlier briefly mistaken for Godfrey Duncannon. Closer to, he was of unusual appearance. His eyes were large and very blue. They should have been magnificent, but were marred by dark shadows around them, as if he never slept sufficiently well. His features were strong, with the same power as Duncannon's, and there was a similar fire of intelligence in his eyes, although Duncannon's were dark.

He greeted Emily politely enough, and with marked interest – no doubt because she was Jack's wife.

'Mrs Radley,' he said warmly. 'Perhaps your husband has not mentioned me. He is admirably discreet. I am one of the lawyers who is drafting this contract we are all so eager to have signed. It will benefit more people than most of us can imagine.'

'My husband has said as much,' Emily replied warmly. 'Although, of course, he does not mention any details.'

'Of course not,' Abercorn agreed. 'But I assure you, if you are a woman of conscience, and compassion for those less fortunate, you will rejoice when as much of it as possible is made public. This will open up vast areas of opportunity, and perhaps right some of the terrible things we committed against the Chinese people during our Opium Wars.'

She could only guess what he was referring to, but she managed to look suitably impressed.

'I count it a great privilege to have a part in it,' he continued. 'It will be the crown of my aspirations to serve my country.'

Emily felt Vespasia tense beside her, with just the slightest stiffening of her already straight back.

'One jewel in the crown, Mr Abercorn,' Vespasia interjected. 'I am sure there will be more.' Her tone was impossible to read.

'I see no further than this, Lady Narraway,' he said blandly. '"I do not ask to see the distant scene, one step enough for me",' he quoted the famous hymn.

'How cautious of you,' Vespasia responded. 'And perhaps wise. Politics can move so quickly it is best not to play all your hand at once.'

'I had not—' he began, then changed his mind and bit off whatever he was going to say.

'Indeed,' Vespasia murmured, as if she had understood perfectly.

Something a few yards away drew Abercorn's attention, and he turned to look. Emily saw his expression change from benign polite interest. For an instant she saw hatred in his face, and pain. It was so deep that she was unaware of anything else. Instinctively she also turned to follow his gaze. The only person she recognised was Godfrey Duncannon. Everyone else seemed to be at least half turned away.

Then the moment passed, Abercorn regained his composure, and Emily was left wondering. She had no time to ask Vespasia what she had observed, because they were joined by others and the conversation instantly became general.

This new group included the woman Emily had seen much earlier talking so earnestly with Josiah Abercorn. This time she was with her husband, Police Commissioner Bradshaw. This relationship, Emily could instantly see, was quite different.

Mrs Bradshaw was a woman of a beauty, which was disturbing because of the haunted look in her wide, dark eyes. Emily was certain within an instant that she had some emotional or physical pain that crowded out pleasure for more than a few moments here or there. Perhaps it was ill-health of such a nature that there was no recovery in view. She listened to the conversation and she laughed quietly at all the right places, but she spoke very little, and she stayed very close to her husband.

Bradshaw was also keenly aware of her and every so often he touched her arm, as if to remind her of his care, even protection.

However, he could not protect her from the pain inside her, and that helplessness was there in his own face in moments he thought unguarded, when someone else made a joke, or a particularly perceptive remark.

Emily wondered how much pain other people carried that passed unnoticed by all but the closest observer. Perhaps the kindest thing was to affect not to have noticed.

Emily excused herself at the first opportunity she found, and made her way over to where Cecily was trying to look interested in the rambling tales of two women as alike as sisters. It was nearly a quarter of an hour before they could extricate themselves with grace.

'Thank heaven,' Cecily said with feeling. 'If it were not the middle of winter, I would go for a walk in the garden. I think I would rather have fallen into the pond than heard any more stories about Rose, or Violet, or whatever her name was.'

Emily turned to her lightly. 'You look worn out. I imagine you have to attend far too many of these receptions. I find after a while that they all seem the same, and I can't for the life of me remember what this particular one was supposed to be about. I can understand why some people call everyone "my dear", or even "your excellency". How does anyone remember all these names?'

Cecily smiled. 'Oh, there are tricks, but they don't always work.'

'Then let us go and look for the room with the Gainsborough portrait in it,' Emily suggested.

'I didn't know there was one!' Cecily said with surprise.

'Then we may well be some time in finding it,' Emily responded.

For the first time in the evening Cecily genuinely laughed. They walked close beside each other, talking of trifles, until they were out of earshot of the main party. A few moments later, out of sight as well.

'Are you just madly bored?' Emily asked gently. 'Or are you concerned about the contract? I have heard nothing to suggest that there will be any problems. I know it is extraordinarily important to you.'

Cecily gave a slight shrug. 'No, I think it is all as it should be. Godfrey is confident. He has certainly worked hard enough at it, and he is meticulous. He leaves no details to chance, or even for someone else to check.'

'Then I think we have no need to worry,' Emily tried to sound as if that were a relief, but none of the anxiety was lifted from Cecily's face. 'It isn't the contract, is it?' she said after another moment or two.

Cecily blinked, and Emily realised with a wave of pity that she was close to tears. She put an arm around her very lightly. 'Come and sit down. There is a sort of small sitting room just through here. I remember it from another occasion. If they thought you were not quite yourself they would be delighted for you to sit a while.'

'It's really nothing,' Cecily hesitated. 'I'm sorry. I must be a little . . . tired.'

'Perhaps you have a slight chill,' Emily said, not as a serious answer, but to fill a silence that seemed to require an explanation. She wanted very much to know what it was that caused Cecily such concern, but it would be clumsy to ask. It would sound more like curiosity than friendship.

They walked into the small room and Emily closed the door. It was, as she had said, a sitting room of sorts. There were three chairs in it, close to each other, and a very small table with a pitcher of water and several glasses. Emily poured two and gave one to Cecily.

'You have children, don't you?' Cecily asked, more as confirmation than an enquiry.

'Yes, a son and a daughter,' Emily agreed. 'And you have a son, Alexander. You've spoken of him once or twice. How is he?'

Perhaps that was what Cecily had been waiting for, but she did not look up at Emily as she answered. 'He had a terrible accident several years ago. His horse fell on him. It damaged his spine . . .'

Emily tried to imagine how she would feel if it were Edward, and she could hardly bear it. 'I'm so sorry . . .' What a feeble thing to say. But what could possibly be equal to seeing your child appallingly injured? Most mothers would sooner it were themselves!

'He recovered . . . quite well,' Cecily said, looking up for the first time. 'The doctor thought his spine had healed, even though it took quite a long time. Alex could walk again, quite well, quite quickly. Even dance. But we didn't realise that without the medicine he was still in a lot of pain.'

Emily nodded, but she did not interrupt. What was there to say that could possibly be of use?

Cecily drew in a shaky breath. 'I thought that it would lessen, and it seemed to. I didn't realise he was sheltering me from much of his pain.'

'And his father?' Emily asked. Although Jack was not Edward's father, he loved Edward deeply as he did Evangeline, who was his. The idea of either of them being hurt would be unbearable to him, every bit as much as to Emily.

Cecily looked away. 'Alexander is . . . very different from Godfrey. Perverse, some people might say. Godfrey is a good man, extraordinarily gifted and dedicated to the causes he works for. Alexander is a dreamer, creative in his imagination and in the arts.' She turned back to Emily almost as if she had read criticism in her. 'And I do not mean he is lazy or impractical, or that he does nothing to realise his visions into form. He has a gift for sculpture. He has made an altarpiece for one of the local churches. And he gets other commissions too. But . . .' She stopped.

Emily guessed that the quarrel with his father went deeper than Cecily wished to say, and in truth, it was a very private matter, even though it was not at all uncommon. Jack had to work hard not to quarrel with Edward now and then. If he had been his own son, he might not have restrained himself so much. Emily had not always been entirely at peace with her own mother, Charlotte even less so. Their sister, Sarah, long dead now, had been the only obedient one.

'Alex lives a different way,' Cecily started again. 'I don't approve of it, but he is still my son. He has friends I don't care for, and I am certain he spends far too much of his time indulging . . . tastes I dislike.' She said it so quietly Emily did not even think of asking what they were. Cecily's pain was all she cared about. Perhaps it happened to most mothers. Edward was a little young for her to worry about his having that sort of troubles, but her own turn could well come, and far sooner than she would ever be prepared for.

'He . . . he had some very unsuitable friends,' Cecily went on, as though now the floodgates were open on the dam that had held it back, she needed to deal with it all at once.

'We all do . . .' Emily responded. 'And some of them turn out to be good.'

'Not like Dylan Lezant,' Cecily said softly, her voice catching as if she found it hard to control.

'Dylan Lezant?' Emily asked.

'A friend Abercorn was very close to. He was a young man of passion and charm, but emotionally fragile. "Too much imagination," Godfrey said. Alexander met him when he was recovering from his accident.'

'He sounds like a good friend,' Emily observed.

'He was . . .'

'Was?'

'He's dead,' Cecily gulped, and turned her head away a little, swallowing hard. 'They hanged him. I think Alexander has never got over it.' The tears spilled and slid down her cheeks. 'He seemed so young! So . . . so very foolish. But I suppose that is the law, and there was no escaping it.'

'The law?'

'He killed a man . . . shot him.' Cecily looked at Emily and met her eyes at last. 'They were buying opium . . . for pain. The police caught them, and in running away, Dylan shot a man, a Mr Tyndale, who was just going home by a shortcut. Alexander refused to believe he was guilty, but of course he was.' She swallowed hard and dabbed her cheeks with the handkerchief from her reticule. 'He still doesn't believe it today. You see . . . Alex escaped. He thought Dylan was right behind him . . . but he wasn't. The police arrested him with the gun in his hand. Poor Tyndale was dead, shot through the heart. That was the worst time in my life. Alexander did everything he could to prove that Dylan was innocent, but of course he wasn't. They tried him and found him guilty. I can remember Alexander's face as if it were days ago, not years. I was terrified he would take his own life, with the grief of it . . . and the guilt. I thought he would never stop . . . that he would . . . damage his heart, quite literally.'

'Guilt?' Emily said slowly, having difficulty with the idea. She ached to help, but what was there anyone could do?

'Because he lived!' Cecily explained. 'They both ran, but Dylan was closer and they caught him. Alexander did everything he could, spent every day and night till he passed out with exhaustion. Spent all his money. But he couldn't prove Dylan's innocence. He couldn't even make anyone listen to him. He hasn't ever stopped grieving over it.'

'If I said I can even imagine how you feel, it would be a lie,' Emily told her. 'But if there is anything I can do in any way at all, please allow me to.'

Cecily was silent for a few moments, as if searching for something to ask of her, then shook her head. 'Thank you . . .'

There were footsteps outside and both of them stood up, not wishing to be caught in what was an acutely private conversation. Gossip could interpret it in too many ways.

Even so, the subject arose in another conversation within the

91

hour, and Emily was determined to turn it to her advantage. She was speaking with Mrs Hill, a woman she had known for some time when they were joined by her brother, Mr Cardon, and his wife, a blunt-faced woman who was wearing rather too many diamonds for the best of taste. However, she had a candour that Emily found a pleasant change from the too common desire to please those considered to be important.

The first reference caught Emily completely by surprise.

'Lestrange,' Mrs Cardon corrected her husband. 'Lezant was the poor young man who was hanged for shooting the bystander in the opium sale, or heroin, or whatever it was.'

Her husband's eyebrows rose so far they wrinkled his brow right up to the point where his hair was receding. 'I don't know why on earth you need feel pity for such a miserable creature. You really should be more careful of the words you choose, my dear. I'm sure you don't mean that. You will give Mrs Radley quite the wrong impression of you.'

'Please don't concern yourself,' Emily said quickly. 'I don't form impressions so rapidly.' That was a lie. She had forgotten the excess of diamonds and gained a greater interest in Regina Cardon.

Mrs Cardon was not so easily corrected. 'I meant what I said,' she told him. 'I read the case very carefully.' She looked at Emily, not her husband. 'Herbert disapproves of my reading such things, but I consider that if it is in *The Times*, then it is fit for all people to read. Don't you agree?' There was no challenge in her voice, but it was intended none the less.

'I think you should read whatever you wish,' Emily replied with more candour than she had originally intended. 'But I agree with your taste. I'm not sure how I missed that story myself. I don't recall it. I feel remiss.' She said it as if she were genuinely interested, as indeed she was.

'Very polite of you, Mrs Radley,' Cardon said. 'But such indulgence is not really necessary.' A shadow of arrogance passed over his face.

Emily drew in breath to argue, then thought better of it. Her chance of learning more was slipping away. 'I have heard something of the matter just by word of mouth, occasional references,' she said, directing her words to Regina Cardon. 'I would be very interested in hearing what *The Times* had to say. It is the most likely to be accurate, at least as to what was indisputable. No doubt opinions vary. They always do.'

'There was no doubt about the young man's guilt,' Cardon said firmly. He gave his wife a warning glance.

Emily plunged on anyway. It concerned Cecily, whom she liked and for whose grief she had a deep compassion. It also might eventually affect Jack, if Alexander Duncannon felt as profoundly about it as his mother believed. If Lezant were innocent, then there was grave error somewhere, and possibly even corruption.

'He confessed?' Emily said with perhaps a little too much innocence.

'No,' Regina Cardon said instantly. 'He went to the gallows denying his guilt in anything except purchasing opium to treat his pain.'

'He should have got it through a doctor, not illegally from some street dealer,' her husband told her brusquely. 'He was resisting arrest, and that is still murder, because it was done while in the act of committing another crime. You have no argument, Regina. Lezant was a thoroughly undesirable young man.'

'If every young man were hanged whom someone three times his age thought undesirable, we should few of us grow to adulthood, Herbert,' she answered coldly.

He looked at her with ill-conceded surprise and arrogance.

'Although I have little doubt you would have made it,' she added.

Emily put her hand up over her mouth as if she were aghast, whereas actually she was afraid of laughing aloud. Cardon might be uncertain as to what his wife meant, but Emily knew exactly – and agreed. With reluctance she rescued the conversation by changing the subject, but she did manage to smile directly at Regina Cardon, to let her know that she both understood and sympathised. She received a flash of gratitude in return.

Later she rejoined Jack, but did not have an opportunity to speak alone with him until nearly two in the morning when they were in their own carriage on the relatively short journey home.

She was tired, but what she wished to say should not be delayed. Discussion on the contract was continuing every day. Only if there were difficulties would it extend beyond Christmas.

'Jack . . .'

He brought himself to attention with an effort.

'I'm sorry,' she said quietly. 'But I feel I should tell you that I had a long talk with Cecily Duncannon this evening, much of it in private.'

He blinked, and in the shifting light of passing carriage lamps she saw the expression of ease go from his face. 'I could see that she was worried. Is it something serious? Is she unwell?'

'Her son, Alexander, is unwell . . .'

He relaxed. 'The poor fellow hasn't been really well since his accident. Godfrey mentions it occasionally. He seems to be recovering very slowly.' He put his hand over Emily's where it rested on her cloak. 'He's a difficult young man. He has chosen a style of life not likely to help him. Godfrey has done all he can to persuade him to change, but I'm afraid it has so far been to no avail. He made some unfortunate friends earlier on, as I suppose many of us do, but in his case it ended in total tragedy, and Alexander refuses to let go of it.'

'He still believes Lezant was innocent,' Emily replied.

Jack looked at her sharply. 'Emily, there was no question. The bystander was shot. The police were there to arrest them, and the dealer, and they saw everything. Alexander was just . . . devoted to this Lezant as a fellow sufferer dependent on opium for the relief of pain. Except Alexander had real and severe pain and this Lezant was just . . . just an addict! I'm sorry for both of them, but it is far beyond time Alexander put it behind him and concentrated on getting his health back.'

'And that's all there is to it?' Emily said with a touch of chill her fur-trimmed cloak and carriage rug did nothing to dispel. 'Is that what Godfrey said to Cecily too?'

'I don't suppose he was quite so blunt, but in substance, yes.'

She did not reply. She had no facts with which to argue, not with Jack, anyway.

Chapter Five

IT WAS an icy morning and Pitt was later arriving at Lisson Grove than he had intended. A dray had slid on the ice in Marylebone Road and everything was held up. It had given him the chance to read his morning newspaper in the hansom, not an enjoyable experience, but necessary.

Stoker was waiting for him, his face pink from the bite of the wind, and his expression dark.

'That missing dynamite from Bessemer's,' he said as soon as Pitt came in at the door. 'It was the foreman who took it, but he's not much help. Either he's scared witless of whoever he sold it to, or he really doesn't know. Either way, it's bound to be anarchists raising funds by selling it on. That's how they get funds.'

'Any idea from other sources who bought it?' Pitt asked without much hope. He pulled out his chair and sat down, looking at the pile of notes already on his desk.

'An Italian called Pollini, who sold it to someone whose name he doesn't know, and whose description could fit half the anarchists in Europe. Most of them are in London anyway. The reports are on your desk. I've looked at them, and I can't see anything useful . . . at least not in regard to the Lancaster Gate business. Got a good line in one or two other cases. It's stirred up the pot a bit, and all kinds of things are coming to the surface. We should be able to tie up the Lansdowne affair.'

Author: Adams, Jane, 1960-
Title: The murder book
Item ID: C901870188
Date due: 3/1/2017,23:59
Date charged: 13/12/2016,
11:54

Author: O'Connell, Carol
Title: Blind sight
Item ID: C901871523
Date due: 3/1/2017,23:59
Date charged: 13/12/2016,
11:54

Author: Jager, Anja de,
Title: A cold case in
Amsterdam Central
Item ID: C902054221
Date due: 3/1/2017,23:59
Date charged: 13/12/2016,
11:54

Author: Perry, Anne,
Title: Treachery at

Lancaster Gate
Item ID: C901207255
Date due: 3/1/2017,23:59
Date charged: 13/12/2016,
11:54

LibrariesNI

Items on Loan

Author: Hannigan, Emma
Title: The heart of winter
Item ID: C90141111169
Date due: 3/1/2017,23:59
Date charged: 13/12/2016,
11:54

Author: McDermid, Val,
Title: Out of bounds
Item ID: C901868149
Date due: 3/1/2017,23:59
Date charged: 13/12/2016,
11:54

Author: Barton, Fiona,
Title: The widow
Item ID: C901865523
Date due: 3/1/2017,23:59
Date charged: 13/12/2016,
11:54

'Good.' Pitt gave a brief smile, took the newspaper out of his pocket where he had slipped it, and dropped it into the bin.

'Did you read the leaders?' Stoker asked unhappily.

'Yes. Most of the demands are worded as looking for justice, but what it really means is revenge on those who attacked the police,' Pitt replied. 'I saw a piece by Josiah Abercorn. He's riding a wave of popularity by defending the police, the ordinary man, people's defence against the rise of crime, and so on. You might see what we know about him . . . I can understand it. The police are our symbol of safety. We resent their interference at times. They can be pompous, authoritarian, full of self-importance, but in the end they are the barrier against violence, loss of property, general chaos. They separate the order we rely on from the barbarism that lies beyond, danger and unreason. To attack them is to attack all of us.'

'That's pretty well what all the papers are saying,' Stoker agreed. 'Least the better ones. Suppose you read that too?'

'I didn't, actually,' Pitt replied. 'I was looking mainly at the foreign news. I don't think this has much to do with anarchists, but I wanted to see if there was anything political of importance, anything happened we should know about.'

'I've looked at the main reports, sir. I'm pretty sure it's just hot air, the usual people ranting on. In fact, from what our blokes are saying, the serious anarchists are upset about the bombing. Stirs everybody up, and some people who used to tolerate them are getting resentful. Got a few of them turned out of their lodgings, even refused in some of the places where they like to eat . . . coffee shops, and the like. Makes people nervous.'

'Interesting,' Pitt said thoughtfully. 'Sounds as if there's no agreement among them, anyway. But we still have to be as certain as we can that there are no new groups that we've missed. I need reports from all the men we have imbedded in those we know of. Let's get it on paper, and see if everything is accounted for.'

Stoker looked at him curiously, alarm in his eyes.

97

Pitt stiffened. 'Do you know of any other certain way to connect everything up so we can see the pattern of it? We need to be as sure as we can that there isn't another pattern we're missing, because we're so used to seeing the one we know.'

'We'll need some help,' Stoker gave in reluctantly. 'Who do you trust enough, sir? Whoever it is will end up learning all the imbedded men's names.' He shook his head. 'Are you sure you want that? Only takes one word let slip, to someone you think you can trust, and before you know it half the Branch knows who's where. We're none of us perfect, sir. We can't talk to wives or sweethearts; we need to be able to talk to each other, now and then.' He came as close as he could to telling Pitt he was wrong.

Pitt bit back the retort in his mind. Stoker was right: he was not suggesting someone would let information slip out through betrayal, but through stress, exhaustion, and the loneliness of not being able to tell even those closest to you what you were doing, what you knew that was frightening, pitiful, or even funny. The pressure of silence can put strain on all kinds of emotions.

And of course there was also the unfairness of telling people more than they needed to know. Secrets slipped could cost another man's life. Each man's own secrets were enough to carry.

'You're right,' he conceded. 'We'll work with what we have, and then ask questions to fill in the blanks, if there are any. Send Blake for a pot of tea.'

It took the whole of the day before they were satisfied that as close as it was possible to tell, there were no incidents that did not fit into the patterns they already knew. They saw no new or unexplained behaviours among the groups already known to exist in London. No one had suddenly made contact with lots of people, there were no unusual meetings, no more travel than usual.

It was not a profitless exercise, however, because several things emerged. There was some old information that could be discarded and a few new ideas noted to follow up on.

'Next job is to look more thoroughly at the victims,' Pitt said wearily, when they finally locked all the papers and notes away.

'Don't think Ednam's going to make it,' Stoker said quietly. 'If you need to see him again I think it's too late. He's slipped into a coma. The nurse said they'd do everything they could for him, but he's not responding. Maybe there's worse inside him than they know. Bossiney's holding his own, but those burns aren't going to heal much. The scars'll be there for ever – poor devil. Yarcombe's very quiet, but his fever's down, and the stump of his arm is healing.'

Pitt said nothing. He had thought Ednam would make it, and maybe Yarcombe would not. Ednam was older, and he had been more seriously burned. The shock to his body must have been worse than Pitt had appreciated. He had not particularly liked the man, but he knew nothing to his discredit. If he died there was going to be a whole new outcry against the bomber. No doubt Abercorn, and men like him, would climb on the bandwagon to call for more and swifter action.

Could one man have planned this bombing and carried it out? Yes, if he were careful and clever. It was beginning to look as if he had no connection with any of the anarchist groups they were aware of.

That raised the chill question Pitt had thought of in the dark hours of the night. Was there a whole cell of anarchists that Special Branch had missed? Perhaps an English group, or one from Scotland or Wales? He was pretty sure it was not a new group from Ireland. That was what Special Branch had been created for, to stop the Fenian bombers. It still employed a large section of men specifically dedicated to that. Fitzpatrick was in charge, a brilliant Anglo-Irishman that Narraway had known for thirty years, and trusted completely. So far he'd been proved right.

Pitt tidied up, read the last reports, then an hour later he locked up the office and walked out into the wind and the rain. It was milder. The ice was gone from the pavements and they were awash from the downpour. If the wind blew the clouds away it would freeze hard by morning, lethal as oiled glass.

The lamps had been lit long ago and shone like fitful moons in a long loop around the curve of the street. It was wet and bitter, yet it had its own kind of beauty, man's beacon masts into an unknown distance. As he passed each one and left it behind him the next one loomed into sight.

He wished he could see further ahead in the case. Perhaps he was not investigating the victims carefully enough? Were they just police as far as the bomber was concerned? Did he regard all police as tokens of a government, an order he hated? Or was he more interested in killing people who would gain them the most attention? Could the whole abomination be something to divert Special Branch's attention from something else? Something more long-lasting, more deeply injurious to the country?

Was it a practice run for a larger attack on an iconic building such as the Houses of Parliament, or even Buckingham Palace? Whitehall? Or in another country altogether? Tomorrow he would have Stoker contact all the foreign officials they knew and see if anything tied in with French or Spanish plots.

He turned the corner but kept on walking. He was stiff after sitting all day bent over papers. The cold air cleared his head and the rain had eased off.

He splashed through another puddle at the edge of the road as he crossed it, his mind whirling with unanswered questions.

Was this a matter of terrorism at all, or just a particularly horrible murder? Was one of the men an intended victim and the others were killed collaterally, just to mask the motive for the one?

What kind of a lunatic bombs five men to be sure of injuring one? Pitt asked himself, was he avoiding looking at that because he was afraid of what he would find? Perhaps it was someone he knew, like some deeply evil men he had found in police departments in the past? Names, faces came to his mind.

But even the worst of those had committed only single crimes to start with, and to gain power, not simply cause destruction.

Had there been threads of it before that they had not seen? That he, specifically, had not recognised? Maybe he lacked the perception and the overall vision and experience that Narraway had had. That had been his fear all day – that he was in a job too big for him. He was a policeman, a detective who had solved complex and fearful murders. But he was not a politician, a spymaster, a man who instinctively understood treason and betrayal, as Narraway had.

Had someone slowly and carefully infiltrated Special Branch so Pitt could be misled, blinded by what he thought was his own understanding? He wished he could believe that was impossible.

When he finally stopped a hansom and requested it to take him to Keppel Street, he was so tired he was afraid he might go to sleep in the cab and have to be roused. He climbed in and sat back gratefully, but his mind would not leave the subject alone.

He arrived home, took off his wet coat and boots and was very soon sitting beside the fire with a slice of bacon and egg pie and a second cup of tea. Still he could not let go of the knots in his shoulders, or the need to keep on trying to unravel tangles in his mind.

This was one case he could discuss with Charlotte because it was totally public anyway. It was talked of on every street corner meeting by everyone from messenger boys to washerwomen, and probably over every garden fence, and over glasses of whisky at every gentlemen's club.

It was she who broached the subject.

'Gracie came to see me,' she remarked. 'She's going to have another child.'

He smiled. It was the first good news he had heard since the bombing. 'Excellent! Can I congratulate Tellman, or am I not supposed to know?'

'I would prefer that you didn't, at least not just yet,' she said gravely. 'That wasn't what she came about.'

'Oh . . . what was it?' The warmth inside him drained away.

'She's afraid for Samuel. He's such an idealist she thinks it's going to hurt him very much if he discovers real corruption in the police,' she answered. The gaslamps shed a warmth over her face, a softness, but it did not hide the anxiety in her eyes. She did not need to put into words her need for a reply, or that comfort would be a denial, not a help.

'I know,' he admitted. 'But there's nothing we can do but look more thoroughly. We've exhausted every avenue we can take about known anarchists. If there's an unknown group then that's what they are: unknown to us, invisible. We've pieced together every fragment of information we have.' He would not tell her about the sources, the informers, domestic and foreign, or his own men long embedded in anarchist cells. 'Which is a great deal. There are no incidents unconnected, nothing that suggests a movement we don't know about.' He said that with a degree of confidence.

But she knew him too well. 'So if it is anarchists, then there is a movement that has managed to remain invisible.' She spoke the fear aloud: 'And you think Victor would have seen it?' Charlotte had learned a little more tact over the years, but she could still cut with surgical precision when she wanted to. She met his eyes without a flicker. 'Have you got rid of all the men in Special Branch that he had? Isn't there someone left that you can be absolutely sure of?'

Did she really think that of him? 'No! Of course not!' he said a little sharply. 'I haven't got rid of any of them. Two left, one for injury, the other because he retired. He was nearly seventy! A very wise man, and I was sorry to lose him.'

She smiled quickly. 'Then why would they suddenly miss something as important as a new movement in anarchy, or nihilism, or general desire for social change?'

'They wouldn't,' he agreed, moving in the chair to ease his locked muscles. 'Of course they wouldn't.' He didn't want her to realise how irrational he had been, how far he had allowed the anxiety to eat into him, so he did not admit how much he had needed that sharp reminder of sanity.

Her tact reasserted itself. She smiled ruefully. 'Then you have to consider that the bombing really was directed at the police. Tellman is going to be very unhappy, but you can't defend someone effectively if you refuse to acknowledge where they are vulnerable.'

'You've been thinking about it, haven't you?' he observed, sitting up a little straighter. 'What did Gracie say?'

'Only that he's an idealist, still, and he doesn't like what he's finding.'

Pitt wondered if that were the full truth, or if she was protecting a confidence. He could easily guess what it was. He had worked with Tellman long enough when they were both police to know his belief in the law, and the police as the front line against those who broke it. His opinion of lawyers was much less generous. They crossed sides far too easily, and their loyalty was to be bought. He would grant in argument that that was necessary. They fought for the innocent as well as the guilty. But his heart was with the police, always.

Corruption in the police was a dark thought in the warmth of this room where he had known so much happiness, but it would not be dismissed.

'Thomas?' Charlotte prompted.

He turned his attention back to her. 'It's possible. I hope it's just one man who feels a personal grudge for some wrong, real or imagined.'

'Bombing police, injuring three and killing two?' she said with doubt. 'It must have been a very great wrong.'

'It could become three,' he corrected. 'Ednam isn't doing well. They don't think he'll live.'

'Oh . . . I'm sorry.'

'But you're right, it is a very violent way to protest. It could easily have killed all five.'

'Is it part of something larger?' she asked. 'If you discover whatever the corruption is, the newspapers will make a big issue of it. Politicians will argue about it, lay blame wherever they want to.' She leaned forward. 'Could that be the purpose of it, do you think? Could it be real Special Branch business? I mean a foreign power trying to weaken us, distract us from some other attack? Make us look at this so hard, we miss something else? Thomas, be very careful what you do about it, how you handle it. The Government will be nervous. They may put pressure on you to cover up the details, and then when some really persistent journalist finds out what you've hidden, the newspapers will make it far more important than it is. They'll blame you for hiding it, suggest you are a liar and then ask what more you are hiding. How bad is the real truth?'

She was right and he had no argument against it.

'In public life it isn't people's wrong acts that destroy them, it's the lies they tell to cover them,' she went on gravely. 'Haven't you noticed that? In politics it happens again and again. I don't know how anybody could fail to notice this! An admission and apology can be forgiven. It's the same in Society. It's the lie that kills.'

'I wish I knew what the truth was!' he said. 'And, please God, it is one I can expose, not something that has to be covered up because it would betray government secrets of diplomacy we can't afford to reveal.'

She caught something in his voice. 'Thomas . . .'

'The man leading the negotiation of this contract with the Chinese – Alexander Duncannon is his son. He had a bad fall from a horse and injured his back.' He answered the unasked questions. 'He took opium for the pain. Still does. Like many young men, he has a desire for social change, and some of it centres on the police. I hope he keeps his opium on a low key, at least until this contract is signed. Jack asked me not to involve Alexander in an investigation, at least until then.'

'And did you agree?'

'I can't. But Alexander was of no help, except to suggest, unintentionally, where I might look for police incompetence and perhaps bad judgement.'

'And will you look?'

'I think I have to look a great deal more closely at the five men who were at Lancaster Gate. I would much rather not, but I can't protect what I don't know.'

'Will you make it public?'

'I don't know if I'll find anything. If it's just error, no, I won't. We need to believe in our police. And most of them are good, brave, honest men doing a difficult job, quite often in danger, and for little enough money. We owe them our loyalty. It's the very least we can give, if we continue to expect them to help us when we're in trouble, keep order so we can sleep at peace in our beds, and go safely about our business the next day. We all depend on it. Respect for the law, and those who guard it, is the bedrock of a civilised society.'

Charlotte leaned forward in her chair and put her warm hand over his where it rested on his knee.

'I know that, and I've been proud of what you do since the day I married you . . .'

'Not before?' he said wryly, in part to conceal a wave of emotion he would have governed rather better had she not been so kind. He remembered the arguments they had had before that, when she was still a young woman of the gentry who resented police, thought them interfering, and socially about as welcome as the bailiff or the rat catcher.

'Before I was married to you, my dear, I had no right to share credit in anything you did,' she responded.

'Or to meddle,' he added. 'But it didn't stop you.'

She gave a little shrug. 'I know. And I'm going to meddle now. Maybe you can think of everything, but just in case you don't, have you wondered if it is a new, different group of people who want the police to be disgraced publicly? If I were to plan a revolution, of any sort that required getting rid of the order that exists, I would start by destroying people's belief in the law. If the police don't protect you, then you have to protect yourself. You must enact your own justice, and for that you need weapons, co-operation, a new force to replace the old one, which you have shown does not work.'

'Charlotte . . .' he protested, but the argument died before he could find words for it. What she was suggesting was extreme, but the breaking of trust in government was the beginning of anarchy. And it would not be the first time.

'Frighten people, make them angry,' she went on. 'And they can be persuaded to do all kinds of things. If I were in danger and the police would not protect me, wouldn't you do so yourself?'

'You don't need to labour the point. I understand,' he said a little sharply. It was the thought he had been trying to reason away. It was extreme. 'But all we have so far is one appalling act of violence. It is quite specific. Panic is the last thing we want . . .'

'I want you to be right,' she insisted. 'Always right! I want you to have thought of everything. You have to. It takes only one lunatic with a vision and enough brains to put it into action, and we have twice the battle to fight than if we had seen it coming, and acted in time.'

He knew that she meant it. She was fiercely protective in that reckless, wholehearted way only women can be. He put his hand over hers and closed it gently.

'I shall consider that very dangerous possibility,' he promised. 'It is one of the many things we need to watch for. As you say, if you want to ruin a nation, begin by ruining their trust in the law. Then each man will take it into his own hands, and you have anarchy. Now I'm going to bed.' He rose to his feet and pulled her up gently also. 'And so are you,' he added.

Pitt could not get Charlotte's words out of his mind. He and Stoker had searched every report from the last half-year, all catalogued so that every thread was easy to follow. The membership of each separate group was listed, constantly updated, including reports and requests from foreign governments. They could see no break in the patterns familiar over the last decade or so.

He mentioned to Stoker the possibility of a diversion created by a foreign group of some sort, but with English help.

'If they exist, they're damn clever,' Stoker said unhappily, staring at the latest reports on Pitt's desk.

'Could it be someone we would be very unlikely to suspect?' Pitt suggested. 'That's how we missed him?'

'Like who?' Stoker asked. 'A Member of Parliament? Or someone in the law, the judiciary?'

'Yes. Or one of us?' Pitt answered more quietly, as if even in here they could be overheard.

Stoker's bony face went even paler. 'Yes, I suppose it could. That would mean we couldn't trust our own reports. And if it's one of them, then until we know who, it's all of them. I've known these men for years, sir. I don't believe that.'

'I know,' Pitt agreed. 'And Tellman doesn't believe it of the police. I can't blame him. Perhaps the real damage would be suspicion itself?'

Stoker shivered. 'Once we start turning in each other, that's really the beginning of the end.'

'We're not going to entertain that one,' Pitt said bluntly. 'But I was thinking, on the way in this morning, if someone really intended to create chaos, and then take over, he would have to have a force of some size behind him. You can't do that with half a dozen here and there.'

'The police?' Stoker's eyebrows rose. 'No. The odd one might be rotten, but they're good men and they'd never take to anything like that. They're part of the people. You're wrong. Hell! You used to be one of them!' He was angry now.

'I wasn't suspecting the police,' Pitt corrected him. 'Anyway, the police generally have no weapons except truncheons. I've been thinking a bit more along the lines of a disaffected group from the army. Ednam used to be army, fifteen years ago.' He saw Stoker's face tighten. 'Thinking back on one or two incidents we got reports of – how about that bit of unpleasantness with General Breward? He's junior, as generals go, only about forty-five, but pig-headed, much admired by his more bloody-minded juniors. Got a few inflated ideas of his own importance.'

Stoker had been a merchant seaman before joining Special Branch. He was used to authority, but he despised a leader who put his own men in jeopardy unnecessarily. Like most sailors, he had intense respect for the sea. No man took it lightly and escaped. He had the same respect for the terrain over which a battle might be fought, and for the men who fought it beside him.

'I'll look into it, sir. He's certainly arrogant enough – and stupid, in his own way. Plenty of cleverness, and damn all wisdom.'

'Thank you,' Pitt agreed. 'I'm going to go back over the victims again. See what they might have done together. Just in case . . .'

'Yes, sir.'

'Good men, all of them,' Chief Superintendent Cotton said an hour later as Pitt sat in his office. He was superior to Whicker, whose responsibility was only at local level. Now Pitt needed someone with more authority.

Cotton tipped his chair back a little and stared at Pitt. He was about Pitt's own age, and sunken-cheeked with black, hooded eyes. 'Why the devil are you asking?'

'To clear their names,' Pitt said with slight surprise, as if the answer should have been obvious. 'You've no doubt heard what the newspapers are suggesting, even if you haven't read them.'

Cotton's smile did not reach the steady eyes, which were unreadable because they were so shadowed by his brows. 'You think they were targeted deliberately?'

'It's possible. I have to explore it. Disprove it, if I can.'

'Why? Because you were once in the police yourself?'

'Because I want to find the man who did this,' Pitt told him. 'And for that I need to know why. It's not any of the anarchists and general troublemakers we know.'

'Sure of that, are you?' Cotton righted his chair before it slipped out of his control.

'Yes.'

Cotton let out his breath. 'Bad business.' For the first time he regarded Pitt with some respect. 'Those five men had worked together on and off for several years. No better or worse than most. Ednam, poor devil, was a bit self-important, bossy, wouldn't be told what to do if he thought different. Army background, I suppose. But he wasn't often wrong. But his men looked up to him. He was loyal to them, good or bad. It was appreciated.'

'Good or bad?'

'He turned a blind eye to a few mistakes, or even a few things done on purpose.'

'What sort of things?' Pitt pressed.

'For God's sake, man!' Cotton said violently, slamming his chair back on all four feet. 'The usual sort of things! A bit too much to drink . . . the odd brawl . . . laying into a suspect to persuade him to stop lying . . . one or two arrests a bit rougher than necessary. Find me the policeman that hasn't crossed the line some time or other, and I'll show you a boss that doesn't know his men.'

'Were they disciplined?' Pitt tried to keep his tone neutral, but with difficulty.

Cotton raised his black brows. 'I have no idea. I didn't ask, and neither will you, if you've any sense.'

'What about losing evidence? Accepting the odd gift from someone to turn the other way?' Pitt could not let it go yet.

Cotton stared at him.

'Or framing someone for a crime they committed, but we somehow just couldn't get the proof?' Pitt went on. 'Or helping themselves to a little evidence, like a bottle of whisky or a box of cigars? Petty theft a member of the public wouldn't know, or care about. Being beaten to give false testimony, or disabled in a violent arrest is a different matter. And being framed for a crime they didn't commit is another matter altogether. Is that what we're talking about?'

'No!' Cotton said angrily. 'Not in my command, and not that I know about. Do you?'

Pitt was startled. 'No I don't!'

'Swear for all your men, would you? Tellman, for example?' Cotton said, meeting Pitt's eyes with a totally unreadable expression.

'I would swear for his honesty, yes,' Pitt said without hesitation. 'Or any of my men in Special Branch.'

'For his honesty? Interesting,' Cotton observed. 'Then what would you not swear for?'

Pitt had to think for a moment. Cotton would remember every word he said, and trip him on it if he could. He would repeat it where he thought it served his purpose. If Pitt denied any possible fault it would mark him as absurd, incompetent, or a deliberate liar.

'He's an idealist,' he chose his words. 'And loyal. He might see what he hoped to see, and be blind to something uglier. I don't know if he would necessarily report a man's error, if he believed it to be genuine. A man who shows no loyalty can't expect to receive any. Trust goes both ways. If you take advantage of a man's error, he'll take advantage of yours, and we can none of us afford that.'

'Naïve? Is that what you'd call him?' Cotton smiled, showing his teeth. 'A loyalty that inclines him to look the other way? An idealist who doesn't see his men's weaknesses? Dangerous, don't you think? Do you operate like that, Pitt? Special Branch Commander Pitt? Is that who has our country's safety in his hands? A man who puts protecting his men from their faults before catching the bombers who would sink our country under a tide of violence and chaos?'

Cotton had taken a step too far, and he knew it the instant he saw the change in Pitt's face.

'My junior officers make mistakes,' Pitt answered. 'If they don't learn not to, they stay junior. What about yours? Ednam was a loyal bully. What about Yarcombe, Bossiney? The others?'

'I don't tell tales on dead men.' Cotton shuffled his chair forward again and looked at Pitt directly across the desk. He was not used to being questioned, even though Pitt outranked him.

'Never investigated a murder then, have you?' Pitt responded.

'Is that what this is? Three murders?' Cotton asked.

'Isn't it? And two attempted?'

'Looks like it. All right, I'll give you all I know on those five men. And you'd better bloody well bring me back someone to answer for them!'

Pitt stood up. 'Thank you.' He knew that in a sense he had accepted a challenge.

He met Tellman again the day after to hear what he had learned further. He summarised the reports that Cotton had given him, the good and the bad.

Tellman's face grew tighter and a flush mounted up his thin cheeks.

'He said that about his own men?' he asked when Pitt had finished. The disgust in his voice was palpable, and a deep emotion as if he were now facing a reality he had long dreaded.

Pitt understood at least in part. He knew the weaknesses of his own men. He was of little use to them if he did not. He knew their skills and their inabilities. He also had a strong feeling in which direction their fears lay, and what most stretched their courage, where their blind spots were, and who worked well with whom. He knew some of their temptations. But he would never have spoken of these faults to anyone else. Trust and discretion must go both ways; all loyalty must.

'I pressed him,' he said as some excuse for Cotton. 'We have to know exactly who was crooked, and how much.'

'I do know!' Tellman said instantly. He was speaking out of bravado, and Pitt was quite aware of it. In fact, this was predictable from Tellman.

'No you don't,' he contradicted. 'At least I hope to God you don't! If you knew that of them and did nothing, then you're part of it.' Even as he said it, he knew that Tellman's reaction would be instant defence.

Tellman's body was rigid, his face white but for the spots of colour burning in his cheeks. 'I'm damn well not part of it!' he shouted. 'I've never taken a thing that wasn't mine. I've never arrested anyone with more violence than was necessary, and I've certainly never hit a man that was down, or cuffed. And if you don't know that, then you're a fool! And you shouldn't be in charge of a newspaper stand, never mind a body of men that risk their lives to carry out your orders. You're a fool . . . and a bitter, damaged man!' The words came out rasping, as if the passage through his throat hurt him.

Pitt swallowed hard. He was taken aback by Tellman's rage, although perhaps he should have expected it.

'I know my men, and I trust them,' he replied as levelly as he could, but he heard his own emotion roughen his tone. 'They know that. They know I also know their weaknesses, as I dare say they know mine. The difference is that it's my responsibility not to put them in the path of the things they can't handle. I understand fear, confusion, pity, clumsiness now and then. But I don't accept lies, stealing, loss of temper until you beat someone.

I don't accept taking bribes or giving them. It's a betrayal of everyone else, and any man caught in those things goes . . . if it's possible, he serves time.'

He drew in his breath and met Tellman's eyes without flinching. 'Turning a blind eye because you don't want to know is not compassion, it's cowardice, and it's a betrayal of the good men. It's not them you're guarding, it's your own feelings, because you don't want to deal with it.'

'And is that what you think I'm doing?' Tellman's voice was high and tight, his eyes blazing.

'I hope not. But you'd better tell me . . .'

'So what? So you can have me put in prison?' Now it was just raw anger.

That stung Pitt into temper as well. 'Maybe so I can save you from being blown up by a bloody bomb!' he shouted back. 'Or didn't you think of that?'

Tellman was silent. Pitt could see in his face the pain of a reality he had long refused to look at, refused to believe was anything but the lies of those who resented the police, or were afraid of them, for just cause.

'You're branding them all because of a few, one in a hundred, that's rotten,' he said bitterly. 'Damning the good with the bad!'

Pitt tried to grasp the situation back into control. He did not want this quarrel.

'We've got to find the bad, before they sink us all,' he told Tellman, but he lowered his voice as well. 'None of us wants to think the people we work beside are corrupt, but looking the other way condemns us all. For heaven's sake, Tellman, choosing not to see something because it's ugly, or it damages your peace of mind, is deliberately allowing it. It's collusion by consent. And you know that as well as I do. We can't prosecute it in people who witness and then refuse to testify, who walk by on the other side, carefully not looking. But we despise it, and we require better of each other!'

'You pompous bastard!' Tellman said furiously. 'You think you know every damn thing . . . and you know nothing! Nothing of what a man thinks or believes . . . nothing that really matters!' And choking on his own grief, he turned and walked out of the room.

Pitt did not call him back. This was not going to heal easily. It had nothing to do with him, he knew, although Tellman would not forget that Pitt had seen the wound of disillusion in him, and he would not be able to forgive him easily for that.

Chapter Six

EMILY WAS dressed in cream and gold, colours she did not often wear, but this gown was the height of sophistication, slender, rich and up to the minute in its styling, especially about the shoulders. She knew it flattered her even before she left her dressing room, but admiration from a number of men, and a burning curiosity from women, reaffirmed it to her now as she and Jack were attending yet another party where the edges of politics and vast business empires interacted.

Again, of course, Parsons, Abercorn, Godfrey Duncannon and many others were gathered. Another major clause in the contract had been successfully negotiated and they were here both to celebrate and to prepare for the next step. It was beginning to look possible they might complete enough of it soon to take a few days' break from negotiations, maybe even go to the country in time for New Year.

Emily was at the edge of a conversation, half listening. Her eyes were on Godfrey Duncannon, elegant, courteous, always appearing to be interested. She wondered how he achieved it. He must have been bored almost to sleep, and yet he was smiling at everyone, nodding now and then as if he approved.

Where was Cecily? No doubt listening dutifully to someone. Emily's eyes swept around the room, trying to recall what colour Cecily was wearing. She saw a figure in a bronze and black gown, striking, almost wintry, but beautiful. Her dark head was bent, the light of the chandelier striking fire from the jewels in her hair.

She straightened up, and Emily realised it was Cecily. As she turned away from the people she was with, Emily saw the tension in her face. Then she looked back at her, her temporary retreat controlled again, hidden.

Was it Emily's imagination, or was Cecily even more troubled than before? Why? Something to do with her son, or her husband? Or possibly it was something completely different.

Emily was drawn back into the conversation around her.

'How interesting,' she lied smoothly. She had no idea what they were discussing, but that seemed an innocuous enough thing to say. Everybody wanted to be thought interesting.

Still she glanced at Cecily when she could. Once she observed her talking to Josiah Abercorn, and watched them discreetly for some moments. Abercorn was immaculately dressed, with almost too much care, as he had been each time she had seen him. There was no ease in it. She knew nothing to his discredit and yet she understood exactly why Cecily stood as far from him as she could without being discourteous, and there was a rigidity to the line of her body, as if he made her uncomfortable. Was that very slight self-consciousness in him something she was aware of too? Did he have any idea? He was smiling as he spoke to her, but Emily was much too far away to have the faintest idea what the conversation might be about.

With Abercorn instrumental in the legal drafting of the contract, Emily thought that perhaps she should get to know a little more about him, for Jack's sake. Cecily nodded agreement in the conversation, and moved a step back from Abercorn.

He gave a self-deprecating shrug, a slight gesture of one hand, and took a half-step forward, maintaining the former distance between them.

For a moment Emily thought Cecily was going to move back again, even excuse herself and walk away altogether. Was the conversation about the contract? Something she feared would hurt Godfrey? Emily already knew that Godfrey's reputation and possibly something of his future might suffer if the contract failed now that he had so publicly allied himself with it. She had asked Jack, and gathered more from his refusal to discuss it than she might have from a reply.

Was that what Cecily was worried about? Abercorn knew the details of the contract; maybe he was warning her, and she wished to be alone to consider what it might mean to her husband. But surely Abercorn was for the contract. Or was it that his intense support came at a price? Could it be one that Godfrey was unwilling to pay?

Emily should learn more about Abercorn. Jack had said he was politically ambitious, and he had very considerable private means. Emily could see, however, that he lacked the grace of one born to privilege, and his arrogance was one of achievement, not of birth.

She wondered if she should ask Jack, or discern for herself. The latter, definitely the latter. It seemed a trifle disloyal, but real loyalty would be to learn the truth. She would have to be discreet.

Like Cecily, Emily herself had not had to be concerned about money for a long time. But restricted circumstances – even moving to a smaller house, maintaining fewer servants, entertaining less often – were far less damaging to happiness than the feeling that one was a failure. She could remember with painful clarity how Jack had suffered when his previous hopes had been dashed. He knew it was a misjudgement, or at least in part it was. Most of Emily's attempts to dissuade him only made it worse. It was the fact of loss that mattered, not always its degree.

Is that what Cecily was worried about? Not the reality of failure but the injury it did to the mind. Emily could see Duncannon, the public man now, thick, iron-grey hair flashed with silver gleaming as he inclined his head to listen to some diamond-tiaraed woman. He looked superbly confident.

But Cecily knew the private man, the one who might sit up alone half the night with a decanter of whisky, then go to bed alone to grieve over the broken image of what he had dreamed himself to be.

Emily looked about, wondering who she should ask about Abercorn. Someone who would be discreet, yet tell her at least something of what she needed to know, and accurately. Such people were few.

How would she explain her wish to know? It must be totally believable.

The idea came quickly: Jack was thinking of inviting him to take a government office. It would be important. Nothing unfortunate was known of Abercorn, but one could not be too careful. He was not married, so the question arose, had he ever been? What was his . . . behaviour? One did not wish details, only assurances.

She had heard such enquiries made before. She knew the questions, and knew how to phrase them.

But then why was she doing this, and not Jack himself?

The answer came to that also . . . *Between women, my dear! We are so much more observant, don't you think?*

And far more likely to pick up the gossip that might, when unwrapped, come very close to the truth.

Now who to choose? Who would be certain not to take the nature of her enquiries straight back to Abercorn himself – or, for that matter, indirectly back.

Of course! Lady Parsons. Emily thought not much would escape her discerning eye, even if it did not pass her carefully guarded lips.

While pretending to listen to someone's wedding arrangements, she looked around the room and after several minutes saw Lady Parsons some distance away in a silver-grey gown that did not suit her at all. She would have been much better in a warmer colour.

As soon as she could without offence, Emily excused herself and, avoiding catching anyone else's eye, she made her way over towards Lady Parsons. She was going to be perfectly candid with her. Anything else would be sensed immediately and she would have lost not only the lady's attention but her respect.

Walking across the room, avoiding meeting the eyes of anyone she knew too well to pass by, she considered how frank to be with Lady Parsons. The judgement should be exactly right. She must not compliment her gown. If Lady Parsons had any idea how it appeared Emily might be suspected of sarcasm.

In the moment their glances met, Emily decided on total candour.

'Good evening, Mrs Radley,' Lady Parsons said with a flicker of amusement in her pale blue eyes. 'You look as if you have business yet to accomplish.'

Pretence would now be absurd. 'Good evening, Lady Parsons,' Emily replied. 'I am beginning to feel that there is always business to be done. The moment I think I have discharged it all, and am free simply to enjoy myself, something else arises.'

'Really?' Now Lady Parsons was quite openly amused. 'If it is your duty to try to persuade me of the virtues of this famous contract, so I may influence my husband's objections to it, I shall try not to be discourteous in discouraging you. But, my dear, we would be far better employed in discussing something of interest. I know what you are going to say, and I believe you know what I will reply. May we consider it accomplished, and move on?'

Emily smiled back at her without the least need to pretend. 'I had already taken that liberty,' she replied. 'I came for a completely different purpose.'

'How very sensible. What is it?' Lady Parsons enquired.

'A little information . . .'

'From me?'

'I think you will put a little less varnish on the truth than most people. And you will have made it your business to know it . . . at least as much as it is available,' Emily explained, wondering if she was being too rash, and whether Jack would be furious with her. But then she had no intention of telling him, at least not until necessary.

'I am intrigued,' Lady Parsons admitted. 'What can it be that I know, and you do not?'

There was no purpose to being evasive. 'My husband is in a position to offer an advancement to Josiah Abercorn. I am concerned that his judgement may be over-generous, but possibly it is my own prejudice speaking to me. I find myself unable to learn much about Mr Abercorn's life. I hear only praise for his professional acumen, and his charitable work.'

'And you wish to know more?'

'Wouldn't you? If it were your husband's reputation involved?'

Lady Parsons' eyes opened wide. 'Indeed I would. And I would need precision in the answer . . . which I cannot give you. I dislike him intensely, because he dislikes and is trying to discredit my husband, because we are on opposing sides of the contract with the Chinese. It is for a free port on the China Sea. I dare say you know? No – I see you did not!'

'Not in detail,' Emily said evasively.

Lady Parsons laughed. 'Ah, my dear! Not so well fielded. Your eyes gave you away. Still – the information. Josiah Abercorn is a man of elusive background. Apparently his father died before Josiah was born. His mother remained a widow and raised him alone. A woman of unquestionable virtue, she managed to find sufficient means to have him given an education. He later received a scholarship. He is undoubtedly brilliant in certain areas.'

'But self-made,' Emily pointed out. This was something to be praised, and yet in many people's eyes it also carried a certain stigma, an implication of awkwardness, a lack of culture. Could that be what made Abercorn tentative at times? A memory of childhood exclusion, the scholarship boy, the boy without a father, almost without a heritage.

Suddenly her slight irritation with him turned to sympathy, and a degree of respect. She had been born into the gentry and raised into the aristocracy. She had carried social place only by being both naturally extremely pretty, and quick-witted enough to learn how to use charm and intelligence. But confidence makes many things easy.

Lady Parsons was regarding her with interest, waiting for the next question and anxious as to what it would be.

'Nice to be respected,' Emily said. 'He has never married, I'm told. Is that true?'

'So I believe.' Lady Parsons' mouth twitched in a slight, ironic smile, not without pity. 'I dare say he was not considered good enough by the parents of the young woman he considered good enough for him. Something of a dilemma . . .' She let the words trail, leaving Emily to finish them as she chose.

'There is still time,' Emily observed. 'He looks no more than his mid-thirties, at the outside. Quite a suitable age for a man to marry. Perhaps he does not care to.' She imagined his childhood memories, and perhaps a sense of loss he was not yet ready to risk facing again. Some wounds run very deep.

'Many things are possible,' Lady Parsons agreed. 'I don't care for the man myself. There is something in him that I find . . . closed off. But had I walked his path, perhaps I would be a good deal less sanguine myself. Have I been of assistance?'

Emily gave her the widest smile. 'You have explained a great deal, and without once descending to gossip. I thank you.'

'I am delighted,' Lady Parsons responded drily. 'Perhaps when this interminable contract is finished, we may go out to luncheon one day? Or possibly visit a gallery, or some such?'

'Most certainly,' Emily agreed, and turned the conversation to something quite trivial.

Emily caught up with Cecily maybe a quarter of an hour later.

'It might be over by Christmas, don't you think?' Emily said with as much warmth as she could.

Cecily looked at her with a moment's blankness.

'At least the main part of it,' Emily elaborated. 'Just details to tidy up. Then we could take a long weekend . . .' She saw Cecily struggle to focus her attention, and realised it was not the contract that disturbed her. If it were, she would have understood immediately.

'Oh . . . yes,' Cecily said with a forced smile. 'That would be very nice. You have a house in the country, don't you?'

'Yes. Just a few days' escape . . .' Emily did not know how to finish. She had not meant to be clumsy, but now that she had, she was looking for a way to redeem the situation.

'So have we,' Cecily agreed, avoiding Emily's eyes. 'But I'm not sure if I want to go. There seems to be . . . so much here . . .' She too stopped.

'Can I help?' Emily said gently. 'You look desperately concerned. I thought it was the contract, but it isn't, is it?'

Cecily looked startled. 'Am I so obvious? I'm sorry. No, there is nothing anyone can do. But thank you . . .' She seemed about to go on, then changed her mind.

'It is your son . . .' Emily began, then seeing the pain in Cecily's face and the quick stiffening of her shoulders, she wished she had not. It was intrusive, but it was too late to retreat.

'He is still grieving for Dylan,' Cecily explained. 'He doesn't say anything about this fearful bombing, but I can see the change in him when it's mentioned. He hates the police, because they said it was Dylan who was guilty, and Alexander is convinced it wasn't. There's nothing Godfrey can say to him that changes his mind. He won't even look at the possibility, even now!' She stared at something inside herself, her eyes blank to the colour and movement around her, the swirl of dresses and glitter of jewels. It was as if she could not hear the laughter.

Emily searched for something to say, and everything that came to her mind was banal, and would only sound as if she didn't have the slightest understanding.

'Godfrey and Alexander had another quarrel about it yesterday,' Cecily went on, her voice so quiet Emily had to concentrate to hear her. 'I don't think Alexander will come back home again for a long time.' The loss in her face was bleak and total.

Emily remembered Cecily saying that he had his own flat. That was surely quite usual at his age. A decision to be independent was a part of growing up. He would certainly have the financial means, from Cecily if not from his father. She would sell her jewels, if necessary, to support her son. Emily understood that. She would have done the same.

'Sometimes you have to believe in your friends,' she said aloud. 'Even if nobody else does, and all the evidence seems to be against them. Actually, when you are young, and loyalty is passionate, especially then. I think you will have to allow him to accept reality when he is ready to, and perhaps not make any comment. The friendships of youth can be very strong. It's all tied up with what we believe to be honour. I'm so sorry.'

'You're right,' Cecily said with a faint smile. 'It is a matter of loyalty. They were there together. Alexander escaped and Dylan didn't. He feels as if he is alive at Dylan's expense. Sometimes I'm terrified he'll take his own life, as if he didn't deserve to have it.' She searched Emily's face, trying to see if she understood.

Emily put her hand very lightly on Cecily's arm, a touch so soft only the warmth of her would be felt. 'All of us would take the pain ourselves for those we love, most especially our children. We still try to, even when we know perfectly well that we can't. Right from the time we first held them in our arms, all through their growing years; we pick them up when they stumble, encourage them, believe in them when no one else does, weep for them when they are hurt. The tragedy is if we don't. No one should be unloved.'

Cecily blinked hard but the tears slid down her cheeks anyway.

'Thank you,' she said huskily. 'Now I think I had better excuse myself and go and talk to someone I dislike enough to mask all my feelings from them. Please don't chastise yourself. I feel far less alone.' And without adding anything more she turned and walked away towards a group of people deep in enthusiastic argument.

It was the following evening before Emily had the chance of speaking to Jack about any of the events at the party. By dinner time in the evening, when Edward and Evangeline had left the table, the sudden silence that lay between them required some remark before it became awkward. She did not want to discuss the contract, or what she had learned of Abercorn, but perhaps it was necessary.

She was not certain how much not only Jack's career but also his own money might rest upon its success. She did not like to ask if he had invested earlier in any of the companies that could be affected. It was highly improper for government ministers to place their own money in businesses whose profits their decisions could affect. It was more than dishonourable, it was a criminal offence.

But money invested earlier, before the issues of the contract existed, would not have been removed and reinvested. That too could be a signal to those who were clever enough to see it, of advantage to come.

For that matter, her own fortune might be involved. Both the house in the city and Ashworth Hall were entailed, and would pass to her son, Edward, who was actually titled Lord Ashworth since his father's death. But what of the rest?

How much was Jack not telling her, which caused the anxiety she could see in his face now where he sat opposite her across the polished table? He had protected her on several occasions, from one sort or another of pain or unpleasantness. She was happy to allow him to, not because she needed it, but because it was important to establish the balance of their relationship.

She had been Lady Ashworth when they met, beautiful, titled

and rich. He was handsome and charming, but the third son of a family with neither wealth nor connection to the aristocracy except of the most distant sort. What could he offer her? It did not matter in the slightest to her; she already had such things. But she quickly learned that it mattered to him. A couple of thoughtless mistakes had shown her that wounds to one's self-belief were deep and did not heal easily. Like broken bones that had knitted at last, a change in the weather could make them ache all over again like new injuries.

'Are you still going to recommend Abercorn a government position?' she asked him.

'Yes. I think he's a good man, and he's going to stand for office next chance he gets . . . I mean when there's a seat open, even before the next general election. Why?'

'What about Godfrey Duncannon? He wouldn't agree with you, would he?'

A shadow crossed his face. 'I work with Duncannon on this particular project; I don't have to agree with him over everything.'

'So he doesn't agree?' she said quickly. 'But it's more than that, Jack. I caught a glance at Abercorn yesterday evening, and for an instant there was hatred in his face. I don't mean just dislike, or a difference of opinion. They were nowhere near each other, and Abercorn looked across at Godfrey with . . . with a terrible expression in his eyes.'

Jack shook his head, his lips tight. 'You're probably imagining it. I dare say he was bored to death with the conversation. And what makes you certain it was Godfrey he was looking at, if he was as far away as you say? They don't like each other. I know that. They are of very different social backgrounds. Godfrey comes from aristocracy and inherited privilege, Abercorn from relative poverty, and making his own way. There are bound to be differences. Heavens, Godfrey is for the Establishment, and keeping everything the same. Abercorn is for change, and what he believes to be social justice, or at least something close to it.'

Emily wanted to argue. What she had seen was not political difference, it was hate, but she could think of no argument that Jack would listen to and believe.

'They agree on the contract,' he went on. 'They are both experts on China, and sea trade, in their own way. You don't have to like someone to work with them. It's politics, Emily, not lifetime partnership!'

She knew better than to argue any further. She changed the subject.

'Do you think we should go to the country for Christmas?' she asked, trying to keep emotion out of her voice.

He hesitated, watching her, trying to read how much it mattered to her.

She did not want to be too obvious. Condescension could deliver the deepest cut of all, like a fine razor. You did not even know how deep it was until you couldn't stop the bleeding.

'I think it would be rather nice to have it here, for a change,' she went on. His failure to answer told her more than he knew. 'Perhaps we should invite Charlotte and Thomas over for dinner? We haven't done that for ages. If Thomas can come, of course? This horrible bombing at Lancaster Gate is taking all his time.'

'On condition we don't talk about it,' Jack said with a smile.

'For heaven's sake!' she exclaimed. 'He wouldn't even think of it. I imagine he dislikes it a lot more than you do. Besides, he's not allowed to talk about his work. It's not like it was when he was in the police.'

Jack leaned back a little in his chair. 'I know that. And I think it would be an excellent idea. Frankly, I would prefer not to spend a day travelling, and be out of touch with any developments in this contract. But I owe Duncannon every support.'

Did he know how distressed Cecily was? Looking at him across the table she could not read his face well enough to decide if he had no idea, or if he was deliberately protecting her from an anxiety she could do nothing to help. Did Godfrey know how deeply disturbed his son was?

Did Emily owe it to Jack to tell him? Or was it kinder, more adult to keep silent? There was nothing to do to help, and meddling might only make it worse.

'Of course,' she agreed. 'It's quite a relief, really. It's going to be cold, and possibly even snowing. It would be nice not to have to go anywhere. I'll tell the staff. And tomorrow I'll invite Charlotte. I hope I haven't left it too late. It does look a bit last minute, doesn't it?'

'Yes,' he agreed with a smile.

She stood up and walked around to his chair. She put both hands on his shoulders and gently kissed his cheek. 'Well, if they can't come, it will just be us. I would be very happy with that too.' She felt the tension ease out of him. He said nothing, but put his hand up to cover hers.

Emily went to see Charlotte, as she had promised. Normally neither of them would stop in the middle of the afternoon for tea. It was a meal no one really needed, but it was a nice excuse to sit and talk. Charlotte had baked fresh mince pies.

'My favourite Christmas food,' Emily said as she sat down at the kitchen table.

'Better than roast goose or Christmas pudding?' Charlotte said with much surprise.

Emily did not bother to answer. Even with silver sixpences in the pudding and brandy butter on top, it still did not beat hot mince pies.

She had rehearsed in her mind a dozen times what she would say, but it never sounded as she wished it to. Underneath their differences in taste, social position into which they had married, and the entire styles of their lives, they knew each other too well.

'Jack doesn't discuss this contract very much, but I know it is extraordinarily important . . .' Emily began.

'Are you afraid it's not going to be ratified? Or that it's not what it is purported to be?' Charlotte asked.

'You don't give me any room to come at it sideways, do you!' Emily protested with a slight smile.

'Your tea will get cold . . .' Charlotte's meaning was obvious, but she said it gently, and pushed the plate of mince pies over towards Emily's side of the table.

Emily took one and bit into it. It was exquisite, sweet and sharp, and its pastry melted in her mouth.

'I don't actually know what I'm afraid of,' she confessed. 'In the face of it, it's foolproof. Jack was so hurt the last time. I mean . . .'

'I know what you mean. There may not be such a thing as an honest politician, but there are degrees. Is it Godfrey Duncannon you distrust, or the people behind him?'

'I think it's circumstances,' Emily replied, finishing the mince pie. 'I know Cecily Duncannon. I like her. Their son's closest friend was Dylan Lezant, a young man who was hanged for murdering a passer-by when he was arrested at a major drug purchase. Alexander is convinced Dylan was innocent, and he can't or won't let the matter rest. He believes the police are corrupt . . . that they let the real killer go and planted false evidence to implicate Dylan.'

Charlotte put down her half-eaten mince pie. 'That's pretty serious. I suppose Alexander is not terribly grieved then that several police have been killed in a bomb blast. I hope to heaven he doesn't say so. He wouldn't, would he?'

'I don't know. I suppose that is what Cecily is afraid of. I hadn't quite put it so directly.'

'Or does she think that he might have had some part in causing the blast?' Charlotte gave words to the thought Emily was trying to avoid.

'Great heavens! I hope not. No, he's angry, but he's not insane!'

'If he's still in great pain, and on opium – as I understand from Thomas – is it not possible that he *is* a little mad?' Charlotte had gone too far not to complete the thought.

'I don't know . . . maybe . . .'

They sat in silence for a moment. Emily took another mince pie.

Charlotte took one too. 'He's a young man, Emily.' She went on with the thread, following it all the way. 'If he feels an injustice has been done and his friend was an innocent man, hanged for a crime he did not commit, if he has any decency at all, he must have tried to save him. It's too late now, but won't he try to clear his name, at least?'

'Yes, Cecily said he has tried repeatedly to do that. But bombing the house in Lancaster Gate isn't going to do that!'

'It's certainly caused a great deal of attention,' Charlotte pointed out. 'Special Branch will have to look into his possible involvement if they don't find anyone else guilty of it. I understand people who know about bombs can make them quite easily, using dynamite, which is tightly controlled, but it's used in quarries, and demolition. Occasionally it gets stolen.'

'You think Alexander Duncannon would have broken into a quarry's storehouse and stolen dynamite?' Emily said incredulously.

'No, I think it's more likely someone else stole it and sold it on. Does Alexander spend his time in his parents' home in the city, or in the country? Or has he his own apartment and lives on his private means, attending parties, or whatever amuses him?'

'He has his own place,' Emily agreed quietly. It was all becoming dreadfully clear as a possibility. Now Cecily's fear was hideously real. 'And he keeps some odd company.'

'Most young gentlemen with time to spare do,' Charlotte pointed out. 'Which you know as well as I do. Some of them have a few very odd ideas. Some are aggressive, a great deal more are idealistic, longing for reform, for greater fairness, freedom . . . however they see that.'

'But his family . . .' Emily began, but knew before Charlotte spoke the words the foolishness of what she had been going to say.

'Have you ever listened to Aunt Vespasia tell you about fighting on the barricades of the revolutions right across Europe in '48?' Charlotte asked earnestly. 'It was a noble cause. They nearly won . . . in some places.'

'Yes, I know,' Emily said quietly, looking down at the crumbs on her plate. 'And then the repression clamped down again like an iron lid, and, if anything, it was worse than before.'

'We need the young to believe that they will one day succeed,' Charlotte said urgently. 'If they have no dreams, no passion to change the injustice and create something better, then we are as good as dead. It doesn't matter whether it's political freedom across Europe, or fairer pay for people in hard and dangerous jobs, or women's rights to their own property, or against disease, usury . . . bad plumbing . . . or anything you like. We have to care. Alexander Duncannon isn't wicked because he wants to fight against police corruption, but if he's guilty of the Lancaster Gate bombing, that's a totally different thing. Is that what his mother is afraid of?'

'Yes, I think so,' Emily answered. 'Is it impossible?'

Charlotte took a breath to answer, and then let it out again silently.

Emily waited.

At last Charlotte smiled, picking her words carefully, and reluctantly.

'I think Thomas is afraid that there is some pretty deep corruption, at least where those particular men are concerned. He doesn't want to investigate it, but he's going to have to. The trouble is, as soon as he starts it will become clear what he's doing, and why. There's going to be anger and, worse than that, fear. Suspicion can make people do all sorts of stupid things.'

'What are you thinking?' Emily was uncertain, her imagination darting in several directions. 'Lies? Blaming others, innocent

people? Thomas isn't in any danger, is he? They wouldn't try to—'
She saw Charlotte's face and stopped herself, but it was too
late.

'I don't think so,' Charlotte said slowly. 'Of course it's possible,
especially when the people who are the victims could also be part
of the crime. Nobody wants to believe it, but when we're frightened we can act without thought. We lash out at the people who
are telling us what we don't want to know.'

Emily wanted to say something helpful, but no words would
come. There was no point in suggesting the corruption could be
slight. It was the fear of it, the possibility, that was poisonous.

She thought of Cecily Duncannon and her fierce, protective
love for her son. Did she think he was guilty, or was it just
the fear she needed to name in order to dispel it?

In carefully chosen words she told Charlotte, as exactly as she
could remember, what Cecily had said.

'May I tell Thomas?' Charlotte asked gravely when she had
finished.

'Of course. I wouldn't tell you then bind you to silence.'

'It would explain why they can't find anything among all the
anarchists they know of. And no foreign power would attack us
that way. It's . . . too slow, and it leaves only a broken nation to
conquer,' Charlotte said slowly. 'A bomb in revenge against a
force he believes to be corrupt seems like a believable answer.'

Emily bit her lip. 'So does attack from another country,' she
argued. 'Weaken us and we'll fall a lot more easily. Look at the
chaos we hear about in other countries where the law has begun
to break down. Poison from within makes anyone easier to conquer.
We could be so busy trying to keep our own people in some kind
of order, if the police are corrupt and the law has lost people's
respect, and then we begin to take the law into our own hands. If
we avenge crimes personally rather than trying people in the courts,
then I suppose we execute them too.' She shivered.

Charlotte sat up straight. 'We are way ahead of any reality. We still have time to find out who the bomber is, and deal with him. Even if it's Alexander Duncannon. Actually, it does seem more likely that someone who is against this contract, for whatever reason, probably financial, is trying to make it look like Alexander, so as to discredit his father. Apparently the success of the nego- tiations depends a great deal upon him.'

'That's what Jack says,' Emily agreed. 'He's not only gifted, but he has all the right contacts. People like him, and trust him, and the trust is what matters. Alexander being even suspected, never mind charged, might affect that pretty badly.'

'We don't have a really good alternative theory of what's behind the bombing,' Charlotte said unhappily, 'except police corruption of who knows what quality. It could be petty theft and the odd bit of rogue behaviour here and there. But it might be a great deal more: swearing to false evidence, violence, blackmail. Samuel Tellman is so hurt by it, so afraid of disillusion that he can hardly bear it. I think even Thomas is going to find it far more painful than he expects. I've watched him . . . I can see it in his face. Emily, I'm frightened too. It's the destruction of things we've believed in all the time I can remember.'

Emily did not argue; there was no denial to be made.

Chapter Seven

TELLMAN SAT in his chair in the sitting room. Perhaps it should more properly have been called a parlour, but it had too nice a fireplace not to use it themselves, whether they had company or not. And, to tell the truth, with a small child and another on the way, they had little inclination to invite people to visit.

Tellman stared around the room and its comfort seeped into him, like warmth from an open fire, such as burned up in the hearth now. The wind and rain outside only made it feel even better in here. It was what he had wanted for as long as he could remember: a place of his own, clean and warm, full of the things he valued. There was a painting over the fireplace of a scene in the country, with big trees leaning across a stream, and a wooden bridge with two figures on it, barely discernible in the shadows. He always thought of them as friends, even lovers. There was a bookcase against one wall and lots of books in it, mostly his favourites, but also some he would read one day, when he had more time.

There was a small table by the opposite chair, where Gracie was sitting quietly, her head fallen forward as if she were asleep, the sewing slipped out of her hands. Beside her was a basket of needles, cottons and various other sewing things. He liked to watch Gracie sew. She looked so comfortable, even though she had to concentrate hard. She found cooking came to her far more naturally. He realised with pleasure how much he was still in love with her. They had been married long enough to expect a second child, but the surprise and delight had not worn off yet.

Even his present distress did not shadow his happiness more than on the surface. He hated quarrelling with Pitt, and he knew that he had behaved miserably. He would not tell Gracie. It would only upset her, and, if he were honest with himself, he was ashamed of it now. Pitt did not want to find corruption in the police any more than Tellman did. It might not cut quite as deeply for Pitt, however. Pitt had other heroes to admire, other men and other causes, even if he had begun much as Tellman had. He, too, had joined the police as soon as he was old enough.

Tellman's father had been born into desperate poverty, the kind where you live from one meal to the next, and go to bed hungry every night. He had worked hard and died young in an industrial accident. Other victims of the accident had survived, but his body was not strong enough to heal from the broken bones, and septicaemia had eventually killed him.

Tellman himself had been slight as a child, some might say scrawny. He had been too clever to be easy friends with other boys, who were afraid of his intelligence, and lashed out at him the only way they knew how, with fists and boots. Even sitting here by his own fire, he could feel the sweat of fear in his body, and then the chill, as he remembered standing facing them in the street, knowing what was coming.

There had been three boys in particular who had held at bay their own inadequacies by hurting him. He could hear the high-pitched giggle of one of them even in his nightmares. He could remember the pain from one time to the next, as if it were going on even before it happened. But it was the humiliation that was the worst. He wanted more than anything else on earth not to be afraid of them, but it was beyond his power. It was the fear they fed on, the spur it gave them to terrify the boy who consistently outdid them in the classroom. Even if he said nothing, pretended he did not know the answers when he did, they knew it; it had happened too often. The need to succeed at something had driven him on. Perhaps the master had known too, but his intervention would only have made it worse.

The time he could not bear to remember was the one in the school yard, near the rubbish bins, when he had been so afraid that he had wet himself. The fat boy with the giggle had laughed so hard he had choked, and called him 'pisspants' for the rest of his schooldays. Tellman still flushed hot at the memory. He had had daydreams about beating the boy to a pulp.

He had never told anyone about that. He had tried to forget it, deny its existence in his mind. Over the years he had all but succeeded.

So why did it come back now, this quiet evening in front of the fire with Gracie sitting not two yards away?

Because the certainties that made him strong were crumbling. He had seen in the police a force for good, a protection of the ordinary man or woman who was victimised, physically or had their belongings stolen or damaged. He was used to poverty and he knew that a few shillings was a fortune to some, the difference between eating and going hungry and cold. One pair of boots might be all a man had. Theft was a major crime to such people.

And for a boy without brothers and sisters, belonging to a group was of intense importance. The friendship, the loyalty, the unspoken trust were rewards greater than the money, although pay was regular in the police, and it meant he could rent a room, eat every day, be warm in the winter. Above all, he could look at his own thin, lantern-jawed face in the glass when he shaved, and see a man he could respect, a man others looked to for help and were not failed. That was happiness.

Thomas Pitt had been his first hero. He was human, and certainly fallible, but he was never dishonest, and even when he seemed beaten, he never gave up. Rumpled, wild-haired, pockets bulging, he knocked on the front door, speaking quietly, and insisted on going in.

Tellman recalled vividly the first time he got in the middle of a street fight to protect a man alone and terrified, and Pitt had praised him. He had stood in the street, his uniform muddy, boots soaked from the gutter, burning with pride.

Police were better regarded now, and Pitt was head of Special Branch. No one treated him lightly; he knew too much about them.

Yet Pitt thought the police were corrupt, so much so that they had brought upon themselves the terrible bombing at Lancaster Gate. Tellman could still smell the smoke and the charred flesh in his dreams. He could see Ednam's white face the last time he had visited him before he died.

No one deserved to die like that!

Not that Pitt had said they did, he was just afraid that the bombing could be in revenge for some injustice rather than an anarchist lashing out at the Establishment. They were seen by him not as the Government or the aristocracy, or the bankers of the city, but ordinary men who had to guard against crime, and catch those who preyed on others.

Tellman hated having quarrelled with Pitt. It was stupid. They had both been tired and, more than that, afraid. The old order was falling to pieces and suddenly they had to face the fact.

Pitt was right, even if he had been clumsy in the way he put it. And perhaps Tellman had been too quick to take offence, striking back without thinking.

Gracie woke and smiled at him, finding the sewing again. The piece she was working on was finished. It was one of his shirts. She was turning the collar. He tended to fray them running his finger around the inside when he was worried. He liked her carefulness. She had learned that from Charlotte, when Pitt was still in his early days.

'So are yer going ter tell me,' Gracie asked, 'or sit there all evening letting me worry about yer?'

'There's nothing really wrong,' he lied. He did not want to tell her the truth. She would have no respect for him if she knew how much he depended on his belief in the men he worked with. If he tried to explain, it would all lead back to the school playground, and he could not bear that. She must never know about that.

'Just feel badly about the Lancaster Gate bombing,' he added. 'We aren't really getting anywhere. Not yet.'

Her face crumpled a little. She knew he was evading answering her properly. He felt guilty, but he must not tell her all the things that were churning in his mind. It was his duty to protect her from them. He should make an effort to change his expression and occupy his thoughts with something else. He mentioned one or two other things in the news.

'Don't change the subject, Samuel,' she responded. 'Yer got a face on yer like a burst boot! There's something wrong real bad.'

'Ednam died,' he answered. 'We thought he'd make it. He was the most senior officer. We have to defend his reputation, now that he can't do it.'

'And that in't going to be easy, eh?' she replied.

She was too quick. She could read him as if he were an open book. It made him feel exposed. Her opinion of him mattered more than anybody else's – in fact, more than everybody else's added together. She needed to believe that he was strong enough to look after her, especially now that she was going to have another child. How could she possibly do that if she could even imagine the terrified, humiliated boy he had once been? She needed to believe in the police too. The whole city was full of millions of people who needed to believe that the police were both honest and brave. If that belief went, so eventually did everything else.

How was he going to deal with it, if Pitt was right and the whole force had crumbling patches in it, men who were corrupted, like rotten wood holding up a house? If the bad bits fell, buckled, couldn't take the weight, then the good bits fell with them! Everything came down, and there was no shelter left at all.

'Samuel!' Gracie said sharply, cutting across his thoughts.

He looked at her, and saw the fear in her eyes.

'There's summink bad that yer won't tell me,' she went on. ''Ow can I do anything about it if I don't know?'

He smiled and felt a sudden rush of emotion. How like Gracie, all five foot nothing of her, thin as a ninepenny rabbit, but ready to fight anybody to protect her own. He was being selfish shut- ting her out, and he recognised it at last. By doing it he was leaving her frightened and alone, as if he didn't think she was capable of helping, or worth trusting. He could see it in her eyes, the hurt far outweighing the fear. He wasn't protecting her, he was protecting himself.

He sat in silence for several moments, trying to find the words that would frighten her least. She had all the courage in the world, but she was still so very vulnerable. She had a child who was not yet two years old, and in another six months she would have a second one. How could he look after her properly if he put himself in jeopardy also?

She was waiting. He could see it clearly in her face, the begin- ning of hurt that he did not trust her. He had been selfish. He must repair that.

He started with the worst part. 'I quarrelled with Pitt.' He could hear the reluctance in his own voice, the raw edge of it. 'He thinks we need to find out if certain accusations against the police are true . . .'

'Why?' she said instantly. 'Who said anything? Does 'e believe it, or is 'e trying ter prove it in't right? Yer can't just stick yer 'ead in the sand an' pretend it's all right. Yer wouldn't if it was about anyone else. People've got a right to trust the police.'

'I know that. But the fact that we're looking into it means it could be true,' he explained. 'And the police know that, and so does everyone else. It must be possible, or we wouldn't be looking!' It was so reasonable, and yet it pained him even to think of it.

'What d'yer think they've done?' she asked, staring at him very solemnly, her sewing forgotten. 'Why don't yer tell me straight out? Don't yer want ter look, 'cos yer afraid o' what yer'll see?'

He drew in breath to deny it vehemently, then he met her eyes and the denial melted away. She would know he was lying: she always knew. Not that he did lie, but sometimes he evaded telling her everything. Gracie had gentleness, and great patience with her child, but she had no equivocation in her whatever when it came to telling the truth. He had seen her tell people to mind their own business, but never had he heard her prevaricate. With people you loved, an evasion was the same thing as a lie.

'I suppose so,' he admitted. Now that the subject was begun it was not as difficult as he had expected. In fact, it was almost easier than continuing to evade it. 'The more we investigate the bombing, the less it looks like an anarchist gone mad, and a lot like it could be somebody that meant those police in particular to be killed,' he finished.

'Ow d'yer work that out?' Her face was totally sober and she asked as if she were another detective asking for facts. He remembered with a jolt that that was probably how she saw herself. When she was still working for Charlotte and Pitt she had overheard most of the long discussions of cases that had gone on around the kitchen table. She had not been afraid to put her own suggestions in. Once Pitt had actually sent her to work undercover as a maid at Buckingham Palace. She didn't refer to it often, as if out of a kind of loyalty, but her eyes lit with pride when she did.

'Because of the way they were lured to the house in Lancaster Gate,' Tellman answered. 'It looks as if someone got them there particularly. He sent a note, very brief. He'd informed them of opium sales before, and been right, so they trusted him.'

'So it were planned,' she said with certainty. 'Mebbe weeks before 'e did it?'

He had not looked at it that way before. She was right. 'Yes,' he agreed. 'But we don't know why he did it because we have no idea who he is.'

'Then Mr Pitt's right: yer gotta look at them police what was baited to go there, and see wot they done so bad someone'd want ter blow 'em all up. An' yer gotta look back ter before 'ooever it was began ter give 'em information about opium and that. Samuel, yer can't just look the other way 'cos yer don't like ter think it were a revenge for something as really 'appened! Whoever did this may be wicked, or mad even, but that's not ter say 'e don't 'ave 'is reasons! Or think 'e does, any which way. Yer can't afford ter—'

'I know that,' he cut across her. 'But they were good men, Gracie. They've been in the police for years. Of course there are things that go on that aren't right. I hate to think of it, but there'll be those who lost their temper with someone who was beating a woman, or a child, and they gave 'em a good belting back.' He took a breath. 'And sometimes we lose evidence, or don't take it the right way, and then even make up a lie so it can still be used, when we know damn well a man's guilty. And sometimes we let people go when we shouldn't. But you don't set off bombs that kill everyone in sight because of something like that. Even if you maybe get him in a dark alley one night, an' beat him back!'

She looked at him very gravely, her small face without a flicker of light in it. 'Then it must be summink worse. Mebbe yer gotta look for someone as is dead?' she told him. 'Someone as died pretty 'orribly, and somebody, even if they're crazy, could think it was the police's fault. It don't matter if it were or not, Samuel; someone thinks as it were. Yer can't get away from that. An' yer can't afford ter pretend as yer can't see it. Blind people walk over the edge o' cliffs, and I don't want that to 'appen ter you . . . ter us.'

The emotion welled up inside him till his throat was tight and his eyes stung.

'I know that. I will look, I promise.'

'Good. An' remember as it's a promise, Samuel Tellman! Life don't take no excuses. "I didn't see" in't no good if wot you mean is "I didn't look neither"!'

'I know that . . .'

At last she smiled. 'Yer want a cup o' tea? I got cake?'

He nodded, swallowing back the feelings inside him. He wanted her to go into the kitchen, and leave him a moment to compose himself. It all mattered too much. He had everything in the world to lose.

In the morning Tellman began straight away, going back to the station where Ednam had worked. He hated doing it, but once he had accepted the necessity, there was no point in putting it off. On the contrary, doing that made it worse. It served no purpose, and it made him feel like a coward. That was a word that haunted him like a badly healed bone break. The fear of it had at times made him rash, not brave but foolhardy. It was all back to the school playground again, standing up to people bigger than you were, to prove to yourself that you were not afraid.

Was there reason to fear this time?

He reported to the sergeant at the desk and insisted, against some show of reluctance, that he see Superintendent Whicker again. He waited ten minutes before he was shown to his office.

He began with an expression of sympathy for Ednam's death.

He looked at Superintendent Whicker's face, and could read nothing in it. Was that a man concealing his grief in front of a comparative stranger? Or was his expression deliberately blank because his feelings were more complex, perhaps equivocal, towards men he had not liked?

'Going to catch who did it, sir,' Tellman added grimly. 'Looks as if it could be anarchists, but just in case they were killed by someone who thought he had a grudge, I'm going to look through as many of the old cases as I can. I shall need your assistance, if you can spare a man, please, Superintendent.'

'Yes, Tellman. I'll spare you who I can. You'll understand we're a bit short-handed, having lost five men.' He reminded Tellman of it bluntly, and with an undisguised resentment.

'Of course, sir. I'll try to be quick.' Tellman took a chance. 'You'll have read what some people are saying in the papers. We've got to get at the truth before anyone else does. Need to protect our own from accusations that come out of old grudges, or fears gone wild.'

'Yes, Inspector,' Whicker agreed.

Tellman looked at him more closely. If there was any emotion in him, he was hiding it. Why? People expected anger, grief, even fear of what might happen next. What was it that was so deep within him that he showed nothing?

'Where would you like to start, Inspector?' Whicker asked tartly.

Tellman thought of what Gracie had said. 'Let's say a month or so before the first tip-off you had from this fellow that calls himself Anno Domini,' he answered.

Whicker looked surprised. 'Before?'

'Yes, please. Let's see the cases that Ednam, Newman, Yarcombe, Bossiney and Hobbs were on.'

'They didn't work together that often, Inspector.'

'No, I imagine not. I'll just look at the cases in general, and see if I can find anything that gives me an idea.'

'Did Special Branch put you up to this, Inspector?' Whicker asked with raised eyebrows.

'Not at all, sir. Don't know I'm doing it,' Tellman said truthfully. 'If there is anything, I'd like to get there before they do.' He watched Whicker's face, waiting for the reaction.

Whicker's black eyes were unreadable. 'You can have the same room as last time, and I'll have Constable Drake bring you the records, Inspector.'

'Start a month before the first contact from Anno Domini, if you please, sir. And come forward from that, a case at a time,' Tellman told him.

'Yes, Inspector.' Whicker turned on his heel and left Tellman to wait.

It was going to be a very long task, and Tellman was perfectly aware that the amount of co-operation he received might be deliberately small.

Drake was a young man whose fair hair and a fair skin probably barely required him to shave. Tellman thought he looked too innocent to be a policeman of any effect at all, until he caught a glimpse of laughter in the man's eyes that changed him altogether.

'That's the month before the Anno Domini tip-off, sir,' Drake said, putting a thick bundle of files on the table in front of Tellman. 'I'll bring the next lot up for you, sir, as soon as I get them all sorted.'

'Thank you.' Tellman eyed the foot-high stack without pleasure. 'Are any of the men who worked on these cases available, if I need to talk to them?'

'Yes, sir. But best read them first, sir,' Drake replied, meeting Tellman's eyes for an instant, and then leaving without asking permission.

Tellman worked all morning. He stopped for tea and a ham sandwich at lunchtime, and then went on again. It was so dull he had trouble keeping awake. It was exactly the sort of police work he was accustomed to. The notes were those such as he had made a score of times himself. He could have been any of these men. Their words were like his, probably their lives were too, and many of their ideas and memories. Their choice of words and their handwriting was individual, but now and again an exact phrase was repeated, as if they had agreed on what to write.

It was only when he realised that several files were out of order, and he rearranged them, that he began to see a pattern. He went back and read them again. There was one case in particular of a man who had been injured in a brawl who had later given information, been charged with theft, and found not guilty. It was Yarcombe's case, then passed to Bossiney.

When Tellman put those reports in the right order, the story looked very different. The dates had been changed, very carefully.

Which made him realise the case had begun with Yarcombe, gone on to Bossiney and ended with Ednam taking charge of it. The events had happened in a different order. The brawl had come last, when two of the named participants had already been in gaol. The only conclusion was that it had been a beating by someone quite different, and the information made no sense.

It was the witness who had been beaten, and who had refused to testify against the man charged.

Was this the error of a tired man confused, trying to get it right, and failing? A misunderstanding? Or even carelessness? Perhaps the injured man was not well enough to testify, or worried about his family? And the error had been covered by the officer's colleagues out of loyalty for him?

Tellman put the files aside and read the following cases. He found more mix-ups, stories that did not make sense when looked at closely. Many notes appeared merely hasty, as if written up by busy men made to work out details too long after the events, and making mistakes in good faith. That was what he wanted to think. He had made errors himself. It was easy to do. You started seeing something another way, and then got the whole pattern wrong. You had to find the chance to go back and put it right.

He forced himself to study the files long into the evening. The errors added up to a few people not being convicted because evidence was lost. A few people had had accidents rather conveniently, and were unable to testify. Whoever was looking after evidence was selectively careless. Some people were arrested quite often, but never seemed to get convicted. He could not avoid seeing the pattern.

The next day he asked for other files, of cases not involving Ednam. He searched for the same carelessness, and did not find it. He also compared the rates of conviction for certain crimes, and found them lower than for Ednam, especially where theft was concerned.

There was little he could prove because some sorts of evidence was consistently missing, but by the end of the second day he was certain that there was a lot of well-concealed graft going on, favours for certain people, evidence deliberately misplaced.

Was Ednam overzealous? Now and then was he taking the law into his own hands when he felt certain a man was guilty, but he could not prove it legally, so he resorted to doing so illegally? Was he exercising his own form of justice? Or was he driven by his own ambition? Please heaven all of this was not for his own profit?

No! Tellman refused to think that.

Had somebody felt a rage hot enough to plant that bomb in Lancaster Gate as revenge for being framed for a crime they had not committed?

Tellman wondered how much the other four men had collaborated with Ednam and how far outside the law they had gone. Had they knowingly convicted an innocent man, possibly not even caring or were they just being obedient? It was possible they might even be afraid of Ednam, who was, after all, their senior.

He thought of what he had learned from their notes of the different men. Newman he had known himself, and liked. He was cheerful, outgoing, prone to thinking the best of people – more than Tellman himself did. That was what Tellman had liked about him.

Suddenly it hurt all over again, recalling seeing him blown to bits on the floor of the house in Lancaster Gate. Had he trusted Ednam when he shouldn't or was he afraid to fall out with his comrades? There was no hint of guilt in his notes.

Yarcombe's notes were terse, saying no more than they had to, like the man.

Bossiney wrote a lot. Was he drowning the truth in too many words?

Hobbs's notes were careful, written in a schoolboy's hand. It was a job he disliked.

It was Ednam whose words wrapped it all up, taking care of the omissions.

But even so, that did not justify the appalling bombing at Lancaster Gate, though it might well have been the cause of it.

Had Drake, this young constable detailed to help him, reordered the files intentionally? He thought so. But when he left late on the second evening, there was nothing in the innocent face to make him certain.

There was still a great deal more to find out. And he had tied it to nothing that related to the informer, Anno Domini. He had found the letter with the information, and the report of the opium sales and the amounts. Actually, to have had a successful police action would not have been a major victory, simply one they would not have had without the specific details. And there was nothing about the letter of information from which he could deduce anything further.

Tellman chose to walk a good distance before even looking for a bus to take him the rest of the way home. The bitter cold edge of the wind kept his thoughts sharp, a knife edge inside to match the one cutting his face.

He must have been terribly naïve to have kept his ignorance of dubious police behaviour for so long. He dealt with the worst aspects of humanity most of the time so none of this should come as a surprise. Yet it did! And it hurt!

He knew the police were fallible, because everyone was, but he had believed they were honest, loyal to the best in themselves. They would face what they saw, the violence and the pain, because they also knew the good.

Ednam had soiled that! He had twisted and distorted it. His betrayal was unforgivable.

Tellman pushed his hands hard into his coat pockets and turned the corner off the main street to take a shortcut. Suddenly he felt shattered. He stopped leaning into the wind and stood straighter, then began walking again.

He came out at the far end of the alley and faced the wind again. It seemed even harsher. Ednam had betrayed his men. And he had betrayed Tellman as well, because in a way he stood for all leaders that men had believed in.

He knew exactly what Gracie would say to that, and he smiled ruefully. She would be right. Did he want to be like Ednam really was? Or did he want to be what he thought Ednam was? That was a question not even worth asking. Just because Ednam had gone that way didn't mean he had to.

He quickened his pace towards the omnibus stop. It was too cold to walk the streets any longer. He was very much needing to go home.

He told Pitt what he had done when they met at Lisson Grove about mid-morning the day after. Tellman was tired and his head pounded from all the reading by lamplight. But at least his cold was beginning to go away. He forgot about it for hours at a time. Perhaps he was simply too angry about the dishonesty and the violence he had found to care about a hacking cough, or aching chest.

Briefly he told Pitt what he had found. He did not apologise for their last meeting. He thought his actions since then were admission enough. He did not want to remind Pitt of it, if he were willing to forget.

He watched Pitt's face and saw the sadness in it. It was only then that he realised the disillusion was as sour to Pitt as it was to him, just maybe not as much of a surprise.

Maybe Pitt's awakening had come some time ago. Perhaps it had dawned when his superiors, far above Cornwallis, had bowed to pressure over the business in Whitechapel and dismissed him from the police. Special Branch had been the only place still open to him to make his living in the profession he knew. That seemed like a long time ago now, but old wounds don't stop aching. They are always under the surface, ready to remind one of the original injuries.

Pitt told him about Alexander Duncannon and his belief that his friend Dylan Lezant had been wrongfully accused, that the evidence had been lied about, and he had been hanged for a crime he had not committed.

Tellman stared at him, slowly grasping the enormity of what he had said. 'Do you believe him?' he asked a little huskily. He wanted him to deny it. This was far more than a minor dishonesty, it was a form of murder by police! 'Do you?' he insisted.

'I believe Alexander thinks so.' Pitt chose his words with care. 'Whether he wants to because he can't think his friend was guilty, or whether he has to blame someone other than himself for getting away when his friend didn't—'

'Getting away?' Tellman interrupted. 'He was there?' He remembered the account of Lezant's arrest had said there were two men, but the other one had escaped.

'So he says, but for how long I'm not sure he even remembers. He says Lezant didn't have a gun, but all that means is that he doesn't remember him having one, or he didn't know he had.'

'Or he's chosen to forget!'

'Or that. But it doesn't matter now—'

'Doesn't matter!' Tellman's voice was high and sharp. 'It doesn't matter if the police lied about evidence to convict an innocent man and see him hanged for a crime they knew damn well he didn't commit? Then, for God's sake, what does matter?' He could feel the desperate, helpless emotion rise up inside him again until he could hardly breathe.

'I meant it doesn't affect Alexander Duncannon's actions whether it's true or not,' Pitt explained. 'He believes it's true. To him it is fact, even if actually he is mistaken.'

Tellman caught his breath, and swallowed hard. 'And is he right?'

'I don't know,' Pitt admitted. 'He could be. From what you tell me about Ednam and those he leads . . . led . . . they were not above bending evidence, misusing money, telling the occasional lie to get what they thought was a bigger truth. They might have been right in some cases, and wrong in others. Perhaps they reached the point where the truth was so blurred they lost sight of it altogether. They believed what they wanted to.' His smile was bitter. 'Like Alexander . . . maybe.'

'*Could* Lezant have been innocent?' Tellman found it difficult even speaking the words.

'It doesn't look like it. But if he was, then one of the police was guilty, and the rest covered for him. Or there was someone else there that they're all lying to cover for.'

'And Duncannon placed the bomb in Lancaster Gate to make us pay attention? Now? The Lezant case was over two years ago,' Tellman pointed out. 'Why didn't he say something at the time?'

'He said he did.'

'There was no record of it at the station.' Tellman knew as he said it that that meant little. It was still all possible . . . or not. He also knew before Pitt spoke again that they were going to have to look into it a lot further, before the Lancaster Gate case suddenly solved itself, and brought chaos, disbelief and violence on all of them.

'More records lost,' Pitt said unhappily. 'Or not written in the first place. I'll go back to Alexander and get as many names and dates as I can. You go on with this.'

When Tellman returned to his own station he found a message waiting for him to report that afternoon to Commissioner Bradshaw. He was not aware of having done anything wrong, and yet he found his hands sweating. What had he missed? Did Bradshaw expect a result already?

It was a beautiful office, elegant, the furniture antique and worn smooth and comfortable by generations of men who held command and on whom it sat easily. Bradshaw with his gracious office, his smooth hair and his well-cut clothes, fitting him as only a personally tailored jacket can, seemed to be placed by birth and education above the anxieties of the ordinary man. But was he?

'Yes, sir?' Tellman said politely.

'Sit down, Tellman,' Bradshaw waved his hand towards a chair with slender legs and a delicately carved mahogany back. His own chair was roomier, the seat leather-padded.

Tellman obeyed. Even if he preferred standing, one did not argue with the Police Commissioner.

'Sad thing about Ednam's death,' Bradshaw said gravely. 'Poor man can't even defend himself now. We've got to do something about the rumours that the press are beginning to stir up. I suppose it was inevitable someone would stir up trouble! Whicker tells me you were on to that yesterday and the day before . . .' He had not phrased it as a question, but he left it hanging in the air unfinished. His face was furrowed with anxiety.

'Yes, sir,' Tellman replied. 'I need to be in a position where I can say I've looked into it. If I don't, they'll leap on it, sooner or later.' Silently he thanked Pitt for forcing him to. 'I hate doing it, sir. It's as if I think there's something to it, but the rumourmongers will twist it if I don't.'

'Yes, yes, I know,' Bradshaw nodded. 'Rotten business altogether. Pitt tells me he has no leads from the Special Branch, no anarchist groups they can pinpoint, except to know who sold the dynamite, but not what happened to it after that. Damned stuff seems to be for sale to God knows who, once a thief gets hold of it.'

'Yes, sir. I've been working with Commander Pitt. Seems most of the anarchists he knows about are more or less accounted for.'

Bradshaw looked up at him. 'Are you suggesting there are others he doesn't know about?' His voice was impossible to read. Was he hoping there were, so it would take the attention away from the police? Or afraid there were, and they were all on the edge of more violence, and perhaps worse?

Tellman thought about it for a moment. Loyalty said he should deny it. Loyalty to whom? To Pitt, with whom he had worked for years? Or to his own force, the police? Pitt had been willing to blame the police, and so far as Tellman knew, had not even looked into the competence or honour of his own men.

No, that was unfair. Tellman would not know whether he had or not. He might have torn them apart! It was the evidence. Alexander Duncannon was blaming police for Lezant's death, not Special Branch.

'It's a possibility, sir,' he replied, still sitting upright in the carved-backed chair. It offered more beauty than comfort. But nothing would have made him comfortable in this interview. 'But unlikely, I think,' he added.

Bradshaw nodded slowly, turning it over in his mind. He looked miserable, as if something were worrying him so deeply he was having trouble concentrating on Tellman.

Tellman began to be concerned in case there was important information that Bradshaw knew, and he did not. Could it be about Pitt? Or about the police?

Tellman noticed in a small alcove in the bookcase a framed photograph of a woman, more than a decade younger than Bradshaw, maybe even two decades. A daughter? A wife? It was possibly an old picture. Its colour was soft, as if a little faded over time from sitting in the light. The woman was beautiful, soft-featured, her hair falling a trifle out of its pins. It was an informal picture, and she was smiling. There was an innocence about her that was instantly appealing. She was a woman of a social class he did not personally know, yet there was something in her that awoke a gentleness in him. She looked young, unaware of what would hurt her.

He moved his gaze. He should not be looking at her. It was a very personal photograph. One day he would like to have enough money to be able to pay someone really good to take a photograph of Gracie, looking happy like that, quite unstudied. He would have it on his desk too, or somewhere that he could see it all the time.

Bradshaw had said something, and he had missed it. He must pay attention.

'. . . anything that makes sense,' Bradshaw added. 'We must give the newspapers something, or they'll make things up. What did you find when you looked into Ednam's records? Who is this Anno Domini Pitt told me of, the informer that led the men to the house in Lancaster Gate ? What grounds did they have for believing him? Can we at least say that much? Is he a suspect, this informer? He has to be. Why haven't we found him yet?'

'We're looking, sir, but no one in the general neighbourhood seems to have any idea who he is.'

'So this man could be anyone, possibly a serious political threat?' Bradshaw looked suddenly afraid, as if the whole issue had ballooned into a new and far more serious crime.

'No, sir. But not an ordinary petty thief or scam artist. And we can't ask Ednam now, poor . . . man. But every other tip this informer has given them has proved genuine.'

'To set Ednam up?' Bradshaw asked grimly.

'Perhaps. But then again, maybe someone was setting the informer up. Sir . . .'

He already had Bradshaw's attention. He must continue now, get it over with . . . or lie.

'Sir, I found a degree of sloppiness, inaccuracy and lying to cover petty theft, in Ednam's station.' He chose his words carefully. 'Quite a bit of unnecessary violence in making arrests. One or two people pushed into changing their evidence when it got to court, or even taking it out altogether. It won't look good if a journalist gets wind of it, sir.' He drew in his breath to go on, then changed his mind. He was already talking too much. He felt awkward in this quiet room where there was a decanter on the side cabinet with a silver label around the neck, and an ashtray for cigars.

Bradshaw nodded, looking at Tellman all the time.

'I see. Thank you for the warning. In the time being, Inspector Tellman, keep it to yourself. The more I look into this thing, the worse it gets. Keep the report off paper, for the moment. Tell me anything else you discover. And you'd better be quick about it. I won't mince words. Your job hangs on how well you manage to keep control of the rumours. I'll have no choice but to replace you, if you can't do it.'

'Yes, sir.' Tellman stood up, but felt the room sway around him. His job! How could he keep this from Gracie? She would be worried sick, even if she did everything she could to hide it from him. And she would!

He must do better than this. He stiffened his shoulders and looked down at Bradshaw in his padded chair.

'We have a suspect, sir, but we need to make certain he is the right man before we tell anyone at all as it will cause a certain amount of concern among some people. I will report directly to you, sir. If I may be excused to continue?'

'Who is it?' Bradshaw asked, in spite of Tellman's saying that he would not divulge the name.

'Need to be certain, sir,' Tellman replied. He met Bradshaw's gaze without the slightest flicker.

Eventually Bradshaw blinked, and then gave a grim smile.

'Very well, I expect to hear from you soon. You may go.'

'Thank you, sir.'

Chapter Eight

PITT RETURNED his attention to the physical evidence of the bombing again, hoping that the break would bring him fresh perception. He concentrated on that which was incontrovertible and had no alternative interpretations.

'Sorry, sir,' Stoker said when they had re-examined everything, all the fragments from the building, sketches and photographs of what was left of the house at Lancaster Gate, and the architect's drawings of what the house had been like before the bomb.

They reread every report from the police that had survived, and from the fire brigade. Separately they went through the medical reports on those alive, and the police surgeon's autopsy reports on the dead.

They checked the information provided by the informer who called himself Anno Domini, and went over every noted time so there were no discrepancies. Was it Alexander Duncannon? Trying yet another way to force police attention? It looked like it to Pitt.

They could trace the dynamite from the quarry from which it had been stolen, through the thief and to the first man to whom he had sold it. From then on it disappeared. 'An anarchist' was all the description they could gain. Dark-haired, young, which could apply to three-quarters of all the anarchists, nihilists and fugitives from European and Russian law that they knew of.

'It's not any anarchist group we know,' Stoker said when they had finished. 'And we are as sure as we ever can be that we know them all. I've even looked at all the odd military or would-be military groups, or arrogant young 'would-be' generals. We can't hide it any more, sir. We've got to look at Duncannon. I don't care who his father is.' He stood facing Pitt, his lean shoulders square, his eyes undeviating. Every angle of his body said he disliked it as much as Pitt did, and therefore he was bent on getting it over with. If he held any hope that they could disprove it, it was not there in his face.

Neither of them had said so, but both of them knew that the rather delicate relationship between Special Branch and the police would be strained by even the suggestion that the murdered men were in any way responsible for their own appalling deaths, or the burns that Bossiney would carry for the rest of his life, or Yarcombe's lost arm. To look into it at all would be seen as a slur on the maimed and the dead, and an insult to every other officer or man who daily worked to keep the law and serve the public.

What would it do to the future co-operation between the forces that Special Branch in particular relied on? The whole idea of a police force, with power to search a man's house, question his servants or even his family, was a relatively new idea among the general public, and, with some, still unpopular.

Special Branch, on the other hand, was accepted by patriotic men, so long as they did not bother people too much, and did not intrude into any man's private affairs. It was agreed that there had always been spies, recognised and dealt with discreetly, since the days of Queen Elizabeth, and her spymaster, Walsingham. It was something one did not refer to, except in private with one's most trusted friends. Best to keep on the right side of the fellow in charge of it, who was usually a gentleman anyway, more or less.

It was the regular police whose toes they trod on occasionally, and whose co-operation they needed a sight too often.

Pitt was angry, mainly with himself.

'Looking into this will turn the whole force against us,' he pointed out, staring at the papers spread out on the table between them.

'You think Tellman's wrong?' Stoker said with raised eyebrows.

'No,' Pitt admitted. 'He hates this even more than we do.'

'I don't hate it,' Stoker contradicted him. 'Any policeman who thinks it's all right to tamper with evidence, pick and choose what bits he'll show and what he'll hide, lie about things, change times and records, take money if he thinks he can get away with it, or beat the hell out of a few witnesses or villains if he's in a bad temper, is a disgrace to the force and should be got rid of, before he poisons everyone. When they're no better than the men they're chasing, we've all had it! I don't care how much they resent it. If they'd got rid of those practices themselves, then we wouldn't have to!'

Pitt gave him a long, cold look. 'You want them to come and take a close look at us?'

Stoker coloured faintly. 'That's not exactly fair, sir. If you caught any one of us doing anything like that we'd be charged with treason, and be out in a day. It's a much tougher service, and you know that.'

'Yes, it is,' Pitt conceded. 'But the police still have to trust each other. You don't want to go into any sort of a fight if you can't trust the man who's always there beside you, watching for you.' He looked at Stoker's face. 'All right, I know: I just made your point for you. But this is still going to cause a hell of a lot of ill-feeling. The next time we need police help, we may be damn lucky to get it!'

Stoker's hard, blue eyes widened. 'We may clear their good name, sir!'

'Don't be so damn stupid!' Pitt snapped, hating himself for the situation he had walked into, and Stoker for his perception of it. He was even annoyed with Tellman for caring so much, and still having gone on and on after Ednam and his men. 'I've got to know more, with proof, before I face them with it. I wish to hell there were a way out of it, but there isn't.'

Pitt needed to talk about it with someone who understood what damage it might do, both if he did as Stoker had suggested – and he knew he must – or if he did not. He had long ago learned what good and honest argument could do. At the very least it would force him to defend his decision, and see the flaws in it before it was too late.

In times past, with ordinary civilian murder cases, he had talked things through with Charlotte, but this was different. There was only one person who would understand it perfectly, and be willing to counteract him with both reason and passion. That was Victor Narraway. He might even have faced a similar decision himself, although Pitt had looked through the records of Narraway's years, and found nothing to compare it with.

But then he himself had made no written notes. It was not something he wanted to have on paper. Narraway might have felt the same.

Vespasia was out when Pitt visited her home. It was now only three days before Christmas, but this was the first reminder of the joy of the season that he had become aware of. There was a tree in the hall, decorated with coloured balls and golden tinsel. Delicate angels of spun glass hung from the upper branches, their gossamer wings seeming to trap and hold the light.

In the sitting room Narraway poured Pitt a very small portion of brandy, ignoring his protests, and they sat on either side of the fire, smelling the faint fragrance of burning applewood. There was a plate of warm mince pies on the small table beside them.

Pitt explained the situation and watched Narraway's face grow more and more serious.

'And you're going to start digging into this trial of Dylan

157

Lezant tomorrow?' Narraway said finally. 'Is the timing intentional, or just inescapable?'

'I would be delighted to escape it,' Pitt replied ruefully. 'But I don't see how I can.'

'What do you expect from me?' The firelight accentuated the shadows on Narraway's dark face, the concentration in his expression.

'An analysis of the political fallout,' Pitt replied immediately. 'And any advice you have as to how best to go about it. What procedure do I use, if the evidence is there, and I need to contain it?'

Narraway did not answer for several minutes. There was no sound in the room except the whicker of flames in the hearth. Somewhere outside, beyond the window and its curtains, came the distant sound of carol singers in the street.

Pitt noticed how much more masculine the room had become since Narraway had moved in. Vespasia's paintings were still on the wall, scenes from her youth, and from generations even earlier. But there were some of Narraway's favourite charcoal drawings of bare trees as well. They were a total contrast, and yet they complimented each other. It completed the sense of balance in the room, and Pitt liked it. He would have said so, but this was not the time for such observations.

A log settled in the hearth, sending up a shower of sparks. Narraway leaned over and took a fresh one from the box, putting it on top of the others. The flames burned up quickly to accept it.

'If what Tellman says is true,' he said at last, 'then you have to start immediately. And Tellman is a good man. I think he would not say this if he could escape it. I assume he has no history with Ednam? Or any of the others? No, I assumed not. You have to know if it is just bad practice at that station, petty corruption that you can discipline the men for, perhaps get rid of the worst of them . . . although, God help us, it rather looks as if young Duncannon may have done that for you.'

'Of course Tellman hates it,' Pitt agreed. 'I could think of a strong argument for dealing with it as discreetly as possible, with some acceptable story for the public, if I were sure there was no more than Tellman found. But if it has any connection at all with the shooting for which Lezant was hanged, then it can't be left. For a start, Duncannon will open it up again, whatever else we do on a smaller scale.'

'If it is Duncannon!' Narraway pointed out. 'Better find out about Ednam and his men on one hand, and about Lezant on the other. Put them together if you have to. I assume you've gone over the bombing evidence with a fine-tooth comb?'

'Of course. There's nothing definitive in it.'

'And this "Anno Domini"?' Narraway gave a wry smile. 'You think that's Alexander Duncannon?'

'No way to be sure,' Pitt replied. 'But I think so, and I have to investigate his story about Lezant.'

'I can't see a way out of it either,' Narraway said unhappily. 'But the cost could be high, and I think it will be. For God's sake, be careful, Pitt. You don't know how far this goes.'

Pitt felt the coldness close up tightly inside him, like a lump of ice. New possibilities took form in his imagination: corruption deeper than merely that of Ednam and his men.

Narraway was watching him intently. 'Be prepared for the worst. This may go very deep. If Alexander really believes his friend was innocent—'

'He does,' Pitt interrupted. That was about the only thing he was certain of. Whether he was losing his grip on sanity, confused, blinded by love or hate, fuddled with pain, or the opium that dulled it, however he had begun and what he recalled or had invented, Alexander now believed that Dylan Lezant had been innocent. 'Right or wrong, he believes it,' he said again.

'Then be prepared for what that means,' Narraway warned.

'He may be right,' Pitt agreed a little tartly. 'I know that!'

'Not only that.' Narraway's face was bleak. 'It means the police lied under oath to get Lezant convicted and hanged. That's not only a particularly terrible and deliberate kind of murder, it's a perversion of the law that affects everyone in England. It is the safeguard for all of us, of the system itself. Those who offend against it have to be recognised, and punished. Surely I don't have to explain the core of that to you?'

'No you don't!' Pitt heard the sharpness in his own voice and regretted it, but he resented Narraway telling him as if he might not have understood it.

'The Lezant case was a couple of years ago,' Narraway went on.

For an instant Pitt thought that he was referring to the fact that Narraway himself had been in charge of Special Branch then, not Pitt. Did that make any difference? Was he saying, obliquely, that he had known something about it?

'Did it involve Special Branch?' Pitt asked sharply. Was this even blacker than he had thought? What could possibly have concerned Special Branch that would have made Narraway connive at such an abysmal miscarriage of justice? What would be important enough to pervert justice to hang an innocent man? Who had Dylan Lezant been that they destroyed him that way?

'No, it bloody well did not!' Narraway was staring at him incredulously. 'But if Alexander Duncannon always believed Lezant was innocent then you need to know why, and who he believed was guilty. Is he so far over the edge that he had no reason but his own emotions to think so? If that's true, why didn't his father have him put away? Or has Godfrey no idea what's going on? Did Alexander tell him, or not? How bad is the relationship between them? And why? What does the mother know, and what did she do, if anything?'

'Probably nothing,' Pitt said quietly. 'She would have her loyalty to her husband as well . . .' He tried to imagine the conflict within her. What would Charlotte have done? He knew the answer to that: she would have faced him with it and demanded an answer – for him to resign his position, if necessary.

And what would he have done? Put his family before his career? Yes. But what if the member of his family, his son, were wrong? Then the answer would have to be different. You did not sell your own honour, whatever the cause, or you had nothing left to give anybody. Was that what Narraway was thinking of?

The room seemed suddenly overwhelmingly silent.

'Think hard before you act, Pitt,' Narraway warned. 'Alexander has had two years in which to try to get somebody to listen to him. Setting a bomb off that killed three policemen, and badly injured two more, is the very last resort, even of a man desperate and emotionally unbalanced. You met him, you liked him. Was he a raving lunatic?'

'No . . . at least I thought not . . .'

'You listened to him. You believed him sincere, if misguided,' Narraway went on quietly. 'Who else did he speak to in a position to help him, and who did they believe? What did they do? They didn't stir up any trouble, and they certainly didn't arrest Ednam, or anyone else. You'd better make damn sure you know why not!'

For a moment Pitt thought Narraway meant that the charges were completely unfounded, and Pitt would be making a fool of himself. Then he saw the darkness in Narraway's face, and realised it was far worse than that. He meant that the charges were true, and someone had made sure they stayed covered up. Someone higher than Ednam was conniving at an appalling murder, and they would react powerfully, perhaps violently, to Pitt's attempt to expose them all, from the most junior policeman involved, all the way through the ranks to the top, maybe even into the Government.

He swallowed hard. His throat felt tight. What the hell had made him take this job? He was not fit for it, not prepared. The decisions were too wide and deep. He had not the knowledge, or the connections to survive it. He had made enemies that would be only too happy to see him brought down.

'I can't let it go.' The moment the words were out of his mouth he realised that he had done exactly what he had believed he would not. He had placed his job before his family. If he were destroyed, how would they survive?

But if he backed away because he was afraid, if he connived at covering up whatever the truth was about Dylan Lezant, how would he survive that? Charlotte would probably be loyal to him. Love would survive, but respect would turn into pity. The whole balance of their relationship would change. And he would hate himself.

A wave of fury boiled up inside him against Ednam, or whoever was responsible. How dare they create a corruption that was going to drown all of them in its tide of poison?

'I can't let it go,' he repeated, but this time his voice was almost strangled in his throat.

'I know you can't,' Narraway said gently. 'Neither can I, now that I know. But for God's sake be careful! Know everything you can about what you're dealing with before you take the cover off, even if you have to lie as to what you're looking into, and why.'

Pitt said nothing. The enormity of it overwhelmed him. It was like a dark storm on the horizon racing towards him. The first wind of it was tingling on his skin already; the first needles of ice began to hurt.

He slept badly, even though he was exhausted. His dreams were full of dark passages that led nowhere, locked doors, paths through grass that crumbled under his feet and slid away.

He was glad to get up early and take a quick breakfast. The maid who had replaced Gracie, Minnie Maude, was busy already, clearing out the ash in the oven and piling in more coal. She was good at it, and the kettle boiled in a matter of minutes.

She had grown used to Pitt's manner, and his odd hours, and made him tea and toast without surprise. She offered to cook more, but he declined. The bread was fresh and she made the toast crispy, as he liked it. There was new marmalade, tart, with a real bite to it, almost aromatic. It was a good start to a cold, unwelcoming day. Two days to go until Christmas. He would take that one day off. He had chosen a gift for Charlotte some time ago, so that was taken care of. He had agreed to share with Charlotte and get both Jemima and Daniel something special. Charlotte would shop, wrap and deliver gifts to all the other people to whom they gave presents, too. But perhaps he should remind her to do something nice for Minnie Maude as well. Or would she have thought of it anyway?

He finished breakfast, thanked her, and collected his coat and scarf from the hooks in the hall. He went out and closed the front door gently, then turned into the wind and walked to Russell Square. From there he would catch a hansom to the Public Record Office and begin by searching the records of the trial of Dylan Lezant. He would read the account carefully, note who had presided, who prosecuted and who defended. He would find and note all the witnesses and what they had said. He would consider finding Alexander Duncannon and asking him who he had consulted in trying to get justice for Lezant, but that was a decision he would leave until later. This side of Christmas, many people had already left the city, and nobody's mind would be on an old case that was ugly, tragic, but long since considered closed.

It was afternoon by the time Pitt had read and noted all that he had set out to find. Reading the trial transcripts was a long and miserable job, but he became so absorbed in it that when he finally reached the end and stood up his back was stiff. His neck ached, too, and he realised his mouth was as dry as the dust he disturbed when he put the mounds of papers back where he had found them.

'Thank you,' he said to the clerk as he was leaving.

'You're welcome, sir,' the man replied, pushing his spectacles back up his nose. They slid again immediately.

Pitt turned back. 'Oh . . . by the way, has anyone else had those out recently, do you know?'

'No, sir. And I'd know. No one has had this lot out in close to two years.'

'You'd know the name of whoever read it?' Suddenly Pitt did not wish to have it known he had enquired, let alone taken the transcripts. 'Who took them?'

'Not took them, sir, just read and put back again. Can't take them off the premises.'

Pitt had produced his identification to get them in the first place. The clerk would have read his name, along with his rank.

'You don't recall who took them?'

'No, sir. Sorry.'

'I would be obliged if you could be as forgetful of my name as well, if you please.'

'Yes, sir.' The man looked startled. 'If you wish . . .'

'I do wish, Mr . . .' he struggled to remember the name he had given, '. . . Mr Parkins. Thank you.'

The clerk paled, but said nothing more.

When Pitt finally got to Lisson Grove he had a message waiting for him that he should see Commissioner Bradshaw as soon as possible.

'Seemed a bit upset, sir,' Dawlish told him with a rueful half-smile. 'Expect he wants to get off for Christmas.'

Pitt did not need to ask what it was about.

'Thank you,' he said, merely as a matter of civility.

In the hansom on the way back into the heart of the city, he considered what he would say to Bradshaw. It was his force Pitt was investigating. It would be a courtesy to inform the man of his intent, but it would also be an unwise thing to do. Bradshaw would be offended, and maybe more worried than he would show. Let him have what Christmas he could, rather than sit worrying when there was nothing he could change or protect now.

He found Bradshaw impatient, pacing the floor. The fire was low in the grate but the room was still warm and it was easy to ignore the rain spattering against the window.

Bradshaw barely observed the civilities.

'Thank you for coming,' he said briskly. 'Filthy night. Before I leave, I want to know exactly what it is you are looking for regarding the men who were killed at Lancaster Gate. Do you think their past records are going to turn up something? What, for example?'

Pitt was already prepared. 'The identity of Anno Domini, the name assumed by their informer, sir. It's possible those particular men were there just by chance and nothing to do with the fact that he had informed them before, so they would take him seriously—'

'We had all got that far, Pitt!' Bradshaw said impatiently. 'You didn't need to have someone go digging through the station records for that!'

Pitt ignored his interruption. 'It is also possible that this informer chose them intentionally, targeting them from the beginning.'

Bradshaw jerked his head up.

'Why? What are you suggesting?'

'That he had some personal issue with one or all of them, and this was not just anarchy, but the desire for revenge over something that happened, or that he believed happened.'

Bradshaw looked pale, and suddenly very tired. 'What do you have in mind? Most criminals resent being arrested. It's always someone else's fault, never theirs. A man caught stealing will blame the man who arrests him, not himself for committing the crime. Did you spend twenty years in the police force with your eyes shut and your ears muffed?'

'No, sir. But neither did I ever have to investigate a revenge bombing and the murder of three officers and horrible injuries of two others.'

Bradshaw sat down behind his desk. He looked almost as if he were punch drunk at the end of a big fight. Pitt was left to sit or stand as he chose.

Pitt was stung with a sense of pity for him, but he could not avoid telling him at least something of the truth. To do less now would be insulting. He glanced beyond Bradshaw to a framed photograph of a lovely, delicate woman in the niche on the shelf.

Bradshaw caught the instant. 'My wife,' he said, as if the explanation were necessary.

'She's beautiful,' Pitt said quite genuinely.

'Yes . . .' There was pain in Bradshaw's voice. 'That photograph catches her perfectly. It's . . . it's a few years old now.'

Was she dead? Pitt could hardly ask. At any time it would have been intrusive. Now, the day before Christmas Eve, it would be even more painful.

'No, sir,' he answered the earlier question. 'I know that men make mistakes, and that petty thieves, embezzlers, men who can't control their fists or their tempers usually blame somebody else for their misfortunes, police or victims they beat or robbed. I am looking for some incident that links the men at Lancaster Gate together, as a starting point.'

'What have you found?'

'It was my police associate who found a series of errors rather more than usual. Most of them were very well covered up, largely by Ednam.'

Bradshaw's face paled.

'The man's dead, Pitt! Is there really any point in raking that up now? He isn't here to defend himself or explain what really happened. His widow has little but grief for Christmas, and that to spend alone. Is this really going to serve anyone?'

'The rumours are already there, sir,' Pitt pointed out. 'In the newspapers, magazines, in the talk in clubrooms and public bars all over the city. Are the police corrupt? Are we riddled with anarchists, nihilists, men with bombs waiting to blow us up any day or night? Where will the next explosion be? In a house, a church, a shop, on a train? Can the police stop them? Can anyone? Or are the police part of it? Do we, each man, have to look after his own—'

'All right!' Bradshaw snapped. 'I can read as well as you can! I know what the public is saying, and what most of the newspapers are saying. And I realise how damned dangerous it is, and that we can't stop it. If we're not careful, we'll have half the citizens taking up their own arms to carry out whatever law they see fit. It'll be chaos. Have you thought that that is exactly what some foreign power might want? Or is that too hideous to contemplate, and that's why you're trying to make this look like one bad police station, and that's an end to it?'

'Are you sure it's only one?' Pitt returned. 'I'd love to think it's Ednam and half a dozen of his men. But shutting our eyes to any other possibility is exactly what allows it to happen.'

Bradshaw started up out of his chair. Then he looked at Pitt's face, and the rigidity of his body, ready to hold Bradshaw in check by force, if necessary. He slumped back again.

'We have to be able to trust the police,' Pitt said very gravely. 'We must not only get rid of the doubtful men, we must show the public that we have and we will go on doing so.'

'By blaming Ednam for his own death?'

'By finding out who Anno Domini is, and if he placed that bomb in the house at Lancaster Gate, and if he did, then why.'

'And have you the faintest idea who it is?'

'Yes. And if I'm right, I also know why. I'm sorry, sir, but if it is so, it's going to be very ugly indeed. The only thing worse would be to let it go. If I am right, the man who did it did so to draw attention to a terrible injustice. If we address it, we can bring it to an end. If not, he will go on bombing until we do. I am not going to be responsible for that, and I imagine you have no wish to be either.'

Bradshaw sighed heavily. 'I hope you know what the hell you're doing.'

Pitt hoped so too. He did not want Bradshaw to have any idea how much he dreaded having to conclude this case, but there was no way out of it. Once Alexander Duncannon detonated that bomb in Lancaster Gate, the course was set.

★　★　★

Pitt arrived home tired, wet and very cold. He had to make an effort to join in around the dinner table with the excited chatter of his family. Tomorrow was Christmas Eve. The day after that they would all be with Emily, Jack and their children.

Daniel put on his exaggeratedly patient face and made sure everyone noticed it. Before pudding had been served, Jemima had her own back by teasing him over the sister of one of his friends, and Pitt was startled to see how easily vulnerable he was. His children were growing up.

He relaxed a little as the good dinner restored his sense of wellbeing, and he was no longer cold. Once, for an instant, he thought of the widows of the men killed in the bombing, and wondered if there were anything on earth that would lessen the terrible grief of their Christmas. Perhaps the only gift worth having would be to know that they had been innocent, and he was not at all sure that he could give them that.

The children were upstairs about their own plans, amid quite a lot of running around, and occasional calls for Charlotte's help to find ribbons or more paper. She was upstairs on one of those errands when the doorbell rang. Pitt went to answer it.

He found Jack Radley on the step. In spite of having come in a carriage, which was waiting at the kerb, the shoulders of his elegant coat were soaked dark with rain.

'Come in,' Pitt invited him, standing back and holding the door wide. 'Is your driver all right out there?'

'I suggested he might go around to the kitchen. Hope you don't mind,' Jack answered, standing in the hall and dripping on to the carpet. 'But I won't be long . . . I hope.'

'Send him around to the back door, and I'll get Charlotte to give him a cup of tea, or better, cocoa,' Pitt directed him.

Jack obeyed. Pitt took the stairs two at a time to give the request to Charlotte. Five minutes later it was all accomplished. Pitt sat in his own chair while Jack stood with his back to the fire, warming himself.

'Of course, you're coming to dinner Christmas Day,' Jack remarked, 'but I wanted to speak to you privately.'

'What is it, Jack?' Pitt asked with a chill of apprehension.

Jack gave a very slight shrug, with little more than a movement of his shoulders. He was standing gracefully, but nothing in him was relaxed. All his body was as taut as the strings of a violin.

'You can let this investigation go for three days at least, can't you?' He seemed about to add something more, then changed his mind.

'Is that what you wanted to know?' Pitt said curiously.

Jack faced him at last. 'Yes, it is. This contract is more important than I can tell you. Worth a vast amount of money, jobs for over three thousand men, good jobs that will mean the renewal of a wide section of industry, and more in another few years. Marvellous for import and export everywhere. Just hold off this investigation of yours until it's signed.'

'What has it to do with police corruption?' Pitt asked. He sat forward in his chair; there was no more relaxing possible.

'Nothing!' Jack moved from the fire into the centre of the room, still too tense to sit down. 'I don't think police corruption comes into it, but I don't know. I have no idea what happened, I just know that Alexander Duncannon is a very disturbed young man who has delusions as to his friend's guilt or innocence. The fear of what he may have done is driving poor Godfrey frantic. Thomas, this contract will help the lives of thousands of people, their families, and their towns. Don't jeopardise it for the sake of a few days.'

Pitt looked back at Jack's face, which showed the earnestness with which he asked. Pitt knew something of the magnitude of the contract, and he could imagine the hopes that rested on it. He had faced being out of work himself, his family cold, frightened and hungry, and even without a home, when he had been thrown out of the police through no immediate fault of his own. It was moving to Special Branch that had saved him.

Jack must have seen the thought in his face. Perhaps he remembered it too. Emily would have known, and understood.

'This injustice has waited for two years,' Jack said. 'Let it wait until the New Year now. Don't go wakening ghosts just before Christmas. If there is anything to find, it will still be there in four or five days' time. Ednam, God help him, isn't going to do any more harm.'

'I have to solve the case,' Pitt warned him. 'It isn't going to disappear on its own. Ednam and his men may have sent an innocent man to the gallows.'

'Is that really likely?' Jack's eyebrows rose. 'Alexander is nice enough, but for heaven's sake, Thomas, he's addicted to opium! He has been ever since his accident when they gave it to him for the pain. He can't help it now, but there are times when he's completely crazy! Frankly, he sees and hears things that aren't there. Ask a doctor: opium addiction is a terrible thing. I dare say it'll kill him in the end.'

Pitt did not answer. Was that really all that was behind Alexander's actions? The blind loyalty of an opium addict, the guilt because he escaped driving him relentlessly to try to excuse his friend? It would be easy enough to believe.

'Dylan Lezant was no better,' Jack went on, sensing Pitt's doubts. 'Another young man severely addicted and sinking further and further into a life of depravity. Godfrey says he went through periods of delirious hallucinations, being dreadfully ill, soaked in sweat. And then he would do something desperate to obtain money, and opium, and then, at least to the casual observer, be perfectly all right again. I'm afraid it is very easy to believe that if opium was involved – and the police say it was an illegal sale that they were intercepting – then his cravings could have driven him to kill, if he thought they were going to deny him his opium, which of course they would.'

As Jack said, it was easy to believe. In fact, it made more sense than anything else. Why had Pitt listened to Alexander with such a willingness to believe him? Pity? Had he been looking at a young man who seemed to belong nowhere, filled with physical pain that he had had no hand in causing – although that was irrelevant? Or was it Alexander's emotional pain he had seen, the trauma of being stretched between two worlds, neither of which really accepted him? Pitt himself could have ended in such a no man's land when his father was convicted and sent to Australia.

Pitt's bitterness could have consumed him then, and he could have turned to theft or violence, believing there was no justice. There had been times when that seemed to be true. It was Arthur Desmond's having taken him into the private schoolroom of his own son, to spur him on, to be a friend and a competitor that had saved Pitt's sense of perspective. That was why he had joined the police: to find the justice for others that had passed by his own family.

But he believed Alexander Duncannon's pain was physical more than emotional, at least to begin with.

'The fact that Alexander might be totally deluded about what really happened that night doesn't mean he doesn't believe it himself,' he pointed out. 'And if he did believe it, and his protests were never taken seriously, as far as he could see, then he could still have felt he had a grudge against Ednam and his men. I have to look into that, Jack. I can't leave it alone.'

'Follow another line of inquiry, for the moment,' Jack argued, but he could see that Pitt was moved. 'Please. Just over Christmas. The contract will be signed in a few days.'

Pitt hesitated.

'The creation of a free port in China will be worth a King's ransom to Britain, if we lease it from them,' Jack said urgently. 'That's what this is, Thomas! Morally it will be something of a reparation to the Chinese for the wrongs of the Opium Wars – and God knows, they were wrong!' He went on more eagerly, his face alight, 'That's why Abercorn is willing to work with Godfrey Duncannon, even though he loathes him. I've no idea why, but

171

it doesn't matter. Abercorn has huge interests in China, and Godfrey has the political and diplomatic weight to see this through. Please . . . don't do something that could ruin Godfrey, for the sake of a few days!'

'Until after Christmas,' Pitt conceded.

'Thank you!' Jack held his hand out and clasped Pitt's so strongly that for a moment Pitt had to concentrate not to wince from the power of it.

After Jack was gone, Charlotte returned to the sitting room, having given the coachman hot tea with a dash of whisky in it, and two rather large mince pies.

She looked at Pitt's face and saw both the relief in it, and the shadow of a remaining anxiety. 'Well?' she asked.

'Has Emily said anything to you about this contract Jack is working on with Godfrey Duncannon?'

'Yes,' she answered guardedly, waiting for him to explain. 'Why? Is that what he came about?'

'Yes. I can see why it's so important to him – to Britain. But I can't let it go altogether . . .'

She looked at him gravely, but she did not ask anything of him.

'I can't let it go,' he said quietly. 'If Alexander is guilty of the bombing, it is because, in his eyes, the police were corrupt to the degree that they deliberately lied, and manufactured evidence. They swore on oath in court that Dylan Lezant was guilty of murder, sending him to the gallows knowing that he was innocent! Then what exactly was Alexander guilty of? Taking the law into his own hands, when the law of the land had so terribly failed him.'

She said nothing, but the grief in her face was answer enough.

'Who else would do that, if it is proved?' he went on. 'Who will help the police, give them simple information? Who will come to them and when they were in trouble, attacked and outnumbered?'

He shook his head. 'Is it an accumulation of events, a kind of seventh wave? Coincidence? Or is there some power behind it, anarchist, nihilist, or another country carefully trying to bring us down for military or industrial power? That's real, Charlotte, and far more of a danger than the odd attack on an outpost of the Empire, or even at sea. It is at the heart, like a spreading disease, and disease can kill.'

'I understand,' she said quietly at last. 'But can't you at least warn Jack?'

'He knows I'm worried, and why I am,' he told her. 'All he asked was that I wait until the contract is signed. Just a few days.'

She smiled, but there was no relief in her. 'It's late. I think we should go to bed. Tomorrow's Christmas Eve, and there's a lot to do, even if we are going to Jack and Emily's on Christmas Day.'

It was just before daylight when Pitt was woken by a loud and persistent knocking on the door. He had slept later than he meant to. He threw the bedclothes off and stood up, shivering in the bedroom that has lost its warmth overnight.

The knocking on the door had stopped. Charlotte must have answered it. Pitt had time to dress hastily, putting on heavy underwear and thicker trousers. He splashed water over his face. There was no time to shave before he found out who it was, and what had happened. No one would dare call him on Christmas Eve, at this hour, if it were not serious.

He went down the stairs quickly in his stocking feet, his hair still tousled.

Stoker was standing in the hall, his eyes hollow, his face white. He did not wait to be asked.

'There's been another bombing, sir,' he said gravely. 'Also near Lancaster Gate. Another empty house. No one hurt this time, but it's a hell of a mess. Still burning, last I heard.'

Pitt stood motionless on the second to last stair.

Charlotte was standing in the hall.

'Shave,' she said quietly to Pitt. 'I'll get Mr Stoker a cup of tea.' She turned to Stoker. 'Have you eaten anything yet?'

'No, ma'am, but—'

She did not let him finish. 'I'll make you some toast. You can eat it while he gets ready. Come with me.'

Stoker did not argue. He was shaking with cold, and the beginning of a new nightmare. He looked as if he had already been up for hours, but his visible fatigue was probably only from the exhaustion of too many long days and short nights.

Pitt shaved too quickly, cutting himself on the chin, but not badly. It was only seven minutes later that he went into the kitchen and took a plate of toast and a cup of tea from Charlotte. Five minutes after that he had his boots on and his coat and led the way out of the front door into the street, Stoker on his heels. The hansom that Stoker had arrived in was still at the kerb. Stoker gave the man the address, and they moved off into the dark, wet early morning.

Chapter Nine

THIS BOMBING was on Craven Hill, a street not a hundred yards from Lancaster Gate. A weak daylight breaking through the cloud showed what was left of the house, smaller than the first but also apparently unoccupied. The blast had woken neighbours who had called the fire brigade. They must have come very quickly because there was little still burning, although the acrid stench of charred wood was heavy in the air and there was debris all over the garden and the road.

Two fire engines stood in the street, horses uneasy, moving from foot to foot, tossing their heads as if eager to leave. In each case, one man stood by them, talking gently, comforting, encouraging.

Pitt looked along the street. It was a quiet, domestic neighbourhood, indistinguishable from Lancaster Gate except the houses were a little smaller. As he watched, he saw a couple of curtains move. He would have been surprised had they not. People were curious, but above all they would be frightened.

Was this the same as the last? Alexander Duncannon again? Or was he wrong about that, and it was anarchists after all?

He turned as the chief fireman approached him.

'Morning, sir,' the fireman said gravely. It was the same man as before. Natural, since it was so close.

'Morning,' Pitt replied. 'Any casualties?'

'No, thank God,' the fireman replied. 'Seems police weren't

called to this. But definitely a bomb. Hell of a blast, so the neighbour said who called us. About an hour ago, just over. Still dark.'

'Single explosion?' Pitt asked him.

'That's what he said, and looks right, from what we can see.
But it's as safe as we can make it. Look for yourself.'

Pitt followed the fireman, stepping carefully through the rubble
and fallen beams, being careful not to touch anything, even accidentally. The firemen could not make it safe without moving
things, and he needed to see it as it was first.

'That's where the bomb was.' The fireman pointed to what had
been the sitting-room fireplace. 'Blast went up the chimney, or at
least part of it did. Brought them all down, which caved a lot of
the roof in. Big chimneys clumped together, these houses. Sweep's
boy could climb from one to another.'

'Best place to plant the bomb?' Pitt thought so, but he wanted
the fireman's professional view as well.

The fireman frowned. 'You'd need a long fuse. You wouldn't
want to be near it when it went off, 'cos the whole damn roof
could land on you . . . which it did . . . fall in, I mean.' He shook
his head, staring at the big pile of bricks and stones that rose
almost to the ceiling. This obviously had been the main load-
bearing wall, with the strength of the central part, and the weight
of the chimneys on it. 'Take a big charge to do this much damage.'

'How much? Four sticks?'

'About that . . . high-quality stuff,' the fireman agreed. He
turned to look at Pitt. 'Any idea who you're looking for, sir? It's
been empty houses so far, but that could change.'

'I know that.' Pitt did not mean to sound terse, but he knew
he did. 'Does it look to you like it was the same man as Lancaster
Gate? He seems to know exactly where to put it for maximum
effect. And this house was clearly unoccupied . . . but he didn't
call the police . . .'

'What I'd like to know, sir, is if he wanted to get the police last
time, what's changed so he doesn't this time, eh?'

'I wish to hell I didn't know the answer to that,' Pitt told him. 'But I think I do. I want to look around a bit further. See if there's anything else to learn.'

'I'll come with you.' It was a statement not an offer.

Pitt nodded acknowledgement. 'I don't intend to move anything.'

'Damn right you don't! But I'm coming with you anyway.'

They walked carefully through the rest of the downstairs of the house. The stairs were half blown away and the cellar door was blocked by rubble it would be dangerous to move.

It was on the table in the scullery that Pitt found the piece of white cloth. He picked it up carefully. It was a gentleman's large handkerchief, made of fine lawn and embroidered with initials in one corner. It was high quality, tasteful and expensive. He knew what the initials were before he looked at it. A. D.

'Mistake, sir? Or a message?' the fireman asked.

'A message, I think,' Pitt replied. 'I didn't take the last one seriously enough.'

The fireman took a deep breath, regarded Pitt for a moment, then changed his mind about saying what was in his mind.

Outside again in the street it was lighter, and a small crowd had gathered almost twenty yards away. As Pitt and the fireman came out on to the pavement a man of about sixty broke away from the others and came striding across the road towards Pitt. He was solidly built with wings of grey at his temples.

'Are you in charge of this, sir?' he said in a voice edged with anger, and perhaps also fear.

'Yes, I am.'

'Then you'd better do it rather more successfully! Decent people are afraid to go to bed in their own homes. Decent policemen are getting killed doing their jobs, and there's no justice for them, or their families. We're suspicious of everyone out alone after dark, or with a package in their hands. Some people are saying it's anarchists, but others are suggesting it's revenge for police corruption—'

'Where did you get that from?' Pitt interrupted him.

'Irresponsible newspapers,' the man replied, not backing an inch. 'Left wing. Lunatics, some of them. But is it true? Have we got corrupt police?'

Pitt thought rapidly. This question had to come, but he had hoped it would have been longer before it did.

'Someone has said we have, but it is only one man making that claim. And yes, he could be the bomber, or just someone trying to take advantage of a tragedy to make his own point,' he answered.

'Well, if you don't do something, some people are going to start doing it themselves,' the man warned. 'And I'm speaking for all of us.' He glanced back at the growing crowd watching him.

The fireman was looking at Pitt also, waiting for him to respond.

Pitt hated this. Being at odds with the very people he was meant to protect was the beginning of true anarchy, the loss of trust, the fear that sowed seeds of chaos.

'It's one man,' he said very clearly. 'And I'm going to see him, now that I have evidence I believe sufficient to charge him. I can't hold him without it.'

'But—' the man protested.

Pitt stared at him. 'Do you want me to have the power to arrest someone without proof, sir? A gentleman . . . as respectable as you are? He's not known to the police for any offence at all.'

'Oh . . . well . . . just do your job!' The man turned on his heel and walked away, straight through the puddles on the road, and rejoined the still growing crowd.

The fireman nodded. 'That'll hold them for a while. Is it true, that the man you're after is a gentleman?'

'Yes.' Pitt did not want to give explanations.

'Right, sir. Good luck.'

Pitt thanked him and left. He walked away cold, wet and deep in thought. There was no escaping the inevitability that this was

Alexander Duncannon again, giving a violent reminder that no one had checked what he believed was police corruption, maybe general, more likely very specific to the case of Dylan Lezant.

Should he send Stoker to see if Alexander were at his flat? If he were in, or not, what would it prove? Unless he had dynamite on the kitchen table, nothing. And this second explosion accounted for all the rest of the dynamite they knew had been stolen. Without proof, arresting Alexander would do more harm than good. Godfrey Duncannon could prevent any further effective investigation, if he wished to. And given the issue of the contract, he well might. Pitt remembered his promise to Jack the previous evening, but the situation had now changed and he couldn't do nothing this morning.

He found a small café open and sat with other workmen, late for duty, and ate a bacon sandwich with a cup of scalding-hot, over-stewed tea. The bitter taste of it was oddly welcome. He was anonymous in the crowd, just another tired man with wet hair, hands red with the cold, and boots once good, but now scuffed and smeared with mud. Maybe it was time he treated himself to a new pair. He could afford to. Possibly he could much less afford not to. A man was judged less by his jacket than by his boots.

He must investigate the Lezant case and either prove the police right and Alexander Duncannon wrong, or else blow the whole matter wide open, with all the questions and the blame that would follow. There would be endless turning over of one old case after another, everything that Ednam had investigated over the last ten years of his career, at least.

Perhaps Tellman was right, and regardless of errors, both practical and moral, they deserved a loyalty that did not look too closely.

Except that it was unworkable, whatever anyone wanted, or could forgive. There would always be the Alexander Duncannons, the people who would see injustice and not accept it, whatever the cost.

Pitt found his way into the flat because the door was unlocked.

Alexander was sitting at the kitchen table looking desperately ill. His face was sheened in sweat, his skin was pale and he was shaking as if he had a raging fever. His shirt was soaked.

He saw Pitt and for an instant his eyes were filled with hope, then he recognised him and the hope died. He slumped forward again with a gasp, his arms wrapped around himself as if some pain within him were almost intolerable.

'Alexander,' Pitt said gently, sitting in the chair next to him at the table. 'Do you need a doctor? Can I get you anyone?'

Alexander's teeth were clenched and he moved very slightly, as if he would rock himself, were he able to bear the pain in the bones and muscles if he moved.

'No . . .' he said through clenched teeth. 'There's nothing . . .'

'There has to be something . . .'

Alexander grimaced. 'You don't happen to be carrying a spare twist of opium, do you?' The hope in his voice was for a moment greater than the misery.

Pitt tried to think if he knew anyone who could supply such a thing. The police surgeon? He might carry it in his first-aid kit, for pain. But Pitt would have to explain why he wanted it, and could he?

'Where do you get it normally?' he asked instead.

Alexander looked at him. 'So you can arrest him?'

'So I can get you some.'

'And then arrest him. No. He'll come. He always does. Being late is just a reminder to me of what it'll cost if I turn him in. A touch of real power . . . in case I get out of line.' He stood up, bent double, and staggered across the room towards the bathroom and toilet.

Pitt could not help. The least he could give him was privacy – if Alexander even cared about that any more. Pitt did not often feel violent, but whoever did this to anyone, as a reminder of power, deserved to be beaten till he hurt like this. Right now, Pitt would have liked to be the one to do it to him.

He lingered for a few moments, glancing around the room to see if there were any signs of Alexander having been out very recently. He must have worn a heavy coat to go to Craven Hill. The night was bitter. He stood up and walked over to the cupboard near the door. He pulled it open silently. There was an overcoat on the hanger. He touched the shoulders. The cloth was still wet. Had he been to Craven Hill, or simply to look for more opium? He leaned forward and sniffed, but there was no odour. He could have left before the blast anyway.

Should he stay in case Alexander collapsed and needed his help even to get back into his room and the chair? Might he be alone and unconscious on the bathroom floor? Or was the supplier waiting until Pitt was gone before he would appear with help? Anything that delayed that, even for minutes, was prolonging the torture.

He would go, and then come back again later, to make certain Alexander was all right. Perhaps he would find a doctor he could trust to be discreet? If there were any such thing?

He got up and went to the bathroom door just as Alexander opened it and came out. He looked white, but relieved of some of the pain.

'Let me take you to a hospital,' Pitt asked. 'They'll give you something immediately.'

'One dose,' Alexander replied. 'What about tomorrow? And the next day?'

Pitt had no answer.

One thing he could do was find out what had really happened in the Lezant case.

But who could he find to tell him, on Christmas Eve?

'I'll come back and check you're all right,' he said. What was that worth? Anything?

Alexander smiled and thanked him.

Pitt walked down the narrow stairs and out into the rain again. It was cold, but the wind had dropped. He caught a hansom to the Public Record Office and checked the names and present addresses of the lawyers who had prosecuted Lezant, and those who had defended him. He also checked on the judge, and found that he had since retired and gone to live overseas.

The lawyer who had prosecuted the case was Walter Cornard. However, Pitt was told, with some surprise that he should ask, that Mr Cornard had left for the Christmas holidays, and was not expected to return until 27 December.

Pitt had introduced himself simply with his name and rank. Now he met the man's startled look grimly. 'Of Special Branch,' he added. 'I am sorry to inconvenience your Christmas, and my own, but there has been another bombing, and I'm afraid the matter will not wait until we have enjoyed Christmas dinner.'

The man blanched. 'I assure you, Commander Pitt, if we had any knowledge at all of such matters, we would already have informed the police.'

'I need to speak to Mr Cornard regarding an old case. You will be good enough to give me his address,' Pitt replied. 'Immediately.'

The man lifted his chin sharply into the air in a gesture of defiance, but he complied.

An hour later Pitt was sitting in the rather chilly library of Mr Walter Cornard's home, listening to the occasional bursts of laughter from the withdrawing room where clearly family guests were enjoying themselves. He had passed the huge, brightly decorated tree in the hall, and many garlands and wreaths of holly and ivy, woven with scarlet ribbons. Cut-glass bowls of chocolates and candied fruit sat on the side tables, and red candles burned on the mantel.

The library fire was unlit and not much warmth crept through from the rest of the house. Clearly this room was not intended to be used today.

Pitt stood up and paced back and forth to stop himself feeling even colder. He hoped Alexander Duncannon's supplier of opium had turned up. At least Alexander had enough money to pay for it. Probably the man would come. It was his business.

This wretched thought was interrupted when Cornard finally arrived. His face was flushed with warmth. He had probably been enjoying the pre-Christmas delicacies.

He did not hold out his hand to Pitt. His resentment at the intrusion was palpable.

'Pitt, my butler said,' he began. 'What on earth is it that makes you intrude on a man's family at this hour on Christmas Eve? This had better be damned important, or I'll know the reason for it!'

'I would rather be at home with my family too,' Pitt replied tartly. 'And I'm sure Inspector Ednam would, instead of in his grave, with his widow and children sitting with a funeral wreath on the door rather than one with red ribbons on it.'

Cornard shut the door hard. 'What the devil are you talking about?' he demanded. 'My man said something about bombing. I know nothing about bombs, anarchists, traitors or anyone else in your . . . area of work. I'd be obliged if you would explain yourself as briefly as possible, and then be on your way.' He remained standing, a statement that he intended their conversation to be very brief indeed.

Pitt sat down in one of the armchairs and looked up at Cornard. Once he would have been intimidated by such a man, even if he had managed to conceal it, but that time was long past.

'I will be as quick as I can, Mr Cornard. The case at the root of my inquiry is that of Dylan Lezant, who was hanged for the murder of James Tyndale, some two years ago. August the ninth, I believe, was the date of his death, if you need reminding.'

'I do not need reminding,' Cornard snapped back. 'It was a clear-cut case. Tragic. The young man was addicted to opium and it had ruined his life. Damaged his brain, it would seem. He went to meet a dealer in an alley. The police intercepted him. Lezant shot Tyndale, apparently a passer-by, although that is open to question. The police arrested Lezant right there on the scene. Gun was in his hand. You would have read all that in the court records, or in the damn newspapers, for that matter. What on earth are you doing here?'

'You must have looked at the evidence very closely,' Pitt observed.

'Of course I did. What is your point?'

'If the police arrested Lezant, in spite of the fact that he was armed, and clearly more than willing to shoot, why did they not also arrest the seller of these drugs? Was he armed as well? There is no record of that. I looked specifically.'

'He probably wasn't. Why would he be?'

'Why was Lezant? Tell me more about him. Where did he come from? Who were his family? How did he become addicted to opium?'

'I have no idea!' Cornard was annoyed. 'It was my job to prosecute him, not to defend him. I have no idea how he became an addict, nor do I care. I certainly don't know why he had a gun, but unquestionably he did! Maybe he intended to rob the dealer rather than pay him!' He raised his eyebrows, his eyes wide. 'Surely not a great stretch of the imagination?'

'Yes, it is,' Pitt agreed. 'To shoot the man he needs so desperately seems a particularly idiotic thing to do.'

'The man was an opium addict, for God's sake!' Cornard said angrily, the colour deepening on his cheeks. 'He did it. The police saw it, and they all testified to it. The facts are beyond doubt.'

'What about the other man who was there, and escaped? Did you ever find him?'

Cornard gave a little snort of derision.

'Alexander Duncannon? He came forward. There's no proof whatever that he was there, and the police deny it.' Cornard took a deep breath and let it out with a sigh of patience far stretched. 'Look, Pitt – or whatever your name is – it was a wretched case. What began as a grubby transaction between an addict and his supplier was apprehended by the police. The addict panicked and shot Tyndale, who may or may not actually have been the supplier.'

'Had he any opium?' Pitt interrupted.

'No. It seems more likely the supplier never came.'

Cornard shifted his weight. 'He may have been as innocent as he looked. For heaven's sake, man, dealers in opium can be anybody! Just as users of it can be. You would be amazed who takes the stuff! It's no respecter of rank, money or profession. Some people become addicted after one use of the stuff, others take it on and off all their lives, and can leave it if they choose. God knows what pain people have and find they can't endure.'

'Either of the body, or of the mind,' Pitt agreed. 'What did you learn about Tyndale? Any income he couldn't account for by whatever he did for a living? What did he do? The court records didn't say.'

Cornard sighed and sat down in the chair nearest the fire. He took a box of matches from the scuttle and lit the paper, wood and logs that were laid out. He watched it for a minute or two while the flames licked upwards, and he was sure it was going to take.

'He was a seller of rare books and manuscripts,' he replied at length. 'His income was erratic because his sales were, but it seemed he was gifted at it, because he made a very comfortable living, and his records were all in order. He had an excellent accountant, and we checked it all.'

'So you looked and found no evidence of his buying or selling opium, or dealing it with anyone else?'

'None. Which isn't to say he didn't, but we found nothing we could take to court.'

'Did you believe he was a dealer?' Pitt said bluntly, staring at Cornard's face.

'No, honestly I didn't.'

'Then he was a perfectly innocent passer-by?'

'Apparently.'

'So why did Lezant shoot him, instead of the closest policeman to him? Seems a stupid thing to do.'

'For God's sake, man, I don't know! Maybe Tyndale saw what was happening and got in the way, thinking he was helping? Or misunderstood the whole thing, and thought the police were robbers attacking Lezant?'

'Weren't they in uniform? The report suggests they were. If they weren't, then maybe Lezant took them for robbers also? Maybe he thought they were all out to steal the opium?'

'Hardly likely, since the dealer hadn't turned up!' Cornard pointed out.

'Unless Tyndale was the dealer after all?'

'Then why the devil would Lezant shoot him?' Cornard said reasonably.

'That was Duncannon's claim,' Pitt pointed out. 'Lezant didn't shoot him. He says the police did.'

'That's patently ridiculous,' Cornard shook his head. 'For a start, they weren't armed.'

'So they said. Lezant also said he wasn't armed.'

Cornard was incredulous. 'And you think the court should have taken the word of a drug addict come to buy opium illegally, over the police who apprehended him? What's the matter with you, man?'

'Then it comes back to the question as to why Lezant would shoot Tyndale, a passer-by? By all accounts he was a thoroughly decent man who has nothing whatever against him. And the police did check very thoroughly. He lived locally, and it is the obvious conclusion that he was on his way home, and stumbled on the police raid on an opium sale. Except that the police have no dealer to show for it, Lezant said there wasn't one, the police are denying that Duncannon was ever there, and Tyndale is dead.'

'So it's a mess!' Cornard said irritably, poking at the fire again. 'No one is denying that. But Tyndale was shot, a gun of the right

186

size and calibre, recently fired, was taken from Lezant. What other evidence is there . . . reasonably?'

'Not a lot of choice,' Pitt admitted. 'But Duncannon's story is that he was there, and Tyndale was shot by accident, by the police. He escaped, and Lezant didn't. The police shouldn't have had a gun, and certainly weren't going to admit having fired it wildly, and hit a respectable citizen passing by. Even if they did jump to the mistaken conclusion that he was the dealer they were expecting.'

Cornard was looking increasingly unhappy. 'Why would they shoot him, rather than arresting him?' he asked.

'Because he wasn't the dealer, and maybe refused to stop. He couldn't hand over the opium, because he didn't have it. Perhaps he argued with them? Challenged them?'

'If a citizen's getting in the way, arguing with you, you don't shoot him dead.' Cornard turned away, disgusted. 'You warn him, and then you arrest him. For heaven's sake, man, they would see the police uniforms! If he had any honest business there, he would have explained it, and gone on his way.'

'What if the police weren't in uniform?' Pitt suggested. 'And they looked like a gang of men setting on one man, to rob him or worse.'

Cornard gave a heavy sigh and moved his shoulders uncomfortably, as though suddenly his jacket did not fit him.

'That wasn't put forward as a possibility,' he said. 'It . . . it seemed as if there were really very little to argue about. There still is. I'm not sure why you are pursuing it?' Now he was openly questioning, his eyes bleak and curious.

Pitt hesitated before answering. How much should he tell this man? Cornard had been open with him, even though Pitt had intruded into his home on Christmas Eve, interrupting what was clearly a family occasion. Did something about the case still trouble him? Or was it just a professional courtesy?

'What was Lezant like?' Pitt asked, suddenly realising he knew only Alexander's view, no one else's.

Cornard looked taken aback. He seemed to search his memory and then look for words. He was unhappy when he answered. 'Quite a decent sort of young man. Over-emotional, but I think he knew even then that he hadn't a chance. He was good-looking, in a quiet sort of way. Very fine eyes, darkest blue I ever saw.'

'Did he ever admit his guilt?'

'No, never. I don't know what he told Hayman, who was defending him, but he insisted to me that he was innocent, right to the end.' Suddenly emotion choked his voice. 'I hate prosecuting a young man to the gallows! Why on earth did you have to come and remind me of this on Christmas Eve, of all days? And in my home!'

'Because the case isn't over,' Pitt answered candidly. 'At least I don't think it is.'

'He's dead and buried!' Cornard stared at him. 'What has it to do with Special Branch? Whoever blew up your buildings, it wasn't Dylan Lezant.'

'Are you certain now that he killed Tyndale? I know what the jury said, but what about you?'

'No, I'm not. But beyond a reasonable doubt? I don't know that either. Why? He wasn't an anarchist. I don't think any mad bomber is trying to avenge him, if that's what you're imagining?'

'I don't think it's vengeance,' Pitt said honestly. 'I think it's an effort to force us to re-open the case and look at it again. Not for revenge . . . to clear Lezant's name.'

'By whom? He has no family. And why now? He's been gone over two years?'

'By Alexander Duncannon. What if he was telling the truth, and he was there?'

'And the police shot Tyndale? Why? That makes no sense.'

'Accident? Stupidity? Panic? I don't know. But Duncannon has tried for two years to say that that particular police station was corrupt, and no one would listen to him. Now he's lost patience.

He's ill himself. Perhaps he doesn't think he has all that much time to play with.'

Cornard looked pale. 'So he's bombing police until someone does listen?'

'There were no casualties in the bombing this morning. But we were beginning to let the case go, at least until . . . for a while. Over Christmas and New Year. Now I can't, much as I would like to.'

'I see.' From the expression on Cornard's face, he really did see. 'Hell of a business. I think Duncannon's mad. If he's into the opium as well – and why else would he have been there at that buy? – then it's eating away at his brain. I've heard it can give people delusions, hallucinations. Poor devil . . .'

'It would be a convenient explanation.'

'You'd better go and see Hayman. He won't appreciate it at this hour, but we can't have any more bombs. Don't know who'll be next. Maybe not another empty building.'

Pitt had not needed reminding of that. He did not argue. Cornard gave him Hayman's address, and he thanked him and left.

The house was not far away, but it took Pitt nearly three-quarters of an hour through rain and heavy traffic before he was reluctantly admitted into Hayman's morning room. It was another ten minutes after that before Hayman himself came in. He was a slender man wearing a dark blue velvet smoking jacket, clearly having relaxed after dinner and begun the lazy part of the evening when he could do as he pleased. He looked to be in his late fifties, and possibly had no children still at home.

'What is it you think I can do for Special Branch, Mr Pitt?' he said with a frown, rather more of confusion than annoyance. His face was lean, his colourless hair receding off a high forehead. 'Do sit down, man!' he added, taking the green leather armchair opposite the one nearest Pitt. It was a pleasant room and the embers of the fire were still warm.

Pitt obeyed. The comfort of the chair made him momentarily aware of how tired he was. His back ached and his feet were cold and wet.

'Do you recall the Dylan Lezant case, Mr Hayman?'

Hayman frowned. 'Of course I do. Miserable business. Why does Special Branch care? He was an unhappy young man, something of a rebel against society, because he was out of step with it. Not an unusual thing for a young man with time on his hands, and perhaps too much imagination. But he was no serious anarchist. Wanted social change, certainly, but so do many of us. He wouldn't have bombed anyone to get it. Anyway, he's been dead a couple of years now, poor devil.'

Pitt felt a quickening of interest, and discomfort. He was not sure what he wanted to find, but he was afraid of learning that Alexander was right, and the police were as badly wrong as he believed. Sitting here in this quiet, well-used morning room of a man he had not heard of until today, he was touched with a new chill as to what this would mean. He had understood Tellman's need for belief in the general trustworthiness of the police, the vast force for order that was there in every town and village in the country, reassuring that underneath each surface ripple of violence or dishonesty, there was a groundswell of decency that would always prevail in the end.

He wanted it to. Perhaps everybody did. It was the difference between trust and fear. There was always medicine, law and the Church, everywhere you would want to call 'home'. The medical profession did not know all the answers, but it would never stop trying. The Church was run by fallible men, but it stood for certain unchangeable principles. But what if the law were without honour?

Hayman was staring at him, waiting for him to explain himself.

'The bombings,' Pitt said rather too bluntly. 'I have to investigate every possibility. One of them is that they are related to the Dylan Lezant case.'

Hayman's eyes widened. 'The bombings at Lancaster Gate? How?'

'You defended him?' Pitt asked.

'Not very effectively, I'm afraid. The evidence was over-whelming . . . by that I mean that it overwhelmed me, and I think possibly a good deal of the truth was obfuscated by lies in the interpretation of those facts.'

Pitt was still hoping for an argument, something that would take him in a different direction. He was being a coward. He should face the facts and allow them to lead him wherever they may.

'What evidence was there, Mr Hayman? Apart from police testimony? Could they prove that Lezant had had the gun, or any gun? Had he a history of violence? Why would he shoot Tyndale? Did anybody ever find the opium? Or proof that Tyndale was anything but the passer-by he appeared to be? Could Alexander Duncannon have been telling the truth that he was there, and saw the police shoot Tyndale?'

Hayman thought for several moments, all the light gradually dying out of his face.

'Duncannon was a bad witness,' he said at last. 'I didn't put him on the stand. He was willing enough to testify, but his father exerted all the pressure he could to prevent it. The prosecution would have done what they could to discredit him, and would have succeeded. He had been in an appalling accident and was still under the influence of the opium given him initially for the pain. No doubt you are familiar with opium addiction. He would have been exposed as an addict, his supplier very probably exposed too, and his legality questioned. It was not his doctor: that I know because I found out for myself.'

'Who was it?' Pitt asked.

The barrister shook his head.

'I know only that it was not his doctor, because I went into his medical history very thoroughly.' His face was filled with pity. 'Alexander wanted to testify that they both went to buy opium from their dealer, who did not turn up. The police did. Tyndale came by, purely by chance – he was not the dealer. The police panicked and shot wildly, hitting Tyndale and killing him immediately. With a spot of very quick thinking, they arrested Lezant, but Alexander escaped, presumably thinking Lezant was behind him.'

Pitt could see the hopelessness of it. It was exactly what Alexander had told him. Which, of course, did not necessarily make it the truth!

'And Lezant?' he asked.

'Lezant was my client. He refused to have Alexander called. He said it would ruin Alexander without helping Lezant himself. I had to acknowledge that he was right. It would have been a pointless sacrifice. But whether it would have helped or not, I had to do as Lezant wished.'

'Did you believe him?' It was a very blunt question, but Pitt needed an answer, even if it was only in the mounting surprise in Hayman's eyes, and then the discomfort.

'I don't know,' he said after a brief hesitation. 'You have looked into it, with hindsight? Do you?'

Pitt had not expected Hayman to challenge him. 'I think Alexander believes it,' he replied. 'But whether that makes it true or not is another matter. How close were they?'

A flash of humour lit Hayman's face, and then vanished. 'Friends in affliction, I think. The desperate loyalty of people who have understood one another's pain, and perhaps shared in many beliefs. Lovers, if that's what you mean? No, I don't think so. I've seen that before, and I would be very surprised. Love, of brothers in grief, yes.'

'Again, do you believe Lezant was guilty?'

'Of shooting Tyndale? No, I don't think so.'

'Thank you.'

'I . . . I wish I could have saved him. I look back now and

wonder if I tried hard enough.' He stopped abruptly. He had been going to add something more, but perhaps he knew it would make no difference now.

Pitt rose to his feet. 'Thank you, Mr Hayman. I appreciate your honesty.'

Hayman stood also. 'Not much point in wishing you a Merry Christmas, is there? I don't envy your job, sir. You have a nasty mess that won't be either opened or closed easily.'

It was just after midnight when Pitt finally got home and went to bed. It did not feel like Christmas morning, a day of celebration, a new hope for the world; if the Church were to be believed, the dawn of a new redemption.

He must make an effort, for his family's sake, no matter what he felt like: he must smile, go to church, let the music and the bells, the sound of happy voices drown out all other sounds. He owed his children that, even if Charlotte knew him well enough to read the shadows inside.

It was the day after Christmas, traditionally known as Boxing Day, named for the boxes of money or other gifts the well-off gave to their staff, tradesmen or others less fortunate. Pitt did not call on Tellman and Gracie for this reason, although he did take them a hamper of gifts from Charlotte and himself, because they were old friends. It had nothing to do with social position. Also, it was the perfect opportunity to leave the last shred of the quarrel behind. They both wanted it forgotten and that was what the heart of Christmas was about.

While Gracie prepared their tea and rich, fruit-filled Christmas cake, Pitt sat with Tellman in the parlour. The fire was burning up well and the whole room was decorated with home-made, brightly coloured paper chains. Dark red candles flickered on both ends of the mantel.

Pitt looked around at it and smiled. Every touch in it spoke not of money, but of care. A child's toys were placed in one corner, as if it were her part of the room. There was a stuffed rabbit, a box of bricks, and a doll with a home-made pink dress on. Pitt was absolutely certain that the little girl would have a dress of the same fabric. Years ago Jemima had had the same. He remembered Charlotte stitching it, and Jemima's face when she had opened the parcel.

It seemed almost a blasphemy to force a conversation about violence and corruption. It should not be permitted to intrude in a place like this. But that was the evil of it. It intruded everywhere, until it was stopped.

'I saw the lawyers for the prosecution and the defence for Lezant on Christmas Eve,' Pitt said, biting into the cake. It was excellent. He would immeasurably have preferred to eat it, and think of nothing else. Gracie's cooking was very much to his taste, and it had improved all the time over the years.

Tellman cut straight to the point. 'They think he was innocent?'

'Of shooting Tyndale, the defence thought so, yes. The prosecution thought Tyndale could have been the drug dealer, but that it's not likely. We've no choice but to investigate further. I hate dragging dead men's names through the mud, but there's no alternative now. At least it will stop Alexander Duncannon from setting off any more bombs.'

'He's as mad as a hatter!' Tellman said bitterly.

'Probably. But that doesn't mean he's wrong about this. If he is, I'll be delighted, but I need to prove it.'

Tellman did not argue. It was as if the comfort and sanity of Christmas had robbed him of the anger he had felt before. 'Where are you going to start?' he asked. 'Ednam's dead, and I doubt Yarcombe or Bossiney'll tell you anything useful. They don't want to be tarred with the same brush.'

'I doubt it too,' Pitt agreed. 'They tried to trace everything they could about poor Tyndale at the time, but we could go over it again. I think he was just in the wrong place at the wrong time. But I'd like to know who the dealer was, and why he wasn't there. What happened to him? And why did any of the police have guns? Had all of them? Or just one? Who was he shooting at when he killed Tyndale? And why? The only people there were other police, Lezant and Duncannon.'

'They said Duncannon wasn't there,' Tellman pointed out.

'Best thing to say to discredit him,' Pitt answered. 'If he wasn't there then his testimony was useless. Anything he said had to be a lie.'

Tellman's face was grim. 'No way to verify that. Of course, they could have been shooting at Duncannon to prevent his escape, and got Tyndale instead.'

'We need to go to the place and see exactly where the shots were fired,' Pitt said unhappily. 'Read the testimony over again, and get the other men who were there to repeat their statements. If that was done at the time, it didn't come out in court.'

'Because everyone took it for granted that Lezant was guilty.' Tellman's voice was hard. He found the words difficult to say. 'Of course, it could be that it was so absurd they didn't bother,' he added.

Pitt gave him a cold look, and did not add any words.

Tellman coloured slightly. He was uncomfortable with it, fighting to cling on to his old certainties.

Gracie came in with the tea and set it down. Without asking, she poured for each of them. She possibly knew Pitt's taste even better than she knew Tellman's.

'Wot yer going ter do, then?' She looked from one to the other. 'Yer gonna bury it and leave it till it poisons everything, or yer going ter dig up all the roots until yer got it all, an' yer can burn it? An' anyone wot's still hanging on to it like a fool?'

'We're going to dig it up,' Tellman answered before Pitt could swallow his cake and form the words.

Pitt did not find it so easy to get any conversation alone with Alexander this time. His mother must have persuaded him to come home for Christmas, or else he had felt well enough to offer her that, perhaps the best gift he could give her.

The fog curled thick as smoke over the city and the street lamps were hazy yellow, seeming to move as the rising wind twined the vapours across them like scarves.

The house smelled of mulled wine, spice, the perfumed greenery of wreaths and the burning of applewood, cigar smoke, and thick, coloured wax candles. A Christmas tree in the hall was hung with glass ornaments reflecting the glitter of the chandeliers in their faceted sides.

Over Godfrey Duncannon's protests, Pitt was conducted to the morning room. The fire was burning up well, dispelling the gloom of the winter evening as he sat alone with Alexander.

'I'll keep it brief,' Pitt said the moment the door was closed and they were alone. 'I've read all the records of Lezant's trial, and the police reports. I've talked to both Cornard and Hayman. There are a lot of unexplained elements in the story. There is certainly a possibility that errors have been made, and unques- tionably some lies have been told. I see why you wanted to be called to the stand, and why Lezant wouldn't allow it. You wouldn't have been believed anyway. You would have got yourself hanged as well, for no cause.'

Alexander looked startled. 'I didn't shoot Tyndale!'

'I know that. But he was shot while you were in the act of committing a crime. That makes you guilty, even though you didn't pull the trigger.'

'Neither did Dylan! It was one of the police,' Alexander said hotly. There was a flush in his pale face and his hands were clenched on his knee.

'Why? Was it an accident? Was he shooting at you? Why shoot at all? Are you sure you didn't have a gun, either of you?'

'Yes, of course I'm sure!' Alexander's voice was raised. 'Why would we take guns? If you're addicted to opium you don't shoot your supplier, for God's sake! He's your lifeline! If he's dead, you're cut off.' The panic rose in his voice as if the threat were there in the room with him now.

Pitt fought the urge to believe him and was overwhelmed. It was the truth, and he could not refuse to see it.

'Did the supplier come?' he asked.

'No.'

'It wasn't Tyndale? You're sure?'

Alexander was incredulous. 'Of course I'm sure! He didn't come. Or if he did, he saw the police and went off without them or us ever knowing he was there.'

'Who was he?'

Something inside Alexander closed down, some shield behind the eyes.

'I can't tell you.'

'You mean you won't!'

'Yes. I won't. Without the opium I can't stand the pain.' It was a simple statement of a fact he must live with day and night, every moment he was conscious, and threaded through all his dreams, too.

'How did you know who the policemen were?' Pitt asked. 'How were you certain enough to kill them?'

Alexander's face was bleak, tight with pain.

'They testified in court, remember? They swore to their names, and to being there.'

Of course. And Alexander was not called to testify.

'I got your handkerchief at Craven Hill,' he said. 'No more bombs!'

Alexander nodded.

He asked Alexander to go over the events of that day one more time, step by step. He could compare it with whatever Yarcombe or Bossiney might say. Newman, Hobbs, Ednam, Lezant and even Tyndale were all dead.

Half an hour later Godfrey Duncannon came in. He did not knock, which, since it was his house, was perhaps acceptable. All the same, Pitt found it an intrusion.

Alexander rose to his feet, his wince of pain almost inescapable.

'Commander Pitt was just leaving, Father.' He turned to Pitt with a sudden, gentle smile, which for a moment illuminated his face and showed the man he could have been. 'Good night, sir.'

Chapter Ten

CHARLOTTE PUT hot porridge in front of Pitt and passed him sugar and cream, then poured him a second cup of tea.

'Thomas, I think you should at least see the newspaper, even if you don't read it all. Perhaps some of the letters . . .'

He looked up at her. 'I know,' he said quietly. 'A good many people are concerned not only to find the Lancaster Gate bomber, but even more to allay this suspicion of the police, and the disgrace of corruption. It is doing a lot of damage.' He heard the strain in his voice, even though he had tried to hide it from her.

'It's more than that,' she replied, not moving away even to put the teapot down, or resume her place opposite him. 'I haven't mentioned this before, because I hoped he would leave it, but he's getting worse . . .'

'Who is?'

'Josiah Abercorn. I didn't know much about him, so I asked Emily if he was important. I'm sorry, but apparently he is.'

She had his attention now. 'I haven't heard of him, except now and then socially, and as something of a philanthropist,' he replied. 'Is he talking about police corruption too? I suppose it's to be expected.' He was desperately tired of the subject, and angry with the people who wrote letters to the newspapers with easy outrage, having no idea how hard police work actually was. They so often spoke as if there were absolute good and evil, and little between,

199

whereas in fact the vast majority were simply poor, hungry, cold and too often desperate.

Charlotte refilled her own cup and sat down.

'No, he is very much for the police. He wants justice for those who were murdered, and all police treated with more respect. He wants the bomber found and hanged, and for Special Branch to stop maligning them, by implication.'

'And does he have any practical suggestions as to how we should do that?' Pitt said bitterly. 'Most of us want to believe that the police are strong, clever and honest. They are the shield between us and the reality of crime.'

'Of course he's saying what everybody wants to hear,' she said patiently. 'He's ambitious to be a politician, no doubt destined for high office! What else would he say?'

'Is he?' He was surprised. He should have remembered the name, but he could not place it.

'He's not elected yet,' she said with a downward turn of her mouth, 'but he aims to be, and he'll succeed.'

'You don't like him,' he observed.

She looked surprised. 'Of course I don't! He's clever, opportunistic, and he's criticising you. But you can't ignore him.'

He smiled. 'What should I do? Write to *The Times* myself? And say what? "Regrettably the police are imperfect, and it is beginning to look very possible that they were in too much of a hurry to close a particularly ugly case in which they may have contributed rather a lot to hanging the wrong man"? I would like to be sure of that before I say it. I'd like to be even more sure that there is a better answer than that.'

'And is there?'

He let out a sigh. 'I don't think so. But I'm not going to say anything until I know for certain, and can prove it. Has anyone replied to Abercorn?'

'Not to this letter yet. But Victor did yesterday. It was rather neat, actually. He explained why Special Branch business is secret, and anyone who read it would see Abercorn as being irresponsible. But people tend to see what they want to. Narraway is playing to reason – Abercorn to panic. Panic usually wins. I'm sorry.'

Pitt did not argue. She was right. He read Abercorn's letter and appreciated exactly what he was doing, fanning the indignation and the fear at the same time. He could also understand it: frightened people act. Saying 'everything is under control, leave it to me' doesn't soothe any anger or grief. It sounds like the indifference of someone who is not himself in any danger.

Charlotte was watching him, waiting for his response.

'I know,' he conceded. 'There's little I would like more than to clear the police of any wrong, in Lezant's death, or anything else beyond ordinary errors now and then. But I can't.'

She did not reply, as if waiting for him to explain. There was no reason of secrecy why he should not. As far as the general public were concerned, everything was known anyway. It was a relief to share it with her. He had not realised how much until he began to tell her. His tea went cold and he did not notice.

When he had finished she looked sad, a pity in her face, which he knew was for Cecily Duncannon. Charlotte imagined herself in Cecily's place, and her emotions were quick to respond.

'If it wasn't Lezant, then who shot Tyndale, and why?' she asked. 'Was it just panic, and stupidity? Or could they have had a reason?'

'From what Alexander says, it was probably Ednam. But they all had to cover it up and blame Lezant. Only Yarcombe and Bossiney are alive now.'

'And Lezant is dead, and Alexander probably a mass murderer, at least in the eyes of the law,' Charlotte added. 'Who is Tyndale? Could he have been the opium dealer?'

Pitt stood up. 'I'm going to see Tyndale's family. I don't suppose I'll learn much, but I have to try.'

She nodded and gave him a quick kiss on the cheek as he turned and went towards the hall, and the front door.

★　　★　　★

Pitt knew Tyndale's address and caught a hansom in Russell Square, giving the driver instructions. Then he sat back and considered what he would say to Tyndale's widow. There was very little about her in the notes from the original case. Perhaps the poor woman had been too shocked by her sudden and pointless bereavement to say anything. She might even have collapsed and no one had attempted to interview her. Ednam had left no description. Pitt wondered if not speaking to her sooner was an oversight that could matter.

He also thought about Josiah Abercorn. If Charlotte were correct and he was busy courting public support, he would find a great deal of it. The bombing had stirred up a powerful undercurrent of fear. Most people were frightened by the spectre of uncertainty, disorder, and panic in the streets. There were more and more immigrants in London, and they were easy to identify. They looked different, sounded different. Too many of them were poor, and willing to work harder than other people, and take less money. They also ate different food and seemed to worship different gods. They were an easy focus for the fear that displayed itself as anger.

Was Abercorn was feeding that fear, and hoping it would in turn feed him? It was despicable, but he certainly would not be the first, or the last, to use it for his own ends.

And perhaps he was also quite genuinely afraid that social upheaval was already awake and restive. Worse could follow: violence imported from Europe, where revolution had been suppressed, speech restricted, and there was poverty and overcrowding so bad it seemed to suffocate the breath in your throat.

His work at Special Branch had necessitated Pitt talking to a lot of foreigners, many from Russia, and the countries lying on its borders. Their desperation was in their faces, in the threadbare clothes they wore, the food they ate, the odd, sometimes colourful phrases they used as they tried to become used to English and its eccentricities.

He thought of the peaceful countryside of his youth, to some boring, and bare of idea or adventure. Now it seemed like a place of lost peace. The world was changing too rapidly, like a train careering towards the horizon, out of control, threatening to crash.

He arrived at the Tyndale house, alighted and paid the driver. He stood on the pavement and stared around him as the hansom moved away. It was a quiet neighbourhood, and a little shabby. A million people lived in houses like these, outwardly much the same, inside, each one unique, with the possessions and the record of one family, perhaps several generations of it.

He walked up to the door of number fifty-seven and knocked. As he stepped back, so as not to threaten whoever opened it, he noticed that the bricks needed repointing in half a dozen places. A slate in the roof was loose, but well away from the door. If it fell it would land harmlessly in the garden, in among the perennial flowers, which were now neatly cut back, ready to grow again next year.

The door opened and a maid looked out curiously. She was young, not more than fifteen or sixteen. She reminded him of Gracie, when he and Charlotte had first married. One young girl was all the domestic help they could afford. He found himself smiling at the memory.

'Yes, sir? Can I 'elp yer?' she asked.

'Good morning. My name is Commander Pitt, of Special Branch. Will you please ask Mrs Tyndale if she can spare me a little of her time? It is important.'

It took her a moment to grasp what he had said, but after the initial amazement, she nodded, dropped an awkward curtsy, and asked him in. She left him in a rather chilly parlour, and went off very swiftly to fetch her mistress.

Pitt looked around. One could tell a great deal about both past and present from the parlour of a family home, or, in wealthier houses, from the morning room. It was usually a mixture of what one wished people to believe was part of one's ordinary life: the books, the pictures, the ornaments, the best furniture; and also the things one thought well of, but did not actually find comfortable: straight-backed chairs, vases given as gifts by relatives one could not afford to offend, books one ought to have read but never would.

Mrs Tyndale came in five minutes later. She was a slender woman with a grave, interesting face and a streak of white across the front of her dark hair. When she spoke, her voice was husky, and had a faint foreign accent he could not place. Instantly she shattered all his preconceptions.

'Good morning, Commander,' she introduced herself. 'I am Eva Tyndale. What can I do for you?'

He answered her quite candidly. 'I apologise for intruding on you, but recent events have obliged me to look into police conduct at the time of your husband's death. I am sorry to have to raise the matter again. This should have been done at the time, but it wasn't.'

She raised fine, black eyebrows. 'Recent events?'

'The death of three policemen and injury of two more in the bombing at Lancaster Gate.'

'Oh. I see.' She made a very slight gesture with one hand, inviting him to sit down. 'I have no idea how I can help. I did read enough about it to realise that they were the same men who investigated the shooting of my husband. I had assumed it was coincidence. Presumably they often work together, and their job is a dangerous one. But how does my husband's death concern Special Branch? He was killed by accident, by a young man addicted to opium, and seeking to buy it illegally. Why is Special Branch involved in that?'

'Because there is a possibility that the two events are connected,' Pitt answered levelly. 'If not in fact, then in someone's imagination.'

'My husband was there purely by mischance.' She sat in the chair opposite him, her hands folded gently in her lap, very white against the black of her dress. She was not beautiful, but there was an intensity of character in her face that held his attention, and he found it pleasing. He regretted having to ask this of her. It had to be painful.

'Mr Tyndale did not normally pass that way?' he asked.

'Seldom. He had come home and gone out again, to look for our dog, which had chased a cat and disappeared.' She took a deep breath and quite openly steadied her voice, keeping her self-control with difficulty as memory of that night returned. 'He never came back. But the dog came home an hour or two later. It has an absurdity about it, doesn't it? Life can be both tragic and ridiculous at the same time.'

'Indeed. The police record says very little about him . . .' he began.

A bitterness made her face bleak for an instant, then she mastered it. 'They asked a great deal at the time, but all in an effort to find out if he could have been the dealer in opium their trap was set to catch. Apparently that man never came . . . if he existed at all. The young man was arrested and charged with shooting my husband to death.' She twisted her hands in her lap, just a tiny movement. 'He denied it. I didn't know whether to believe him or not. I can think of no reason in the world why he would shoot James. Or the drug seller either, for that matter.' She gave Pitt a small, sad smile. 'I would have thought it far more likely he would shoot one of the policemen, or even more than one, and then make his escape. Wouldn't you?'

'Yes,' Pitt admitted. 'I found no evidence at all, but then I am on the scene a couple of years too late. I understand your husband dealt in books, Mrs Tyndale?'

'Yes, he sold rare books and manuscripts,' she replied.

Pitt had already looked around the room and seen that a once very comfortable style of life had suffered a little since Tyndale's death. There was a slight shabbiness, obvious from cushions worn and not replaced, net curtains carefully mended, the loose slate on the roof, old paint here and there, a cracked paving stone in the garden. How wide a tragedy can spin its web.

'Did Inspector Ednam, or any of his men, ask you about your husband's business, or his habits at the time? Anything about him?'

'Are you suggesting there was something to hide?' she said, almost without expression. How many times had she fended off the intrusive questions of neighbours? Why Tyndale, why not their husbands, or sons? It is easier to think misfortune is somehow deserved;, then you can make yourself safe from it.

'No, Mrs Tyndale. I am wondering if they did not ask precisely because they knew your husband's death was completely random, exactly as you said. There has been some suggestion that Lezant shot him deliberately. But since he had never met him that seems very unlikely.'

'Then why did he?' At last the pain came through her voice.

'There is a young man, another one, who says he was there also, and escaped. He claims that Lezant did not shoot your husband, but one of the police did. He always claimed so throughout the trial right until Lezant's own death, but he was not believed.'

'Except by you?' Mrs Tyndale asked, her eyes widening.

'I'm not sure,' he admitted. 'There are questions unanswered, things that don't appear to make sense, as you have pointed out.'

She looked at him steadily, and then averted her eyes. He caught the bright light for an instant on tears. Then she moved and the shadow changed.

'I would be grateful if you proved without any doubt that my husband was a chance victim, and nothing more. It is all I can do for him now.'

'Has anyone suggested otherwise, apart from the police, who are now under far closer scrutiny?'

She looked back at him. 'Those who wish to protect the police,' she answered. 'Specifically Mr Abercorn, with his letters to the newspapers. I can understand why. We all need to believe the police are strong, honest, brave, everything that will stand between us and the violence and darkness we are afraid of, whether it is real or not. We are afraid of what we hear and can't see, the images of a danger that has no recognisable shape and therefore we have no weapon against it.'

He knew exactly what she meant: immigrants, strangers, people whose ways were different, people who had nothing and therefore threatened what we had.

He spoke with her another twenty minutes, learning more of James Tyndale, and then excused himself and left. He would check everything she had said, but the more he considered it, the less did he believe that Tyndale was anything more than a bystander caught fatally in someone else's disaster.

Tellman also had read Josiah Abercorn's letter to the newspapers, and found that the man who had taken Ednam's place was in profound agreement with it.

'Thank heaven somebody's speaking out for us,' Pontefract said as Tellman closed the door behind him and sat down opposite the desk.

Tellman felt it would be foolish at this point to do anything but agree.

'Indeed.' He nodded. 'I hope that very soon this kind of defence won't be necessary.' He had felt uncomfortable reading the letter at his own breakfast table. There was an anger in it that suggested, without saying so outright, that any questioning of police morality was a sympathy with anarchists. And yet he understood that. It was his own instinctive response. He disliked change. The old values were good, familiar to everyone, proven over the years. It all came down to trust.

'We need to win the public back on our side,' he added, watching Pontefract's face. He hated having to, but he was far too good a detective to take anyone's innocence for granted. He

207

was disturbed to find that he wondered if Pontefract were involved himself, even if it were no more than to turn a blind eye, for fear of seeing something he would prefer not to, something that might require him either to be involved, or deliberately to speak out against . . . what? Bribery? Concealing a fatal crime, and sending an innocent man to the gallows? Murder?

How far had he come from just a couple of weeks ago that such a thought would even come into his mind? It made him feel chilled inside, and slightly sick.

'Of course,' Pontefract agreed. He seemed to be weighing what he would say next, searching Tellman's face. Finally he came to a decision. He leaned forward a little across the desk and lowered his voice. 'I have looked a great deal more closely at Ednam's record over the past several years. To be frank, Tellman, I've discovered a few things that are very disturbing. He seems to have been blind, perhaps intentionally, to quite a few . . . regrettable things. Mostly slight, you understand, but allowing a pattern of dishonesty to develop. I'll see that it stops. Good men, basically, but grown a little lax. We need discipline, just like anyone else.'

He looked at Tellman very steadily, trying to read his face.

Tellman was unpleasantly aware of it. Under the palliative words, there was a battle beginning. Tellman was being told to leave it alone. Should he do that? Allow the situation to heal itself? But would it? Wasn't that turning the blind eye, as he had been all along? Only now it would be worse, because he knew.

'A good man, Abercorn,' Pontefract went on. 'On our side. We need more like him. Understands the job. Not just that, he knows we are the line between safety and lawlessness. It's not Special Branch who need to enforce order, for all their responsibility for security and, I dare say, much higher pay – it's us.' He nodded. 'Got to keep public respect. I know you can see that. You've always seen it. The ordinary working man, with a family to care for, and nothing to do it with but what he earns. Duty to them. Damn Ednam and his slack ways, little lies here and there, pocketing the odd shilling to let things slip. Over-zealous in some things, too lenient in others. We'll put it right.' He stopped and waited for Tellman to reply.

The silence grew heavy.

'Glad you agree,' Tellman said at last. 'We'll have to begin with this opium dealing disaster a couple of years ago.'

Pontefract shook his head. 'Ah – no. Can't do much now. All the poor devils involved in that are dead, or as good as.' He shrugged. 'Nothing really to look into. We'll never know if Tyndale was the dealer or not, but since he's dead too, it's over with. Now – there's the matter of Trumbell and whether he lost his temper and hit . . . what was his name? Holden? Yes . . . Holden. Nasty piece of work. I think a good caution, perhaps dock a week's pay, and that'll be settled. He won't do it again. Give him a fright and show that we haven't forgotten it. What?' He smiled as if Tellman had already agreed with him. 'And keep better records of all things taken as evidence. Make sure it's double-checked, and there's a signature on everything. Carelessness, not malice, you know?'

Tellman could see by the bland smile on Pontefract's face that nothing he said was going to make any difference. The defence was prepared and he was not going to be allowed to break through it, not without injuring himself, and making enemies.

Pitt had been right. There was an ugliness here that would hurt all of them, one way or another.

Tellman persisted in listing and clarifying everything, out of stubbornness rather than belief he could win, and by the time he left for home it was dark outside. The east wind had a biting edge to it. The ice was already hard on the pavement and his weight cracked it where he stepped on shallow puddles.

He began intending firmly not to tell Gracie anything about it. However, she too had read Abercorn's letter, albeit repeated in an evening newspaper.

''E's wrong,' she said bleakly after they had finished supper and Christina had been put to bed. Tellman always liked it if he could get home in time to talk to his daughter. She listened wide-eyed, watching his face and trying to mimic him, copying his tone and now catching many of his words, even if they were ones she did not understand at all. It was an intense pleasure to him and he had been known to go and waken her deliberately, if he were home late, just for the pleasure of watching her, and seeing the recognition and the excitement in her eyes.

Tonight he had not done so. She was teething and Gracie had just settled her. She herself looked tired and worried. She picked up his moods as if she could read the thoughts written in his face, or perhaps the weariness of his step in the hall, the way he sat with his feet before the fire.

'Is he?' He was referring to Abercorn, in reply to her observation. 'If it's put right then isn't it time to forgive and move on? Maybe Ednam was the only bad apple in the barrel?'

'They in't apples,' she argued stubbornly. 'And you know that! When did you ever blame them above yer for things yer done wrong? You get 'ot enough under the collar if they take credit for what other people do right!'

That was true.

'It's not the same thing—' he began.

'In't it? Looks just the same ter me. You saying they're just like machines? Yer push this button an' this 'appens, push that one an' summink else does.'

'No, of course not! But if Ednam was bad, he's gone. I don't like Pontefract, self-satisfied . . .' He left out the word he was thinking. He was careful not to swear in front of her; he thought better of her than to do that. 'But he's right. We've got to forgive somewhere, and the sooner the better. We rely on each other. Trust men and they'll trust you. It can be hard out in the streets, Gracie.'

'I know that, Samuel,' she agreed quickly. 'An' don't think I don't worry about yer, 'cos I do. Yer can forgive someone 'oo 'urt yer yourself. Yer got the right to do that. But someone what 'urts other people, if yer the law, yer gotter draw a line an' say, "If yer do this, then it'll cost yer." If yer don't, then they know they can do anything they like, and yer won't ever do anything.' She drew in her breath. 'Yer got no right ter do that, Samuel. Yer'd be lying to everyone.'

'But—' he started.

'No!' she said hotly. 'If yer tell a child "no", but what yer doing means "yes", then they don't know what you mean. They'd stop trusting yer because yer in't telling the truth. And yer really in't protecting them the way yer promised. Yer in't leading them right. I can tell yer one thing for sure, Samuel, yer in't teaching my child that! It's wrong.'

He looked at her where she sat stiff-backed in front of him, her face set, her eyes meeting his without a flicker.

He thought for an instant of asking her if she would make exceptions for certain cases, then knew that she would not. She would tell him to say what he meant in the first place, and stick to it.

'Is it bad?' she asked when he still didn't answer.

'I think so,' he said grimly. 'There've been too many lies. They should have done something years ago. It's going to be hard . . .'

A moment of fear flickered in her eyes and her lips tightened. 'Yer'd better be careful, then, 'adn't yer!'

He kept on thinking he knew her, and she wouldn't surprise him any more, and again he was wrong.

'Have you got any cake?' he asked.

She knew she had won, and she smiled at him, taking a deep breath. She had not wanted to be right. It would have been so much easier to tell him to leave it alone.

'Yeah,' she said airily. 'I got one piece left. I'll get it for yer.'

In the morning Tellman began on other cases since the death of Tyndale, ones that Ednam had worked on, and particularly those that included Newman, Hobbs, Bossiney and Yarcombe. He had a piece of testimony that had been key to a conviction, and was returning down an alley towards his own station when he heard footsteps behind him, light and rapid, like someone attempting to catch up with him. He turned as a man bumped into him, knocking him off balance. He fell against the wall, bruising his shoulder.

He righted himself immediately, regaining his stance and ready to fight. The man stood in front of him. He was young, strong and on the balls of his feet, like a boxer.

This looked as if it were going to be ugly. He felt a sharp tingle of fear. They were alone. Tellman had learned how to defend himself. He was wiry, and very fast, but what if the man had a knife?

The man stared at Tellman unblinkingly.

'Sorry, Inspector,' he said with a very slight smile down-turned at the corners of his mouth. 'Didn't mean ter scare yer. Not a very good neighbour'ood, this. Mebbe yer shouldn't be 'ere alone, like. I'll walk yer to the main road.'

Tellman felt a sweat of relief break out on his body. He racked his memory to recall where he had seen the man. His face was vaguely familiar, but he could not place it. It was recently, and they had spoken only briefly. He knew the intonation, and the man had addressed him by rank. Had he arrested the man for something? There was challenge and dislike in his eyes.

Tellman swallowed, and calmed his breathing. 'It's not far,' he dismissed the suggestion. He did not want the man with him. More than that, he could not afford to have the man know how much he had startled him . . . no, that was less than the truth. For a moment he had been afraid. His heart was still hammering in his chest. It was a long time since he had walked the beat, aware of the dangers around him.

Now suddenly he knew who the man was: Constable Wayland, one of Whicker's men.

'No trouble, sir,' Wayland said, falling into step beside Tellman as he started to move again. 'Just make sure yer all right, sir. We gotta look out for each other, right? Even off duty . . .'

'Thank you, Constable Wayland.' Tellman forced his voice to be calm, level. Should he let the man know he had understood the implicit threat? If he didn't, then maybe it would be repeated, less pleasantly. Or was he imagining it? Making himself ridiculous, as if he had a guilty conscience?

They walked in silence along the narrow pavement, matching step for step, until they came to the main thoroughfare, and then stopped at the kerb.

'You'll be right now, sir,' Wayland said, nodding with satisfaction. 'Good day, sir.'

'Good day, Constable,' Tellman replied, and then watching the traffic carefully, he crossed the road, still uncertain, turning it over in his mind. Had Wayland done this out of concern? Or was it a warning of how easily Tellman could have been attacked, killed, without anyone knowing.

Neither was the following day a good one. He continued to look over records, find discrepancies because now that he was looking for them, there were figures that did not match, even a couple of times statements that had been altered very carefully, very cleverly. He could feel his stomach knotting as he began to appreciate how deep the corruption ran.

He met with resistance everywhere, sometimes even open dislike. One constable fetched him a cup of tea and spilled it all over his jacket and trousers.

'Oh! Terribly sorry, sir!' he said, barely concealing his smile.

It was hot, almost hot enough to scald, if Tellman had not moved quickly enough to miss most of it.

There was a snigger of amusement from one of the other men, quickly changed into a cough, then another. The two other constables in the room also began to cough, as if in a chorus.

Tellman tried to make light of it, but he was sharply aware of how much worse it could have been. He was wet from the tea, and it would be very uncomfortable, not to mention embarrassing, when it got cold. It would be obvious, all down his front, as if he had wet himself. Hotter, and it might have taken the skin off his belly. He forced the childhood memory out of his mind. It was unbearable. A wave of the old helplessness swept over him at the memory of the laughter, the mocking. He forced it away, banished. He was superior to all four of the men in this room. They were all pretending to be helpful and everyone knew they were either guilty of changing evidence or stealing money themselves, or they had turned a blind eye to whoever was.

Was his pretence not to know a mark of cowardice? They would smell fear. Bullies always did. How rash would it be to let them know he knew, face them? If he did not, was he then telling them he did not dare to?

What would Gracie think of him? What would he rather do? Face them and possibly be attacked? Or retreat, and be ashamed of himself, not be able to tell Gracie, in fact lie to her, even if only by omission?

'Don't worry about it, Constable,' he said. 'It's unimportant.' He looked the man in the eye and saw a faint flush in his cheeks. 'You seem to be afflicted with carelessness. You can't add your figures right either. There are some very odd mistakes here. Oddest thing about it is that it's always short! Never money over. Noticed that, did you?'

The constable's jaw hardened but there was fear in his eyes. 'Can't say as I did,' he answered. 'But when yer done a long day on the streets, ye're so tired yer can 'ardly see straight, an' yer feet 'urt something terrible, could be as figure work in't perfect.' He leaned forward a little too close to Tellman.

Tellman did not retreat; he stayed exactly where he was.

'Yer ever done that, Inspector? I 'spec you did, way back when you were a constable, like? When yer dealt wi' people yerself, instead o' tellin' others to. When yer broke up the fights down by the dockside, or in the dark alleys where most folk got the sense not to go.' He cleared his throat and went on. 'When yer knew that yer mates were be'ind yer? When yer'd bin in fights, got beat up, punched, sworn at, put on the ground an' kicked. An' yer never told on others, 'cos they was the ones as came an' got yer, risked their own necks ter see yer were all right!' He took a hissing breath. 'An' when yer made a mistake, they picked up after yer, and kept their mouths shut. Yer know about that, do yer? Or 'ave yer forgot, like, now as yer don't do that any more?'

Tellman felt cold right through to his bones, as if the chill came from inside himself. There was no point in saying anything to this man, was there? They both knew what was behind the argument. If you expect loyalty, then you give it . . . all the time. You don't pick and choose, do it only when it doesn't cost you.

But there was an anger in Tellman as well, a rage for what was happening to good and bad men alike. Above all for him at least there was the destruction of an ideal that mattered. It had been at the heart of his purpose since he was that boy in the playground, humiliated and needing something to believe in, to drive him forward. To get him up again when he fell, made mistakes, was too tired to think clearly.

'I understand,' he said quietly.

For an instant there was pain in the constable's eyes, and then he smothered it. 'Easy to say . . .' He forced the words through a tight jaw. 'Got children ter feed, 'ave yer?'

Tellman wanted to lie, to protect his family, then he realised how pointless that was. Anybody could find out, in moments. Now he was really afraid.

'Yes, I have,' he answered, but his voice was shaking. 'Why? Would you hurt them too, if I don't keep silent and cover for your thefts?'

The man paled. 'God in 'eaven! Wot d'yer think I am?'

Tellman answered honestly. It was too late for lies, and no one would have disbelieved him anyway. 'A man who began honest, doing a job that's hard, at times dangerous, and gets paid too little, but who was obliged to realise that he depended on the loyalty of others. In your case that price was that you turned a blind eye to corruption . . . to petty theft, the occasional lie, lost evidence, sometimes more violence than you needed. Each step leads to the next one, until you're too far in to get out again.' He looked at the pain in the man's face. 'Now tell me I'm wrong,' he went on. 'Tell me this is what you want.' He hated saying it. He knew how deeply it would cut into himself. 'Tell me this is how you want your kids to see you: a man who dishonours his job, when it gets tough. That's what you want them to be too – when it's hard, too much trouble, then cheat.'

The constable's muscles tightened, stretching the fabric of his uniform, and his fists clenched. Now there was hatred in his eyes, at Tellman, for making him see and despise himself. He struggled for words, and found none.

'You raised the question of family,' Tellman added. 'Did you think to threaten mine because someone has threatened yours?'

The man was breathing heavily, struggling with himself.

Tellman waited.

'No,' he said at last. 'No, of course not. What the 'ell do you think we are?'

'Caught,' Tellman said grimly. 'All caught.'

The man let his breath out. 'What yer going ter do, then?'

Tellman had given himself no time to think. He had to answer straight away, or he would look weak, even stupid. 'Give you the chance to put it right,' he replied. 'Whicker knows. Special Branch knows, so getting rid of us will only make it worse. Kill me, and you'll hang.'

'Gawd! Wot's yer—' He stopped. He had not even imagined such a thing, and it was clear in his face.

Neither had Tellman thought of it when he began, but now it was too obvious to evade. In minutes he had moved from petty theft, failure to report a stupid incident and have it dealt with, a disciplinary action a sergeant could have taken, a bad note on the man's record, maybe a stop of pay. Now they were talking of murder, and the gallows. How the hell had he allowed this to go so far?

Easy . . . inevitable even, if Lezant were innocent.

'You have a choice,' he said. 'But you have to make it quickly. And I'll take a constable with me, from now on, so don't get any stupid ideas.'

The constable looked like a man who had been struck from behind, and found himself on the floor, bruised and bleeding, without even knowing how it had happened.

When Tellman left that day and walked away from the station, he tried not to increase his speed. He must never let anyone see that he was afraid.

He reported it all to Pitt, not so much because Pitt needed to know, although he did, but for Tellman's own safety. And he would do as he had told them he would.

He was glad to see that Pitt appeared to be as distressed about it as he was himself. He had said that they must find the corruption, if it was there. He had even worn an expression as if he expected it, but now that it was real, it hurt him too. Disillusion was a deep and ineradicable pain, even if the beliefs had been unrealistic, taken for granted and built to protect one's own dreams.

Pitt was sent for by Bradshaw again. It was five o'clock, well after dark and the lamplight glittered on frost as the hansom pulled to the side of the road. Pitt got out and paid his fare. He walked carefully across the ice-covered pavement and up the steps. His breath was visible in the air for a moment, there and then gone again.

Upstairs in his office Bradshaw was waiting for him, standing by the window looking out at the lights of the city, the glittering reflections on the river. He turned as Pitt was shown in. He looked pale, bleached not only of colour but also of energy.

'Your man Tellman has been creating hell all over the place,' he said bitterly. 'Have you thought one step ahead of what you're doing? Have you given the consequences even a moment's consideration?'

'He's not my man, sir,' Pitt reminded him. 'He's regular police, and he hates doing this as much as any of us. But since the bombing at Lancaster Gate, there's no alternative.'

'Of course there are alternatives!' Bradshaw replied, but there was more desperation in his voice than anger. 'Get whoever did it, and put an end to this . . . witch-hunt! Ednam's dead. For God's sake, leave what's left of the man's reputation. For the police force's sake, and the man's family.'

'It's going to be very ugly.'

'Uglier than dead policemen all over the wreckage of a house, burning debris in the streets, and accusations of police corruption through half the city?' Bradshaw demanded. There was pain in his voice and in his eyes, and another thing: a shadow Pitt thought was fear.

'Yes, sir,' Pitt said quietly. 'The injuries and deaths are unchangeable. The fires are out and the debris is cleared up. The accusations are only words, so far. With care, we can settle most of them without prosecutions.'

'We've got to prosecute whoever set those bombs!' Bradshaw slashed his hand in the air to emphasise the point, and perhaps because he was so filled with unbearable tension that he needed some violent action to release even a little of it, just for a moment, before it built up again.

'Of course,' Pitt agreed. 'I meant prosecution of police who have committed theft, embezzlement, perjury and possible uncalled-for violence.'

Bradshaw closed his eyes and blasphemed under his breath.

'I meant prosecution of the bomber, you fool!' he retorted. 'You can't prosecute dead men! And so help me, Pitt, I'll have your job if you try. I have friends in high places too!'

Pitt did not resent the abuse, or even the threat. He could see that Bradshaw was a man at the end of his endurance. There seemed to be some deep and appalling pain beyond the revelation of corruption, one that he could not speak of. Why should he share it with Pitt anyway? They were not friends, were no more than professional acquaintances, and seldom met.

'Yes, sir,' he said quietly. 'And it will be public, as all court cases are, unless it involves spying, and secrets that cannot be revealed for reasons of state. To suggest such a thing as that would only make it worse – and so far as we know, it is not true. That also would come out, eventually.'

'Of course it would be public!' Bradshaw kept his voice under control only with difficulty. 'Making it public is the most important part of it! People need to believe in the police, that we are efficient and powerful and will protect them from anarchists, lunatics and random violence. Why the devil am I explaining this to you?'

Pitt felt his own muscles tightening, but the power of emotion in the other man outweighed his own. He breathed in and out slowly.

'Whoever it was had a reason, sir. The second bomb, which destroyed property but injured no one, makes it pretty clear that he intends to draw attention to something, and is prepared to go to any lengths at all to do it.'

'To the length of being hanged?' Bradshaw said with surprise.

'Yes, sir, I think so.'

There was a flicker of hope in the Commissioner.

'Is he insane? Do you know that for certain?'

'If it is who I believe, then he is addicted to opium. Do you know anything about severe opium addiction, sir?'

Bradshaw's face drained of all colour until he was ashen. For a moment Pitt thought he might actually faint. Then as Pitt took a step forward, Bradshaw straightened himself and seemed to regain his self-control.

'What . . . what are you talking about?' His voice wavered and for a moment hit a falsetto note. He cleared his throat. 'Are you saying that one or more of our men are . . . addicted . . . to opium? I doubt very much that that . . . could be true.'

Pitt struggled to keep the conversation impersonal, as if he had not noticed Bradshaw's emotion.

'No, sir,' he said levelly. 'But I think the man who set the bombs may be.'

'Opium addiction does not make a person violent, Pitt. I don't know where on earth you got that idea from. It's nonsense – dangerous nonsense. I would have thought that a man in your position would have been less . . . ignorant.' He almost spat the word. Then he seemed to regret it. 'I'm sorry . . . that was . . .'

'I am aware of the causes of opium addiction,' Pitt spoke quickly, to rescue him. 'In many cases it is medically prescribed, for severe pain. Some people can give it up easily enough when the pain is gone. Others can become addicted on a single dose. I mentioned it because I believe the bomber may be addicted, through no fault of his own.'

'It does not make people violent!' Bradshaw repeated intently, his face still almost bloodless.

Pitt's mind was whirling. Bradshaw spoke so passionately that there had to be someone he loved who had experienced addiction, or did so even now. A son, perhaps? Was he as damaged as Alexander Duncannon? It must be terrible for any parent, but for one in the police, who saw what it actually brought, not in nice clean words, but in the reality of the flesh, the real pain, the nightmares and nausea, the fears and despair, it must be even worse – if anything could be!

What was the kindest thing he could do? Say he understood? He didn't, not in more than imagination. Or pretend he had not seen? Give the man an illusion of privacy?

He must answer.

'No, sir. I think it possible that his occurred because a friend of his was victim of police corruption, or so he thought. This friend, a fellow addict, was blamed for a crime our man was certain he had not committed, but on police testimony he was tried, convicted and hanged. Our man has attempted since then to get the case reinvestigated, and no one will listen to him. At least this is his belief.'

Bradshaw cleared his throat again, as if he did not trust his voice. 'Is this . . . is this true?'

'I don't know. It is his belief. And for the purpose of driving his actions, that is all that would be necessary.'

'And he is still addicted to opium?'

'Yes. It is killing him, which he knows, so he has very little to lose.'

'Poor devil. Do you know who his supplier is?' Bradshaw's voice was not much more than a whisper.

'No. He won't tell me. I am not surprised. The man stands between him and the agony of withdrawal. I believe if it is sudden enough, in some cases it can lead to a terrible death.'

'Indeed,' Bradshaw said hoarsely. 'You cannot expect that of him.'

Pitt hesitated, looking for something to say that was not shallow, as if he had not either brain or heart. He could not help believing that Bradshaw had someone intensely close to him who was in just such a private hell.

'What are you going to do?' Bradshaw asked.

'I don't know,' Pitt answered carefully. 'First of all I must make sure that it is as I believe.'

'And if it is?'

'Arrest him. If we hold him in custody I will see that the police surgeon gives him sufficient to manage his pain. I can't leave him free, he'll bomb again. He wants us to reopen the case.'

'But you said the other man was hanged!'

'He was. Our man's whole purpose is to clear his name.'

'Who is it?'

'I'll tell you that, sir, if I am right. Until then I must save those close to him from any breath of scandal.'

Bradshaw's face was grey.

'For God's sake, be careful. Suppliers of opium, or any other drug, have no pity. They'll kill you, if you threaten them. I mean it, Pitt. They will!'

'Yes, I dare say they will,' Pitt agreed.

Bradshaw started to say something else, and then changed his mind.

Pitt ended the awkwardness by excusing himself, closing the door behind him. He walked away exhausted by the pity that had seared through him for Alexander, for his family, for Bradshaw, whom he was now certain was trapped in the same hell, unable to imagine any escape except death.

Even as he went down the steps into the street, he was aware that such grief could touch anyone. Happiness was fragile, and infinitely precious.

Chapter Eleven

THIS TIME Pitt found it even harder to contact Alexander, but it was imperative that he do so. He could not much longer put off arresting him, and when that happened he would lose the chance to question him and learn the answers to the major facts he was still missing.

Had he really tried to gain a hearing on the Lezant case, over and over, and no one had listened to him? What had been a long-simmering anger that had been consistently ignored, and what was simply his own imaginings, re-created after the bombing?

Would Alexander have used someone else's act of violence to draw the attention he had failed to get before? It was possible. Pitt needed to know. He did not expect Alexander to tell him, but if he wanted to be believed, then he would be able to give a list of the people he had spoken to, the times and places, at least roughly. Pitt could check them. An example of Alexander's handwriting could be compared with the Anno Domini notes. It all needed proving. Above all, there was the question of the identity of the supplier who had failed to turn up at the meeting where Tyndale had been shot. Why? How did Ednam even know of the proposed rendezvous? There was something major missing.

More than that, Pitt needed to find proof that Alexander really had tried to raise the Dylan Lezant case again and make someone listen to his account. He could start looking without knowing when, and to whom, but it would certainly take far longer than if Alexander told him.

And of course there were other issues to be considered all the time. Earlier on Pitt had seriously wondered if the whole matter of the bombing in Lancaster Gate were only a blind to take the attention of Special Branch away from the real issue that would then happen somewhere else, designed by cleverer anarchists than those that had already come to the notice of Special Branch. That could be anything: theft of documents, an assassination, military or industrial espionage; the list of possibilities was long.

But he believed that Alexander Duncannon was a man in extreme pain, both mental and physical, knowing he was coming towards the end of his life, and determined to clear his friend's name. And possibly even more important to him, whether he knew it or not, was to vindicate his own escape, and survival, even if it were only temporary. His name was clear of any crime, while Dylan Lezant had been hanged for murder.

Pitt found Alexander eventually, at about eleven o'clock in the evening, staggering along an alley a hundred yards from his flat. He had bumped into a lamppost and was standing, leaning against it, dazed in its ghostly light.

Pitt was tired, cold and short-tempered. It was the third time he had passed this way and he had been ready to give up and go home.

Then he saw Alexander's face and the thought of his own anger vanished. He stepped forward and took the young man by both arms, as if he expected to have to support his weight.

'Alexander!' he said. 'Alexander!'

Alexander blinked and looked at him hard for a moment before recognising him. 'Oh. It's you. What do you want now?' He sounded not aggressive, just infinitely tired.

'When did you last eat?' Pitt asked him.

'No idea. Why? Does it matter?'

Pitt did not know. Food did you little good if you could not hold it in your stomach long enough to digest it.

'Come with me,' he said firmly, as if he would not accept a refusal. 'At least get warm. There's a place along here that's open all night.'

Alexander stared at him. 'What do you want?'

'Details. I want to know all the things you did to try to make them listen to you and look further into Lezant's case.'

'Why?' Alexander stared at him, still leaning his weight against the lamppost. He blinked several times trying to focus his mind.

'I want to know who ignored you,' Pitt replied.

Alexander shrugged. 'Who gives a damn now?'

'I do.'

Alexander slumped and Pitt was obliged to hold him up so he did not slide into a heap on the pavement. He would be hard to raise up again.

'Come on!' he said sharply. 'You'll freeze out here. Come and get warm inside, and at least have a hot cup of tea.'

Alexander made an effort, and allowed Pitt to lift him. Possibly because he hadn't the energy to fight any more.

Half an hour later they were both warmed by the pleasant clatter of a café open for workers all night. They had hot, over-strong tea with too much sugar in it. Pitt all but gagged on it, but Alexander drank it without apparent awareness of its taste. He ate half a bacon sandwich, and seemed rather better for it.

He looked at Pitt curiously. He returned to the earlier subject. 'Why do you want to know so exactly? Are you going to prosecute me for it? No, of course not. It's evidence, isn't it? It gives me a motive for killing Ednam and his men. They ignored me. And if I had found proof, then they would have hanged, and not Dylan.' He blinked, knowing he had made an error. 'No . . . that's out of order, isn't it? I mean, out of sequence. I went on trying to make them listen, after Dylan's death. It's to hang me, isn't it . . . for the bombing? Give me a motive. Otherwise why would I?' He shook his head very slightly. 'No evidence. No one saw me, or you'd have arrested me already.'

Pitt looked at him across the narrow wooden table, the light coming from oil lamps set at each end. The shadows were sharp, throwing Alexander's features into an exaggerated hollowness.

Pitt smiled. 'So I would. But isn't that what you want? If not, why blow up a second building?'

'You know I did that?' Alexander's expression was unreadable. It could have been anything from irony to tragedy in his face.

'Of course. You left the handkerchief for me,' Pitt answered. 'But whatever you want, I want to know who killed Tyndale, and why. If it was accidental or deliberate, and if police knowingly sent an innocent man to the gallows.'

Alexander winced at the word 'gallows'. In that moment Pitt knew that the pain was still there, still deep, and that whatever he had done, Alexander would not stop until the truth was exposed, or he was dead, whichever came first.

He was going to die. The shadow of it was already across his eyes. Pitt stopped trying to deny it to himself, and was overwhelmed with his own anger and pity. He knew he would do anything he could to see that justice came while Alexander could still see it.

'Tell me all the people you saw,' he urged. 'Or tried to see, and how far you got with them. If possible, tell me approximately when.'

Alexander nodded, smiling, as Pitt took out his notebook and held the pencil ready.

Having had just five hours in bed altogether, Pitt woke early the next day, and after a quick cup of tea he began to visit the people whose names Alexander had given him.

The first was a man called Lessing who was in charge of the process of appeals. Pitt gained an immediate appointment because of his position, which he was more than willing to use to its utmost.

'I don't see what this has to do with the security of the nation,' Lessing said irritably. 'This office is extremely busy!'

'Then let us not waste your valuable time in explanations as to why I cannot tell you the reasons for my request,' Pitt replied with a straight face, and an equally tart tongue. 'Did Alexander Duncannon, or anyone else, ask you to look further into the circumstances of the case against Dylan Lezant?'

'It will take me some time . . .' Lessing began, his lips pursed as if in distaste.

Pitt gave him the date, and approximate time of day Alexander had said he called.

Lessing glared at him. 'It seems you already know,' he pointed out with a touch of sarcasm.

'I know what was told to me,' Pitt replied. 'I expect you to either confirm it, or deny it. Preferably with written records, which I presume you have?'

'We don't let such records out of this office.' Lessing looked at Pitt with little patience. He expected a man of Pitt's position to know that without being told.

'I want to read it, not take it!' Pitt stared at him almost unblinkingly. 'Don't waste my time or your own, Mr Lessing. Was the request made, or not?'

'We don't keep records of every frivolous request that comes to our doors . . .' Lessing began.

Pitt raised his eyebrows. 'Police corruption is not regarded as frivolous by Special Branch, Mr Lessing. Most particularly when it involves manslaughter, perjury and judicial murder. And now it would appear multiple murder in a bombing. We see it as very serious . . . indeed.'

Lessing looked pale, and furious. He had been caught off balance by what he regarded as deliberate deceit.

'It involved a rather hysterical young man accusing reputable police officers of having shot a bystander in a drug deal to which there were at least four witnesses, and the man concerned had been tried by a jury, found guilty and hanged,' he said all in one breath. 'There was nothing to investigate. And what is more, the young man complaining was clearly under the influence of drugs himself. He was staggering, slurring his words, and at times almost incomprehensible. He spoke of the dead man as if they were lovers.' He said the last word with a heavy intonation of disgust.

'I know who the complainant was.' Pitt's own voice was tight now with barely controlled rage. His own helplessness to heal pain drove his response. 'He is a young man of excellent family; his father highly respected. Unfortunately the young man suffered a severe injury from which he will never recover. Extreme pain can cause a man's behaviour to be erratic. Drugs were prescribed to him in order to make the pain bearable, at least most of the time. The hanged man was like a brother to him, a companion in suffering. Perhaps that is not something you have experienced. But it is unfortunate that you should put such an interpretation on it. It says more about you than it does about either of the young men.'

Lessing's face flamed hot with colour, but he knew better than to lose his temper with the head of Special Branch. Pitt realised that without surprise. He had seen that flicker of fear when men looked at Victor Narraway, but never recognised it so clearly with himself. It was gratifying, and alarming. Please heaven he never got used to it.

'Did you inquire into the issue?' he asked with a smile that was more a baring of his teeth.

'Of course not!' Lessing attempted to be derisive. 'The case was tried and decided.'

'I thought appeals were your business? Do you always decide ahead of inquiry that the verdict was unquestionable? Then there hardly seems any purpose to your existence!'

'Of course not! But usually it is. "Twelve good men and true" are generally right in their decisions. Do you always question the jury's verdict?' He mimicked Pitt's tone with some satisfaction.

'Yes, if it seems to make little sense,' Pitt snapped back.

'It made perfect sense,' Lessing told him. 'Lezant went to

purchase opium to feed his addiction. He intended to meet his supplier in an alley, but when he got there he found the police waiting for him. He panicked and shot at them, and unfortunately he killed a bystander. Or possibly the bystander was actually the dealer.'

'You are slandering an innocent man, Mr Lessing,' Pitt told him coldly. 'Tyndale was investigated exhaustively – I have since done so again myself – and his record is without blemish.' He was exaggerating very slightly, but he was furious with this man. There was no evidence whatever against Tyndale, but his involvement was not as impossible as Pitt was suggesting.

'All right!' Lessing said with equal anger. 'So he was merely a passer-by. So much the more tragic that Lezant should have shot him.'

'Why should he? He was in the opposite direction from the police – in fact behind Lezant,' Pitt told him.

Lessing's eyebrows shot up.

'Really? Who told you that?'

Pitt could not tell him that Alexander had.

'The evidence,' he responded. 'If you had read it you would conclude so yourself. The alley had two entrances, and a small cutting through which one might make a shortcut from the main road to where Mr Tyndale lived. He was on that cutting, making his way home.'

'How do you know?' Lessing demanded.

'I have been there and compared it with the police drawings, and their testimony,' Pitt told him. 'If you looked at it yourself, where Tyndale's body was found, and the bullet holes on the wall of the building, you would see that Tyndale was behind Lezant, but in front of all four of the police.'

'Five,' Lessing corrected.

'Four,' Pitt repeated. 'One of them, Bossiney, was not actually present. He was repeating what he was told.'

'Are you saying that five policemen lied, and one hysterical opium addict, who was not even there, is telling the truth? You're crazy! You must be on some kind of a—' He looked at Pitt's face and bit off the words he was going to say.

'If you go to the scene instead of reading other people's accounts of it,' Pitt told him very carefully and in a measured voice, 'you will see that what the police say doesn't make any sense. And Alexander Duncannon says he was there. In fact he had the money to make the opium purchase.'

'He said so?'

'Yes.'

'And of course you believe him!' Now Lessing's voice was derisive again. 'Isn't that a little . . . gullible . . . sir?'

'Well, Lezant didn't have it,' Pitt pointed out. 'His possessions were carefully listed when he was arrested, on the spot! The gun, a pocket handkerchief, one pound, seventeen shillings and six pence in change. No money to buy opium, and no opium itself. If there was no one else there, no dealer, no companion, where was the money, or the opium?'

'Tyndale . . .' The moment he has said it Lessing realised his error.

'Really?' Pitt widened his eyes in amazement. 'Did he have the opium, or the money, or both? I wonder why it never turned up. And the police failed to mention it. You did not see fit to inquire into that, I see.'

Lessing was fuming, but the point was just.

'I have no idea. It was two years ago now. Mistakes happen now and then . . .' he protested.

'Resulting in a man being hanged?' Pitt let all his sarcasm show. 'That's rather more than a "mistake", Mr Lessing. I think you owe a considerable accounting as to why you did not examine it at the time.'

Lessing's mouth drew into a thin, hard line. 'Well, if their lordships request it, no doubt we will do what we can,' he said grimly. 'In the meantime, I have other work to do.'

Pitt made a note on the bottom of his page, and closed his notebook. 'Indeed, as have I,' he answered with a bleak smile. 'Quite a lot of it!'

Pitt went to see all of the people Alexander had listed in his attempt to get anyone at all to reconsider Dylan Lezant's case. Few of them were as hostile as Lessing, but the pattern was all the same in the end.

'I felt sorry for him,' Green, the clerk at Lezant's lawyer's chambers said sadly. 'He seemed a decent young man, terribly cut up about his friend's death, and sure that he was innocent.' He shook his head. 'Hope if I'm ever in trouble I have a friend as loyal. But there wasn't anything we could do. He offered to pay us all he had, which was considerable. But there really were no grounds for appeal. I wish there had been. I would like to have helped him, simply because he was so desperate.'

'There was no merit to the case?' Pitt pressed.

'Morally, perhaps,' Green conceded. 'But legally not. Once a man has been convicted, there has to be a fault in the way the case was conducted, which there was not, or some overwhelming new evidence, which also there was not. I'm sorry.' He looked as if it grieved him. Pitt wondered how many desperate relatives he had had to turn away, people who could not bear to believe that one of their own, a husband, a son, even a wife, could be guilty of a crime so grave they would pay for it with their lives.

All the accounts, compassionate or not, sad or dismissive, even angry, when put together painted a picture of a lonely young man, idealistic, emotional, and in both physical and mental pain, driving himself to exhaustion in the effort to save his friend. And after Lezant's death, he strove at least to retrieve his reputation.

Every name and office that Alexander had given him, Pitt checked and found that he had been there, and in one manner or another had been turned away. Everyone had been either unwilling or unable to help. No one had taken it higher. No one had felt the need to reconsider the issue or question the police report.

Should they have questioned further, re-examined the facts, questioned the witnesses again? Lessing, definitely. He had chosen to believe the easiest account, and ignore the inconsistencies. At the other end of the spectrum, Green had regretted the fact that he could do nothing. The loopholes were with the police, possibly with the conduct of the case, but not with the law itself.

By the end of the third day Pitt was sitting beside the fire in his own parlour, weighing up all he knew. It had begun at the level of the five police: Ednam, Newman, Hobbs, Yarcombe, and then Bossiney. It had been covered up by those immediately above, and seriously questioned by no one.

Where else was such a thing happening? That was a question he would much rather not have to ask, but it was now unavoidable.

He was thinking of this when there was a knock on the front door. Since Charlotte was upstairs talking to Jemima, Pitt answered and found Jack Radley on the doorstep. He was wearing a heavy winter overcoat and yet his shoulders were hunched, spoiling his usual highly fashionable appearance.

Pitt let him in, took his coat and hung it in the hall, then invited him into the parlour. He offered him whisky rather than tea, but Jack declined it anyway. He sat in Charlotte's chair by the fire, his feet close to the hearth. He came straight to the point of his visit.

'You'll remember that I have been working with Godfrey Duncannon on this contract for a British free port on the China coast . . .?' he began.

Pitt nodded without interrupting.

Jack smiled with bleak humour. 'I haven't forgotten my past misjudgements of character. Only a fool gets caught in the same mistake twice, and I would expect to be thrown out if I do it again. It may be totally trivial, and I'm being too easily alarmed.

I suppose that's as bad a fault in the opposite direction. But there are small things that worry me. If I speak to you, is it in confidence?'

Pitt could see the tension in him, very little hidden by his attempt at lightness.

'Of course it is. But if I have to act, I can't guarantee that no one will guess my source. What is it that disturbs you?'

'Emily noticed it before I did,' Jack said almost as an apology. 'Duncannon and Josiah Abercorn are both very keen for this contract to succeed, for different reasons. For Duncannon it would be the crowning achievement of his career. For Abercorn, who is at least twenty years younger, it would be an investment that would probably make his fortune for the rest of his life, and guarantee his political career, with a good deal of independence. He's well on the way to getting a safe seat in Parliament.'

Pitt was puzzled. 'You don't need Emily to tell you that. What bothers you?'

Jack looked down at his hands. 'I used to think that it was just a difference in age, and social background. Abercorn has no family to speak of, only a mother, who is now dead . . .'

'The point, Jack.' Pitt reminded him.

'Abercorn hates Duncannon.' He raised his head again. 'Hate is a very extreme word, but I mean it. Emily just noticed it, but once she told me, I could see it in small things. It sounds petty, but it builds up. A tone of voice, a facial expression when he assumes no one is looking at him, double-edged remarks that seem civil until you realise the alternative meaning. I thought at first that he was just less sophisticated with words, until I caught the look in his eyes, the slight sneer, gone the instant he knows you are looking at him. I know, it sounds absurd. But Abercorn knows I've seen it, and now he avoids me, and he's much more careful when the three of us are in the same discussion.'

'Is Duncannon aware of it? Does he feel the same?'

Jack smiled. 'Godfrey Duncannon really doesn't care what

anyone else thinks of him, as long as they do what he wishes. And Abercorn is certainly doing that, at least at the moment.'

'People dislike each other for all sorts of reasons,' Pitt pointed out. 'Could it be a debt? A woman? Could Duncannon have done something as simple as blackball Abercorn from some club he wants to, or needs to be, a member of? People can care passionately about these things. It matters a lot to a social or political career. And usually those two are linked. They shouldn't be, but they are.'

'Not dislike, Thomas,' Jack corrected. 'I wouldn't give a damn about that. I don't trust Abercorn. There's malice in him, a deep pain. I can't help thinking he knows something about Duncannon that I don't, and when it suits him, he's going to use it. I would love it if you could tell me for certain that I'm wrong.'

'What are you afraid of, Jack? Specifically?'

Jack took a deep breath. 'That Abercorn knows something about these bombings, and he'll produce it when it can most damage Duncannon.'

'Alexander's guilty,' Pitt said quietly. 'But I think you already know that as well as I do. Isn't that why you asked me to delay arresting him until the contract is signed?'

'Yes. But my fear is that it goes deeper than that; I'm not sure how. Abercorn is championing the dead police as the victims of anarchy and lawlessness. He's calling for revenge on those who were putting anyone at risk by attacking the very defence against crime that everyone relied on. Some of his most outspoken remarks even suggest that to fail in support for the law, and those who represent it, is to invite anarchy, even to give support to revolution.

'In one article he says that the specific duty of Special Branch is to safeguard the security of the Crown, and the nation,' Jack continued. 'He asks if you are involved in the Lancaster Gate bombing case precisely because that, through attacking the police, both violently with murder and insidiously by speaking of corruption, there is a thinly veiled prologue to revolution by violence. He likens it to the revolution that all but destroyed France in 1789.'

'For heaven's sake—' Pitt began.

But Jack overrode him. 'The fact that we are now at the beginning of the last year of this century was not lost on most of his readers,' he added. 'There are more than enough eccentrics, even lunatics, predicting the end of the world, without men otherwise respected adding to the hysteria. Be realistic, Thomas. Men don't invest fortunes if they don't expect to gain something from it, either even more money, or value of some other sort. Are you sure Alexander committed this atrocity? Absolutely sure . . . and on his own?'

'Yes, I am.'

'Why? Because he's dissolute, and addicted to opium? Not all opium addicts are violent.' Jack leaned forward earnestly. 'He lost his way – no one is arguing that – but he's a decent man, underneath the eccentricity, and the pain. Perhaps he got in with some bad people. Godfrey says Lezant was a pretty good rotter. Considering what happened to him, that much seems unarguable. He must have been off his head with the opium, or why else would he have shot a completely innocent passer-by?'

'Is that what Godfrey Duncannon says?' Pitt was curious. He had not spoken to Alexander's father, nor did he intend to, on that subject. According to Alexander, Godfrey knew very little of the incident in particular, or of Alexander's life in general. 'Easiest thing to blame the friend,' he agreed. 'I might do the same, if it were my son. It's not what Alexander himself says.'

Jack shook his head sharply. 'For heaven's sake, Thomas! He's a quixotic young man, severely injured in an accident and all his future blighted by pain. Like a lot of us, he formed some strange and unfortunate friendships. It happens, especially to those who don't have to work for a living, or support a family. He's lonely, shut out of the sort of career and society he would have had if

235

he were able to follow in his father's steps. Unfortunately he fell in with a really bad one in young Lezant.'

There was some truth in what Jack said, but only a little, and even that was irrelevant now.

'Whether Lezant was guilty or not doesn't change anything if Alexander set the bomb in Lancaster Gate,' Pitt pointed out. 'Yes, he is young and quixotic. He was over-loyal. He refuses to believe that Lezant was guilty. Have you considered the possibility that he was actually there, and he saw what happened? Maybe he isn't guessing. Perhaps he *knows* that Lezant wasn't guilty. Then trying to save him wasn't quixotic. It was simply the decent thing to do.'

'Lezant was tried and convicted,' Jack argued.

'And juries are infallible?'

'Do you think this one was wrong? Come on, Thomas! Five police, all lying? Two opium addicts, one of whom probably wasn't even here! Who do you believe?'

'There is police corruption, Jack, and it's a lot deeper than I thought.' It hurt to have to say that.

'To the level of shooting a bystander then lying to get another man hanged for it?' Jack said with open disbelief.

'Yes, it looks that way,' Pitt replied. Then a sudden weariness overtook him, filling him with grief. 'It's more than that, Jack, it's a creeping dishonesty. This didn't happen suddenly. Good men don't turn bad overnight. There were small thefts, a few shillings here and there: lies to cover a man's incompetence, absence without explanation, being drunk on duty, losing evidence, threatening a witness, turning a blind eye when it suited them, using more violence than necessary to arrest someone, or get a statement. None of them alone is terrible, but added up, they are. And, in this case, it looks as if someone lost his self-control, panicked, and then found he'd shot Tyndale, the passer-by. The only way out of it was to arrest Lezant, put the gun next to him, and say that Tyndale either was the dealer, or Lezant thought he was.'

'Why the hell would Lezant shoot his own dealer?' Jack asked.

236

'He wouldn't. He didn't,' Pitt agreed.

'Where was Alexander?'

'They both ran for it, he was faster and got away. Or perhaps Lezant deliberately covered for him. It would explain even more powerfully why Alexander is willing to pay such a high price to clear Lezant's name. From all I can find, he tried to his wits' end to clear Lezant at the time. Nobody believed that Alexander was even there.' He disliked what he said next, but he still said it. 'I don't think Lezant's father was anyone of note. Godfrey Duncannon certainly is. Perhaps no one wanted to lay the blame at that door, if they could find an easier one. Alexander would hate him for that.'

A sudden tightness filled Jack's face, then with an effort he dismissed it. 'I . . . don't know,' he confessed, the conviction suddenly seeping out of him.

But it was too late. 'Yes, you do,' Pitt told him. 'I've watched Alexander's face when his father's name is mentioned. He may well suspect that he got off because of his father's name, even if Godfrey never actually said anything. If you're powerful enough, you don't have to.'

There were several conflicting emotions in Jack's face. A momentary tenderness was replaced by anger, then guilt. Was he thinking of his daughter, Evangeline, so like Emily, so quick, so admiring of her father? What would Jack do to save her, if he had to?

What would Pitt do to save his children? How can you ever know, unless you are tested?

'I'm sorry, Jack,' Pitt said gravely. 'If I have to arrest Alexander, then I will do. He wants a trial. He's dying and he knows it. That's why he did all this. It's not revenge; it's to force us to look at Lezant's case again!'

Jack's face was racked with pity, but it did not change his mind.

'I understand that, Thomas, but it doesn't change my fear that Abercorn has something planned against Godfrey. He might even be going to try to implicate him in the bombings . . . I don't know. I would like to say Godfrey might try to save Alexander, but I don't believe that myself. I've tried to find out more about Abercorn, but I can't discern anything except a hard-working mother, no apparent father. Birth certificate simply says 'deceased'. He looks to be illegitimate, but that's irrelevant to this. From what little I can learn, his mother was a decent enough woman who may have anticipated marriage, and then had the misfortune for her would-be husband to be killed just before the wedding. I don't want to crucify her for that, for God's sake! Half the aristocracy sleeps around where they shouldn't. And believe me, I know that. I've been to enough country house weekends. Lots of lordships' children are not who they think they are.'

Pitt looked at Jack's face, the humour in it, and behind the charm, the deep anxiety, almost fear.

'I'll see what I can find out,' he promised. 'Special Branch doesn't know Abercorn, except what the general public know. But Narraway might know something personally. There's a lot that isn't committed to paper.'

The tight muscles loosened and Jack suddenly sat easily in his chair. 'Thank you,' he sighed. 'I . . . appreciate that. If it turns out to be nothing, I apologise.'

Pitt smiled back at him. He did not think it would be 'nothing'.

Pitt got up early the next morning, and had a snatched breakfast in the kitchen while Minnie Maude prepared for the day. She had already cleaned out the stove, boiled the kettle for him and stirred the porridge. Now she was encouraging the old embers to catch the new coal and burn up ready to cook for the rest of the family.

He thanked her and ate the porridge quickly. He would far rather have stayed and eaten properly, with the rest of the family. Stoker had been on watch all night, but there was no guarantee that Alexander would remain at his parents' home, where he was currently staying, beyond eight or nine o'clock.

Charlotte was standing at the bottom of the stairs, holding her dressing gown around her to keep warm.

'Are you sure you want to arrest him at his parents' home?' she asked anxiously. 'This early his father will be there. He won't make it easy for you.'

'I know that.' He touched her arm gently. 'But at least he will be there to be some support to his mother. If I wait it will look as if I've deliberately done it behind Godfrey's back. I can't afford to leave it, Charlotte. He's very likely to do something more, and there could be someone else killed.'

'I know . . . I know.' She was arguing for no reason, and they both understood that. She just could not accept it easily. Silence might imply consent.

He kissed her, then, without looking back, put on his coat. He added a thick scarf, which was definitely unfashionable, but was a remembrance of the old days when he was simply a policeman, and he did not have to think more than superficially about politics. He jammed his hat on at an unintentionally rakish angle, and went outside.

The traffic was beginning to get heavy, but even so, he arrived at the Duncannons' house far sooner than he wished. But it was a delusion to think that he would ever be sufficiently prepared for the emotional tragedy that was about to play out.

He found Stoker tired and cold about fifty feet away from the house, half-sheltered from sight by a tree.

'Still there,' he said quietly as Pitt came up to him. 'We going to take him? Will two of us be enough?'

'Yes. He wants to go . . . poor devil,' Pitt said quietly. 'Come on. Let's get it over.'

The butler looked startled to see him, especially with Stoker at his back. Pitt did not expect violence, least of all from Alexander, but he would be a fool if he did not prepare for the possibility.

'Good morning, sir?' the butler said coolly. It had been a footman who answered the door when Pitt came here on Boxing Day. Pitt did not look like the usual kind of gentleman who called on Godfrey Duncannon. His hat was too casual, the scarf was a disaster. What kind of man wore such a thing? He did not notice Pitt's beautiful boots, which were an indulgence he had continued ever since the first expensive pair he had been given. A policeman is on his feet too much to ill-treat them.

'Good morning,' Pitt replied. He put his card on the silver tray in the butler's hand. It carried his rank in a discreet print that was nevertheless highly legible. 'I require to see Mr Godfrey Duncannon and Mr Alexander on business that cannot wait. If you would be good enough to present my card . . .? I will wait in the morning room. Sergeant Stoker will wait in the hall.'

The butler blinked. Clearly he considered arguing, and then thought better of it. He pulled the door wider open and allowed them both inside. The house was old and long cared-for with both money and dedication. At another time Pitt would have admired the carved mahogany balustrade and the portraits on the walls. Today he thought only of what was ahead of them.

He was shown to the morning room, which was cold because the fire had barely caught. The dark wood panelling and the green leather furniture made it feel even colder. It was early in the new year, and the cheer of Christmas had already faded.

Pitt stood as the minutes ticked by. Did Duncannon already know why he was here? Surely he must. An escape would be an undignified admission of guilt. The newspapers would make a far bigger issue of it. This was as discreet as it was possible to be.

Finally Godfrey Duncannon came in and closed the door behind him. He faced Pitt grimly, his skin pale and papery, his thick hair immaculate, but somehow looking lifeless.

'I understand you wish to see me, Commander Pitt,' he said, meeting Pitt's eyes unflinchingly. 'It must be urgent indeed for you to interrupt breakfast. You had better tell me what it is you wish.'

Could he really be so unaware? Or did he know, and he was playing out the charade to the bitter end?

'I know it is early,' Pitt replied. 'I considered waiting until later in the day, but I thought it the better thing to do while you were at home, and able to offer your wife some comfort, and decide in private what steps you wish to take.'

'Regarding what, for heaven's sake? Spit it out, man!'

'I have come to arrest Alexander for the bombing in Lancaster Gate, and the resulting deaths of three police officers, and the serious injury of two more.'

Duncannon stared at him. He stood absolutely motionless, and the last vestige of colour drained from his skin. In that moment Pitt had the wild idea that he had actually never considered this possibility. Had he refused to acknowledge it? Or imagined that Alexander would not be charged?

'That . . . is . . . that is absurd!' he said at last. 'Why on earth would my son do such an appalling thing?' His voice shook. 'The idea is preposterous! Is this some political ploy to stop the contract going through? Is that what you're after? Who's behind it?'

Pitt was embarrassed for him. He was making a fool of himself.

'I very much hope the contract does go through, sir,' he said gravely. 'But whether it does or not, I can no longer put off arresting your son for the Lancaster Gate bombing.'

'Why on earth would he do such a thing? You are making yourself ridiculous!' Duncannon tried one more time.

'To draw attention to police corruption the only way he knows how,' Pitt replied. 'No one would listen to him—'

'For God's sake!' Duncannon's rage exploded at last. 'He's addicted to opium, man! He's off in a fairy land of his own! He can't face it that his friend, what's his name – Lezant – was guilty. He can't bear to think it. He needs rest, in a hospital of some sort.'

'That might have been an excellent idea a few months ago,' Pitt agreed. 'It's too late now—'

'You've got your facts twisted,' Duncannon cut across him. 'Taking the easiest answer. It's anarchists of some sort, whom you damned well should have found. The city is full of them.' He turned towards the door.

'Sir! I intend to arrest him. We can either do this in a discreet way, or you can make an incident out of it, and I shall be obliged to do it by force. I don't think that is what you wish, for your son or for your wife.'

Duncannon's eyebrows shot upwards. 'Are you threatening me, sir?'

Pitt hated doing it. He could imagine how he might have felt if someone had come to arrest Daniel. But he would not be bluffed.

'If you wish to look at it that way, then yes, sir, I am. The law applies to your family just as it does to any other man's. I give you the courtesy of doing it in private, and in your presence. I could as easily have waited until he left, and arrested him in the street.'

'You are a disgrace to your service, sir!' Duncannon spat the words, but he snatched the handle and flung the door open. He turned back and looked at Pitt disdainfully. 'Then you had better come and arrest my son in the dining room where he and his mother are having breakfast. I trust you will not expect me to offer you tea?'

Pitt did not reply. He followed Duncannon across the hall, nodding to Stoker as he went, and then into the dining room.

Cecily Duncannon was sitting at the foot of the table, Alexander beside her. He looked gaunt and very pale, but he faced Pitt without surprise. If he was afraid, now that the moment had come, he did not show it. He rose from his seat slowly, swayed for an instant, then straightened himself.

'I imagine you have come for me at last,' he said to Pitt. 'I am obliged that you did it here, and not somewhere more comfortable for you. Now we will all know at the same moment. Perhaps not easier, but then nothing would make it easy, but at least discreet. My father can pretend it was simply a social call . . . a little early in the day.' He made a good attempt at a smile.

'You are not going with them, Alexander,' Duncannon said firmly. 'We will contact Studdert, and then go in at our leisure.'

Alexander looked past his father towards Pitt. 'Studdert is our family solicitor. I don't wish to consult him. Mr Pitt and I already understand each other. Thank you, Father, but I will take care of my own affairs.' He moved away from the table just as Cecily stood up also. She did not look confused, only desperately unhappy. Pitt was certain in that moment that she already knew how this would have to end. Indeed, she too had been expecting it.

'Do what you must, Alex,' she said gently. 'But know that whatever happens, I love you.'

For a moment Alexander swayed and Pitt was afraid he was going to collapse. Then he straightened himself, but did not trust his voice. He touched his mother, brushing the side of her cheek with his finger, and then turned to Pitt. 'I am ready.'

'Nonsense!' Duncannon interrupted. 'You will do as I tell you, Alexander. You are in no state to represent yourself.' He gestured towards Pitt without looking at him. 'This man is trying to say that you are guilty of the murder of three policemen. For God's sake! Don't you understand that if they find you guilty they'll hang you!' He all but choked on the word, and he was struggling for breath.

Alexander raised delicate black eyebrows. 'You mean like they hanged Dylan? Yes, I know that, Father. Perhaps I know more about it than you do. They assured me that actually when you get as far as having the rope around your neck, it's quite quick. The only difference is that Dylan was innocent. I am not.'

'How dare you say that in front of your mother?' Duncannon's voice was high with fury.

Pitt had seen it before. Rage was less painful than fear, and far easier to own.

For an instant Alexander's face filled with scorn.

'You think I should protect her? From what? Reality? She's always faced reality, Father. It's you who doesn't. She knew my back would never heal. She never said so, but she knew. She knew the time would come when I couldn't take the pain and I'd go back to the opium. She sold her diamonds to get it for me. She believed me that Dylan was innocent. You can't protect her from the truth now, and I don't think you ever did!' Without waiting for his father to react, he moved away from the table and walked towards Pitt. He held out his hands, palms down, wrists very slightly exposed from his white shirt cuffs.

'That's not necessary,' Pitt told him. 'But it is very cold outside. I think you should have your butler bring your coat.'

Alexander made an attempt at the ghost of a smile. '"If it were done when 'tis done, then 'twere well it were done quickly",' he quoted, then he walked beside Pitt and into the hall. Not once did he look back.

It was late afternoon and already hastening towards dusk when Pitt was sent for to Bradshaw's office. The lampposts were a curving chain of lights along the river's edge and the wind was blowing hard from the east.

'What the hell are you playing at?' Bradshaw demanded the moment Pitt had closed the office door. 'Release Duncannon immediately. If you have to say anything at all to the press, and avoid it if you can, tell them he was helping you with reference to an old case. Let them assume what they like. I'd have thought you'd have had the sense to realise that you cannot arrest him until this . . . this damned contract is agreed. It may well be no more than a few days. Whatever possessed you to do it today? And at his father's home, for God's sake!'

Pitt was tired and cold, and he had hated arresting Alexander. The young man had trusted him, perhaps for all the wrong reasons. Alexander was searching for justice, and he might well have had no idea what it was going to cost him. Pitt was not even sure if he was completely sane. Perhaps pain, the opium, and grief over the friend he had in his own mind let down had robbed him of balance.

'For precisely the reasons you mentioned,' he answered, leaving off the courtesy of calling him 'sir'. They were of equal enough rank, extraordinary as that seemed to Pitt. 'I went there discreetly and his parents were present so they did not have to be informed.'

'What did you charge him with?' Bradshaw asked.

'Murder. Three policemen are dead.'

Bradshaw sat down very slowly. He looked exhausted, as if he were facing defeat after a long battle. 'Why now? Why couldn't you have waited?' It was a cry of despair, not accusation.

'Because he was trying to be arrested,' Pitt replied, sitting down in the chair opposite the desk. 'He let off the second bomb because we took too little notice of the Lezant case after the first. I couldn't afford to leave him free to do it again.'

'Are you so sure, Pitt?'

'Yes, I am. He left his monogrammed handkerchief for me at Craven Hill.'

Bradshaw put his elbows on the desktop and his head in his hands. 'Oh God! But you're still going to have to let him go.'

'Why? He's guilty, and he doesn't deny it. He refused to have his father's lawyer represent him.'

'He's out of his mind.' Bradshaw's voice dropped even lower. 'Opium addiction does that to you in the later stages. It's . . . a very slow and terrible death.'

Pitt heard the pain in Bradshaw's voice; saw the beaten, aching slump in his shoulders. He was speaking of a terrible pain that he was enduring himself. Pitt realised this as profoundly as he was aware of the quiet room around him, the lamplight and the wind loudly rattling the windows.

He stared beyond Bradshaw at the photograph in the alcove, the one of his lovely wife, who looked so happy. It would be cruel, inexcusable to ask if she was the addict he referred to. Was she still alive? Disintegrating in front of him, like Alexander Duncannon? Had she also suffered some agonising disease from which there was no escape but death?

'Sir,' Pitt began almost gently, 'I have to arrest him. If I don't, he'll blow up something else, and there may be other people dead. We were lucky last time. He got it right, and destroyed an empty building.'

Bradshaw raised his head and stared at Pitt.

Pitt did not say anything more.

Bradshaw pushed his hand through his hair. 'I thought you were going to say that Josiah Abercorn was crucifying us in the papers, and we have to do something.'

'Damn Abercorn!' But Pitt knew that what Bradshaw said was true. Every day there were more letters, more articles by people agreeing with him. They defended the police, the good, honest men who risked their lives every day to protect the public from the violence and pain of crime. 'Now there are questions in the newspapers as to why we aren't doing anything. Put up by Abercorn, no doubt!'

Pitt did not often swear, but he felt like it now – except that to give in to fury was just the reaction men like Abercorn counted on. It was an admission of defeat.

'By-election coming up soon, is there?' he said bitterly.

Bradshaw looked at him. 'I suppose it's obvious, isn't it? There are times when I hate politicians, Lords or Commons.'

'"A plague on both your houses",' Pitt replied with a twisted smile. 'Do you still want me to release Duncannon?'

Bradshaw's voice was very quiet, and he looked away, as though the words were forced out of him. He did not meet Pitt's eyes. 'Yes. For the time being. But put a watch on him. For God's sake don't let him blow up anything more.'

Bradshaw stood up, moving stiffly, as though his body ached. 'Was there police corruption?' he asked.

'Yes, sir. Ednam and his immediate men, at the least. Probably more,' Pitt replied.

Bradshaw winced as if he had felt a sudden stab of pain, and there were tears in his eyes. 'Let Alexander go anyway.'

Pitt kept his word to Jack. He went straight from Bradshaw's office to Vespasia and Narraway's home. He considered speaking to Narraway alone, then realised how foolish that was. Vespasia might well know more rumour about Josiah Abercorn than he did, certainly more personal gossip, which frequently was the first step towards the truth, however unwelcome.

He sat beside the fire in Vespasia's great sitting room.

'Highly ambitious,' Narraway answered Pitt's questions. 'And a man who likes to owe no one anything, so if he has accepted favours, and few people attain high office without, he will be as quick to pay them off as he can.'

'Godfrey Duncannon?' Pitt asked.

'I doubt it. I've never known Godfrey to act except in his own ultimate interest.'

'You don't like him,' Pitt observed, and saw Vespasia smile.

'Not a lot,' Narraway admitted. 'But he is exceptionally competent, and I know nothing to his discredit. He's just . . . chilling.'

'Invulnerable,' Vespasia said quietly.

Both Pitt and Narraway looked at her curiously.

'You do not like a man who is invulnerable,' she said to Narraway.

A shadow passed across Narraway's eyes, a moment's hurt.

'Do I always have to have power?' he asked very softly.

She reached over and put her slender fingers on his arm.

'Not at all, my dear. It is not his weakness you need; it is the humility it brings, and the understanding of others. Without such things he is no use to any of us, ultimately, least of all himself.'

Narraway put his hand over hers, and said nothing.

Pitt knew he had witnessed a very private moment, of both

247

pain and joy. He had never imagined such raw vulnerability in Narraway, or imagined him so intensely human after all.

Vespasia looked back at Pitt. 'Godfrey married Cecily for her money, you know. There was a very great deal of it, and he has multiplied it many times.'

'Are you sure?'

'On both counts. I am perfectly sure. The enlarging of her fortune, now his, is common knowledge, but you can easily check it, if you wish.'

'No . . . that he married Cecily for her money. Does that have anything to do with Abercorn?'

Vespasia's smile was extremely sad. 'Of course it has, Thomas. It was Abercorn's mother Godfrey Duncannon jilted to do it.'

Pitt and Narraway both stared at her, and neither of them spoke.

Chapter Twelve

TELLMAN HUGGED his daughter so tightly she giggled, then gave a little squeak of protest. He let her go, reluctantly. For him Christina was still a kind of miracle, and her laughter touched him so deeply he was a little embarrassed by it.

He tickled her gently, and pulled faces at her, just to hear her laugh again. He kissed Gracie softly and more lingeringly than he had done for some time, then he went out of the front door and walked off down the road without looking back at them. Perhaps they were not at the window any longer, but if he turned round and saw them, he would remember all the things that mattered to him, and he might lose his resolve to follow the story of Ednam's corruption to the very end.

Someone was protecting Ednam, someone far more powerful than he was. There had to be a reason. He had to think more clearly, imagine all the possibilities, even the ones most morally or emotionally painful to him.

If Lezant were innocent, what were all the things that followed from that? It was what Pitt was thinking, which was why they had quarrelled. Tellman had refused to follow that path of thought, because of where it would lead. It was time to face the truth.

He crossed the street and carried on along the icy pavement, his collar turned up against the wind, although he was so deep in thought he was barely aware of it.

Why would Lezant have taken a gun? He bought opium regularly.

It was an arrangement both he and the supplier needed. Neither of them would jeopardise it. Tellman wished the police had been able to find the supplier. There were plenty of records of Ednam trying at the time, but whoever it was had been too careful and too clever for them.

Or had Ednam not tried at all, because he did not need to? Was it possible that he knew? That was a hideous thought. Tellman racked his brain for some reason why it could not be true. He found none.

If protecting the seller of opium were Ednam's real corruption, it would explain why they had never found the man; why, in fact, the seller had not turned up at the arranged place at all that fateful day. Ednam had warned him before the ambush was ever laid!

But why had Ednam, or any of his men, brought a gun? Who had they meant to shoot? Not the dealer. Then it could only be either Alexander or Lezant. Or did they fear some third person turning up, and then mistaken Tyndale for him?

Neither Lezant nor the supplier would have wanted a confrontation. Had they known of it they would simply have chosen another place – or waited for a better time, even a different day.

Ednam would not want to capture them, but what of the other men – Hobbs, or Newman perhaps? Shooting would be the final solution, arrest and information would have been better. Where had Ednam obtained the gun? No official source had admitted giving it to him. And if he were really in the pay of the seller, then he could not afford the risks carrying a gun entailed.

Tellman loathed even the thought of it – but it fitted all the facts he knew.

Damn Ednam!

The first thing to do was look more closely at the exact record of the gun; even better, to find it in the evidence of the case. An exact description of it would be necessary, its make, calibre and so on. Then he could check back through all records to see if such a gun had ever been taken into police possession as evidence. Guns were rare in towns, especially handguns. Shotguns were common enough in the countryside. Most farmers had at least one, more likely several.

At the station he was greeted with some irritation by Whicker.

'What is it now?' he said, looking up at Tellman standing in front of him. His face was pinched and his skin had the pallor of a man who had lost too much sleep and shaved with more haste than care.

'I need to see the gun Lezant used to shoot Tyndale,' Tellman replied.

Whicker's anger was instant. 'Whatever for?' he demanded. 'Damn waste of time. Haven't you got anything useful to do? How about finding the bloody lunatic who killed three of our best men? Or is that too much for you?'

'I want to do more than catch him,' Tellman replied grimly, keeping hold of his temper with some effort. 'I'd like to make sure there's no question about him doing it. I want a clear chain of evidence right from beginning to end. Isn't that what you want?'

Whicker was taken aback. Obviously he had not expected a complete and slightly aggressive answer. It caught him off balance.

'Thank you,' Tellman said, as if Whicker had agreed. It was neatly done, but it gave him no comfort. He did not like being at odds with another man in the force. They should be on the same side.

The sergeant at the evidence room made heavy weather of it. He did not like men from other stations re-examining old cases. Had Tellman not outranked him, he would have questioned what he wanted it for. As it was, he moved with unnecessary deliberation while Tellman moved from one foot to the other and finally paced the floor. He took a full half-hour to report that it appeared to have been mislaid. He could not say when, or by whom, and smiled at Tellman as if that were an achievement.

Tellman felt his temper slipping. If he lost it he would have given victory to the sergeant.

'Then I'll have to make do with second best,' he said levelly. 'Look at your records and tell me when it was first logged in, who by, and connected with what crime.'

'I don't know that I can do that, sir. Take me a long time. I got other things to do.' He looked at Tellman blandly.

'Then you'd better get on your knees, praying that it doesn't turn up in another crime, hadn't you!' Tellman snapped back. 'Since it was last in your keeping, you'll be the first on our list of suspects.'

The blood ebbed out of the sergeant's face like a receding tide. 'Things get lost! People take 'em out an' don't bring 'em back!'

'Didn't give it away to someone, did you? Sell it, maybe?' Tellman suggested.

'Of course I didn't!' There was now a fine sheen of sweat on the sergeant's skin. 'You can't say that!'

'Then show me the records,' Tellman insisted. 'Unless you've been told not to by someone? Who would that be? Ednam's dead. Who else needs to cover it up?'

The sergeant gasped. 'I'll get what we 'ave.' Before Tellman had to argue any further, the man turned away from the counter where they had been speaking, and disappeared into another room.

Tellman waited a full quarter of an hour before the sergeant came back, carrying two large ledgers in his arms. He set them down on the countertop.

'There you are, sir. You'll find them all under the correct dates.' He clearly was not going to assist any further, so Tellman took them from him and started to search for himself. He knew the date of Tyndale's death, so the reference was not difficult to find. The gun was logged in with an accurate description of its make, calibre and the fact that it was empty of bullets at the time it was repossessed by the officers in charge.

Tellman made a note of the details, and then started to look backwards in the inventory for any guns taken into evidence and held for any length of time. It was a tedious and very time-consuming task because the ledger was full of property of all sorts. However, although there were a large number of weapons, mostly knives or cudgels of various sorts, there were relatively few guns.

It took him almost two hours before he found another gun exactly like the one that Lezant had apparently used, the same make, the same calibre, only this one had been fully loaded. The bullets had been taken out by the sergeant when it was put away.

'Do you remember this?' Tellman asked him.

'No, sir. Can't 'ave been me on duty then,' he said blandly.

'Looks like your signature here,' Tellman pointed out. 'Looks like your writing and your name.'

The sergeant's face was a careful study in blank insolence. If he was trying to disguise it in any way, he failed.

'You asked if I remember, an' I don't! Yer ought to leave that alone, Mr Tellman. You're one of us, or yer was! Yer didn't ought ter do this. One o' these days yer goin' ter need someone ter forget something, or not see it in the first place. And yer goin' ter find it won't 'appen. Them as can't give another man a little leeway finds, when 'e needs a little room 'isself, there's nobody willing to stick 'is neck out.'

Tellman felt cold, and profoundly vulnerable. He found his voice husky when he spoke. 'What is it you're asking me to forget, Sergeant? That a gun and bullets went missing from property, and turned up later in a murder committed by Dylan Lezant? And no one here knows how it got from here into his possession?'

'Mistakes 'appen.' He stared at Tellman with flat, angry expression. 'An' five men are dead, or as close to as matters,' he went on. ''Ow'd yer like to 'ave yer face so burned yer own mother wouldn't know yer? Or lose one o' yer arms?' He looked Tellman up and down. 'Still find that uniform fits yer, do yer? Still think yer got the right ter wear it?'

Tellman's hands were shaking.

'Yes, Sergeant, I do. Ednam's gone, and no one else is going to risk his neck covering for you.' He pushed the ledgers back across the counter, then turned and walked out.

Outside in the street there was a very light snow falling and it was bitterly cold, more than Tellman remembered from when he'd arrived.

The next thing to follow up was the time of the information regarding the drug purchase. How had Ednam known where it would be, when, and who would be involved? To take other men with him, he had to have a story to account for how he had learned the information.

The inquiry led him eventually to a Sergeant Busby who, under considerable pressure, admitted that he had owed Bossiney a favour for some time: a mistake overlooked. He had mentioned information to Bossiney about an upcoming drug sale, but might have forgotten to tell all the appropriate superiors as well. Perhaps the information had lost its way somehow? He was no longer certain exactly where it had originated.

Tellman did not press him any further. There were lies within lies. What had happened to the written reports? No one knew. Perhaps in the haste and shock of Lezant shooting at them, and admitting killing poor Tyndale, things here and there had been lost. He defied Tellman to prove any differently.

Late in the evening when the snow had stopped and an icy wind sliced in from the east, Tellman did what he had dreaded he must. He went to see Bossiney at his home.

The hospital had released him, but they had warned Tellman that he was still in a very bad state.

It would be a long time before he returned to work, if ever.

Even then, it could only be some kind of desk duty, where the public would not see his face.

Tellman found him sitting beside his own fire, dressed in a nightshirt and a thick jacket to keep him warm. Even so he was rigid, as if knotted against some cold no one else in the stuffy room could feel. Bossiney's wife, small and frail-looking, left them alone as soon as she had received a nod from her husband that she should do so.

Tellman took the other chair and forced himself to look at Bossiney's face. It was scarred hideously, and still inflamed so that his right eye was almost invisible. How could Tellman inflict further pain on him by asking questions about past wrongs? There was too much suffering altogether. Newman and Hobbs were dead, and now Ednam too. And, of course, Tyndale and Lezant. Nothing anybody said was going to alter that.

For that matter, Alexander Duncannon was destined to die no matter what happened. If he wasn't hanged, the opium would kill him, only more slowly. Did the truth matter so much? It would hurt deeply and endlessly, regardless of his acts.

'What do you want?' Bossiney asked him.

Tellman took a deep breath and let it out slowly. His heart was hammering in his chest as if he had been running.

'The drug sale that went wrong.' He cleared his throat. 'When Tyndale was shot . . .'

Bossiney stared at him from his one good eye. His face was so badly disfigured it was impossible to read any expression in it.

Tellman began again. 'The drug dealer that didn't turn up. Did you ever get him?'

'No,' Bossiney answered. 'Why do you care now?' Part of his mouth was scarred, but it did not slur his speech.

Tellman chose his words carefully. 'I don't, except that I'm wondering who gave you the information that set up the operation in the first place.'

'Don't know,' Bossiney replied. 'I'd say ask Ednam, but he's dead, isn't he!'

There was something in his answer, not the words but a change in the tensions in his body, even in his twisted face, that made Tellman believe he was lying, if not in total then at least in part.

'Yes, you do,' he said. 'Nobody sets up a five-man operation like that unless there's pretty good information about it. It wasn't just a petty sale. Five of you! And armed!' He was taking a chance and he knew it. He hated doing it. These were his own men, not the enemy! Friends, more than that, allies. 'You were expecting something hard and dangerous.'

Bossiney sat motionless, except that his left hand curled over, gripping the thick fabric of his jacket.

'We weren't armed. Lezant had the gun. He shot Tyndale.' He said the words as if by rote, with no hesitation, not even any emotion. He seemed tired of repeating them. Did that mean they were lies? Or simply that he did not care any more? Perhaps the tide of violence and tragedy had drowned such things in him.

Then would he be ready to tell the truth at last?

Tellman felt brutal. He was attacking a beaten man. Did the truth matter enough for that?

Yes, it did.

'As you said, Ednam is dead,' Tellman said flatly. 'You can't protect him any more. There's only you and Yarcombe left.'

'Then it doesn't matter, does it?' Bossiney said bitterly. 'Leave it alone. Let him rest in peace.'

'Who? Ednam? He was the one who shot Tyndale?'

There was silence, absolute except for the ashes settling in the hearth. Who would pay for coal, for food, for anything, if Bossiney were dishonourably discharged from the police?

'I don't care if it was you,' Tellman said rashly. 'I have to know the truth to get Alexander Duncannon. He keeps swearing Lezant was innocent. That's why he blew up the house! Is he wrong? Maybe he didn't put that bomb there, then?'

Bossiney blinked his good eye.

Tellman waited.

'I don't know where the tip-off came from,' Bossiney said at last. 'I got it from Busby, but . . . but he told me later that it was false. I never told Ednam. I forgot, until it was too late, then I never said. We had a lot of bad things going on then.'

'So Ednam took the gun . . .' Tellman said quietly, as if he knew.

'Yes . . .'

'And he shot Tyndale?'

'We thought it was the drug seller come . . .' Bossiney must have realised how futile that sounded now.

'And then made it look as if Lezant shot him,' Tellman finished.

'They were drug addicts anyway! Both of them!' Bossiney protested.

'Were they?' Tellman's heart was beating so hard it almost choked him. 'Are you sure?'

'Of course I'm sure! They were pale-faced, sweating, shivering, like something out of a nightmare. Both of 'em.'

'Duncannon and Lezant?' Tellman held his breath.

'Yes . . .' Then Bossiney realised what he had said. They had been close enough to see their faces, to recognise Alexander, whom they said had not been there! He seemed to crumple up inside, and shrink as if suddenly he had become a smaller, older man, robbed of part of himself.

'Duncannon escaped and you put the gun into Lezant's hands. What did you do? Knock him out, then put it beside him and swear it was his?'

Bossiney did not answer, but nor did he deny it.

'And you let him hang.' It was a statement. There were not many questions left now, but Tellman had to ask them. 'Why?' he said. 'You knew he was innocent.'

Bossiney breathed in and out, slowly, for so long that Tellman thought he was not going to answer.

Did Gracie have any idea what she had asked Tellman to do?

Bossiney was watching him. His face was puckered with scars, his skin purple-red, his mouth pulled at one corner. It was impossible to read.

Tellman felt a rage burn up inside him, not at Bossiney, who God knew had paid an unimaginable price, but at Ednam, who had put him there, and the whole system that had conspired to allow the rot to creep through so far.

'I didn't want to know,' Bossiney said at last. 'Ednam said it was the right thing to do, and I believed him because I wanted to. Going against him would have cut me off from all the rest of the men. I'd 'ave been on my own. I wouldn't 'ave lasted. Don't you know what it's like to be out there with everybody against you? What about my family? Who'd look after them if I'm gone?'

Tellman said nothing. He hated everything Bossiney was saying, and everything he had failed to do. And yet he was choked by the pity inside him.

'You don't know what power he had,' Bossiney went on. 'He knew people a lot higher up than us. You can't win. Best to hang on to what you got, an' not look at what you don't want ter see.'

Is that what Tellman had done himself? He would like to think it wasn't, but it would be a lie. There were things he must have seen, half seen and refused to recognise for what they were. He had turned a blind eye, and called it mercy, when perhaps cowardice would have been a truer name for it.

It was not only punishment or exclusion he was afraid of, it was the truth of weakness, a momentary lapse by someone. Above all it was of not being part of the group, the men he believed in. It was the breaking of illusions that cut deep. The reflection of what he wanted to see was perfect, until someone threw a stone into the water, and it fractured into countless pieces.

He stood up. What could he say to Bossiney? The man had paid more than enough. Tellman could not bring himself to make it worse.

'I'll find proof of it without you,' he told him, knowing how much he might regret those words, but he had to say them now. 'I know where to look.'

Bossiney did not answer. Tears filled his good eye.

Tellman turned away. He went out of the room closing the door behind him, and out into the street again. He must find who had protected Ednam, and why. Had Ednam blackmailed someone? Or was that person using Ednam, paying him, and protecting him?

'Just delay it, that's all we're asking,' Jack said desperately. It was late the following day and they were sitting in Pitt's office. Outside the fog was closing in like a blanket, wrapping them in a muffling darkness that denied even the sharp sound of horses' hoofs on the road.

'I can't,' Pitt told him. 'I have to charge Alexander. I can't hold him unless I do.'

'Then release him into his father's custody,' Jack protested. 'For God's sake, Thomas, do you think Godfrey won't keep him safe? He'll have him locked in his room, if that's what you want?'

'What I want is to have him locked in a hospital ward,' Pitt said tartly, 'with a doctor who'll give him some sort of treatment. The man's a wreck.'

'Then let him be at home.' Jack's face lit with hope as if at last they had reached some meeting point. 'We're nearly there with the contract. The Chinese have no arguments left!'

Pitt kept his patience with difficulty. It was what Bradshaw had asked him to do, but the seriousness of the case far outweighed political or diplomatic expediency.

'I can't let him go, Jack. He killed three policemen, and he's told me to my face that if I don't try him for the whole thing, both bombings, he'll do it again.'

Jack was exasperated. He jerked his hands in a gesture of futility.

'He's manipulating you, Thomas!'

'Of course he is.' Pitt's own voice rose. 'He's manipulating all of us. God knows, we've done it enough to him.'

'The law has, maybe.' The colour rose hot up Jack's face now. 'Not his family, and certainly not the Government.'

Pitt's eyebrows rose. 'Do you think he sees a distinction between the Government, the law and his family? Don't be so naïve!'

Jack winced.

Before Pitt could frame a gentler answer, one that took account of the disappointment of yet another major hope crashing because of individual vulnerability, he was interrupted. There was a sharp rap on the door, and without waiting for permission to enter, Stoker walked in.

'Sir,' he barely inclined his head to acknowledge Jack. 'I just got a message. Inspector Tellman's gone after some of the bent coppers by himself, and he's in bad trouble.'

Pitt froze. For a moment it was as if he could not command his muscles. Then he forced himself to stand. 'Where?' he demanded. 'Where is he, man?'

'Word to me was Tailor's Alley,' Stoker replied. His face was very pale and there was a slight nervous twitch in one temple. 'I've got a cab waiting, sir. I only came for you because you know the business he's been about. He's stirred up a right hornets' nest.'

Pitt wanted to know how, but there was no time for questions. He turned to Jack. 'I'm sorry but this can't wait.' He had no idea whether Jack understood exactly what he meant, but he would just have to make the best of it.

Jack's face was grim. He glanced at Stoker, then back at Pitt. 'I'm coming too—'

'You can't,' Pitt cut him off. 'It could get very nasty.' Perhaps he owed him something of an explanation, a few words at least. He spoke as he went over to a heavy cupboard. He took the key ring from his pocket and unlocked the door, then an inner safe door beyond that.

'Tellman's been running down police corruption,' he said to Jack. 'Last message I had from him, he's got proof and admission that Lezant was innocent. It's a whole network of debts and favours, lies.'

'I'm coming with you,' Jack repeated.

Pitt took a revolver out of the safe and closed the door, then the outer door.

Jack did not move. In the gaslight he looked older, greyer at the temples than Pitt had realised. The lines in his face showed more deeply.

Pitt was in no mood for another battle, nor was there time. Tellman could be in very bad trouble. They could be too late already.

Stoker put out his hand, the light gleaming on the barrel of the gun he was offering Jack.

Jack took it, not even glancing at Pitt. He handled it easily, as if he had used such a weapon before.

'I've got another one,' Stoker looked briefly at Pitt. 'We should go, sir.'

Jack put the gun in his pocket and went out of the door a step behind Stoker.

The hansom was waiting at the kerb, horse restless in the hard, cold wind.

'Tailor's Alley,' Stoker told the driver, and stepped up quickly, Jack and Pitt behind him.

They moved off at a rapid pace, the sudden motion jerking them momentarily out of their seats, then back again. They rode in tense silence.

Tellman had told Pitt that Duncannon appeared to be telling the truth about Tyndale's murder. Lezant was innocent, which meant that Ednam and his men had lied, carefully and deliberately, to get him hanged and save themselves. What else had followed after that could be guessed. How wide the lies spread was another matter. So also was what had happened to the original dealer in opium who had not turned up at the meeting. A tragedy of errors, or a deliberate act? No one had ever named the dealer, and nothing Pitt had said had persuaded Alexander Duncannon to reveal his name.

They swept on past lights blurred by fog. They were out of the main streets now, keeping up speed even in stretches of near darkness. The fog made them blind, as if they were suddenly in an unknown city. Distances were distorted. It seemed miles to the Edgware Road. Nothing was quite where you had thought it was. Praed Street Station came and went in an instant. Even sounds lost distinction and echoed as if the walls of fog were solid. The journey had the repetitive, nonsensical quality of a nightmare.

Pitt felt his muscles clench with fear. Would they find Tellman already dead?

The cab swung round the corner a little fast, pitching them on to one another. By the time they had righted themselves they were at another corner, slower this time, then pulled to a halt.

Pitt leaped out first. Through the gloom ahead of him he could see the entrance to a narrow opening and, just below the lamp, the name 'Tailor's Alley'. There was a man huddling in a doorway and propping himself up against it. He looked to be either drunk or asleep.

Stoker was out beside him. There was just a breath of wind, clammy, cold, and the fog moved sluggishly.

'Keep the cabby!' Pitt ordered.

'He'll wait,' Stoker assured him. 'Haven't paid him yet.'

Pitt held his hand over the gun in his pocket and moved forward, his feet silent on the rough cobbles. He strained to listen, but he could hear nothing except the faint drip of water from the eaves. The man in the doorway stirred and lifted his head. He was a stranger.

Where was Tellman? Would they find only bodies, injured or dead, in the alley? No, that was absurd. The man would hardly be sleeping in the doorway if there had been a battle. Perhaps he wasn't asleep, just drunk?

They were too early. Or wrong. It was all misinformation. Pitt half-turned to look at Stoker.

Stoker glanced up at the sign, now behind them, and then before Pitt could stop him, he went round the corner. He swivelled and strode back in barely two seconds.

'Wrong place,' he said, his voice tight. 'There's no one there!'

Stoker broke into a run, reaching the cab and grasping the driver's coat-tails to demand his attention. 'Is there another Tailor's Alley?' he asked as Pitt and Jack reached the cab and climbed back in.

'Tailor's Row a mile away,' the cabby replied.

'Then get to it!' Stoker ordered him. 'Fast as you can!'

Grumbling, the cabby obeyed. They jolted forward again and followed back alleys, avoiding the main traffic. Pitt was totally lost. They lurched and slithered like a drunken eel through one shortcut after another until they pulled up again, and this time there was no mistake. The sound of gunfire was clear even before their feet touched the cobbles.

Stoker threw a few coins to the cabby, then followed after Pitt and Jack.

Another gunshot rang out, then a crack and a whine as the bullet hit stone, ricocheted and was lost.

The fog closed over them, muffling sounds. From what Pitt had heard, the shots were coming from the other end of the alley, fired towards them. Now the silence was heavy. He strained his ears, and heard brief, slithering footsteps, a voice, and then nothing.

Jack was beside him, gun in his hand. Stoker was a few yards away, on the other side of the alley and moving towards the corner where he would be able to look into the other alley and see what was happening.

'Tellman!' Pitt called out, then immediately moved a few yards.

A shot rang out, ricocheting off the stone wall where Pitt had been.

There was a shout from ahead, then silence.

The fog drifted, constantly changing the shape of things.

Suddenly there was another shout, and a thudding of feet. Someone swore and there were more shots, then a cry as if at least one bullet had found flesh. More shouting. Voices Pitt did not know.

Stoker was out of sight, already in the alley.

Pitt inched round the corner. He could see a figure flattened against a doorway opposite him, bent over a little as if to protect one arm. His other held a gun. The man was average height, and thin, like Tellman, but his face was turned away so in the meagre light Pitt could not be sure.

In the deeper shadow ahead of Pitt someone raised an arm, then as he fired towards the figure near Pitt, another man ducked and ran closer, holding his fire until he was almost opposite the doorway. He was thick, heavy-set.

From the other side of the alley, Stoker fired at him and he went down immediately.

The fog cleared for a moment and four figures appeared at the far end of the alley and there were several more shots fired. A bullet struck the stone wall next to Pitt and sent up splinters that stung his cheek.

Pitt shot back. He was now almost certain that it was Tellman in the doorway, standing awkwardly, as if he had been hit.

The men at the far end of the alley were inching forward. There was no cover except the slight alcove of doorways, no more than six or eight inches deep.

Stoker fired two more shots, which were answered immediately.

Four men. Was that all? Could there be a fifth, or even a sixth, moving around behind them?

'Watch your back!' Pitt called out to warn Jack and Stoker. 'May be more behind us.'

Jack swore, his voice a little high as if his throat were closing up, but he turned sideways to look. He was just in time. He knocked into Pitt's shoulder to send him sharply to the right, almost losing his balance, as another volley of shots rang out, all close around them. One actually tore the sleeve of Pitt's coat.

Jack let out a sharp cry, muffled instantly. His breathing became rapid, turned to gasps for a moment, then steadied again.

'You hit?' Pitt asked, his heart pounding.

'Not badly,' Jack replied. 'Just my arm.' He raised his own gun and shot back, three times. There was a cry as the man behind them staggered and fell.

Ahead there was a shout of rage and three men at the far end charged forward.

Pitt fired at them until his gun was empty. To his right there seemed to be bullets everywhere. Tellman crumpled and slid down the doorpost into a huddle on the ground.

Pitt reloaded and went forward, shooting at the men ahead. He aimed for their bodies; there was no choice. All he could think of was Tellman, wounded, perhaps bleeding to death. Between all three of them they probably had only a few rounds left. Every shot must count.

One of the men coming towards them floundered and fell face down on the cobbles, his gun clattering over the stones.

More shots came from the others, and Stoker and Jack were both firing.

Another man fell. For an instant his police uniform was clearly visible. What the hell had they come to that they were killing each other in a fog-bound alley?

Then another thought forced its way into Pitt's understanding. If anyone had heard the gunfire and called the police, they would see Pitt, Stoker and Jack in civilian clothes, firing on police in uniform! Tellman would be in uniform, but who was to say they had not shot him too! Not Tellman if he were dead! Was this what had happened to Lezant? Who was to say what had happened and who had shot whom? Only the survivors!

Pitt raised his gun and shot straight at the man ahead of him. It was as if he were a boy again, on the estate, shooting pheasants. You aimed for a clean kill. He squeezed the trigger. Handguns had little aim, not like a rifle. But they were close to each other, just a few yards.

The man went down.

One of the men shouted, 'Don't shoot! I give up!' And the next moment his gun clattered on the stones.

The other man hesitated.

A shot crackled a yard from him.

'I give up!' he shouted, a high-pitched sound in the dark and the fog. Then his gun too fell to the ground.

Jack stood holding his gun in his good hand while Stoker cuffed both men with their own manacles.

Pitt ran over to Tellman. He was crumpled up, but definitely still breathing, although his face was creased with pain and there seemed to be a lot of blood on his arms and chest.

'Hang on,' Pitt said as gently as his own ragged breath would allow. 'Let me see.'

Tellman relaxed a little, allowing Pitt to look at his wounds, but the fear did not leave his face.

There was shouting behind them now, and a clatter of horses' shod feet on the stones.

Stoker was shouting but Pitt could not make out the words.

Someone came up behind him.

'Let me see,' he said firmly. 'Need to get him to a hospital.' He put his hand on Pitt's shoulder. 'You've done all you can. I'm a doctor. Let me see!'

Then there were more people, other police from somewhere. The gunshots had been heard and help sent for.

Jack was beside Pitt. In the gas lamplight his face looked pale.

There was blood on his sleeve and his coat was ruined, but he looked relieved, almost happy.

Two men were lifting Tellman. Pitt followed them to a cab, then turned to help Stoker explain to the sergeant who seemed to be in charge.

'Special Branch,' he said simply. 'Sorry about this. It's about the Lancaster Gate bombing . . .'

'Yes, sir. Good job done, then. Now get into the cab and let's take you all to hospital.'

Pitt did not answer. There was nothing he could say that was adequate, and his arm was burning like hell where the bullet had torn the skin. It was nothing, barely even a decent flesh wound. All that mattered was, would Tellman make it?

Chapter Thirteen

IT WAS long after midnight when Pitt finally got to bed. There had been four police cornering and attacking Tellman, all of them from Ednam's old station. Three of them were dead, the fourth not expected to survive.

Pitt was extremely sore where the bullet had torn its way through the flesh of his arm, and the hospital had stitched it and bound it up for him. He knew it would probably feel worse before it was better. All his concern had been for Tellman, who was lucky he had not bled to death. Jack also had needed careful stitching and bandaging, and had gone home in some pain.

Gracie had shown up at the hospital white-faced and clinging on to her self-control with a desperation she could not hide. Charlotte had gone to stay with her now, and would be back when she judged that Gracie was all right on her own. Pitt missed her, but he never for an instant hesitated in the decision – not that Charlotte had asked his permission. She had informed him, with the assumption that he would wish it as much as she did.

Still, he was lonely and sore when he fell into a restless sleep.

He woke several times in the night, jerked into consciousness as if by some loud noise. But the house was silent.

When he finally awoke to a grey daylight it was nearly nine o'clock. His head was pounding and his arm was stiff and on fire. It took him a moment to remember why, and then as he saw the empty place beside him in the bed, and the white bandage, he remembered.

Before washing or shaving, he put on his dressing robe and went downstairs to the telephone. He called the hospital and, as soon as he was connected, he asked about Tellman. He was told that he was in a lot of pain, and very weak from loss of blood but he was expected to recover fully, in time.

That was all he needed to know. Tellman would recover. He had not looked like he would last night.

In the kitchen Daniel and Jemima were both still at the table and both stood up as soon as he came in.

'Are you all right, Papa?' Jemima said anxiously. 'You look . . .'

'. . . awful,' Daniel finished for her.

Pitt thanked them wryly, and assured them that he was all right. Minnie Maude came in from the pantry, looked him up and down and decided he needed quiet, and some breakfast. She was right, and for once he did not argue. He wrote a note and gave it to Daniel, with his cab fare, and told him to take it to Charlotte, to assure Gracie that he had telephoned the hospital and been told that Tellman was doing well.

It was going to be a long, tedious morning, with a lot of paperwork to give exact accounts of what had happened in the alley, before the Home Secretary, or anyone else, could ask for them, or misinform the newspapers. Minnie Maude was right: he needed a good breakfast.

After dinner, when Pitt was thinking of going to bed, Narraway called. He walked into the parlour as Minnie Maude directed, and looked Pitt up and down ruefully.

'Hurts, doesn't it?' he said, but it was impossible to tell from his expression whether that was sympathy, or merely an observation. 'It'll take a while to heal,' he added. 'Thank God poor Tellman's going to survive.' He sat down in Charlotte's chair and crossed his legs.

'If you want whisky, it's over there,' Pitt indicated the decanter.

'Not yet, thank you,' Narraway replied.

Pitt's heart sank. He could tell from Narraway's face that he came with bad news. 'What is it?' He wanted the blow quickly, rather than drawn out in tension, however well-intended.

'Alexander Duncannon will face trial,' Narraway replied.

'I know that,' Pitt said tartly. 'You didn't come over here in the mud and ice to tell me something we all know. What's the real reason?'

'Abercorn is trained in criminal law, did you know that?'

'No.' Pitt was surprised. 'What does that matter? I know he's behind a lot of the heat to get justice for the police. He's been playing to the gallery all the time since the bombing. I presumed it was for political advantage. He'll give the prosecution all the help he can. I expected that, didn't you?' He looked at Narraway more closely. 'Godfrey Duncannon can afford the very best lawyers in the country. And whatever he feels about his son, for his own sake, he'll pay to defend him. Politically he can hardly afford to do anything else.'

'Quite,' Narraway agreed. 'Probably with a defence of insanity, due to opium addiction.'

'That's foreseeable,' Pitt agreed. It bothered him. It was a miserable end to Alexander's brave and desperate attempt to save Lezant's name, and find some justice. He wouldn't find the mere deaths of Ednam, Hobbs and Newman sufficient. That was no more than vengeance.

Narraway was watching him, as if he could see the thought behind his eyes.

'Alexander won't like it,' Pitt said aloud. 'But if he's being defended as insane, his lawyer won't allow him to testify, and even if he did, it would carry no weight.' He felt unreasonably defeated himself. He wanted to say more, to give words to his sense of injustice on Alexander's behalf, as if he himself had been injured by the failure. An innocent man had been hanged, deliberately, and the one friend who knew it had been beaten by the system, and his own terrible frailty.

He felt for Abercorn, both pity regarding his mother, and Godfrey Duncannon's treatment of her, but also an unreasonable dislike. He would do his best to see that the lawyer Godfrey chose for him could make the insanity plea unbelievable. He could not blame him for that. Alexander was the legitimate son that Abercorn should have been. But even if he succeeded, Alexander would escape the rope, but die a miserable death in an asylum, alone, in pain and defeated.

Pitt was exhausted and feeling beaten. His muscles, even his bones ached. Whatever he said would sound like a cry of his own failure – to be frank, his own vulnerability.

Narraway was watching him, his eyes almost black in the shadows from the lamplight, his face touched with both pity and anger.

'Abercorn is going to prosecute it himself,' Narraway said quietly.

'What?' Pitt thought he must have misheard. His mind was playing tricks on him.

Narraway smiled bleakly. 'That's why I mentioned that Abercorn has kept his law qualifications current. Never know when they'll come in useful.'

Pitt swore with more pent-up rage than he had felt in a long time. It startled him how profound his anger was, and how helpless.

'So have I,' Narraway said it as if that also surprised him.

Pitt forced his attention back. 'So have you what?'

'Paid my dues and kept my right to practise law,' Narraway answered mildly. 'It's always a good thing to have.'

Pitt was stunned. 'I never knew you had . . .' He let the words tail off. Of course he had not known. There were loads of things he did not know about Narraway, in fact about most of his life. He knew he had been in the Indian Army at the time of the Mutiny, in his youth. He must have come back to England and gone to university after that. Law was a hard discipline, but perhaps the two were in some way aligned?

'What has that to do with Abercorn, or his case?' he asked, feeling stupidly confused.

'If Abercorn prosecutes Alexander Duncannon, then if I can obtain his approval, I shall defend him,' Narraway replied.

Pitt was stunned. He must have misunderstood.

'Why? What can you do that the best lawyer his father can pay wouldn't do, and do it better?'

'Rather ungraciously put,' Narraway said with a flash of amusement. 'But if my plan works, then I can expose the police corruption, and plead some merciful outcome for Alexander, in a hospital rather than an asylum.'

'And if it doesn't?' Pitt refused to allow himself to hope.

'Then he'll probably be hanged,' Narraway replied, his voice tight. 'Which on the whole might be more merciful than the asylum.'

'With a guilty verdict,' Pitt said bitterly.

'It will be a guilty verdict anyway,' Narraway told him very softly. 'It's what he wants . . . isn't it?'

Pitt agreed silently, just a tiny nod, little more than an expression in the eyes.

Narraway stood up and went to the decanter. He poured whisky for each of them, then returned to his seat and continued to explain.

Jack Radley had spent two days in bed. His wound had been stitched and bandaged and he seemed to be recovering without more than a very slight fever, and a lot of pain. He was still shaken enough by the whole event to be very willing to stay at home, most of the time in the sitting room by the fire, wrapped in a heavy dressing gown over his nightshirt. The effort of dressing properly caused considerable pain, wrenching his wound. He was stiff, and it still bled sufficiently for him to be aware that it must be kept bandaged.

He let Emily help him, and was glad of her attention. He was surprised that occasionally he felt a little dizzy.

Normally he had excellent health. He was not used to being so miserable, or so handicapped in all his usual pursuits. It was a sobering thought. It turned his mind to Alexander Duncannon, who was in pain all the time, and knew that it would always be so. How did he bear it?

Thinking of Alexander inevitably forced him to think also of Godfrey.

He looked across the warm, fire-lit room to where Emily was sitting in her chair while he lay sideways on the couch, his feet up. The light was soft on her face; kind to the few lines of anxiety that were just visible on her fair skin. Her hair looked almost gold in its warmth. He had always liked the way it curled.

What she really wanted to know was if the shooting incident was going to affect his career, but she did not wish to commit herself to saying so. It was not the money that mattered. She had enough to keep them both in the fashion they wished. It was what the loss of his position would do to his self-esteem, his vanity.

Did that matter? Compared with the grief the Duncannons would face? Not much. Emily and the children were safe. So was Jack, in essence. The tear in his arm hurt, but it would heal. He would not be crippled by it. It was up to him whether he let the wound to his vanity cripple him.

What wound exactly? He had obeyed the instruction given him regarding the contract. He had been loyal to Godfrey Duncannon, which was a matter of principle rather than emotion. He had not particularly liked him, but that was irrelevant. He had found him a colder man than he affected to be. No laughter or pain seemed to take his attention for long, or even divert his energy from his task. He was unfailingly polite, but he never apologised. He

273

expressed his thanks, but stiffly, with satisfaction rather than pleasure.

Jack had also learned slowly that Godfrey was more ambitious than he appeared at first. But then many in government were like that. It was part of the job to seem affable. It was even more important to be as hard and as resilient as steel underneath. And clever; one must always be clever.

Then the thought that had been on the edge of his mind for weeks forced its way in: was Jack himself actually in the right job? It was the first time he had allowed the thought into his mind in words. He had once believed it was the answer to what he would do with his life, his charm, his judgement and ease with people, and the degree of leisure and choice that wealth gave him.

As a Member of Parliament he would earn Emily's respect, and the public's acceptance as a man of some purpose.

The fire crackled and sank a little. He should ring the bell and have the footman fetch more wood.

Emily was watching him. Had she any idea what was racing through his mind?

'I shall go to visit Cecily tomorrow,' she said with a rueful smile. 'I imagine many of her friends will not. I hope you don't mind?' It was a question, but he had an absolute conviction that, now that he was better, she would go whatever he said.

'Could I persuade you not to?' he asked with a smile.

'Only if you gave me a reason so strong I couldn't argue against it. Do you want to?' She glanced at the fire, and then back at him.

'No. I think you should go. Tell me, Emily . . . do you like Godfrey?'

She stood up, crossed to the bell pull and tugged it. As soon as the footman came she requested more wood, and perhaps a little coal as well. It was a bitter evening. The footman obeyed, taking the scuttle with him.

'Do you?' Jack insisted as soon as the door was closed.

'Pardon?' she asked innocently.

'Do you like Godfrey Duncannon?' he repeated.

'Not very much,' she admitted.

'Why? I want to know.'

'I haven't got a sensible answer. I think he's – cold.'

'That's a sensible answer. Does Cecily love him?'

Emily shrugged. She always did that with great elegance.

'I don't know. I think she once did.' She did not add anything, but he knew she was thinking that that could happen to anyone, and probably did to many. The danger had brushed by them too, just months ago: the drifting apart, the taking for granted, the small faults becoming more important, the loss of laughter, the protests remembered rather than forgiven.

It was Cecily Duncannon who had brought the money to the marriage. Perhaps neither of them had ever forgotten that.

Did Jack forget that he was in a similar situation? When he remembered it, it was with a sense of obligation, the need to live up to it. Did Godfrey feel the same? Or had money been a large part of the reason he married, rather than love?

Did Emily ever wonder how much the money was Jack's reason, and the love a well-played act? It wasn't! But did he make sure enough that she knew that?

'You should go and see her,' he said. 'Please do. And find a way to say how sorry I am about all of this.'

'Thank you.' She smiled at him suddenly. 'I didn't want to argue with you about it.'

'But you would have done?' he said with a smile, to rob the words of any sting.

She smiled even more sweetly. 'Yes.'

She had not asked him how the case coming to trial would affect his future. It could be another failure, tying his name to one more man of importance who had come to a spectacular crisis in his career, albeit none of his own fault. Was it bad luck?

Or Jack's misjudgement? Should he give thought to some other career where his skills were better? For now, he would say nothing. He smiled back at Emily, and tried to ease himself into a more comfortable position. He was fortunate to be so little injured. He could easily have been killed in that alley. If the shot had been only a few inches further to the right . . . It was time to think rather more deeply.

Emily went to the Duncannon house with considerable misgiving. She had no idea whether Cecily would receive her or not. She had brought a note to leave if she were refused entrance. There was so little to say that it seemed rather ridiculous, but friendship required that she did not take the easy escape of claiming that she did not know what to say. There were all kinds of tragedies for which there were no adequate words, nothing that healed the pain, but one did not leave people alone, regardless.

It was a cold morning with a bitter wind from the east. It cut through woollen coats and even fur collars, as if it were straight off the North Sea, which it probably was. She was relieved when the door was opened. A blank-faced butler took a moment to recognise her, and then pulled the door wide and stepped backwards to invite her in.

'Mrs Duncannon is in the morning room, ma'am,' he said gravely. The pallor of his face suggested that he knew they were on the eve of tragedy. 'If you will excuse me a moment, I will see if she is well enough to receive you.' Without waiting for Emily's reply, he closed the front door and walked smartly across the wide hallway and knocked on one of the doors. A moment later he returned to take Emily into the morning room where Cecily Duncannon was waiting.

'Emily. How kind of you . . .' Cecily began, then faltered into an awkward silence. She looked ravaged, her skin pale, dark rings around her eyes as if she were bruised. She seemed beaten physically as well as emotionally. All her old vitality was gone. Perhaps that had been nervous energy anyway, bringing the strength needed to keep the pains of reality just beyond reach. Emily had not understood it at the time, but now it seemed so clear. This day, or a day like it, was always going to come. What courage it must have taken to seize the time before, and live it to the full. Were it Emily's own son, Edward, could she have found the strength to do that?

What on earth was there that she could say that was not trivial, just chatter to fill in her own silences?

She walked over to Cecily and took both her hands, holding them gently, as if they too would bruise at a touch.

'If you would rather have privacy, please let me know. Don't pretend for anyone else's sake,' she said gently. 'But if you prefer not to be alone, then I am here for as long as you wish.'

The tears spilled over Cecily's cheeks and blinking was no help, no disguise. She took a shuddering breath, waited a moment, and then felt sufficiently composed to speak.

'Thank you. I . . . I think I would like you to stay, a little while. Our lawyer, Sir Robert Cardew, is in the study with Godfrey. I have no idea what they will do, but Godfrey says Sir Robert is the very best, not just articulate, and of course brilliant with the law, but wise. He will know what will be best for Alexander, in the long term.'

Emily felt a ripple of alarm, cold and frightening. There was no 'long term' for Alexander. Did Cecily not know that? She must! Emily had seen it in her face, in her eyes when she had looked at him in unguarded moments. It had been there, and then gone again, mastered by good manners, and duty.

Maybe Godfrey really meant the long term for himself. Was that an unworthy thought? If it were Edward in such terrible trouble, would Emily think of Jack, in the long term? And of Evangeline, an innocent inheritor of the stigma that must attach to the family? Who would marry her? What would her future be?

'Of course,' she said quietly. 'You must take whatever advice you think wisest.'

At that moment the door opened and Godfrey Duncannon came in, followed immediately by a man of not dissimilar appearance. He was not quite as tall, but had thick, perfectly barbered iron-grey hair and was immaculately dressed. They both stopped when they saw Emily.

A flash of anger crossed Godfrey's face but he masked it quickly.

'Good morning, Mrs Radley,' he said coolly. He introduced Sir Robert Cardew, explaining that Emily was a friend of Cecily's, who had no doubt come to offer her sympathies and was about to leave.

'I am sure you will appreciate that we are grateful for your concern, but we have urgent family business to discuss.' He turned to Cecily and the shadow of annoyance was back in his face. Or perhaps it was a disguise for fear. Men such as he was would never admit to being afraid; he could not afford to. Enemies and rivals understood fear, and used it. Emily felt a moment's intense pity for him. Perhaps Cecily was too hurt to be any use, any support at all for him in this. Alexander was his only son also!

She bit back the response she had wanted to make.

'Of course,' she agreed, and then turned to Cecily. 'If there is anything I can do, please let me know. Perhaps there are letters to write, errands you wish, or simply to go somewhere not alone.'

'Thank you,' Cecily said quickly. 'But there is no need to leave now. You have barely arrived . . .'

'Cecily!' There was sharpness in Godfrey's voice that was unmistakable.

Cecily stared back at him, terror in her eyes.

It was Cardew who intervened. 'Mrs Duncannon, we have discussed the situation thoroughly and reached what I can assure you is the best plan of action. There is a very good chance that we may be able to prove beyond reasonable doubt that Alexander is not fully responsible for his actions. If we succeed, he will be placed in a secure asylum where he will be well treated, and if your husband deems it wise, you will be able to visit him from time to time.' He smiled at her; but it seemed more out of kindness than encouragement. 'I will do everything I can to see that that is the nature of the trial. I advise you to consider allowing your husband to attend the actual trial in your place. It would be bound to distress you.'

Cecily stared at him with distinct chill. 'Thank you for your concern, Sir Robert, but I will attend. I imagine Mrs Radley will accompany me, to make sure I do not attract attention by fainting at an unsuitable moment.' She was standing close enough to Emily to touch her arm lightly, and for Emily to return the pressure.

Cardew looked taken aback, and then uncomfortable. He glanced at Godfrey.

'We will see,' Godfrey said firmly. 'Thank you very much.' He reached for the bell to summon the butler to show Cardew out.

As soon as he was gone Godfrey looked at Emily.

'You will excuse us.' It was an order, and only just the right side of abruptness.

'Of course.' Emily was reluctant to leave. She knew by the way Cecily gripped her arm that she did not wish to be left, but in the face of such clear dismissal she could hardly remain.

The situation was broken by the return of the butler looking distinctly uncomfortable. He hesitated awkwardly.

'Mrs Radley is leaving,' Godfrey told him.

'Sir, Lord Narraway has arrived and insists upon speaking with you. He . . . he encountered Sir Robert Cardew on the doorstep, sir.'

'For God's sake! What does he want?' Godfrey snapped. He was exasperated, but he knew he could not afford to offend Narraway, who had been, until recently, head of Special Branch. Narraway's knowledge of men and their secrets was encyclopaedic, and he was now a figure of immeasurable importance in the House of Lords; immeasurable literally, because no one knew for certain exactly what secrets he was privy to, but some of them were deemed to be very dark indeed.

'To speak with you, sir,' the butler replied unhappily.

Godfrey straightened his shoulders, and considered for a moment, without looking at either Emily or his wife. 'Show him in,' he said curtly.

Cecily looked puzzled, but Emily knew, in a sudden instant of complete understanding, that Godfrey presumed Narraway would not say anything of a personal nature with the two women present. Emily had a strong feeling that he was mistaken.

Narraway came in. He was, as Cardew had been, immaculately dressed, but slenderer, and an inch or two shorter. However, there was an air of confidence in him, of controlled energy, that made him dominate the room.

'Good morning,' he said politely, including both women in his glance. 'I apologise for calling unannounced. I am sure it is inconvenient, but it is necessary. I am sure that Sir Robert Cardew has told you that Josiah Abercorn is going to lead the prosecution in the opening trial of your son.'

'Of course,' Godfrey snapped. 'I cannot imagine you have come here to tell me something so . . . so obvious, or of so little concern to you.' His manner was ice cold, and barely polite.

Cecily seemed frozen, hanging on to Emily's arm as if for actual, physical support.

'Of course not,' Narraway agreed. 'What you will be unaware of, since it has only been agreed this morning, is that I am going to represent Mr Alexander Duncannon—'

'No, sir, you are not!' Godfrey was furious. 'I don't give a damn who you are, or were! I have engaged Sir Robert Cardew to defend my son. There is nothing further to be said. Good day.'

Narraway raised his eyebrows very slightly. 'It is your son who is on trial, Mr Duncannon. He is of age, and may engage anyone he chooses to represent him. He has chosen me.'

Godfrey was white to the lips. 'He is of unsound mind, as you well know. He is not competent to choose who will represent him. You are not even a lawyer. How dare you misrepresent yourself in this manner? It is despicable! Get out of my house, sir, before I have you thrown out!'

For a moment Emily was afraid the passion, the fear, and the rage were going to descend into violence.

Narraway smiled, although it was perhaps more a baring of his teeth.

'I am as licenced to practise law as Mr Abercorn is. But you must do as you think appropriate, Mr Duncannon. I am informing you as a courtesy. It is fortunate that Mrs Radley is a witness to it, although of course I have lodged the necessary papers.'

'I shall not pay you a penny!' Godfrey replied grimly. 'Mrs Radley is also a witness to that. You may call on any others you wish. You will only make a spectacle of yourself. I cannot imagine what you hope to gain by this, but I promise you, it will be nothing.'

'I do not require payment, Mr Duncannon. Not everything is done for money, at least not by all of us. I have not and shall not ask you for anything whatever. I am defending Alexander, with his consent, because I believe I can bring to pass a certain justice that Sir Robert Cardew cannot. I do not require your consent in this. I am telling you because you have the right to know, not to interfere. Good day, sir. Mrs Duncannon. Emily, perhaps it would be a good time for you to take your leave also.' With a very slight bow of his head to Cecily, he turned and walked out into the hall.

Godfrey used an expletive he would not normally have used in front of women.

Cecily said absolutely nothing.

Emily squeezed her arm very gently, then turned also and went after Narraway.

She caught up with him on the front doorstep where he had hesitated, apparently waiting for her. She did not bother with niceties. The wind was bitterly cold and both their carriages were waiting at the kerb, horses restless.

'What are you doing?' she demanded. A year ago she would have held him in too much awe to have been so abrupt, but since he had married Vespasia, who was Emily's great-aunt, by her marriage to her first husband, she had seen a far more human and vulnerable side to him, to her great liking. 'Can you really help Alexander?'

'He is beyond anyone's help,' he said with startling gentleness. 'He will not live a great deal longer. But I believe I can do as he wishes, and save both his reputation as a man of sanity, and of loyalty to his friend, who was innocent of the crime for which he was hanged. Then Alexander will not have given his life for nothing.'

She nodded, emotion overwhelming her. 'Please let me know if I can help.'

'You can be with Cecily Duncannon,' he replied. 'It will be hard for her, and I doubt her husband will be of much comfort.'

The contract had not been signed, and perhaps now it never would be. There was nothing any of them could do about it, and she found that she did not care enough to make an issue of it. It must be won or lost on its own merits.

'Of course,' she agreed.

He smiled, and waited a moment or two for her to accept the assistance of her coachman. Then he walked briskly over to his own coach and climbed in.

The trial of Alexander Duncannon began late in the morning of the third Monday in January 1899. He was accused of the murder of three policemen and the attempted murder and serious injury of two more. They were all named.

Charlotte sat in the body of the courtroom next to Vespasia. Emily was with Cecily Duncannon, as she had promised she would be. Godfrey might be called as a witness, and much against his will, could not be present. He was still furiously angry with Narraway but he had exhausted all his avenues of objection to his representing Alexander and there was nothing further he could do.

Pitt could not attend, because he was naturally the chief witness for the prosecution. He also had no choice in the matter.

Jack sat next to Charlotte, on the opposite side from Vespasia. They all maintained silence, not because it was appropriate, or good manners, but because there was no longer anything left to say.

All the initial court procedures were carried out. They seemed to go on for ages before finally Abercorn called his first witness. He did it with tremendous gravity, making sure that every eye in the room was on Bossiney as he walked slowly, with help from the usher, up to the witness stand. He climbed the steps one at a time, drawing his left foot up to the next step, then the other level with it, clinging on to the rail.

Finally he reached the top and turned to the court. There were gasps from the jury and the crowded gallery.

Charlotte felt her stomach turn and the sweat break out on her body at the sight of his ravaged face, the scars still red, twisted and hideous.

Even the judge, Lord Justice Bonnington, was pale-faced.

Abercorn stepped forward and looked up at the stand with awe. He listened while Bossiney swore to tell the truth, the whole truth and nothing but, and gave his name and police rank.

Charlotte glanced at Vespasia. What could Narraway, or anyone, do against this horror? No one would forget this.

'Wait,' Vespasia whispered. 'We are a long way from the end, my dear.' She did not look towards Narraway at the defence table, only at Abercorn as he stood in the centre of the court, like a gladiator in the arena.

'Constable Bossiney, we can all see the terrible burns that have altered your face irreparably. How much more of your body do they cover?'

The judge frowned, but he did not interrupt.

If Narraway felt any disgust at such an extraordinary beginning, it did not register in his calm grave expression.

'All down my right side, sir,' Bossiney answered. 'Far as my
knee.'

'I imagine the pain of it was beyond description,' Abercorn
observed.

'Yes, sir,' Bossiney agreed.

The judge looked at Narraway to see if he objected. There had
been no question in Abercorn's remark, but Narraway did not
protest.

'Did you have any mark or disfigurement before the explosion
and the fire at Lancaster Gate?' Abercorn asked.

'No, sir,' Bossiney answered.

'How did you come to be there?' Abercorn went on, his voice
light and courteous, as if it were possible that anyone in the room
did not already know.

'I was on duty. Information had come in to the station that
there was going to be a big sale of opium, sir. We wanted to catch
the dealers.'

'Just so,' Abercorn agreed. 'And where did this information
come from? I assume it must have been a source you considered
reliable?'

'Yes, sir. The source's information has been accurate on several
occasions before.'

'Regarding the illegal sale of opium?' Abercorn pronounced
the word carefully, so no one should miss it.

'Yes, sir,' Bossiney agreed.

'Did you know the name of this informer?'

'No, sir. Just signed 'is letters A.D.' As if involuntarily, Bossiney
glanced up at the dock where Alexander Duncannon was sitting.

'The same person each time?' Abercorn reinforced the
impression.

'Looked like it, sir.'

Vespasia shifted very slightly in her seat. Charlotte knew why.

Bossiney was answering every question carefully, as Abercorn had schooled him, never overstating anything. He would be very difficult to catch out. She wondered how Narraway thought he was going to do it. It must be decades since he had stood up in court to defend anyone. Did he really have any idea what he was doing? She glanced at Vespasia, and met her eyes. Vespasia read her anxiety perfectly, and mirrored it for an instant in her own expression, before she very carefully replaced it with a look of complete assurance. But Charlotte knew now that it was a mask, and that it hid fear.

'How many of you went to the house in Lancaster Gate?' Abercorn continued.

'Five of us, sir.'

'And who were they?'

'Inspector Ednam, Sergeant Hobbs, Sergeant Newman, Constable Yarcombe and me,' Bossiney replied.

'Sergeant Newman and Sergeant Hobbs were killed at the site, and Inspector Ednam later died of his wounds, is that correct?' Now Abercorn looked very grave. His voice was sombre and he stood stiffly, almost to attention. He might have been at the funeral now.

No one in the room stirred.

Bossiney's expression was unreadable because of the damage to his face, but his voice was thick with emotion.

'Yes, sir.'

'Could you describe the house when you arrived, Constable, as well as you can?'

Bossiney did so in some detail. Again Charlotte had the distinct feeling that he had been told exactly how much to say – enough to make it real so the jury could imagine it, smell the staleness in the air, hear the silence, but not enough to lose their attention. It frightened her that Abercorn was so skilled, so very much in control. For the first time she could ever remember, she doubted Narraway's ability. It was deeply disturbing. She had not realised how much she had believed in him, until that belief was broken.

'Thank you.' Abercorn nodded.

Narraway said nothing at all. He did not even move in his seat.

Charlotte's body was tense, her hands locked together in her lap.

'What happened, as much as you can recall?' Abercorn prompted.

Bossiney described the shock of the explosion, the ear-splitting noise, the violence, confusion, and above all the unbearable pain, then nothing, just darkness. He used simple words; none that were not part of his ordinary language. Nothing he said sounded coached or rehearsed.

The horror of Bossiney's description filled the room. Somewhere in the gallery a woman was crying. Emily was sitting close to Cecily Duncannon, holding on to her as if she were drowning.

Charlotte could not even imagine what she must be feeling. She wanted to scream at Abercorn to get on with his questions, and not to let them all sit here imagining the nightmare. But of course that was exactly what he was doing. That was what this was all for: to foster the horror, the fear that somehow it could happen to anyone here; to suggest that as long as people like Alexander were free, nobody was safe.

It was the judge who broke the silence.

'Have you anything more for the witness, Mr Abercorn?'

'No, my lord,' Abercorn said quietly. 'I think we have asked enough of him.' He walked slowly to his chair and sat down.

'Mr Narraway?' the judge asked, and then corrected himself. 'I beg your pardon, Lord Narraway.'

Narraway rose to his feet. 'No, thank you, my lord. I believe Constable Bossiney has told us all he knows that is relevant.' He sat down again.

The judge looked startled. Abercorn was confused, uncertain whether to be triumphant or alarmed.

The judge adjourned the court for luncheon.

Charlotte, Vespasia and Jack walked the short distance to the nearest public house seeking a good, hot meal. They did so in silence, wrapped up against the wind. Vespasia did not mention whether she had been to such an establishment before, but she looked around curiously only once. They all had more pressing weights on their minds than the chatter of the other diners, many of whom had also come from one of the nearby courts or offices.

They spoke briefly of Tellman, and his slow but steady recovery. Vespasia particularly asked after Gracie, and Charlotte smiled for the first time that day as she recounted how Gracie was completely in control and Tellman was for once doing exactly as she told him.

'Perhaps he at last realises how much she loves him?' Vespasia suggested.

'I think so,' Charlotte agreed. 'And he is allowing himself to admit that his family means more to him than anything else.'

Vespasia smiled back, and resumed eating a kind of meal to which she was totally unaccustomed.

Abercorn began the afternoon's testimony by calling Constable Yarcombe. He was better recovered than Bossiney, but he still walked a trifle out of balance for having less than half an arm on one side. He also told of being lured to the house in Lancaster Gate, of how they all were prepared to find a major drug deal in progress, confident that the informer who had previously been so reliable would be so again.

He described the house much the way Bossiney had, but carefully using different words, as if they had not compared notes, or been coached. Again it was enough to feel as if he knew the place, but not swamped in detail, and not so any of it could be contradicted.

He spoke of the explosion with some distress, both for his

colleagues who were killed, and for the searing pain he had felt. When Abercorn asked him, he spoke highly of Ednam.

'Yes, sir, 'e were a fine man. Knew 'im for years, I did. Very brave, 'e were. Very fair. It were a terrible thing that 'e died of 'is injuries. Mind, the pain of it, there were days I wished I 'ad.'

There was an audible murmur of sympathy around the gallery. Charlotte saw one of the jurors muttering something, and then looking up at Alexander, who sat white-faced and stiff. But he was no stranger to pain. He had lived with it since his own accident, and would for the rest of his life, but of course the jury did not know that – and was it relevant to anything? Narraway had not pleaded insanity for Alexander. Why not? If he spoke of Alexander's pain surely the opium he had been prescribed, and then became addicted to, could have driven him mad? And madness was about the only defence for this.

Charlotte wondered what on earth was Narraway doing, and whether Pitt had any idea at all how appallingly this was going. It could hardly be worse.

But when Yarcombe came to the end of his evidence, and Narraway could have done something, again he declined to ask him anything at all.

The ripple of amazement around the court was tinged with anger, even contempt.

And contempt was written clearly on Abercorn's aggressive face. He looked across once to where Cecily Duncannon sat and there was victory already in his eyes.

Charlotte wished she could somehow hurt him, take some weapon and hit him so hard with it that the pleasure in him would vanish for ever. She knew that was ridiculous and childish. It was not really he who was at fault. He was only doing what he was supposed to. But she hated him for enjoying it. And he was! Staring at him, at the shine on his face, she was certain of it. This was a victory against Godfrey Duncannon, because

Alexander was his son and he had what should have been Abercorn's. Godfrey had abandoned Abercorn's mother for Cecily, and left her to the pain of difficult birth and no one to support her. That was where the opium had begun!

Abercorn could do nothing now except proceed. If Narraway had hoped to knock his confidence by behaving so extraordinarily, he was not succeeding.

Abercorn called the senior fireman who had attended the blaze after the explosion. His account was exact, harrowing, but with the expert detail that held the attention of everyone in the court. There was a horrible fascination in the power of fire to cause all-consuming destruction. Here, safely in the courtroom, the fear gave a fusion for excitement.

Abercorn thanked the fireman and turned to Narraway.

Narraway rose to his feet. 'Thank you, my lord,' he said to the judge. 'I cannot think of anything this witness has left out, or indeed of anything that could be interpreted other than as he has done.'

'You've nothing to ask?' the judge said incredulously.

'Nothing, my lord, thank you.'

The jurors looked at one another, puzzled, even disconcerted.

There was a murmuring in the body of the court.

Charlotte turned to Vespasia, and then wished that she had not. The concern in her eyes was unmistakable. Charlotte reached across and put her hand gently on Vespasia's and felt her fingers tighten in response.

Abercorn spent the rest of the afternoon and the beginning of the next morning calling expert witnesses one after another. Most moving were the doctors, both the one who described the pain of those who had survived. The police surgeon described the causes of death of Newman and Hobbs. He also stated that Ednam's injuries were the primary cause of his death, although it occurred a little later.

Again Narraway had nothing to say.

'Surely, Lord Narraway, you have some purpose here?' the judge said in complete exasperation. 'You are hardly giving your client any kind of defence at all! Are you hoping for a mistrial, sir? You cannot claim incompetence. You are perfectly capable of mounting some sort of defence, or I would not have permitted you to undertake it. Do you wish to be replaced?'

'No, thank you, my lord,' Narraway said a little stiffly, as if his neck ached and his throat were dry. 'I have not questioned the witnesses so far because I do not believe their evidence is in error or in any way incomplete. I will have questions later. I do not believe it is in my client's interest to waste the court's time over issues that are not in doubt.'

'Very well. But you had better begin soon, or I shall be obliged to find a more . . . competent counsel for Mr Duncannon.'

'I am engaged, my lord,' Narraway said with a sudden flare of passion. 'Believe me, I am!'

Charlotte gripped Vespasia's hand harder, and found her eyes filling with tears of relief.

Pitt knew it was inevitable that Abercorn should call him as a main witness against Alexander Duncannon. He had spent a good deal of time with Narraway, and knew what he had planned, as well as both the chances, and the risks. He was not surprised when Abercorn called him in for a final discussion before putting him on the stand, the day after he finished with the other expert testimony.

At seven o'clock in the morning Pitt was very reluctantly having breakfast with Abercorn at his home. It was a large, elegant house off Woburn Square. This was an excellent neighbourhood, quiet and exclusive, wealthy but it had been so quite long enough to wear it with ease.

Abercorn ate well. The sideboard held silver dishes of scrambled eggs, sausages, bacon, mushrooms, devilled kidneys, kippers should he have wished for them. There were racks of fresh toast, butter and several kinds of marmalade. Graceful silver pots held tea and hot water, matching the silver cruet sets and the mono-grammed knives, forks and napkin rings.

Abercorn himself was dressed in a suit obviously tailored for him, and a quality of shirt Pitt would have felt extravagant for himself, with a family to support, but he admired it none the less. He did wonder why Abercorn had not married, or if perhaps he had, and tragedy of some sort had robbed him of his wife, and the possibility of children. Perhaps it had been too painful for him to wish to marry again. He did not like the man, but he still felt a stirring of pity for him.

In a brief visit to his study the last time he was here, in earlier preparation, he had noticed the portrait of an elderly woman, dressed in the fashion of some thirty years earlier. And in spite of the ravages of pain, her features bore a noticeable resemblance to Abercorn's. Pitt had assumed it was his mother.

'Sorry for calling you out so early,' Abercorn said almost as soon as the food was served and they began to eat. 'But this is crucial. I think we already have the jury completely. It has all gone perfectly so far.'

Pitt knew this from Charlotte, but he intended to make no mention of that.

Abercorn took another large mouthful of devilled kidneys. He had separated them on his plate – a generous helping. They were apparently a favourite and he meant to indulge himself. Pitt wondered how long he had had his wealth. There was something in him, almost indefinable, a relish, that made Pitt aware that he was not born to such plenty. He still savoured it, just enough to see.

'Narraway did absolutely nothing,' Abercorn went on. 'I thought at first that he would be a dangerous opponent, but the more I watch him, the more I am coming to believe that he is totally out of his depth. I don't know why he took the case on at all . . .' He hesitated, watching Pitt closely.

Pitt did not reply. He sat waiting as if he expected Abercorn to explain.

'You know the man!' Abercorn said impatiently. 'Is he really empty, a paper tiger?'

Pitt was conscious that he must judge his reply exactly, not only his choice of words, but the precise expression with which he said them.

'He's made mistakes,' he began. 'Misjudgements. But then so has everyone. Sometimes it's not the errors you make but how you recover from them that mark the difference between failure and success.'

'I don't intend to give him the opportunity to recover,' Abercorn said tersely. 'So far he's said nothing. Why do you suppose that is?'

Pitt smiled, to rob the reply of any suggestion of sarcasm. 'Possibly you've made no mistakes he could exploit? The evidence of the actual crime seems very clear cut. I tried to make it unarguable.'

'Indeed, you succeeded,' Abercorn agreed. 'But I expected him to say something.' He frowned. 'How long is it since he actually practised law?'

'I didn't know he ever had, until he told me a couple of weeks ago,' Pitt admitted. 'And I didn't ask him. I gathered it was a very long time ago.'

'I looked,' Abercorn nodded. 'I found no trace of his ever appearing in court at all. But he is certainly qualified. Why on earth does he want to defend Duncannon? Do you know?'

It was the first question to which Pitt must answer with a direct lie. He disliked doing it, but he had no choice.

'I imagine it could have something to do with Godfrey Duncannon and the negotiations on this large contract he is presently dealing with. The Government is very keen it should be accomplished successfully.'

A shadow crossed Abercorn's face, and then was gone. 'I agree that the timing is appalling, and I dislike doing the opposition's job for them. But the attack on our police force is even more serious. They are our first line of defence against anarchy and the total chaos of civil disorder, even the prospect of actual revolution.

'The whole of Europe is in civil disorder and within the next ten or fifteen years, at the outside, we will be in chaos if we do not gain some control. Socialism is rising in Russia, Germany, France. The Balkans are on the brink of war. Who is to hold on to order, if not us?'

Pitt did not answer. Everything Abercorn said was true.

'We must not, cannot let down those who rely on us,' Abercorn went on. 'Three men are dead and two more fearfully injured. Bossiney was a fine witness. His disfigurement made a lasting impression on the jury. They'll have nightmares about that for a long time. I'll have that face in my dreams for years.' He winced, for a moment not making any attempt to hide his emotion.

Pitt felt a moment's complete unity with him. Bossiney would carry that for the rest of his life. Whatever he had done in complicity with Ednam, it was a monstrous punishment. But it did not justify the crime or hanging Lezant, or assuage Alexander's pain either.

'What is it you asked to discuss?' he asked.

Abercorn brought his attention back to the present. 'Ah . . . yes. Just details. Attitude perhaps more than facts. They seem to be clear enough.' He looked at Pitt earnestly. 'I know exactly what I am going to ask you. You are my main witness, beyond the facts already established. Narraway has to cross-question you, or he has done nothing at all. I want to make sure he cannot rattle you. He must know you well. He was your superior for several years.' He left the remark in the air between them, forcing Pitt to respond.

'I believe I know what you mean,' Pitt said slowly. 'But if you are plain, then there can be no misunderstanding. We have already gone over the evidence. I shall be precise in answering your questions.'

'And brief,' Abercorn added, still watching Pitt closely. 'Don't offer anything I haven't asked for.'

At another time Pitt might have smiled. He had given evidence far more often than Abercorn had even been in a courtroom. But there was nothing easy, final or to be taken for granted in this.

'I won't,' he promised. He must be careful. He did not like Abercorn, and yet his dislike of him was baseless and probably unfair. His loyalty to Narraway was deep, and his loyalty to what he believed to be right was even deeper. He knew exactly what Narraway meant to do – at least he thought he did. Narraway had been very careful not to tell him in so many words.

Abercorn stared at him, weighing, measuring, and judging. Pitt had a strong sense of the man's power, and his acute under-standing of others that had brought him from obscurity, poverty even, to a place where he was rich and very widely respected. He was almost certainly headed for the next step up the ladder to a political career of some distinction. His might even exceed that of Godfrey Duncannon. There was even something of a physical resemblance between the two men.

If he won this case it would be seen as a victory in the crusade for the ordinary man, the policeman on the beat who protected people's houses, families, even their lives against crime and disorder. A place in Parliament, even in government, was not unlikely, for Josiah Abercorn, to be a springboard for government office, even, eventually, a ministry, such as the Home Office, with all its power to change the law and life of the nation. It would be foolish to take him lightly.

Did any of this have to do with Godfrey Duncannon's success or failure with the contract? Pitt could not see how. Alexander's tragedy had begun with his accident, a fall from a horse, the animal rolling on him. It had been no one's fault, and it had happened years ago.

Pitt had at last learned not to fill other men's silences with words he would rather not say. He ate his breakfast, without enjoyment.

'Narraway must have some plan,' Abercorn said at last. 'You know the man. More to the point, he knows you! Is he going to try to trip you? What does he imagine he can do that Godfrey Duncannon has allowed him to represent the family? I have a powerful feeling that there is something I don't know! What is it, Pitt?'

Pitt was startled. 'What makes you think that?' He was playing for time, studying Abercorn's face, the tension in his body as he sought to probe Pitt's thoughts. Was this what the meeting was really about?

'How well do you know Duncannon?' Pitt asked. It was a thought that had only just occurred to him, and probably it was irrelevant.

Abercorn's expression was extraordinary: a mixture of a terrible humour, bitter and deep, a satisfaction as if tasting something delicate, determined not to gulp it, mixed with a pain that was almost overwhelming.

Or was Pitt letting his own tiredness overtake him, his helplessness to do anything for Alexander beyond giving him room to guide his destruction to some end that mattered to him? The weight of Pitt's own grief at the corruption of men he had trusted was added to by Tellman's disillusion, and the opulence of this room with its velvet curtains and its fire roaring in the grate.

He drew in a deep breath, as if there were not enough air in all that space, though the room was forty feet long.

'Duncannon?' Abercorn said with his eyebrows raised. 'Our paths have seldom crossed. Why do you ask?'

Pitt shrugged, aware now that they were playing a complicated game with no rules to it. 'Looking for what it could be that we don't know,' he answered.

'Why did Duncannon allow Narraway to do this?' Abercorn held his fork in the air, the next mouthful for once ignored.

'Perhaps it was Alexander's decision?' Pitt suggested, knowing that it was.

'Why? Cardew was to be Godfrey's lawyer. He would have been excellent. He would at least have put up a battle.'

'But would he have won?' Pitt asked.

Abercorn pursed his lips doubtfully. 'Insanity, perhaps. Narraway hasn't even put it forward. God knows why. It's all there is.'

'Perhaps he doesn't think it would work?'

'Nothing's going to work!' Abercorn said with a sudden rush of emotion. His big broad hand was clenched on his knife, his face was flushed with a wave of colour. 'He's guilty!'

'Yes, he is,' Pitt agreed. He felt as if the room stifled him. He thought of Alexander bent double with pain, the sweat pouring off his face, his shirt soaked with it. He wanted justice for Lezant. He would die for it. He was going to die anyway. The opium would see to that.

Could Narraway bring about that justice?

There was something Pitt had missed, some connection. He racked his brain, but the pieces still did not fit, not quite.

Chapter Fourteen

WHEN THE trial resumed, Pitt took the stand immediately. He climbed the steps, faced the court and swore to his name, rank and occupation. He was aware of Alexander in the dock, white-faced and motionless. He knew that Cecily would be in the front seats of the gallery, with Emily beside her, somewhere that Alexander could see her. Godfrey would not be there. Abercorn had kept him in reserve as a witness.

Pitt glanced at Charlotte once; she was sitting with Vespasia. Then he turned all his concentration on Abercorn as he stepped forward and began what was intended to be his cornerstone of the prosecution.

'My lord,' Abercorn addressed the judge, 'I shall not ask Commander Pitt more than necessary about the terrible carnage he saw when he arrived at Lancaster Gate on the evening of the bombing. We already know exactly what happened from the two victims who survived that atrocity. Nothing could be more immediate or more accurate than their accounts. We have heard from the firemen, from the ambulance men and from the hospital doctors. We need no more retelling of the horror and the pain.'

He gestured towards Pitt on the stand. 'What I will ask Commander Pitt to tell you is how he investigated the crime, how he put together all the evidence and came to the inevitable and terrible conclusion that Alexander Duncannon was responsible for it. He, and he alone, did this thing. I have no doubt whatever that you will reach the same conclusion.' He gave a very slight bow, a tiny gesture of courtesy, and then he looked up directly at Pitt.

'This must have been extraordinarily distressing for you, Commander,' he began, his voice filled with sympathy. 'You will have seen many disasters, many crimes, but these men whose shattered corpses you found were fellow police officers! Men exactly as you were yourself only a few years ago.'

Pitt thought of Newman's body hunched up, broken. He could smell the charred flesh as if it had been moments since it had happened. His throat was so tight it was hard to speak. The question had come without warning, and he knew Abercorn had done this on purpose. It was brilliant theatre. He appreciated it, and hated him for it at the same moment. Please God, Narraway would be as good at it when it was his turn.

'Yes,' he agreed.

'Did you actually know any of the victims?' Abercorn asked.

There was silence in the courtroom. No one even fidgeted. Pitt was aware that the jurors were all watching him minutely, enthralled, and he had barely begun. He hated it. Everything depended upon him.

'Yes, I had heard the names of all of them, and I knew Newman and Hobbs personally,' he answered.

'It must have been terrible for you,' Abercorn dwelt on it for a moment, allowing the imagery to sink in. He did not leave it long enough for Narraway to object that it was not a question. 'After you had seen the bodies,' he continued, 'and made sure the survivors had been taken to hospital, and that the fires were out and the structure of the building, what was left of it, was safe to examine, what did you do next?'

'Looked for passers-by, possible witnesses,' Pitt answered. 'Unfortunately we learned very little of value. We also did all we could to find any remnants of the bomb, and to work out from the wreckage exactly where it had been placed.'

'Why? What difference did that make?' Abercorn sounded interested. He was not following the pattern he had discussed with Pitt. Maybe he did not wish it to sound rehearsed.

'The more you know about an explosion, the more likely you are to be able to deduce the ingredients of a bomb, the amount of dynamite used, the container, how it was detonated.'

'What good does that do?'

'There are not many sources of dynamite.' Pitt went on to explain the various types of bomb, how they were constructed and used. Abercorn did not interrupt him, and neither did Narraway. The public in the gallery were watching a drama unfold, whether or not they understood where it was leading.

Abercorn nodded. 'The source of this dynamite, Commander – were you able to trace it, in this instance?'

'Yes—'

'Is one lot of dynamite different from another?' Abercorn interrupted.

'Not that you can tell, once it has exploded. But it is very carefully controlled,' Pitt explained. 'No one can prevent the occasional theft, especially from quarries where it is used frequently. One doesn't trace the dynamite so much as the men who steal it, sell it, or buy it. They are usually recognisable.'

'And Special Branch knows who deals in stolen dynamite?'

'Yes.' He did not qualify it. How many dealers they did not know was a matter of calculation. Abercorn had insisted that his testimony remain simple. Complication would confuse the jury.

Not that Pitt needed telling that.

Abercorn paced two or three steps from the place where he had begun.

'And you traced the thief, the seller and the purchaser of this particular dynamite?'

'Yes.' Carefully, in simple detail, Pitt recounted how they had traced the dynamite from the quarry from which it had been stolen, through the thief, his contacts among the anarchists, eventually to Alexander Duncannon. No one interrupted him. Narraway sat as if paralysed. Pitt was careful not to look at him, except momentarily, out of the corner of his eye. He knew Vespasia was beside Charlotte, but he dared not even imagine what she was feeling.

'And it led you to Alexander Duncannon,' Abercorn repeated, unable to keep the victory out of his voice.

'Yes,' Pitt agreed.

The judge leaned forward. 'Lord Narraway, have you nothing whatever to say? You do understand your ability to object, don't you?'

'Yes, my lord.' Narraway rose to his feet as a matter of courtesy. 'So far I have heard nothing to object to. It all seems to be very clear and honest. I shall have a few questions for Commander Pitt, if there is anything that he has not covered by the end of his testimony.' He sounded polite, even untroubled, as if he did not understand what was happening.

Abercorn was not quite as comfortable as before. He resumed after walking a little less gracefully back to his original position in front of the witness stand.

'Did you question the accused about the bomb, the explosion, the fire, the deaths, and appalling injuries, Commander Pitt? Did he deny that he was responsible?'

'Yes, I did question him, and he did not deny it,' Pitt replied.

'So you arrested him?'

'Not at that time. I looked for further proof.'

Abercorn's eyebrows shot up. 'Why?'

'He was ill, and I thought perhaps unstable,' Pitt answered. 'I wanted to be perfectly sure, independently of his words, that he was actually guilty.' He took a breath. 'And of his connections with any possible anarchists. After all, it was from a known anarchist that he had bought the dynamite.'

'Ill?' Abercorn asked. 'Do you mean insane?'

Narraway moved in his seat.

The judge leaned forward.

The jury, as a man, stared at Pitt.

Narraway said nothing.

Someone in the gallery coughed and choked.

'Commander!' Abercorn said loudly.

'I am not a doctor to know the answer to that,' Pitt measured his words carefully. 'But it did not seem so to me, then or since.'

Abercorn smiled. 'Quite so. Thank you.' He turned away, as if to go back to his seat. Then suddenly he swivelled around and faced Pitt again. 'And may we assume that you found all the proof you wished for?'

'Yes.'

'And connections to any anarchists?'

'No, sir, other than the purchase of the dynamite.'

'But Alexander did lead a somewhat dissolute lifestyle . . . such as gave him acquaintance with anarchists, or he would not have known where to purchase dynamite?' Abercorn persisted. It was barely a question, more a conclusion.

'That would seem unarguable,' Pitt agreed.

'Thank you, sir. You have been most helpful.' Abercorn's smile was that of a shark who had just eaten very well. 'Your witness, Lord Narraway.'

Narraway rose to his feet and walked gracefully to the centre of the floor in front of the witness stand.

'Thank you, Mr Abercorn. Commander Pitt, your evidence has been commendably clear and concise. Nevertheless, there are a few points I would like to go over, and perhaps make clearer still.'

Pitt waited.

There was a silence in the room such that one almost imagined the creak of stays as women breathed in and out, or the scrape of a boot sole on the floor as a foot moved an inch.

Narraway spoke quietly, as if all emotion were knotted up inside him.

'Your evidence as to the explosion in the house at Lancaster Gate is perfectly clear, and of the appalling injuries to the five policemen who attended the event in pursuit of an opium sale, which apparently never took place. It didn't, did it?'

'No, sir.'

'But you pursued it? You attempted to find out if it had ever been a genuine piece of information?'

Abercorn rose to his feet. 'My lord, surely it is clear to Lord Narraway that there was never any such sale intended? It was a feint, a lure to get the police to Lancaster Gate!'

The judge looked at him with an expression of impatience. 'I think since we have heard so little from Lord Narraway, as you have extensively remarked, we should allow him to make this point.' He turned to Narraway. 'Please continue, and if you have a point to make that is pertinent to the issue, then please let us hear it.'

'Yes, my lord.' Narraway looked at Pitt again. 'Did you investigate this person known as A.D., and his information, Commander?'

'Yes, sir. It seems that he had supplied information regarding sales of opium on at least three earlier occasions, and on all of them his information had proven correct.'

'What relevance does this have to this case?' Narraway asked innocently.

'I did not appreciate how much at the time,' Pitt admitted. 'It was a routine thing to check. But it did occur to me straight away that since his earlier information had resulted in the arrests of several dealers, the police would expect the same to be true this time, and send along a fairly large body of men to effect an arrest. Possibly they would be the same men as on the earlier occasions.'

'Seems reasonable,' Narraway agreed.

Abercorn moved restively in his seat, as if to stand up, and then changed his mind.

'And were they the same men?' Narraway asked Pitt.

'Probably. It wouldn't be difficult to ascertain—'

This time Abercorn rose immediately. 'My lord, I object most strenuously to Commander Pitt's assumption. He seems to be suggesting that the dead and injured men were somehow responsible for their own fate. That is beyond appalling! It is inexcusable.'

'Really?' The judge looked surprised. 'All I understood from the question was that they could have been a target, the cause of which might have been anything, but the most likely to my mind is revenge, possibly for any of their previous successes. They were very successful in their jobs, I understand?'

'Yes, my lord, but—'

'Your objection is heard, and denied, Mr Abercorn. Please continue, Lord Narraway. Your point is made.'

'Thank you, my lord.' Narraway's face was almost expressionless, nothing visible in it but concentration. He looked again at Pitt. 'So these investigations, which my learned friend had you recount for the court, led you to the conclusion that the officers, both dead and wounded, were deliberately lured to the house in Lancaster Gate where the bomb was detonated?'

'Yes, sir,' Pitt agreed.

'And you discovered what materials were used in the bomb?'

'Yes, sir.'

Again Abercorn was on his feet. 'My lord, I am happy to save the court's time by stipulating to all the evidence previously given in his capacity as my own witness for the prosecution. Commander Pitt of Special Branch is an officer Lord Narraway knows very well, and when he retired he personally recommended Pitt to take his place. Is he now suggesting that Commander Pitt is in some way either incompetent, or dishonest?'

There was a rustle of movement in the gallery and several audible murmurs of surprise, and dissent.

The judge looked at Narraway questioningly.

A flicker of apprehension shadowed Narraway's face for an

instant, and then he banished it. 'Not at all, my lord,' he said to the judge. 'But as any witness is required to do, he answered only the questions asked him. I would like to explain a little further, with the court's permission. I have not so far wasted the court's time, my lord . . .'

'Indeed, it is more than time you took up a little of it,' the judge agreed. 'But please make sure it is relevant. Do not use our time simply to make it appear that Mr Duncannon has had adequate defence.' His tone was sharp, a reminder of his authority.

Narraway acquiesced with a gesture, and continued speaking to Pitt.

'You told my learned friend Mr Abercorn that you followed all the lines of inquiry open to you regarding the source of the dynamite used in the bomb, and also the device used to detonate it?'

'Yes, sir.'

'And you questioned the anarchists known to you?'

'Yes, sir.'

'Did you discover anything at all: any shred of evidence whatsoever to indicate that they were involved, or could have been?'

'No, sir, nothing at all.'

There was a sigh around the room.

Abercorn smiled and leaned back in his seat, as if the danger had passed.

'You were led irrevocably, fact by fact, each one tested, to the conclusion that the bomber was Alexander Duncannon?' Narraway went on.

'Yes, sir, I was.'

Now the atmosphere in the court was electric. There were gasps of indrawn breath. Abercorn looked for an instant as if he could barely believe what he had heard.

The jury stared at Pitt, then at Narraway, then back to Pitt.

The judge was puzzled and unhappy. It was obvious that he was embarrassed for Narraway.

Pitt did not dare look at Charlotte, still less at Vespasia.

'Were you satisfied with the evidence against him?' Narraway smiled, looking deceptively innocent.

The judge frowned, waiting for the answer.

Pitt hesitated.

'Commander?' Narraway prompted him. 'Was there some question in the evidence?'

'No. I was asked not to pursue the case against Alexander Duncannon by Commissioner Bradshaw,' Pitt replied. He had hoped to avoid saying this. He was convinced that Bradshaw had done so because his wife was also addicted to opium for pain relief, and he was afraid the prosecution of Alexander might reveal that. Perhaps they had the same supplier, and Alexander would be pressured to reveal him, and in so doing also cut off Bradshaw's wife's supply. The suppliers had the perfect weapon to blackmail the Commissioner into anything! And God alone knew how many others! It might be incidental to Bradshaw that his own career would be ruined. He would face disgrace, but not financial ruin. He had considerable private means. Pitt believed it was genuinely his wife he feared for. For the first time since he had mounted the witness stand, Pitt was deeply worried for the unknown.

'Did he say why?' Narraway asked.

'It was a political matter which I am aware of, but prefer not to discuss,' Pitt replied. That was not the truth, but he hoped Narraway would leave it alone. The danger was that Abercorn was aware of the truth and would use the exposure to discredit both Narraway and Pitt himself. He could feel the sweat of fear prickle his skin, and then go cold.

'Indeed.' Narraway gave a slight shrug and appeared to dismiss the subject. He walked back a few steps towards his seat, and then turned round. 'From when you first suspected Alexander Duncannon of the bombing that killed the three policemen, did Mr Duncannon take any further action, so far as you know, Commander Pitt?'

Pitt swallowed. They were coming into the most dangerous territory at last. Everything depended on this.

'Yes. He set off another bomb in the Lancaster Gate area, but this time no one was injured.'

Narraway affected to look surprised.

'The evidence led conclusively to him? You are perfectly sure of that?'

Abercorn sat back in his seat and smiled. Now he thought he knew what Narraway was attempting to do, and was doomed to failure. Pitt would avoid that trap. He could not blame anyone else, and thereby raise reasonable doubt as to Alexander's guilt.

There was a palpable tension in the courtroom. Several jurors looked at one another and a couple even passed whispered comments.

The judge looked even more concerned. He waited for Pitt's reply.

'There was very little conclusive evidence,' Pitt replied. 'Not all the stolen dynamite had been used in the first explosion – at least it appeared so.'

'It appeared so?' Narraway said instantly. 'That is hardly proof, Commander Pitt. Yet you say that Alexander Duncannon was guilty. Please explain yourself.'

Pitt was faced by accusing stares. This was the moment. Should he mention the beautifully initialled handkerchief? It was proof to him, as Alexander had meant it to be, but was it in law?

'He admitted it to me,' Pitt said simply.

Narraway's eyes opened wide. 'You asked him, and he admitted it,' he repeated. 'Do you expect us to believe that?'

Now there were rustles of movement, hasty whispers and hisses.

'Silence!' the judge ordered sharply.

'I expect you to believe it, my lord.' Pitt looked straight at Narraway. 'I believe your client will have told you the same. Whether the court does or not, I don't know, and I can't help.'

The judge leaned as far forward over the magnificent bench as he was able to.

'Lord Narraway, are you perfectly sure you are aware of what you are doing? I have told you before, no matter what . . . extraordinary behaviour you exhibit, you have taken considerable pains to assure this court that you are competent to defend your client. I accepted your assurances, and your qualifications. I will not grant a mistrial because of your . . . eccentric conduct now! Do I make myself clear?'

Narraway was stiff, the tension in him like an electric charge in the air.

'Yes, my lord. I understand perfectly. I have no intention whatsoever of asking you for any kind of mistrial on such a basis . . . or any other.'

'Then proceed.'

'Thank you, my lord.' Narraway walked back a couple of paces towards the witness stand. 'Commander Pitt, can you explain this . . . extraordinary statement? My client has given me leave to ask you this question. It will not be grounds for any plea on his behalf.'

Pitt took a long, deep breath, and then another. He could feel his heart hammering in his chest. It was all up to him now. No one else could help Alexander, or find any kind of justice or even mercy.

'He had already admitted to setting the original bomb, which killed three police and terribly injured two more . . .'

There were gasps around the court.

Godfrey Duncannon was in the gallery today, apparently released from any possibility of being called to the stand. He rose to his feet, protesting, but his voice was drowned in the hubbub.

'I will have order!' the judge shouted furiously. 'Lord Narraway, for the love of heaven, control your witness, or I shall be obliged to call for someone to replace you. This has become absurd!'

The tide of noise subsided.

Narraway stood pale-faced. 'With the greatest respect, my lord, I am acting in what my client believes is his best interest.'

'You have not had him plead insanity,' the judge reminded him.

Abercorn was visibly smiling.

'No, my lord,' Narraway agreed. 'I do not think Mr Duncannon was insane within the definition of the law.'

'I don't know what you are playing at, man, but get it over with,' the judge said wearily.

Narraway looked up at Pitt. 'He admitted to setting the bomb in the house in Lancaster Gate, the first one?'

'Yes.'

'Did you ask him why he had done such a . . . monstrous thing?'

'Of course I did. And why the second also.'

'And his reply?'

Abercorn rose to his feet quickly. There was now a distinct pallor to his face, as if he had at last seen the shadow on the horizon. 'My lord, this has descended to farce! We cannot give the accused a platform to air his wild political opinions.'

'Sit down, Mr Abercorn,' the judge ordered. 'Commander Pitt is answering a perfectly reasonable question. You did not offer any motive for this abominable act. It is in order that his defence should offer it, destructive to his case as it may be. I cannot imagine anything that could be a justification. Can you?'

'Absolutely not, my lord!'

'Good. Then sit down and be quiet, so we can get this over with as quickly as possible. Narraway?'

'Yes, my lord. Please continue, Commander Pitt.'

'Yes, I did ask him,' Pitt answered. He was acutely aware that he might well get only one chance to say what he had to. Abercorn would do all he could to stop him. One slip and he would be silenced.

'And his reply?' Narraway prompted.

'I thought at first it was revenge,' Pitt began. He gripped the rail in front of him, aware that his knuckles were white, but it helped to hold on to it. 'He was injured very badly in a riding accident and had been given opium by his doctor, to give some ease for the appalling pain.' He deliberately chose the same word that Narraway had used. 'He became addicted to it, as I am afraid often happens, especially when the pain itself will be for life.'

Abercorn stirred, but the judge glared at him, and he subsided.

Pitt went on quickly, 'A little over two years ago he and a close friend found in affliction, also addicted to opium, for pain, set up a meeting to purchase a further supply. When they got to the appointed place, they were met by a police ambush. Five men: Ednam, Newman, Hobbs, Bossiney and Yarcombe. The drug dealer was not there. It developed into a brief but fatal battle. A passer-by, James Tyndale, a totally innocent man, was shot dead. Alexander Duncannon told me it was by one of the police. Alexander escaped. His companion, Dylan Lezant, who was close behind him, was less fortunate. He was tackled by the police and knocked senseless.'

'Really,' Abercorn began. 'This is—'

'Be quiet!' the judge ordered. 'Continue, Commander Pitt.'

'Thank you, my lord,' Pitt replied. 'The police account of the incident said that Lezant was guilty of the murder of Tyndale. He was tried for it and, on police testimony, found guilty and hanged. Alexander said he was innocent. Neither he nor Lezant carried weapons of any sort. They had no need of them. The last thing a man desperately addicted to opium is likely to do is quarrel with the man who supplies him with the only release he knows from his agony.'

'And did you believe this . . . story?' Narraway asked.

'Not at first,' Pitt replied. 'I and the policeman I most trusted, Inspector Samuel Tellman, investigated at some length. It was extremely disturbing. I was in the police for many years, and Inspector Tellman is still in the force. But we both found

Duncannon's story to be substantially true. Indeed, Inspector Tellman was personally attacked for his part in the investigation, and shot! He is still recovering from his injuries.'

Abercorn was on his feet and shouting now. 'My lord, this is all hearsay! Pitt used to work with Tellman. It is—'

The judge held up his hand and Abercorn restrained himself with difficulty and ill-concealed fury.

'Is this hearsay, Commander Pitt?' the judge asked.

'No, my lord. I was informed of the battle by one of my own men and I went to the scene immediately. I took Mr Jack Radley, MP with me, because he was visiting me at the time. When we arrived Inspector Tellman was cornered in an alley by several armed police and there was a great deal of shooting going on. We managed to rescue him, during which battle Mr Radley was wounded in the arm. However, I'm sure he would testify to this knowledge of the event if you wanted to call him.'

The judge shook his head, his lips pursed. 'It will not be necessary. I am far more concerned with your account of the battle two years ago in which James Tyndale was killed. If what you say is true, then there was a deliberate judicial murder of a man possibly guilty of being addicted to opium, but most certainly not of murder. This will require an extremely grave inquiry. An innocent man may have been hanged by police perjury and corruption.'

'Yes, my lord, I believe so,' Pitt agreed. 'I have no doubt whatsoever that that is what Alexander Duncannon believes, and wished to be tried in this court in order to expose it.'

Abercorn would not be silenced any longer. He began to speak even as he was straightening to stand.

'That is absolute rubbish, my lord! No sane man would believe it. Why didn't he protest to the court at the time of Lezant's trial? Why was he not called as a witness for him? The answer is obvious. He was part of the crime, an accomplice at the very least. How can you give credence to any of this?'

Pitt answered before the judge had time to rule, or Narraway to ask.

'He was not called to testify at the trial,' he answered, speaking to Abercorn directly as if no one else in the huge room were there. 'He wished to, and was not allowed. Lezant refused, in order to protect him, and the prosecutor did not need him. I have that from the lawyer concerned. And he did try to take up the issue with the police numerous times, and no one would listen to him.'

'He's a drug addict, for God's sake!' Abercorn all but shouted back. 'Have you ever looked at where he lives? What he does? The gin-sodden alleys he sleeps in when he's too far gone to find his own home? The drunken, drug-crazed company he keeps?'

'Yes, I have.' Pitt raised his voice back. 'But far more important than that, and far more relevant, I've followed the course of the investigation into Tyndale's death. I've seen how the police lied, mostly led by Inspector Ednam. I've followed the facts, and their story doesn't make sense with the evidence – Alexander's does! He tried over and over again to make someone listen to him, and they closed in a wall of lies or silence to cover their own disastrous error in shooting Tyndale when they panicked because they thought he was the opium dealer. He wasn't! He was an innocent passer-by, no more. The drug dealer never turned up, and was never caught.'

Abercorn was pale, a sheen of sweat on his skin.

'None of that, even if it is true, excuses what Duncannon did to these five policemen!'

'Of course it doesn't,' Narraway agreed. 'He knows that, and is prepared to answer with whatever remains of his life. He has kept his word to his friend, and his own honour. You cannot raise the dead, but Dylan Lezant will be pardoned. What a ridiculous expression! We will pardon him that we hanged him by the neck until he was dead – on the perjury and corruption of five policemen! Three of whom are also dead now, and the two others punished even more terribly.

311

'Alexander himself has been in excruciating pain of body since his accident, and will soon die, either on the end of a rope himself, or in prison. Unless his lordship sees fit to put him in a hospital where at least some of his agony may be relieved.' Narraway's face was filled with pity and his voice was hushed. 'I am not sure if that is justice, but it is the best we have left to us.'

There was a silence of shock, grief, and perhaps fear in the room.

It was Pitt, remembering something from only a few moments ago, and then other things from further back, who spoke then.

'My lord, may I have permission to ask Mr Abercorn a question, or if not, then to speak with Lord Narraway so that he may?'

'If it is brief, and has some relevance to this tragic matter,' the judge replied.

'Thank you.' Pitt turned to Abercorn. 'Sir, you said that Alexander Duncannon lived a life of depravity, in gin-sodden alleys, half-crazed with drugs, filthy and desperate. If I quote your words out of order, I apologise.'

'Do you dispute it?' Abercorn challenged.

'No. No, I don't. Opium addiction is a terrible thing. What I wanted to ask you was how you knew that?'

Abercorn froze for an instant, almost too small to notice. Then he let out his breath slowly.

'I have had occasion to observe opium addicts now and then, even to do what I could to help them.' His expression was one of torn emotions, rage and pity and deep, scouring pain. 'I have learned that it is useless . . .' he stopped. For a moment grief overwhelmed him.

Pitt would like to have given him the dignity of silence, but he would never again have this chance, and it must be taken. Other words came back to his memory, and the moment when he had seen the resemblance between Abercorn and Godfrey Duncannon, and then something Bradshaw had said.

312

'Your mother,' he said. 'She died of opium addiction. You watched as a boy and could not help.'

Abercorn threw his head back and glared at Pitt with a hatred that was inflamed by grief and humiliation.

'It wasn't her fault!' He almost choked on the words. 'She was seduced by a promise of marriage, lied to, and betrayed for a woman with far more money. She was left with child, and disgraced. It was a hard birth and the pain never left her! I watched her die by inches. What would you have done?'

'Probably the same,' Pitt admitted. 'And I would have hated my own father too. But, please God, I would not have taken it out on his son, your half-brother.'

There were gasps. No one moved.

'You knew Alexander was addicted, because you supplied him, as indeed you did Bradshaw's wife, and God knows how many more. You blackmailed him so he would never expose you. How much did you use Ednam to do your dirtiest work? You learned as a youth how to find opium, for your mother,' Pitt went on. It must be done now. There would never be another chance. Even so, the judge could stop him at any moment. 'Ever more and more powerful doses. Did you really hate him so much, because he was Godfrey's legitimate son, the heir to all that should have been yours?'

Now people were moving in the body of the court. Godfrey Duncannon was on his feet, his face purple with fury, but uncertain what to do. Beside him Cecily was staring at him as though she had never really seen him before, not clearly, not like this.

Then Cecily turned away and Emily put her arms around her, letting her hide her face.

Charlotte was on her feet too, holding Jack's hand hard, not allowing him to interrupt Emily at this fearful moment.

Abercorn was dazed. At least he understood. The entire edifice of his dreams had crashed around him and lay in wreckage on the floor, and he knew who had done it, and how, and that there was nothing he could do.

It was Vespasia, ignoring everyone else, who walked gracefully across the floor to Narraway, signalling that the trial was over.

'You were quite brilliant, my dear,' she said quietly, but distinctly enough that those close to her could hear. 'With Thomas's help, I think you have achieved all the justice that is possible.' She looked up at the judge. 'I dare say his lordship will accept your suggestion of a hospital for Alexander to live out whatever days he has left. Won't you, Algernon?'

The judge blushed very faintly, and did his best to retain his composure.

'You are excused, Commander Pitt,' he said a little hoarsely. 'I hope not to see you in my court again. You have made a complete shambles of this trial.'

'Yes, my lord,' Pitt agreed humbly, but he was smiling in spite of the pity that tore him apart.

'But you did it rather well, I suppose,' the judge added.

Pitt bowed his head in acknowledgement, and then made his way down the steps and across the floor to Charlotte.

She took his hand. 'Very well,' she said softly. 'Brilliantly.'